PIP WILLIAMS

Writer and researcher Pip Williams was born in London, grew up in Sydney and lives in the Adelaide Hills with her partner and two sons. Her debut fiction, *The Dictionary of Lost Words*, was the bestselling new novel of 2020 in Australia. Pip began writing the story when she delved into the history of the *Oxford English Dictionary* and discovered that the definition of the word 'bondmaid' had failed to make its way into the first edition.

PIP WILLIAMS

The Dictionary of Lost Words

VINTAGE

3 5 7 9 10 8 6 4

Vintage is part of the Penguin Random House group of companies
whose addresses can be found at global.penguinrandomhouse.com

Penguin
Random House
UK

Copyright © Pip Williams 2020

First published in Vintage in 2022
First published in hardback by Chatto & Windus in 2021
First published in Australia by Affirm Press in 2020

penguin.co.uk/vintage

A CIP catalogue record for this book is available from the British Library

Map © Mike Hall 2021

ISBN 9781529113228

Printed and bound in Great Britain by Clays Ltd, Elcograf S.p.A.

The authorised representative in the EEA is Penguin Random House Ireland,
Morrison Chambers, 32 Nassau Street, Dublin D02 YH68

Penguin Random House is committed to a sustainable future
for our business, our readers and our planet. This book is
made from Forest Stewardship Council® certified paper.

For Ma and Pa

Contents

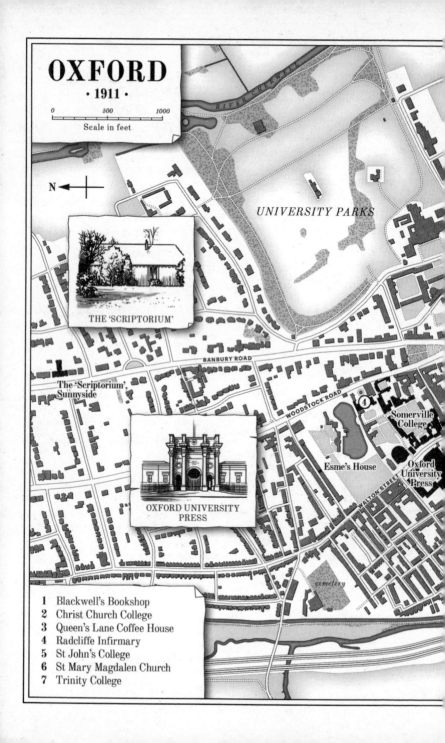

OXFORD
· 1911 ·

0   500   1000
Scale in feet

N

UNIVERSITY PARKS

RIVER CHERWELL

THE 'SCRIPTORIUM'

BANBURY ROAD

The 'Scriptorium',
Sunnyside

WOODSTOCK ROAD

4

Somerville
College

OXFORD UNIVERSITY
PRESS

Esme's House

Oxford
University
Press

WALTON STREET

cemetery

1   Blackwell's Bookshop
2   Christ Church College
3   Queen's Lane Coffee House
4   Radcliffe Infirmary
5   St John's College
6   St Mary Magdalen Church
7   Trinity College

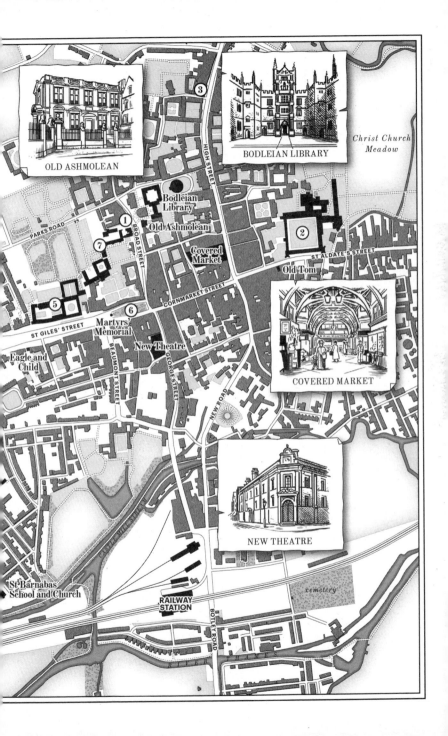

OLD ASHMOLEAN

BODLEIAN LIBRARY

Christ Church Meadow

③

Bodleian
Library

Old Ashmolean

①

PARKS ROAD

⑦

⑤

ST GILES' STREET

Martyrs'
Memorial

⑥

New Theatre

Eagle and
Child

Covered
Market

②

Old Tom

ST ALDATE'S STREET

CORNMARKET STREET

HIGH STREET

BROAD STREET

BEAUMONT STREET

GEORGE STREET

NEW ROAD

CASTLE MILL STREAM

St Barnabas
School and Church

BOTLEY ROAD

RAILWAY
STATION

cemetery

COVERED MARKET

NEW THEATRE

PROLOGUE

February 1886

Before the lost word, there was another. It arrived at the Scriptorium in a second-hand envelope, the old address crossed out and *Dr Murray, Sunnyside, Oxford*, written in its place.

It was Da's job to open the post and mine to sit on his lap, like a queen on her throne, and help him ease each word out of its folded cradle. He'd tell me what pile to put it on and sometimes he'd pause, cover my hand with his, and guide my finger up and down and around the letters, sounding them into my ear. He'd say the word, and I would echo it, then he'd tell me what it meant.

This word was written on a scrap of brown paper, its edges rough where it had been torn to match Dr Murray's preferred dimensions. Da paused, and I readied myself to learn it. But his hand didn't cover mine, and when I turned to hurry him, the look on his face made me stop; as close as we were, he looked far away.

I turned back to the word and tried to understand. Without his hand to guide me, I traced each letter.

'What does it say?' I asked.

'*Lily*,' he said.

'Like Mamma?'

'Like Mamma.'

'Does that mean she'll be in the Dictionary?'

'In a way, yes.'

'Will we all be in the Dictionary?'

'No.'

'Why?'

I felt myself rise and fall on the movement of his breath.

'A name must mean something to be in the Dictionary.'

I looked at the word again. 'Was Mamma like a flower?' I asked.

Da nodded. 'The most beautiful flower.'

He picked up the word and read the sentence beneath it. Then he turned it over, looking for more. 'It's incomplete,' he said. But he read it again, his eyes flicking back and forth as if he might find what was missing. He put the word down on the smallest pile.

Da pushed his chair back from the sorting table. I climbed off his lap and readied myself to hold the first pile of slips. This was another job I could help with, and I loved to see each word find its place among the pigeon-holes. He picked up the smallest pile, and I tried to guess where Mamma would go. 'Not too high and not too low,' I sang to myself. But instead of putting the words in my hand, Da took three long steps towards the fire grate and threw them into the flames.

There were three slips. When they left his hand, each was danced by the draught of heat to a different resting place. Before it had even landed, I saw *lily* begin to curl.

I heard myself scream as I ran towards the grate. I heard Da bellow my name. The slip was writhing.

I reached in to rescue it, even as the brown paper charred and the letters written on it turned to shadows. I thought I might hold it like an oak leaf, faded and winter-crisp, but when I wrapped my fingers around the word, it shattered.

I might have stayed in that moment forever, but Da yanked me away with a force that winded. He ran with me out of the Scriptorium and plunged my hand into the snow. His face was ashen, so I told him it didn't hurt, but when I unfurled my hand, the blackened shards of the word were stuck to my melted skin.

Some words are more important than others – I learned this, growing up in the Scriptorium. But it took me a long time to understand why.

PART ONE
1887–1896
Batten–Distrustful

May 1887

Scriptorium. It sounds as if it might have been a grand building, where the lightest footstep would echo between marble floor and gilded dome. But it was just a shed, in the back garden of a house in Oxford.

Instead of storing shovels and rakes, the shed stored words. Every word in the English language was written on a slip of paper the size of a postcard. Volunteers posted them from all over the world, and they were kept in bundles in the hundreds of pigeon-holes that lined the shed walls. Dr Murray was the one who named it the Scriptorium – he must have thought it an indignity for the English language to be stored in a garden shed – but everyone who worked there called it the Scrippy. Everyone but me. I liked the feel of *scriptorium* as it moved around my mouth and landed softly between my lips. It took me a long time to learn to say it, and when I finally did nothing else would do.

Da once helped me search the pigeon-holes for *scriptorium*. We found five slips with examples of how the word had been used, each quotation dating back little more than a hundred years. All of them were more or less the same, and none of them referred to a shed in the back garden of a house in Oxford. A *scriptorium*, the slips told me, was a writing room in a monastery.

But I understood why Dr Murray had chosen it. He and his assistants were a little like monks, and when I was five it was easy to imagine the Dictionary as their holy book. When Dr Murray told me it would take a lifetime to compile all the words, I wondered whose. His hair was already as grey as ash, and they were only halfway through B.

Da and Dr Murray had been teachers together in Scotland long before there was a Scriptorium. And because they were friends, and because I had no mother to care for me, and because Da was one of Dr Murray's most trusted lexicographers, everyone turned a blind eye when I was in the Scriptorium.

The Scriptorium felt magical, like everything that ever was and ever could be had been stored within its walls. Books were piled on every surface. Old dictionaries, histories and tales from long ago filled the shelves that separated one desk from another, or created a nook for a chair. Pigeon-holes rose from the floor to the ceiling. They were crammed full of slips, and Da once said that if I read every one, I'd understand the meaning of everything.

In the middle of it all was the sorting table. Da sat at one end, and three assistants could fit along either side. At the other end was Dr Murray's high desk, facing all the words and all the men who helped him define them.

We always arrived before the other lexicographers, and for that little while I would have Da and the words all to myself. I'd sit on Da's lap at the sorting table and help him sort the slips. Whenever we came across a word I didn't know, he would read the quotation it came with and help me work out what it meant. If I asked the right questions, he would try to find the book the quotation came from and read me more. It was like a treasure hunt, and sometimes I found gold.

'*This boy had been a scatter-brained scapegrace from his birth.*' Da read the quotation from a slip he had just pulled out of an envelope.

'Am I a scatter-brained scapegrace?' I asked.

'Sometimes,' Da said, tickling me.

Then I asked who the boy was, and Da showed me where it was written at the top of the slip.

'*Ala-ed-Din and the Wonderful Lamp,*' he read.

When the other assistants arrived I slipped under the sorting table.

'Be quiet as a mouse and stay out of the way,' Da said.

It was easy to stay hidden.

At the end of the day I sat on Da's lap by the warmth of the grate and we read 'Ala-ed-Din and the Wonderful Lamp'. It was an old story, Da said. About a boy from China. When I asked if there were others, he said there were a thousand more. The story was like nothing I had heard, nowhere I had been, and no one I knew of. I looked around the Scriptorium and imagined it as a genie's lamp. It was so ordinary on the outside, but on the inside full of wonder. And some things weren't always what they seemed.

The next day, after helping with the slips, I pestered Da for another story. In my enthusiasm I forgot to be as quiet as a mouse; I was getting in his way.

'A scapegrace will not be allowed to stay,' Da warned, and I imagined being banished to Ala-ed-Din's cave. I spent the rest of the day beneath the sorting table, where a little bit of treasure found me.

It was a word, and it slipped off the end of the table. When it lands, I thought, I'll rescue it, and hand it to Dr Murray myself.

I watched it. For a thousand moments I watched it ride some unseen current of air. I expected it to land on the unswept floor, but it didn't. It glided like a bird, almost landing, then rose up to somersault as if bidden by a genie. I never imagined that it might land in my lap, that it could possibly travel so far. But it did.

The word sat in the folds of my dress like a bright thing fallen from heaven. I dared not touch it. It was only with Da that I was allowed to hold the words. I thought to call out to him, but something caught my tongue. I sat with the word for a long time, wanting to touch it, but not. What word? I wondered. Whose? No one bent down to claim it.

After a long while I scooped the word up, careful not to crush its silvery wings, and brought it close to my face. It was difficult to read in the gloom of my hiding spot. I shuffled along to where a curtain of sparkling dust hung between two chairs.

I held the word up to the light. Black ink on white paper. Eight letters; the first, a butterfly B. I moved my mouth around the rest as Da had taught me: O for orange, N for naughty, D for dog, M for Murray, A for apple, I for ink, D for dog, again. I sounded them out in a whisper. The first part was easy: *bond*. The second part took a little longer, but then I remembered how the A and I went together. *Maid*.

The word was *bondmaid*. Below it were other words that ran together like a tangle of thread. I couldn't tell if they made up a quotation sent in by a volunteer or a definition written by one of Dr Murray's assistants. Da said that all the hours he spent in the Scriptorium were to make sense of the words sent in by volunteers, so that those words could be defined in the Dictionary. It was important, and it meant I would get a schooling and three hot meals and grow up to be a fine young lady. The words, he said, were for me.

'Will they all get defined?' I once asked.

'Some will be left out,' Da said.

'Why?'

He paused. 'They're just not solid enough.' I frowned, and he said, 'Not enough people have written them down.'

'What happens to the words that are left out?'

'They go back in the pigeon-holes. If there isn't enough information about them, they're discarded.'

'But they might be forgotten if they're not in the Dictionary.'

He'd tilted his head to one side and looked at me, as if I'd said something important. 'Yes, they might.'

I knew what happened when a word was discarded. I folded *bondmaid* carefully and put it in the pocket of my pinny.

A moment later, Da's face appeared under the sorting table. 'Run along now, Esme. Lizzie's waiting for you.'

I peered between all the legs – chairs', table's, men's – and saw the Murrays' young maid standing beyond the open door, her pinafore tied tight around her waist, too much fabric above and too much fabric below. She was still growing into it, she told me, but from under the sorting table she reminded me of someone playing at dressing-up. I crawled between the pairs of legs and scampered out to her.

'Next time you should come in and find me; it would be more fun,' I said, when I got to Lizzie.

'It's not me place.' She took my hand and walked me to the shade of the ash tree.

'Where is your place?'

She frowned, then shrugged. 'The room at the top of the stairs, I s'pose. The kitchen when I'm helping Mrs Ballard, but definitely not when I ain't. St Mary Magdalen on a Sunday.'

'Is that all?'

'The garden, when I'm caring for you – so we don't get under Mrs B's feet. And more and more the Covered Market, 'cos of her cranky knees.'

'Has Sunnyside always been your place?' I asked.

'Not always.' She looked down at me, and I wondered where her smile had gone.

'Where did it used to be?'

She hesitated. 'With me ma and all our littluns.'

'What are littluns?'

'Children.'

'Like me?'

'Like you, Essymay.'

'Are they dead?'

'Just me ma. The littluns was taken away, I don't know where. They was too young for service.'

'What's *service*?'

'Will you never stop asking questions?' Lizzie picked me up under the arms and swung me round and round until we were both so dizzy we collapsed on the grass.

'Where's my place?' I asked as the dizziness faded.

'The Scrippy, I guess, with your father. The garden, my room and the kitchen stool.'

'My house?'

''Course your house, though you seem to spend more time here than there.'

'I don't have a Sunday place like you do,' I said.

Lizzie frowned. 'Yes, you do, St Barnabas church.'

'We only go sometimes. When we do, Da brings a book. He holds it in front of the hymns and reads instead of singing.' I laughed, thinking of Da's mouth opening and closing in imitation of the congregation, but not a sound coming out.

'That's nothing to laugh at, Essymay.' Lizzie held her hand against the crucifix I knew rested beneath her clothes. I worried she would think badly of Da.

'It's because Lily died,' I said.

Lizzie's frown turned sad, which wasn't what I wanted either.

'But he says I should make up my own mind. About God and Heaven. That's why we go to church.' Her face relaxed, and I decided to get back to an easier conversation. 'My best place is Sunnyside,' I said. 'In the Scriptorium. Then in your room, then in the kitchen when Mrs Ballard is baking, especially when she's baking spotted scones.'

'You're a funny little thing, Essymay – they're called fruit scones; the spots are raisins.'

Da said Lizzie was no more than a child herself. When he was talking to her, I could see it. She stood as still as she could, holding her hands so they wouldn't fidget, and nodding at everything with barely a word. She must have been scared of him, I thought, the way I was scared of Dr Murray. But when Da was gone, she'd look at me sideways and wink.

As we lay on the grass with the world spinning above our heads, she suddenly leaned over and pulled a flower from behind my ear. Like a magician.

'I have a secret,' I told her.

'And what would that be, me little cabbage?'

'I can't tell you here. It might blow away.'

We tip-toed through the kitchen towards the narrow stairs that led to Lizzie's room. Mrs Ballard was bent over a flour bin in the pantry and all I saw of her was her very large behind, draped in folds of navy gingham. If she saw us, she'd find something for Lizzie to do and my secret would have to wait. I put a finger to my lips but a giggle rose in my throat. Lizzie saw it coming, so she scooped me into her bony arms and trotted up the stairs.

The room was cold. Lizzie took the coverlet off her bed and laid it on the bare floor like a rug. I wondered if there were any Murray children in the room on the other side of Lizzie's wall. It was the nursery, and we sometimes heard little Jowett crying, but not for long. Mrs Murray would come soon enough, or one of the older children. I tilted my ear towards the wall and heard the baby's waking noises, little sounds that were not quite words. I imagined him opening his eyes and realising he was alone. He whimpered for a while, then cried. This time it was Hilda who came. When the crying stopped, I recognised the tinkle of her voice. She was thirteen, like Lizzie, and her littlest sisters, Elsie and Rosfrith, were never far behind her. When I sat on the rug with Lizzie, I imagined them all doing the same on the other side of the wall. I wondered what game they might play.

Lizzie and I sat opposite each other, legs crossed, knees just touching. I raised both hands to begin a clapping game, but Lizzie paused at the sight of my funny fingers. They were puckered and pink.

'They don't hurt any more,' I said.

'You sure?'

I nodded, and we began to clap, though she was too soft with my funny fingers to make the right sound.

'So, what's your big secret, Essymay?' she asked.

I'd almost forgotten. I stopped clapping, reached into the pocket of my pinny and pulled out the slip that had landed in my lap earlier that morning.

'What kind of secret is that?' asked Lizzie, taking the slip in her hand and turning it over.

'It's a word, but I can only read this bit.' I pointed to *bondmaid*. 'Can you read the rest for me?'

She moved a finger across the words, just as I had done. After a while, she handed it back.

'Where did you find it?' she asked.

'It found me,' I said. And when I saw that wasn't enough, 'One of the assistants threw it away.'

'Threw it away, did they?'

'Yes,' I said, without looking down, even a little bit. 'Some words just don't make sense and they throw them away.'

'Well, what will you do with your secret?' Lizzie asked.

I hadn't thought. All I'd wanted was to show it to Lizzie. I knew not to ask Da to keep it safe, and it couldn't stay in my pinny forever.

'Can you keep it for me?' I asked.

'I s'pose I can, if you want me to. Though I don't know what's so special about it.'

It was special because it had come to me. It was almost nothing, but not quite. It was small and fragile and it might not mean anything important, but I needed to keep it from the fire grate. I didn't know how to say any of this to Lizzie, and she didn't insist. Instead, she got to her hands and knees, reached under her bed and pulled out a small wooden trunk.

I watched as she drew a finger through the thin film of dust that covered the scarred top. She wasn't in a hurry to open it.

'What's inside?' I asked.

'Nothing. Everything I came with has gone into that wardrobe.'

'Won't you need it to go on journeys?'

'I won't be needing it,' she said, and released the latch.

I placed my secret in the bottom of the trunk and sat back on my haunches. It looked small and lonely. I moved it to one side, and then to the other. Finally, I retrieved it and cradled it in both hands.

Lizzie stroked my hair. 'You'll have to find more treasures to keep it company.'

I stood, held the slip of paper as high as I could above the trunk and let go, then I watched it float down, swaying from side to side until it came to rest in one corner of the trunk.

'This is where it wants to be,' I said, bending down to smooth it flat. But it wouldn't flatten. There was a lump under the paper lining that covered the bottom of the trunk. The edge had already lifted, so I peeled it back a little more.

'It's not empty, Lizzie,' I said, as the head of a pin revealed itself.

Lizzie leaned over me to see what I was talking about.

'It's a hat pin,' she said, reaching down to pick it up. On its head were three small beads, one on top of the other, each a kaleidoscope of colour. Lizzie turned it between her thumb and finger. As it spun, I could see her remembering it. She brought it to her chest, kissed me on the forehead then placed the pin carefully on her bedside table, next to the small photograph of her mother.

☙

Our walk home to Jericho took longer than it should, because I was small and Da liked to meander while he smoked his pipe. I loved the smell of it.

We crossed the wide Banbury Road and started down St Margaret's, past tall houses standing in pairs with pretty gardens and trees shading the path. Then I led us on a zigzagging route through narrow streets where the houses were tightly packed, one against the other, just like slips in their pigeon-holes. When we turned into Observatory Street, Da tapped his pipe clean against a wall and put it in his pocket. Then he lifted me onto his shoulders.

'You'll be too big for this soon,' he said.

'Will I stop being a littlun when I get too big?'

'Is that what Lizzie calls you?'

'It's one of the things she calls me. She also calls me *cabbage* and *Essymay*.'

'*Littlun* I understand, and *Essymay*, but why does she call you *cabbage*?'

Cabbage always came with a cuddle or a kind smile. It made perfect sense, but I couldn't explain why.

Our house was halfway down Observatory Street, just past Adelaide Street. When we got to the corner, I counted out loud: 'One, two, three, four, stop right here for our front door.'

We had an old brass knocker shaped like a hand. Lily had found it at a bric-a-brac stall in the Covered Market – Da said it had been tarnished and scratched, and there'd been river sand between the fingers, but he'd cleaned it up and attached it to the door on the

16

day they were married. Now, he took his key from his pocket and I leaned down and covered Lily's hand with mine. I knocked it four times.

'No one's home,' I said.

'They will be soon.' He opened the door and I ducked as he stepped into the hall.

⁓

Da set me down, put his satchel on the sideboard and bent to pick the letters off the floor. I followed him down the hall and into the kitchen and sat at the table while he cooked our dinner. We had an occasional maid come three times a week to cook and clean and wash our clothes, but this wasn't one of her days.

'Will I go into service when I stop being a littlun?'

Da jiggled the pan to turn the sausages then looked across to where I sat at the kitchen table.

'No, you won't.'

'Why not?'

He jiggled the sausages again. 'It's hard to explain.'

I waited. He took a deep breath and the thinking lines between his eyebrows got deeper. 'Lizzie is fortunate to be in service, but for you it would be *un*fortunate.'

'I don't understand.'

'No, I don't suppose you do.' He drained the peas and mashed the potatoes, and put them on our plates with the sausages. When he finally sat at the table, he said, 'Service means different things to different people, Essy, depending on their position in society.'

'Will all the different meanings be in the Dictionary?'

His thinking lines relaxed. 'We'll search the pigeon-holes tomorrow, shall we?'

'Would Lily have been able to explain *service*?' I asked.

'Your mother would have had the words to explain the world to you, Essy,' Da said. 'But without her, we must rely on the Scrippy.'

❧

The next morning, before we sorted the post, Da held me up and let me search the pigeon-holes containing S words.

'Now, let's see what we can find.'

Da pointed to a pigeon-hole that was almost too high, but not quite. I pulled out a bundle of slips. *Service* was written on a top-slip, and beneath that: *Multiple senses*. We sat at the sorting table, and Da let me loosen the string that bound the slips. They were separated into four smaller bundles of quotations, each with its own top-slip and a definition suggested by one of Dr Murray's more trusted volunteers.

'Edith sorted these,' Da said, arranging the piles on the sorting table.

'You mean Aunty Ditte?'

'The very same.'

'Is she a lexi—, lexiographa, like you?'

'Lexicographer. No. But she is a very learned lady and we are lucky she has taken on the Dictionary as her hobby. There's not a week goes by without a letter from Ditte to Dr Murray with a word, or copy for the next section.'

Not a week went by when we didn't get our own letter from Ditte. When Da read them aloud, they were mostly about me.

'Am I her hobby too?'

'You are her goddaughter, which is much more important than a hobby.'

Although Ditte's real name was Edith, when I was very small I struggled to say it. There were other ways to say her name, she'd said, and she let me choose my favourite. In Denmark she would be called Ditte. Ditte is sweeter, I sometimes thought, enjoying the rhyme. I never called her Edith again.

'Now, let's see how Ditte has defined *service*,' Da said.

A lot of the definitions described Lizzie, but none of them explained why *service* might mean something different for her and for me. The last pile we looked at had no top-slip.

'They're duplicates,' Da said. He helped me read them.

'What will happen to them?' I asked. But before Da could answer, the Scriptorium door opened and one of the assistants came in, knotting his tie as if he had only just put it on. When he was done it sat crooked, and he forgot to tuck it into his waistcoat.

Mr Mitchell looked over my shoulder at the piles of slips laid out on the sorting table. A wave of dark hair fell across his face. He smoothed it back but there wasn't enough oil to hold it.

'*Service*,' he said.

'Lizzie's in service,' I said.

'So she is.'

'But Da says it would be unfortunate for me to be in service.'

Mr Mitchell looked at Da, who shrugged and smiled.

'When you grow up, Esme, I think you could do whatever you wanted to do,' Mr Mitchell said.

'I want to be a lexicographer.'

'Well, this is a good start,' he said, pointing to all the slips.

Mr Maling and Mr Balk came into the Scriptorium, discussing a word they had been arguing about the day before. Then Dr Murray came in, his black gown billowing. I looked from one man to another and wondered if I could tell how old they were from the length and colour of their beards. Da's and Mr Mitchell's were the shortest and darkest. Dr Murray's was turning white and reached all the way to the top button of his waistcoat. Mr Maling's and Mr Balk's were somewhere inbetween. Now they were all there, it was time for me to disappear. I crawled beneath the sorting table and watched for stray slips. I wanted more than anything for another word to find me. None did, but when Da told me to run along with Lizzie my pockets were not completely empty.

I showed Lizzie the slip. 'Another secret,' I said.

'Should I be letting you bring secrets out of the Scrippy?'

'Da said this one is a duplicate. There's another one that says exactly the same thing.'

'What does it say?'

'That you should be in service and I should do needlepoint until a gentleman wants to marry me.'

'Really? It says that?'

'I think so.'

'Well, I could teach you needlepoint,' Lizzie said.

I thought about it. 'No thank you, Lizzie. Mr Mitchell said I could be a lexicographer.'

For the next few mornings, after helping Da with the post, I'd crawl to one end of the sorting table to wait for falling words. But when they fell, they were always quickly retrieved by an assistant. After a few days I forgot to keep an eye out for words, and after a few months I forgot about the trunk under Lizzie's bed.

April 1888

'Shoes?' Da said.

'Shiny,' I replied.

'Stockings?'

'Pulled up tight.'

'Dress?'

'A bit short.'

'Too tight?'

'No, just right.'

'Phew,' he said, wiping his brow. Then he took a long look at my hair. 'Where does it all come from?' he muttered, trying to flatten it with his big, clumsy hands. When red curls sprang between his fingers, he made a game of catching them, but he didn't have enough hands. As one lock was tamed, another escaped. I began to giggle, and he threw his hands in the air.

Because of my hair, we were going to be late. Da said that was fashionable. When I asked him what *fashionable* meant, he said it was something that mattered a lot to some and not at all to others, and it could be applied to everything from hats to wallpaper to the time you arrived at a party.

'Do we like to be fashionable?' I asked.

'Not usually,' he said.

'We'd better run, then.' I took his hand and dragged him along at a trot. We were at Sunnyside ten minutes later, just a little out of breath.

The front gates were decorated in As and Bs of every size, style and colour. Colouring my own letters had kept me quiet for hours in the previous week, and I was thrilled to see them among the As and Bs of all the Murray children.

'Here comes Mr Mitchell. Is he fashionable?' I asked.

'Not at all.' Da held out his hand as Mr Mitchell approached.

'A big day,' Mr Mitchell said to Da.

'A long time coming,' Da said to Mr Mitchell.

Mr Mitchell kneeled down so we were face-to-face. Today there was enough oil in his hair to keep it in place. 'Happy birthday, Esme.'

'Thank you, Mr Mitchell.'

'How old are you now?'

'I turn six today, and I know this party isn't for me – it's for *A and B* – but Da says I can have two pieces of cake anyway.'

'Only right.' He pulled a small packet from his pocket and handed it to me. 'You can't have a party without presents. These are for you, young lady. With any luck you'll be using them to colour the letter C before your next birthday.'

I unwrapped a small box of coloured pencils and beamed at Mr Mitchell. When he stood up, I saw his ankles. He wore one black sock and one green.

A long table was set up under the ash, and it looked exactly as I'd imagined. There was a white cloth covered with plates of food and a glass bowl full of punch. Coloured streamers hung in the branches of the tree and there were more people than I could count. No one wanted to be fashionable, I thought.

Beyond the table, the younger Murray boys were playing tag, and the girls were skipping. If I went over, they would invite me to play – they always did – but the rope would feel awkward in my hand, and when I was in the middle I could never keep the rhythm. They would encourage, and I would try again, but there was no fun for anyone when the rope kept stalling. I watched as Hilda and Ethelwyn turned the rope, counting the turns with a song. Rosfrith and Elsie were in the middle, holding hands and jumping faster and faster as their sisters sped up. Rosfrith was four, and Elsie was just a few months older than I was. Their blonde plaits flew up and down like wings. The whole time I watched, the rope never stalled. I touched my own hair and realised Da's plait had come loose.

'Wait here,' said Da. He walked around the crowd towards the kitchen. After a minute he was back, Lizzie at his heels.

'Happy birthday, Essymay,' she said, taking my hand.

'Where are we going?'

'To get your present.'

I followed Lizzie up the narrow stairs from the kitchen. When we were in her room, she sat me on the bed and reached into the pocket of her pinny.

'Close your eyes, me little cabbage, and hold out both hands,' she said.

I closed my eyes and felt a smile spread across my face. A fluttering danced across my palms. Ribbons. I tried not to let the smile fall; there was a box of ribbons beside my bed, overflowing.

'You can open your eyes.'

Two ribbons. Not shiny and smooth like the one Da had tied around my hair that morning, but each was embroidered on its ends with the same bluebells that were scattered across my dress.

'They ain't slippery like the others, so you won't lose them so easy,' Lizzie said as she started pulling her fingers through my hair. 'And I think they'll look very nice with French plaits.'

A few minutes later, Lizzie and I returned to the garden. 'The belle of the ball,' Da said. 'And just in time.'

Dr Murray stood in the shade of the ash, a huge book on the small table in front of him. He tapped a fork on the edge of his glass. We all went quiet.

'When Dr Johnson undertook to compile *his* dictionary, he resolved to leave no word unexamined.' Dr Murray paused to make sure we were all listening. 'This resolve was soon eroded when he realised that one enquiry only gave occasion to another, that book referred to book, that to scratch was not always to find, and to find was not always to be informed.'

I tugged on Da's sleeve. 'Who is Dr Johnson?'

'The editor of a previous dictionary,' he whispered.

'If there's already a dictionary, why are you making a new one?'

'The old one wasn't quite good enough.'

'Will Dr Murray's be good enough?' Da put a finger to his lips and turned back to listen to what Dr Murray was saying.

'If I have been more successful than Dr Johnson, it has been owing to the goodwill and helpful co-operation of many scholars and specialists, most of them men whose time is much occupied but whose interest in this undertaking has led them willingly to place some of it at the Editor's service, and freely to contribute of their knowledge to the perfection of the work.' Dr Murray began to thank all the people who had helped compile the words for *A and B*. The list was so long my legs began to ache from standing. I sat down on the grass and started pulling up blades, peeling back the layers to reveal the tenderest green shoots and nibbling on them. It was only when I heard Ditte's name that I looked up, and soon after that I heard Da's and those of the other men who worked in the Scriptorium.

When the speech was over and Dr Murray was being congratulated, Da walked over to the volume of words and lifted it from where it rested.

He called me over and made me sit with my back against the rough trunk of the ash. Then he put the heavy volume in my lap.

'Are my birthday words in it?'

'They certainly are.' He opened the cover and turned the pages until he reached the first word.

A.

Then he turned a few more pages.

Aard-vark.

Then a few more.

My words, I thought, all bound in leather, the pages trimmed in gold. I thought the weight of them would hold me to that place forever.

Da put *A and B* back on the table, and the crowd swallowed it up. I feared for the words. 'Be careful,' I said. But no one heard.

'Here comes Ditte,' said Da.

I ran towards her as she came through the gates.

'You missed the cake,' I said.

'I would call that perfect timing,' she said, bending down and kissing me on the head. 'The only cake I eat is Madeira. It's a rule and it helps keep me trim.'

Aunty Ditte was as wide as Mrs Ballard and a little bit shorter. 'What is *trim*?' I asked.

'An impossible ideal and something you are not likely to have to worry about,' she said. Then she added, 'It's when you make something a little smaller.'

Ditte wasn't really my aunt, but my real aunt lived in Scotland and had so many children she didn't have time to spoil me. That's what Da said. Ditte had no children and lived in Bath with her sister, Beth. She was very busy finding quotations for Dr Murray and writing her history of England, but she still had time to send me letters and bring me gifts.

'Dr Murray said you and Beth were proflitic contributors,' I said, with some authority.

'Prolific,' Ditte corrected.

'Is that a nice thing to be?'

'It means we have collected a lot of words and quotations for Dr Murray's dictionary, and I'm sure he meant it as a compliment.'

'But you haven't collected as many as Mr Thomas Austin. He is far more proflitic than you.'

'Prolific. Yes, he is. I don't know where he finds the time. Now, let's get some punch.' Ditte took my good hand and we walked towards the party table.

I followed Ditte into the crowd and became lost in a forest of brown and plaid broadcloth trousers and patterned skirts. Everyone wanted to talk to her, and I made a game of guessing who the trousers belonged to each time we stopped.

'Should it really be included?' I heard one man say. 'It's such an unpleasant word that I feel we should discourage its use.' Ditte's hand tightened around mine. I didn't recognise the trousers, so I looked up to see if I would recognise the face, but all I could see was his beard.

'We are not the arbiters of the English language, sir. Our job, surely, is to chronicle, not judge.'

When we finally came to the table under the ash, Ditte poured two glasses of punch and filled a small plate with sandwiches.

'Believe it or not, Esme, I haven't travelled all this way to talk about words. Let's find somewhere quiet to sit, then you can tell me how you and your father are getting on.'

I led Ditte to the Scriptorium. When she closed the door behind her, the party went quiet. It was the first time I'd been in the Scriptorium without Da or Dr Murray or any of the other men. As we stood on the threshold, I felt all the responsibility of introducing Ditte to the pigeon-holes full of words and quotations, to all the old dictionaries and reference books, and to the fascicles, where the words were first published before there were enough for a whole volume. It had taken me a long time to learn how to pronounce *fascicle*, and I wanted Ditte to hear me say it.

I pointed to one of the two trays on the small table near the door. 'That's where all the letters go that are written by Dr Murray and Da and all the others. Sometimes I get to put them in the pillar box at the end of the day,' I said. 'The letters you send to Dr Murray go in this tray. If they have slips in them we take them out first, and Da lets me put them into pigeon-holes.'

Ditte rummaged around in her handbag and produced one of the small envelopes I knew so well. Even with her there beside me, the neat and familiar slant of her writing brought a tiny thrill.

'Thought I'd save the cost of a stamp,' she said, handing me the envelope.

I wasn't sure what to do with it without Da giving directions.

'Are there slips inside?' I asked.

'No slips, just my opinion on the inclusion of an old word that has the gentlemen of the Philological Society a little flustered.'

'What is the word?' I asked.

She paused, bit her lip. 'It's not for polite company, I'm afraid. Your father would not thank me for introducing you to it.'

'Are you asking Dr Murray to leave it out?'

'On the contrary, my darling, I'm urging him to put it in.'

I placed the envelope on top of the pile of letters on Dr Murray's desk and continued with my tour.

'These are the pigeon-holes that hold all the slips,' I said, waving my arm up and down the nearest wall of pigeon-holes, then doing the same for other walls around the Scriptorium. 'Da said there would be thousands and thousands of slips and so there needed to be hundreds and hundreds of pigeon-holes. They were built especially, and Dr Murray designed the slips to be the perfect fit.'

Ditte removed a bundle, and I felt my heart beat. 'I'm not supposed to touch the slips without Da,' I said.

'Well, I think if we're very careful, no one will know.' Ditte gave me a secret smile, and my heart beat faster. She flicked through the slips until she came to an odd one, larger than the rest. 'Look,' she said, 'it's written on the back of a letter – see, the paper is the same colour as your bluebells.'

'What does the letter say?'

Ditte read what she could. 'It's just a fragment, but I think it might have been a love letter.'

'Why would someone cut up a love letter?'

'I can only assume the sentiment was not returned.'

She put the slips back in their pigeon-hole and there was nothing to show that they had ever been removed.

'These are my birthday words,' I said, moving along to the oldest pigeon-holes where all the words for A to Ant were stored. Ditte raised an eyebrow. 'They're the words Da was working on before I was born. Usually, I'll pick one out on my birthday and Da will help me understand it,' I said, and Ditte nodded. 'And this is the sorting table,' I continued. 'Da sits right here, and Mr Balk sits here, and Mr Maling sits next to him. *Bonan matenon.*' I looked to see Ditte's reaction.

'I beg your pardon?'

'*Bonan matenon.* That's how Mr Maling says hello. It's Speranto.'

'Esperanto.'

'That's right. And Mr Worrell sits there, and Mr Mitchell usually sits there, but he likes to move around. Do you know he always wears odd socks?'

'How would you know that?'

I giggled again. 'Because my place is under here.' I got on my hands and knees and crawled under the sorting table. I peeked out.

'Is it, indeed?'

I almost invited her to sit with me, then thought better of it. 'You'd need a trim to fit under here,' I said.

She laughed and held out her hand to help me out. 'Let's sit in your father's chair, shall we?'

Every year, Ditte would give me two gifts on my birthday: a book and a story. The book was always a grown-up one with interesting words that children never used. Once I'd learned to read, she would insist I read aloud until I came to a word I didn't know. Only then would she begin the story.

I unwrapped the book.

'*On – the – Origin – of – Species*,' Ditte said the last word very slowly and underlined it with her finger.

'What is it about?' I turned the pages looking for pictures.

'Animals.'

'I like animals,' I said. Then I turned to the introduction and began to read. '*When on board H.M.S* Beagle …' I looked at Ditte. 'Is it about a dog?'

She laughed. 'No. H.M.S. *Beagle* was a ship.'

I continued '… *as a* …' I stopped and pointed to the next word.

'*Naturalist*,' Ditte said, then sounded it out slowly. 'Someone who studies the natural world. Animals and plants.'

'*Naturalist*,' I said, trying it out. I closed the book. 'Will you tell me the story now?'

'What story would that be?' Ditte said, looking bewildered, but smiling.

'You know.'

Ditte shifted her weight in the chair, and I manoeuvred myself into the soft sling between her lap and shoulder.

'You're longer than last year,' she said.

'But I still fit.' I leaned back, and she wrapped her arms around me.

'The first time I saw Lily, she was making cucumber-and-watercress soup.'

I closed my eyes and imagined my mother stirring a pot of soup. I tried to dress her in ordinary clothes, but she refused to take off the bridal veil she wore in the photograph by Da's bed. I loved that picture more than all the others because Da was looking at her and she was looking straight at me. The veil will end up in the soup, I thought, and smiled.

'She was under the instruction of her aunt, Miss Fernley,' Ditte continued, 'a very tall and very capable woman who was not only secretary of our tennis club, where this story takes place, but headmistress of a small private ladies' college. Lily was a student at her aunt's school, and the cucumber-and-watercress soup was apparently on the syllabus.'

'What is *syllabus*?' I asked.

'It is the list of subjects you learn about at school.'

'Do I have a syllabus at St Barnabas?'

'You've only just started, so reading and writing are all that's on your syllabus. They'll add subjects as you get older.'

'What will they add?'

'Hopefully something less domestic than cucumber-and-watercress soup. Now, may I continue?'

'Yes, please.'

'Miss Fernley had insisted that Lily make the soup for our club lunch. It was awful; everyone thought so, and some even said it out loud. I'm afraid Lily may have overheard, because she retreated to the club-house and busied herself with wiping tables that didn't need wiping.'

'Poor Lily,' I said.

'Well, you might not think so when you hear the rest of the story. If it wasn't for that awful soup, you might never have been born.'

I knew what was coming and held my breath to hear it.

'Somehow, your father managed to empty his bowl. I was dumb-founded, but then I watched him take that bowl into the kitchen and ask Lily for a second helping.'

'Did he eat that too?'

'He did. And between mouthfuls, he asked Lily question after question, and her face went from that of a shy and awkward girl to a confident young woman in the space of fifteen minutes.'

'What did he ask her?'

'That I can't tell you, but by the time he'd finished eating, it was as if they had known each other all their lives.'

'Did you know they would get married?'

'Well, I remember thinking how fortunate it was that Harry knew how to boil an egg, because Lily was never going to like spending too much time in the kitchen. So, yes, I think I did know they would get married.'

'And then I was born and then she died.'

'Yes.'

'But when we talk about her, she comes to life.'

'Never forget that, Esme. Words are our tools of resurrection.'

A new word. I looked up.

'It's when you bring something back,' Ditte said.

'But Lily will never really come back.'

'No. She won't.'

I paused, trying to remember the rest of the story. 'And so, you told Da you will be my favourite aunt.'

'I did.'

'And that you will always take my side, even when I'm troublesome.'

'Did I say that?' I turned to look at her face. She smiled. 'It's exactly what Lily would have wanted me to say, and I meant every word.'

'The end,' I said.

April 1891

At breakfast one morning, Da said, 'The C words would certainly cause consternation considering countless certifiable cases kept coming.' It took me less than a minute to work it out.

'*Kept*,' I said. '*Kept* starts with a K not a C.'

His mouth was still full of porridge; I was that quick.

'I thought throwing in *certifiable* might have tricked you,' he said.

'But that must start with a C; it's from the word *certain*.'

'It *certainly* is. Now, tell me which quotation you like best.' Da pushed a page of dictionary proofs across the breakfast table.

It had been three years since the picnic to celebrate *A and B*, but they were still working on the proofs for C. The page had been typeset but some of the lines had been ruled out, and the margins were messy with Da's corrections. Where he'd run out of room, he'd pinned a scrap of paper to the edge and written on that.

'I like the new one,' I said, pointing to the scrap of paper.

'What does it say?'

'*To certefye this thinge, sende for the damoysell; and then shal ye know, by her owne mouthe.*'

'Why do you like it?'

'It sounds funny, like the man who wrote it couldn't spell and was making up some of the words.'

'It's just old,' Da said, taking back the proof and reading what he'd written. 'Words change over time, you see. The way they look, the way they sound; sometimes even their meaning changes. They have their own history.' Da ran his finger under the sentence. 'If you took away some of the Es, this would almost look modern.'

'What's a *damoysell*?'

'It's a young woman.'

'Am I a damoysell?'

He looked at me, and the tiniest frown twitched his eyebrows.

'I'll be ten next birthday,' I said, hopeful.

'Ten, you say? Well, that settles it. You will be a damoysell in no time.'

'And will the words keep changing?'

The spoon stopped midway to his mouth. 'It's possible, I suppose, that once the meaning is written down it will become fixed.'

'So you and Dr Murray could make the words mean whatever you want them to mean, and we'll all have to use them that way forever?'

'Of course not. Our job is to find consensus. We search through books to see how a word is used, then we come up with meanings that make sense of them all. It's quite scientific, actually.'

'What does it mean?'

'*Consensus*? Well, it means everyone agrees.'

'Do you ask everyone?'

'No, clever-boots. But I doubt a book's been written that we haven't consulted.'

'And who writes the books?' I asked.

'All sorts of people. Now stop asking questions and eat your breakfast; you're going to be late for school.'

❧

The bell rang for lunch, and I saw Lizzie in her usual place outside the school gates, looking awkward. I wanted to run to her, but I didn't.

'You mustn't let them see you cry,' she said as she took my hand.

'I haven't been crying.'

'You have, and I know why. I saw them teasing you.'

I shrugged and felt more tears spring to my eyes. I looked down at my feet stepping one in front of the other.

'What's it about?' she asked.

I held up my funny fingers. She grabbed them, kissed them and blew a raspberry in my palm. I couldn't help laughing.

'Half their fathers have funny fingers, you know.'

I looked up at her.

'True. Them that work in the type foundry wear their burns like a badge telling the whole of Jericho their trade. Their littluns are scamps for teasing you.'

'But I'm different.'

'We's all different,' she said. But she didn't understand.

'I'm like the word *alphabetary*,' I said.

'Never heard of it.'

'It's one of my birthday words, but Da says it's obsolete. No use to anyone.'

Lizzie laughed. 'Do you talk like that in class?'

I shrugged again.

'They have different kinds of families, Essymay. They's not used to talking about words and books and history the way you and your da do. Some people feel better about themselves if they can pull others down a bit. When you're older things will change, I promise.'

We walked on in silence. The closer we got to the Scriptorium, the better I felt.

After eating sandwiches in the kitchen with Lizzie and Mrs Ballard, I crossed the garden to the Scriptorium. One by one, the assistants looked up from their lunch or their words to see who had come in. I went quietly and sat beside Da. He cleared some space, and I took an exercise book from my satchel to practise the longhand I'd been learning in school. When I was done, I slid off my chair and under the sorting table.

There were no slips, so I did a survey of the assistants' shoes. Each pair suited its owner perfectly, and each had its habits. Mr Worrall's were finely tanned and sat very still and pigeon-toed, while Mr Mitchell's were the opposite: his shoes were comfortably worn with the toes turned out and heels bouncing up and down without pause. He had a different-coloured sock peeping out of each shoe. Mr Maling's shoes were adventurous and never where I expected them to be, Mr Balk's were pulled back under his chair, and Mr Sweatman's were always tapping out a pattern that I imagined as a tune in his head. When I peeked from under the table, he was usually smiling. Da's shoes were my favourite, and I always inspected them last. On this day, they rested one on the other, the soles of both exposed. I paused to touch the tiny hole that had just started to let in water. The shoe waved, as if to shoo a fly. I touched it again and it stopped, rigid. It was waiting. I wriggled my finger, just the tiniest bit. Then the shoe fell sideways, lifeless and suddenly old. The foot it had shod began stroking my arm. It was so clumsy that I had barely enough room in my cheeks to hold all the giggles that wanted to escape. I gave the big toe a squeeze and crawled to where there was just enough light to read by.

We were startled by three sharp raps on the Scriptorium door. Da's foot found his shoe.

From under the table, I watched as Da opened the door to a small man with a large blond moustache and hardly any hair on his head. 'Crane,' I heard the man say as Da ushered him in. 'I'm expected.' His clothes were too big for him, and I wondered if he was hoping to grow into them. It was the new assistant.

Some assistants only came for a few months, but sometimes they stayed forever, like Mr Sweatman. He'd come the year before and, of all the men who sat around the sorting table, he was the only one without a beard. It meant I could see his smile, and he happened to smile a lot. When Da introduced Mr Crane to the men around the sorting table, Mr Crane didn't smile once.

'And this little scapegrace is Esme,' said Da, helping me up.

I held out my hand, but Mr Crane didn't take it.

'What was she doing under there?' he asked.

'Whatever children do under tables, I suppose,' said Mr Sweatman, and his smile met mine.

Da leaned towards me. 'Let Dr Murray know that the new assistant has arrived, Esme.'

I ran across the garden to the kitchen, and Mrs Ballard walked with me to the dining room.

Dr Murray sat at one end of the large table, Mrs Murray at the other. There was room for all eleven of their children in between, but three had flown the coop, Lizzie said. The rest were spread along each side of the table, the biggest at Dr Murray's end, the littlest in high chairs near their mother. I stood dumb as they finished saying grace, then Elsie and Rosfrith waved and I waved back, my message suddenly less important.

'Our new assistant?' Dr Murray said over his spectacles when he saw me lurking.

I nodded, and he rose. The rest of the Murrays began to eat.

In the Scriptorium, Da was explaining something to Mr Crane, who turned when he heard us come in.

'Dr Murray, sir. An honour to join your team,' he said, holding out his hand and bowing slightly.

Dr Murray cleared his throat. It sounded a bit like a grunt. He shook Mr Crane's hand. 'It's not for everyone,' he said. 'Takes a certain … diligence. Are you diligent, Mr Crane?'

'Of course, sir,' he said.

Dr Murray nodded then returned to the house to finish lunch.

Da continued with his tour. Whenever he told Mr Crane something about the way the slips were sorted, Mr Crane would nod and say, 'Quite straightforward.'

'The slips are sent in by volunteers from all over the world,' I said, when Da was showing him how the pigeon-holes were ordered.

Mr Crane looked down at me, frowned a little but made no response. I stepped back a fraction.

Mr Sweatman put a hand on my shoulder. 'I came across a slip from Australia once,' he said. 'That's about as far away from England as you can get.'

When Dr Murray returned from lunch to give Mr Crane his instructions, I didn't sit and listen.

'Will he be here for a little while or forever?' I whispered to Da.

'For the duration,' he said. 'So, probably forever.'

I crawled beneath the sorting table, and a few minutes later an unfamiliar pair of shoes joined those I knew so well.

Mr Crane's shoes were old, like Da's, but they hadn't been polished in a while. I watched as they tried to settle. He crossed his right leg over his left, then his left over his right. Eventually, he wrapped his ankles around the front legs of his chair, and it looked as though his shoes were trying to hide from me.

Just before Lizzie was to take me back to school, a whole pile of slips fell beside Mr Crane's chair. I heard Da say that some of the C bundles had become 'unwieldy with the weight of possibility'. He made that little noise he made when he thought he was being funny.

Mr Crane didn't laugh. 'They were poorly tied,' he said, bending to sweep up as many slips as he could in a single movement. His fingers closed into a fist around them, and I saw the slips crushed. I let out a little gasp, and it made him bump his head on the underside of the table.

'All right there, Mr Crane?' asked Mr Maling.

'Surely the girl is too big to be under there.'

'It's just until she returns to school,' said Mr Sweatman.

When my breathing settled, and the Scriptorium returned to its regular shuffle and hum, I searched the shadows under the sorting table. Two slips still rested beside Mr Worrall's tidy shoes, as if they knew they would be safe from some careless tread. I picked them up and had a sudden memory of the trunk beneath Lizzie's bed. I couldn't bring myself to return them to Mr Crane.

When I saw Lizzie hovering at the door, I emerged beside Da's chair.

'That time already?' he said, but I had a feeling he'd been watching the clock.

I put the exercise book in my satchel and joined Lizzie in the garden.

'Can I put something in the trunk before going back to school?'

It had been a long time since I'd put anything in the trunk, but Lizzie took no more than a moment to understand. 'I've often wondered if you'd find anything else to put in it.'

The slips weren't the only words that found their way into the trunk.

On the floor of Da's wardrobe were two wooden boxes. I found them when we were playing hide-and-seek. The sharp corner of one stuck painfully into my back as I pushed myself into the furthest corner. I opened it.

It was too dark among Da's coats and Lily's musty dresses to see what was inside, but my hand stroked the edges of what felt like envelopes. Then there was a clomping on the stairs, and Da sang '*Fee Fi Fo Fum*'. I closed the lid and shuffled towards the centre of the wardrobe. Light flooded in, and I jumped out into his arms.

Later that night, when I should have been asleep, I wasn't. Da was still downstairs correcting proofs, so I sneaked out of bed and tip-toed across the landing to his bedroom. 'Open sesame,' I whispered, and pulled on the wardrobe doors.

I reached in and brought out each box. I sat with them beneath Da's window, the dusky evening light still good enough to see by. They were almost the same – pale wood with brass corners – but one box was polished, the other dull. I pulled the polished box closer and caressed the honeyed wood. A hundred envelopes, thick and thin, pressed against each other in the order they were sent. His plain white against her blue. They mostly alternated, though sometimes there were two or three white in a row, as if Da had a lot to say about something that Lily had lost interest in. If I read the letters first to last they would tell a story of their courtship, but I knew it was a story with a sad ending. I closed the box without opening a single one.

The other box was also full of letters, but none were from Lily. They were from different people and were tied in bundles with string. The biggest bundle was from Ditte. I slid the latest letter from beneath the string and read it. It was mostly about the Dictionary; about the C words that never seemed to end, and how the Press Delegates kept asking Dr Murray to work more quickly because the Dictionary was costing too much. But the last bit was about me.

Ada Murray tells me James has the children sorting slips. She painted quite a picture of them huddled around the dining table late into the night, barely visible under a mountain of paper. She even ventured to say that she thought this may have been his motive for a big brood all along. Thank goodness for her sense and good humour. I do believe the Dictionary might have faltered without it.

You must tell Esme to stay well-hidden when she's in the Scrippy or she will be Dr Murray's next recruit. I daresay she's bright enough, and I wonder if she would, in fact, be willing.

Yours,

Edith

I put both boxes back in the wardrobe then I tip-toed across the landing. The letter was still in my hand.

The next day, Lizzie watched as I opened the trunk. I pulled Ditte's letter from my pocket and placed it on top of the slips that covered the bottom.

'You're collecting a lot of secrets,' she said, her hand finding the cross beneath her clothes.

'It's about me,' I said.

'Discarded or neglected?' She'd insisted on rules.

I thought about it. 'Forgotten,' I said.

I returned to the wardrobe again and again to read Ditte's letters – there was always something about me; some answer to a query of Da's. It was as if I were a word and the letters were slips that helped define me. If I read them all, I thought, maybe I would make more sense.

But I could never bring myself to read the letters in the polished box. I liked to look at them, to run my hand across their spines and feel them flutter past. They were together in that box, my mother and my father, and when sleep was about to catch me, I sometimes imagined I could hear their muffled voices. One night I sneaked into Da's room and crawled like a hunting cat into the wardrobe. I wanted to catch them unawares. But when I lifted the lid of their polished box, they went quiet. A terrible loneliness shadowed me back to bed and kept me from sleeping.

The next morning, I was too tired for school. Da took me to Sunnyside, and I spent the morning beneath the sorting table with blank slips and coloured pencils. I wrote my name in different colours on ten different slips.

When I opened the polished box later that night, I nestled each slip between a white envelope and a blue. We were together now, all three of us. I wouldn't miss a thing.

The trunk beneath Lizzie's bed began to feel the weight of all the letters and words.

'No shells or stones. Nothing pretty,' Lizzie said when I opened it one afternoon. 'Why do you collect all this paper, Essymay?'

'It's not the paper I'm collecting, Lizzie; it's the words.'

'But what's so important about *these* words?' she asked.

I didn't know, exactly. It was more feeling than thought. Some words were just like baby birds fallen from the nest. With others, I felt as though I'd come across a clue: I knew it was important, but I wasn't sure why. Ditte's letters were the same, like parts of a jigsaw that might one day fit together to explain something Da didn't know how to say – something Lily might have.

I didn't know how to say any of this, so I asked, 'Why do you do needlepoint, Lizzie?'

She was quiet for a very long time. She folded her washing and changed the sheets on her bed.

I stopped waiting for an answer and went back to reading a letter from Ditte to Da. *Have you considered what to do when Esme outgrows St Barnabas?* she asked. I thought about my head popping through the chimney of the schoolroom and my arms extending out the windows on both sides.

'I guess I like to keep me hands busy,' Lizzie said. For a moment I forgot what I'd asked. 'And it proves I exist,' she added.

'But that's silly. Of course you exist.'

She stopped making the bed and looked at me with such seriousness I put down Ditte's letter.

'I clean, I help with the cooking, I set the fires. Everything I do gets eaten or dirtied or burned – at the end of a day there's no proof I've been here at all.' She paused, kneeled down beside me and stroked the embroidery on the edge of my skirt. It hid the repair she'd made when I tore it on brambles.

'Me needlework will always be here,' she said. 'I see this and I feel … well, I don't know the word. Like I'll always be here.'

'Permanent,' I said. 'And the rest of the time?'

'I feel like a dandelion just before the wind blows.'

August 1893

The Scriptorium always went quiet for a while over summer. 'There's more to life than words,' Da said once, when I asked where everyone went, but I didn't think he meant it. We sometimes went to Scotland to visit my aunt, but we were always back at Sunnyside before all the other assistants. I loved waiting beneath the sorting table for each pair of shoes to return. When Dr Murray came in, he would always ask Da if he'd forgotten to bring me home, and Da would always pretend he had. Then Dr Murray would look beneath the sorting table and wink at me.

At the end of the summer of the year I turned eleven, Mr Mitchell's feet failed to appear, and Dr Murray came into the Scriptorium saying very little. I waited to see a green-socked ankle crossed over a pale blue, but there was a gap where Mr Mitchell usually sat. The other feet seemed limp, and even though Mr Sweatman's shoes tapped up and down, they were tuneless.

'When will Mr Mitchell come back?' I asked Da. He took a long time to answer.

'He fell, Essy. While climbing a mountain. He won't be back.'

I thought of his odd socks and the coloured pencils he'd given me.

I'd used them until there was nothing left to hold, and that was years before. My world beneath the sorting table felt less comfortable.

When the year turned, the sorting table seemed to have shrunk. I crawled beneath it one afternoon and hit my head when I crawled out.

'Look at the state of your dress,' Lizzie said when she collected me for afternoon tea. It was patterned with smudges and dust. She beat off what she could, 'It ain't ladylike to crawl about the Scrippy, Essymay. I don't know why your father lets you.'

'Because I'm not a lady,' I said.

'You ain't a cat, either.'

When I returned to the Scriptorium, I navigated the perimeter. I trailed my funny fingers over shelves and books and collected little wads of dust. I wouldn't mind being a cat, I thought.

Mr Sweatman winked at me as I passed near him.

Mr Maling said, '*Kiel vi fartas*, Esme?'

I said, 'I'm well, thank you, Mr Maling.'

He looked at me and raised his eyebrows. 'And in Esperanto you would say?'

I had to think. '*Mi fartas bone, dankon.*'

He smiled and nodded. '*Bona.*'

Mr Crane took a deep breath to let everyone know I was a disturbance.

I considered slinking beneath the sorting table, but didn't. It was a grown-up decision, and I felt a sulk take hold as if someone other than me had made it. Instead, I found a space between two shelves and shuffled awkwardly into place, disturbing cobwebs and dust and two lost slips.

They'd been hidden beneath the shelf on my right. I picked up one and then the other. C words, only recently lost. I tucked them away then looked over to the sorting table. Mr Crane sat closest, and there was another word by his chair. I wondered if he even cared.

'She's light-fingered,' I heard Mr Crane say to Dr Murray. Dr Murray turned my way, and a chill spread through me. I thought I might turn to stone. He returned to his high desk and picked up a proof. Then he walked over to Da.

Dr Murray tried to make it look as though they were talking about the words, but neither looked at the proof. When Dr Murray had moved away, Da looked along the length of the sorting table to the gap between the shelves. He caught my eye and signalled towards the Scriptorium door.

When we were standing under the ash, Da held out his hand. I just looked at it. He said my name louder than he'd ever said it before. Then he made me turn out my pockets.

The word was flimsy and uninteresting, but I liked the quotation. When I put it in his hand, Da looked at it as if he didn't know what it was. As if he didn't know what he should do with it. I saw his lips move around the word and the sentence that contained it.

COUNT
'I count you for a fool.' – Tennyson, 1859

For a very long time he said nothing. We stood there in the cold as if we were playing a game of statues and neither of us wanted to be the first to move. Then he put the slip in his trouser pocket and steered me towards the kitchen.

'Lizzie, would it be all right if Esme spent the rest of the afternoon in your room?' Da asked, closing the door behind him to keep in the heat of the range.

Lizzie put down the potato she was peeling and wiped her hands on her apron. ''Course, Mr Nicoll. Esme is always welcome.'

'She's not to be entertained, Lizzie. She's to sit and think about her behaviour. I'd rather you didn't keep her company.'

'As you wish, Mr Nicoll,' said Lizzie, though neither she nor Da seemed able to look each other in the eye.

Alone upstairs and sitting against Lizzie's bed, I reached into the sleeve of my dress and pulled out the other word, *counted*. Whoever wrote it had beautiful handwriting. A lady, I was sure, and not just because the quotation was from Byron. The words were all curves and long limbs.

I reached under Lizzie's bed and pulled out the trunk. I always expected it to feel heavier, but it slid across the floorboards without effort. Inside, slips covered the bottom like a carpet of autumn leaves, and Ditte's letters rested among them.

It wasn't fair that I was in trouble when Mr Crane had been so careless. The words were duplicates, I was sure – common words that many volunteers would have sent in. I put both hands in the trunk and felt the slips shift through my fingers. I'd saved them all, just as Da thought he was saving the others by putting them in the Dictionary. My words came from nooks and crannies and from the discard basket in the centre of the sorting table.

My trunk is like the Dictionary, I thought. Except it's full of words that have been lost or neglected. I had an idea. I wanted to ask Lizzie for a pencil but knew she wouldn't disobey Da. I looked around her room, wondering where she would keep them.

Without her in it, Lizzie's room felt unfamiliar – as if it might not belong to her. I got off the floor and went to the wardrobe. It was a relief to see her old winter coat with the top button that didn't quite match the others. She had three pinnies and two dresses; her Sunday best, once shamrock-green, was now paled like summer grass. I brushed it with my hand and saw strips of shamrock where Lizzie had let out the seams. When I opened her drawers, all I could see were underthings, an extra set of bed linen, two shawls and a small wooden box. I knew what was in the box. Just the other day, Mrs Ballard had decided it was time I knew about monthlies, and so Lizzie had shown me the rags and the belt that she kept in there. I hoped never to see them again, so I left the box closed and shut the wardrobe door.

There was no chest with games. There were no shelves with books. The little table beside her bed held a swatch of embroidery and the photograph of her mother in its simple wooden frame. I peered at it: a plain young woman in an ordinary hat and ordinary clothes, holding a simple bouquet of flowers. Lizzie looked just like her. Behind the frame was the hat pin I'd found in the trunk.

I kneeled down and peered under the bed. At one end were Lizzie's winter boots; at the other, her chamber-pot and sewing box. My trunk lived right in the middle, its resting place marked by an absence of dust. There was nothing else. No pencils. Of course.

I looked at the trunk, still open on the floor, the latest word lying face-up on all the others. Then I looked at the hat pin on Lizzie's bedside table and remembered how sharp it was.

❧

The Dictionary of Lost Words. It took me all afternoon to scratch it inside the lid of the trunk. My hands ached from the effort. When it was done, Lizzie's hat pin lay bent out of shape on the floor, the beads as bright as the day I'd found it.

Something filled me then, some strange and awful queasiness. I tried to straighten the pin, but it refused to be made perfect. The end had become so blunt I couldn't imagine it piercing the felt of even the cheapest hat. I searched the room but found nothing that would fix it. I placed the pin on the floor beside Lizzie's bedside table, hoping she'd think it had bent in the fall.

❧

For the next few months, I mostly stayed away from the Scriptorium. Lizzie collected me from St Barnabas, fed me lunch, took me back. In the afternoons, I read my books and practised my writing. I alternated between the shade of the ash, the kitchen table and Lizzie's room, depending on the weather. I pretended I was ill when they celebrated the publication of the second volume, the one containing all the words beginning with C, including *count* and *counted*.

On my twelfth birthday, Da picked me up from St Barnabas. When we came through the gates of Sunnyside, he kept hold of my hand and I walked with him towards the Scriptorium.

It was empty, except for Dr Murray. He looked up from his desk as we came in, then stepped down to greet me.

'Happy birthday, young lady,' he said. Then he peered at me over his spectacles, unsmiling. 'Twelve, I believe.'

I nodded; he continued to peer.

My breath faltered. I was too big to hide beneath the sorting table, to escape from whatever he was thinking. So instead, I looked him in the eye.

'Your father tells me you are a good student.'

I said nothing, and he turned and gestured towards the two Dictionary volumes behind his desk.

'You must avail yourself of both volumes whenever you have the need. If you don't, there is no reason for all our efforts,' he said. 'If you require knowledge of a word beyond C, then the fascicles are at your disposal as they are published. Beyond that –' again he peered, '– you must ask your father to search the pigeon-holes. Do you have any questions?'

'What is *avail*?' I asked.

Dr Murray smiled and looked briefly at Da.

'It is an A word, thankfully. Shall we look it up?' He went to the shelf behind his desk and got down *A and B*.

When my twelfth birthday card from Ditte arrived, it contained a slip of paper. A word that Ditte said was *superfluous to need*.

'What does *superfluous* mean?' I asked Da as he put on his hat.

'Unnecessary,' he said. 'Not wanted or needed.'

I looked at the slip. It was a B word: *Brown*. Bland and boring, I thought. Not lost or neglected or forgotten, just superfluous. Da must have told Ditte I'd taken a word. I put hers in my pocket.

I thought about it all day at school. I let my fingers play with the slip's edges and imagined it a more interesting word. I considered throwing it away, but couldn't. Superfluous, Ditte had said. Maybe I could add that to the list of rules Lizzie had insisted on.

When I arrived at Sunnyside in the afternoon, I went straight up to Lizzie's room. She wasn't there, but she wouldn't mind me waiting. I pulled the trunk from under her bed and opened it.

She arrived just as I was getting the slip out of my pocket.

'It's from Ditte,' I said quickly, to stop her frown from deepening. 'She sent it for my birthday.'

Lizzie's frown began to fall away, but then something caught her eye. Her face froze. I followed her gaze and saw the rough letters scratched inside the lid of the trunk. I remembered my anger, blind and selfish. When I turned back to Lizzie, a tear was sliding down her cheek.

It felt like a gas balloon was expanding in my chest, squashing all the bits I needed to breathe and speak. I'm sorry, I'm sorry, I'm sorry, I thought, but nothing came out. She went to her bedside table and picked up the pin.

'Why?' she asked.

Still, no words. Nothing that would make sense.

'What does it even say?' Her voice teetered between rage and disappointment. I hoped for rage. Harsh words against bad behaviour. A storm then calm.

'*The Dictionary of Lost Words*,' I mumbled, not raising my eyes from a knot in one of the floorboards.

'The dictionary of stolen words, more like.'

My head snapped up. Lizzie was looking at the pin as if she might see something in it that she hadn't seen before. Her lower lip quivered, like a child's. When our eyes met, her face collapsed. It was the same look that Da had the day I was caught, as if she'd learned something new about me and didn't like it. Not rage, then. Disappointment.

'They's just words, Esme.' Lizzie held out her hand to pull me up off the floor. She made me sit on the bed beside her. I sat rigid.

'All I had of me mother was that photograph,' she said. 'She's not smiling, and I reckoned that life always weighed heavy on her, even before all us children came along. But then you found the pin.' She twirled it and the beads became a blur of colour. 'I don't know much about her for sure, but it helps me to imagine her happy, knowing something beautiful came to her.'

I thought of the photographs of Lily all around my house, the clothes that still hung in Da's wardrobe, the blue envelopes. I thought of the story Ditte told me every birthday. My mother was like a word with a thousand slips. Lizzie's mother was like a word with only two, barely enough to be counted. And I had treated one as if it were superfluous to need.

The trunk was still open, and I looked at the words carved into it. Then I looked at the pin, so fine against Lizzie's rough hand, despite its bandy leg. We both needed proof of who we were.

'I'll fix it,' I said, and I reached out, thinking I could straighten it by sheer force of will. Lizzie let me take it and watched as I tried.

'Good enough,' she said, when I finally gave up. 'And the sharpening stone might work on the point.'

The balloon in my chest burst, and a flood of emotion escaped. Tears and sniffling and a fractured apology: 'I'm sorry, I'm so sorry.'

'I know you are, me little cabbage.' Lizzie held me until the blubbering stopped, stroked my hair and rocked me, as she had when I was small, though I had almost outgrown her. When it was over, she returned the pin to its place in front of the picture of her mother. I kneeled on the hard floor to close the trunk. My fingers brushed the lettering, rough and untidy. But permanent. *The Dictionary of Lost Words*.

∾

Mr Crane was leaving early. When he saw me sitting under the ash, he gave neither a word nor a smile. I watched him stride towards his bicycle, shove his satchel around to his back and swing one leg over the saddle. He didn't notice when a bundle of slips fell to the ground behind him. I didn't call out.

There were ten slips pinned together. I put them between the pages of the book I'd been reading and returned to the ash.

Distrustful was written on the top-slip in Mr Crane's untidy hand. He had defined it as *Full of or marked by distrust in oneself or others; wanting in confidence, diffident; doubtful, suspicious, incredulous.* I didn't know what incredulous meant and shuffled through the slips for a sense of it. My discomfort grew with each quotation. *Distrustfull miscreants fight till the last gaspe*, wrote Shakespeare.

But I had rescued them, from the evening wind and morning dew. I had rescued them from Mr Crane's negligence. It was he who could not be trusted.

I separated one of the slips from the others. A quotation but no author, no book title or date. It would be discarded. I folded it and put it in my shoe.

The rest of the slips went back inside my book, and when the bells of Oxford rang out five o'clock I went to join Da in the Scriptorium.

He was alone at the sorting table, a proof in front of him, slips and books spread all around. He was bent to the page, oblivious to my presence.

I fingered the pages of the book in my pocket and removed the *Distrustful* slips. When I reached the sorting table, I added them to the disorder of Mr Crane's workspace.

'What is she doing?' Mr Crane stood in the doorway of the Scriptorium, his features hard to make out against the afternoon light, but his slightly stooped frame and thin voice unmistakable.

Da looked up, startled, then saw the slips under my hand.

Mr Crane strode over and reached out as if to slap my hand away, but seemed to flinch at its deformity. 'This really won't do,' he said, turning to Da.

'I found them,' I said to Mr Crane, but he wouldn't look at me. 'I found them near the fence where you lean your bicycle. They fell out of your satchel.' I looked to Da. 'I was putting them back.'

'With all due respect, Harry, she shouldn't be in here.'

'I was putting them back,' I said, but it was as if I couldn't be heard or seen; neither of them responded. Neither of them looked at me.

Da took a deep breath and released it with a barely noticeable shake of his head.

'Leave this to me,' he said to Mr Crane.

'Of course,' said Mr Crane, then he took up the pile of slips that had fallen from his satchel.

When he had gone, Da removed his spectacles and rubbed the bridge of his nose.

'Da?'

He returned his spectacles to their usual place and looked at me. Then he pushed his chair back from the sorting table and patted his knee for me to sit.

'You're almost too big,' he said, trying to smile.

'He did drop them; I saw him.'

'I believe you, Essy.'

'Then why didn't you say anything?'

He sighed. 'It's too complicated to explain.'

'Is there a word for it?' I asked.

'A word?'

'For why you didn't say anything. I could look it up.'

He smiled then. '*Diplomacy* springs to mind. *Compromise, mollify.*'

'I like *mollify.*'

Together we searched the pigeon-holes.

MOLLIFY

'To mollify, by these indulgences, the rage of his most furious persecutors.'

David Hume, *The History of Great Britain*, 1754

I thought on it. 'You were trying to make him less angry,' I said.

'Yes.'

September 1896

I thought I'd wet the bed, but when I pulled back the covers, my nightdress and sheets were stained red. I screamed. My hands were sticky with blood. The ache I'd been feeling in my back and belly was suddenly terrifying.

Da burst into my room and looked around in a panic, then he came to my bedside, worry all over his face. When he saw my bloodied nightdress, he was relieved. Then he was awkward.

The mattress gave in to the weight of him as he sat on the edge. He pulled the covers back over me and stroked my cheek. I knew, then, what it was, and was suddenly conscious of myself. I pulled the covers higher and avoided looking at him.

'I'm sorry,' I said.

'Don't be silly.'

We sat there for an uncomfortable minute, and I knew how much he wished Lily was there.

'Has Lizzie …?' Da began.

I nodded.

'Have you got what you need?'

I nodded again.

'Can I …?'

I shook my head.

Da kissed my cheek and stood. 'French toast this morning,' he said, closing the door as if I were an invalid, or a sleeping baby. But I was fourteen.

I waited to hear his footsteps on the stairs before letting go of the covers and sitting on the edge of the bed. I felt more blood leak from me. In the drawer of my bedside table was a monthlies box that Lizzie had made up especially, with belts and padded napkins she'd sewn from rags. I bunched up the length of my nightdress and held it between my legs.

Da was making a racket in the kitchen, letting me know the coast was clear. With the box under my arm, I crossed the landing to the bathroom and held tighter to the wad of fabric that stopped me from dripping.

❧

No school, Da said. I would spend the day with Lizzie. My eyes welled with the relief of it.

We left the house and began the familiar walk to Sunnyside. As if nothing was different, Da told me a word he was working on and asked me to guess what it meant. I barely knew how to think, and for once I didn't care. The streets stretched long, and everyone we passed looked at me as if they knew. I walked as though nothing I wore was a good fit.

There was a dampness between my thighs, then the trace of a single drop, like a tear running across a cheek. By the time we were on the Banbury Road, blood was running down the inside of my leg. I felt it seeping into my stockings. I stopped walking, squeezed my legs together, held my hand to the place that was bleeding.

I whimpered. 'Da?'

He was a few steps ahead. He turned and looked at me, looked down along the length of my body and then around, as if there might be someone better equipped to help. He took my hand, and we walked as fast as we could to Sunnyside.

'Oh, pet,' Mrs Ballard said as she ushered me into the kitchen. She nodded at Da, discharging him of any further responsibility. He kissed my forehead, then strode across the garden to the Scriptorium. When Lizzie walked in, she gave me a pitying look then went straight to the range to heat water.

Upstairs, Lizzie removed my clothing and sponged me down. The basin of warm water swirled pink with my humiliation. She showed me again how to fit the belt around my waist and the rags inside it.

'You didn't make it thick enough, or tight enough.' She put me in one of her night shifts and made me get into bed.

'Must it hurt so much?' I asked.

'I guess it must,' Lizzie said. 'Though I don't know why.'

I groaned and Lizzie looked at me with an expression of kindly impatience. 'It should hurt less over time. The first is often the worst.'

'Should?'

'Some ain't so lucky, but there're teas to make it better,' she said. 'I'll ask Mrs Ballard if she has yarrow.'

'How long will it last?' I asked.

Lizzie was adding my clothes to the basin now. I imagined they'd all stain red and that would be my uniform from now on.

'A week – maybe less, maybe more,' she said.

'A week? Must I stay in bed for a week?'

'No, no. Just a day. It's heaviest on the first day, which might be why it hurts so much. After that, it slows down and eventually stops, but you'll need the rags for about a week.'

Lizzie had told me I would bleed every month, and now she was telling me I would bleed for a week every month and have to stay in bed for a day every month.

'I've never known you to stay in bed, Lizzie,' I said.

She laughed. 'I really would have to be dying to spend a day in bed.'

'But how do you stop it running down your legs?'

'There are ways, Essymay. But it ain't right to talk of them to a girl.'

'But I want to know,' I said.

She looked at me, her hands in the tub of water; it didn't disgust her to have my blood on her skin.

'If you was in service you might need to know, but you ain't. You're a little lady, and no one will mind you spending a day in bed every month.' With that, she picked up the basin and went down the stairs.

I closed my eyes and lay as still as a plank. Time dragged, but I must have slept eventually, because I dreamed.

Da and I arrived at the Scriptorium, my stockings brimming over with blood. All the assistants and lexicographers I'd ever known were sitting around the sorting table. Even Mr Mitchell, his odd socks just visible under his chair. No one looked up. I turned to Da, but he had already moved away. When I looked back at the sorting table, he was in his usual place. His head was bowed to the words, like everyone else's. When I tried to move towards him, I couldn't. When I tried to leave, I couldn't. When I shouted out, no one heard me.

'Time to go home, Essymay; you've slept through the day.' Lizzie stood at the end of the bed, my clothes hanging over her arm. 'They're toasty warm. They've been hanging in front of the range. Come, I'll help you dress.'

Once again, she helped with the belt and the napkin. She pulled the shift over my head and replaced it with layers of warm clothing. Then she kneeled on the floor and put my feet in the stockings, slipped on my shoes and tied the laces.

❧

Over the course of the next week I created more laundry than I had in the previous three months, and Da had to pay the occasional maid extra to get it all done. I'd been given leave from school, and each day I went to stay in Lizzie's room. I wasn't confined to bed, but I dared not stray too far from the kitchen. The Scriptorium was off limits. No one had said as much, but I feared my body would betray me again.

'What is it for?' I asked Lizzie on the fifth day. Mrs Ballard had put me in charge of stirring a brown sauce while she spoke with Mrs Murray about meals for the following week. Lizzie was sitting at the kitchen table, mending a pile of Murray clothes. The bleeding had almost stopped.

'What is what for?' she said.

'The bleeding. Why does it happen?'

She looked at me, unsure. 'It's to do with babies,' she said.

'How?'

She shrugged her shoulders without looking up. 'I don't know exactly, Essymay. It just is.'

How could she not know? How could something so horrible happen to a person every month and that person not know why?

'Does Mrs Ballard get the bleeding?'

'Not any more.'

'When does it go away?' I asked.

'When you're too old to have babies.'

'Did Mrs Ballard have any babies?' I'd never heard her talk about children, but maybe they were all grown.

'Mrs Ballard ain't married, Essymay. There's been no babies.'

'Of course she's married,' I said.

Lizzie looked through the kitchen window to make sure Mrs Ballard wasn't on her way back in, then she leaned closer to me. 'She calls herself Mrs 'cos it's more respectable. A lot of old spinsters do it, 'specially if they's in a position to order others about.'

I was too confused to ask any more questions.

❧

It had come earlier than he'd expected, Da said, looking apologetic. It was called *catamenia*, and the process of shedding it was *menstruation*. He reached for the sugar bowl and took great care to sprinkle a liberal amount on his porridge, even though it was already sweetened.

New words, but they made Da feel uncomfortable. For the first time in my life I felt unsure about my questions. We fell into a rare silence, with *catamenia* and *menstruation* hanging meaningless in the air.

❧

I stayed away from the Scriptorium for two weeks. When I did return, I chose the quietest time. It was late afternoon, when Dr Murray was visiting Mr Hart at the Press and most of the assistants had gone home.

Only Da and Mr Sweatman sat at the long table. They were preparing entries for the letter F, which meant they had to check the work of all the other assistants to make sure they matched Dr Murray's very particular style. Da and Mr Sweatman knew the Dictionary abbreviations better than anyone.

'Come in, Esme,' said Mr Sweatman as I peered round the Scriptorium door. 'The big bad wolf has gone home.'

M words lived in pigeon-holes beyond the sight of the sorting table, and the words I wanted were crammed into a single pigeon-hole. They were already sorted under draft definitions. That is what Ditte spent so much of her time doing, and I wondered if I would recognise her hand on any of the top-slips.

There were so many words to describe the bleeding. *Menstrue* was the same as *catamenia*. It meant *unclean blood*. But what blood was clean? It always left a stain.

Four slips with various quotations were pinned to the word *menstruate*. The top-slip gave it two definitions: *To discharge the*

59

catamenia and *To pollute as with menstrual blood*. Da had mentioned the first, but not the second.

Menstruosity was *the condition of being menstruous*. And *menstruous* had once meant *horribly filthy or polluted*.

Menstruous. Like monstrous. It came closest to explaining how I felt.

Lizzie had called it 'The Curse'. She'd never heard of *menstruation* and laughed when I said it. 'Probably a doctor's word,' she'd said. 'They have their own language, and it hardly ever makes sense.'

I took the volume with all the C words from its shelf and searched for *curse*.

One's evil fate.

It didn't mention bleeding, but I understood. I let the pages fan past my thumb. There were thirteen hundred in just this one volume, about the same as in *A and B*, and I remembered Da saying there would never be an end to words beginning with *C*. I looked around the Scriptorium and tried to guess how many words were stored in the pigeon-holes and the books and in the heads of Dr Murray and his assistants. Not one of them could fully explain what had happened to me. Not one.

'Should she be in here?' Mr Crane's voice cut through my thoughts.

I closed the volume in a hurry and turned round. I looked to Da, who was looking at Mr Crane.

'I thought you'd gone for the night,' Da said, sounding friendlier than he was.

'This really is no place for children.'

I wasn't a child any more; everyone had told me that.

'She's no trouble,' said Mr Sweatman.

'She's interfering with materials.'

I felt my heart pound and couldn't stop myself from speaking. 'Dr Murray said I should avail myself of the Dictionary volumes whenever I liked.' I immediately regretted it when Da flashed me a cautionary look. But Mr Crane neither responded nor looked in my direction.

'Will you be joining us, Crane?' asked Mr Sweatman. 'With three of us we should get through this work before dinnertime.'

'I've just come back to get my coat,' he said. Then he nodded to them both and left the Scriptorium.

I returned the great volume of C words to its shelf and told Da I would wait for him in the kitchen.

'You are welcome to stay,' he said.

But I was no longer sure. Over the next few months I spent more time in the kitchen than the Scriptorium.

Da read Ditte's letter and shared none of it. When he finished, he folded it back into its envelope and put it in his trouser pocket instead of leaving it on the side table, where other letters from Ditte would sometimes sit for days.

'Will she visit us soon?' I asked.

'She doesn't say,' said Da, as he picked up the newspaper.

'Did she say anything about me?'

He let the paper drop so he could see me. 'She asked how you were enjoying school,' he said.

I shrugged. 'It's boring. But I'm allowed to help the younger ones when I've finished my work. I like that.'

He took a deep breath, and I thought he was going to tell me something. He didn't. He just looked at me a little longer, then said it was time for bed.

A few days later, after Da had kissed me goodnight and returned downstairs to work on proofs, I tip-toed across the hall and into his room. I crawled into the wardrobe and retrieved the shabbier of the two boxes. I took out Ditte's letter.

15th November 1896

My dear Harry,

What a mixture of sentiments your last letter brought. I have been trying to compose a response that Lily would approve of (I have come to the conclusion that that is what you desire above all else, and so I will try not to fail you, or her, or Esme. Try, mind you. I promise nothing).

Mr Crane continues to accuse our Esme of thieving. It is a weighty word, Harry. It conjures an image of Esme sneaking around with a sack slung over her back, filling it with candlesticks and teapots. However, from what I can glean, her pockets contained nothing more than slips that others had been careless with. As to your parenting being unconventional, well, I suppose that it is, but where Mr Crane meant it as a rebuke, I mean it as a compliment. Convention has never done any woman any good. So, enough self-recrimination, Harry.

Now, to the matter of Esme's education. Of course she must continue, but where to go when she outgrows St Barnabas? I have been making enquiries of an old friend, Fiona McKinnon, who is headmistress at a relatively modest (by which I mean affordable) boarding school in Scotland, near the town of Melrose. It is years since I last spoke to Fiona, but she was a formidable student, and I daresay she has fashioned Cauldshiels School for Young Ladies on her own precocious needs. As your sister is less than fifty miles away, it seems an excellent alternative to the far more expensive schools in the South of England.

Esme will not likely celebrate the idea in the short term, but at fourteen she is old enough for an adventure.

Finally, while not wanting to encourage her wayward behaviour, I am enclosing a word that Esme may like. 'Literately' was used in a novel by Elizabeth Griffiths. While no other examples of use have been forthcoming, it is, in my opinion, an elegant extension of 'literate'. Dr Murray agreed I should write an entry for the Dictionary, but I have since been told it is unlikely to be included. It seems our lady author has not proved herself a 'literata' — an abomination of a word coined by Samuel Taylor Coleridge that refers to a 'literary lady'. It too has only one example of use, but its inclusion is assured. This may sound like sour grapes, but I can't see it catching on. The number of literary ladies in the world is surely so great as to render them ordinary and deserving members of the literati.

A number of volunteers (all of them women, from what I can tell) sent in the same quotation for 'literately'. There are six in all, and as none of them is of any use to the Dictionary, I see no reason why Esme cannot have one of them. I look forward to hearing how the two of you employ this lovely word — together we might keep it alive.

Yours,

Edith

❧

It was our last school assembly before Christmas, and I would not be returning to finish the school year. The headmistress of St Barnabas girls' school, Mrs Todd, wanted to wish me well, so I sat on a chair at the front of the hall, facing the assembled girls. They were children of Jericho. Daughters of the Press and Wolvercote paper mill. Their brothers attended St Barnabas boys', and would grow up to work at the mill or on the presses. Half the girls in my class would be binding books within the year. I'd always felt out of place.

There were the usual announcements. I sat rigid, looking down at my hands and wishing the time would pass more quickly. I barely heard what Mrs Todd said, but when the girls began to clap I looked up. I was to receive the history prize and the prize for English. Mrs Todd nodded for me to approach, and as I did she told the school that I was leaving to attend Cauldshiels School for Young Ladies.

'All the way up in Scotland,' she said, turning to me. The girls clapped again, though this time with less enthusiasm. They couldn't imagine leaving, I thought. As I couldn't imagine it. But then Ditte said it would prepare me. 'For what?' I'd asked. 'For doing whatever it is you dream of,' she'd said.

The week after Christmas was wet and dreary. 'Good preparation for the Scottish Borders,' Mrs Ballard said one day, and I burst into tears. She stopped her kneading and came to where I sat shelling peas at the kitchen table. 'Oh, pet,' she said, holding my face in both hands and dusting flour across my cheeks. When I stopped my snivelling, she put a mixing bowl in front of me and measured out quantities of butter, flour, sugar and raisins. She took the cinnamon jar from the top shelf of the pantry and put it beside me: 'Just a pinch, remember.'

Mrs Ballard used to say that rock cakes didn't care if your hands were warm or cold, deft or clumsy. She relied on them to distract me whenever I was unable to accompany Lizzie, or when I was out of sorts. They'd become my speciality. Mrs Ballard went back to her kneading, and I began to break the butter into bits and rub it into the flour. As usual, my right hand felt gloved. I had to watch my funny fingers do their work to really feel the crumbs begin to form.

Mrs Ballard chatted on. 'Scotland is beautiful.' She'd been there when she was a young woman. Walking, with a friend. I couldn't imagine her young. And I couldn't imagine her anywhere other than in the kitchen at Sunnyside. 'And it's not forever,' she said.

Everyone who was at the Scriptorium that day came out to farewell me. We stood in the garden, shivering in the early morning: Da, Mrs Ballard, Dr Murray and some of the assistants. But not Mr Crane. The youngest Murray children were there, Elsie and Rosfrith either side of their mother. They each held the hand of one of the two smallest and kept their eyes on their shoes.

Lizzie stood in the doorway of the kitchen, even though Da called her to come out. She never liked being among the Dictionary men. 'I don't know how to speak to 'em,' she said, when I teased her about it.

We stood just long enough for Dr Murray to say something about how much I would learn and the health benefits of walking the hills around Cauldshiels Loch. He gave me a sketchbook and a set of drawing pencils and told me he looked forward to receiving letters with my impressions of the countryside around my new school. I put them in the new satchel Da had given me that morning.

Mrs Ballard gave me a box filled with biscuits still warm from the oven. 'For the journey,' she said, and she hugged me so tight I thought I would stop breathing.

No one said anything for a while. I'm sure most of the assistants were wondering what all the fuss was about. I could see them moving from foot to foot in an effort to keep warm. They wanted to return to their words, to the relative warmth of the Scriptorium. Part of me wanted to return with them. Part of me wanted the adventure to start.

I looked over to where Lizzie stood. Even from a distance, I could see her swollen eyes and red nose. She tried to smile, but the deceit was too much and she had to look away. Her shoulders quivered.

It would prepare me, Ditte had said. It would turn me into a scholar. 'And when you leave Cauldshiels,' Da had added, 'you can enter Somerville. It's as close to home as any of the ladies' halls, and just across the road from the Press.'

Da gave me a gentle nudge. I was meant to respond to Dr Murray, to say thank you for the sketchbook and pencils, but all I knew was the warmth of the biscuits coming through the box into my hands. I thought about the journey. It would take all the daylight hours and half the night. There would be no heat left in the biscuits by the time I arrived.

PART TWO
1897–1901
Distrustfully–Kyx

August 1897

The garden at Sunnyside looked smaller than it had two seasons earlier. The trees were in full leaf, and the sky was a patch of blue between the house and the hedges. I could hear the clatter of carts and the clop of horses drawing trams along the Banbury Road.

I stood under the ash for a long time. I'd been home for weeks, but only now did I understand what I'd been missing. Oxford wrapped around me like a blanket, and I began to breathe easily for the first time in months.

From the minute I'd arrived home from Cauldshiels, I'd wanted more than anything to be inside the Scriptorium. But every time I stepped towards it, I'd felt a wave in my stomach. I didn't belong there. I was a nuisance. That was why I'd been sent so far away, whatever Ditte tried to say about adventure and opportunity. So I pretended to Da that I had outgrown the Scriptorium. In truth I could barely resist it.

Now, a week before I was to return to Cauldshiels, the Scriptorium stood empty. Mr Crane was long gone – dismissed, too many errors. Da could barely hold my gaze when he told me. Da and Dr Murray were at the Press with Mr Hart, and the other assistants were spending their lunch hour by the river. I wondered if the Scriptorium might be locked. It never had been, but things could change. Everything was locked at Cauldshiels. To stop us getting in. To stop us getting out. I took one step and then another. When I tried the door, it opened with a familiar creaking of hinges.

I stood on the threshold and looked in. The sorting table was a mess of books and slips and proofs. I could see Da's jacket on the back of his chair and Dr Murray's mortar board on the shelf behind his high desk. The pigeon-holes seemed full, but I knew that room could always be found for new quotations. The Scriptorium was as it had always been, but my stomach wouldn't settle. I felt changed. I didn't go in.

When I turned to leave, I noticed the pile of unopened letters just inside the door. Ditte's handwriting. A larger envelope, the kind she used for Dictionary correspondence. I grabbed it without any thought, and left.

In the kitchen, apples were stewing on the range, but Mrs Ballard was nowhere to be seen. I held Ditte's envelope above the steam from the apples until the seal gave. Then I took the stairs to Lizzie's room, two at a time.

There were four pages of proofs for the words *hurly-burly* to *hurry-scurry*. Ditte had pinned additional quotations to the edges of each page. *The red-haired hurlyburlying Scotch professor* was attached to the first, and I wondered if Dr Murray would allow it. I began to read the edits she'd made on the proof, trying to understand how they might improve the entry. Then tears were running down my face. I'd wanted to see Ditte so much, needed to see her, to talk to her. She'd said she would visit at Easter to take me out for my fifteenth birthday. She never came. It was Ditte who'd convinced Da to send me to Cauldshiels. Ditte who'd made me want to go.

I dashed the tears away.

Lizzie came into the room, startling me. She looked at Ditte's pages, splayed on the floor.

'Esme, what are you doing?'

'Nothing,' I said.

'Oh, Essymay, I may not be able to read but I know fair well where those papers belong, and it's not in this room,' she said.

When I made no reply, she sat on the floor opposite me. She was heavier than she used to be and didn't look comfortable.

'These are different from your usual words,' she said, picking up a page.

'They're proofs,' I said. 'This is what the words will look like when they're in the Dictionary.'

'You've been in there then, the Scrippy?'

I shrugged and started gathering up Ditte's pages. 'I couldn't. I just looked in.'

'You can't take words from the Scrippy any more, Essymay. You know that.'

I settled my gaze on Ditte's familiar handwriting on the slip pinned to the last page of proofs. 'I don't want to go back to school, Lizzie.'

'You're lucky you have the chance to go to school,' she said.

'If you had been to school, you'd know how cruel it can be.'

'I guess it's bound to feel that way to a child who's had as much freedom as you, Essymay,' Lizzie soothed. 'But there's no one that can teach you here, and you're too bright to stop your learning. It will only be for a little while, and after that you can choose to do whatever you please. You could be a teacher, or write about history like your Miss Thompson, or work on the Dictionary like Hilda Murray. Did you know she's started working in the Scrippy?'

I didn't. Since going to Cauldshiels I felt further away from the things I once dreamed of. When Lizzie tried to catch my eye, I looked away. She retrieved her sewing box from beneath the bed then walked to the door.

'You should eat your lunch,' she said. 'And you should return those papers to the Scrippy.' She closed the door softly behind her.

I unpinned Ditte's note from the proof. It was an additional meaning for the word *hurry*: this definition was more akin to harassment than haste, and it only had a single quotation to support it. I said it out loud and liked it. I leaned under the bed and was relieved to feel the leather handle and the weight of the trunk as I pulled it towards me. Lizzie must have kept the trunk secret the whole time I'd been away. I wondered what might have happened to her if anyone had found it here.

The thought made me pause, made me think about pinning *hurry* back in its place. But taking it felt like a reckoning. I opened the trunk and breathed in the words. I put *hurry* on top, then closed the lid.

In that moment, my anger towards Ditte faded, just a little, and an idea occurred to me. I would write to her.

I returned the proofs to their envelope and resealed it. As I left Sunnyside to walk home, I dropped Ditte's envelope in the letter box on the gate.

❧

28th August 1897

My dear Esme,

As always it was a joy to come across your familiar hand as I was sifting through yesterday's post. There were one or two letters from the Scriptorium besides yours: one from Dr Murray and another from Mr Sweatman. The letter 'I' is causing a bit of bother — all those prefixes, where should they stop?! I was grateful to put off the work to read about your summer back in Oxford.

But you told me almost nothing, other than that the weather was stifling. Six months in Scotland and it seems you've acclimatised to the chilly damp and boundless space. I wonder if you miss the 'sweep of hills towards troubled sky and the unfathomable depths of the loch'?

Do you remember writing this after your first few weeks at Cauldshiels? I read it and was reminded of your father's love of that place. The rugged solitude restored him, he said. I can't say I shared his view. Hills and lochs are not in my blood as they are in yours.

But is it possible I have misunderstood your descriptions of the landscape; that your beautiful language has disguised your thoughts? Because your request has come as something of a surprise.

From all accounts, you are thriving at Cauldshiels. Near the top of your class in a number of subjects, 'continually questioning' according to Miss McKinnon. This is the fundamental attribute of scholars and liberals, my father always thought.

Your letters, without exception, describe an ideal education for a young woman of the twentieth century. My goodness, the twentieth century! I think this is the first time I have written it down. It will be your century, Esme, and it will be different from mine. You will need to know more.

I am flattered that you think I could tutor you in all you need to learn; so flattered, in fact, and so taken with the idea of having you live with us, that I discussed it for hours with Beth. Between us we could do an adequate job of history and literature and politics. We could add something to what you know of French and German, but the natural sciences and mathematics are beyond us. And then there is the time that would be required. We simply do not have enough of it.

You remind me that I have promised to always take your side, but when it comes to your education I think I would fail you. By declining your request, I hope I am taking the side of an older Esme. I hope you will one day agree.

I have written to Mrs Ballard and asked her to bake you a batch of ginger-nut biscuits. I think they will keep well on the long journey back to school and nourish you well into the first week of the new term.

Please write to me once you have settled back in. The account of your days is always a pleasure to read.

My love, as always,

Ditte

❧

I sat on the edge of my bed and looked over at my school trunk. Up until that moment, I had been sure it would accompany me to Ditte and Beth's house in Bath. I read Ditte's letter again. *My love, as always*. I screwed up the letter, threw it on the floor and ground it under my foot.

Da and I ate dinner in silence. I don't think Ditte had even bothered to discuss it with him.

'Early start tomorrow, Essy,' he said as he took the plates to the kitchen.

I said goodnight and climbed the stairs.

Da's room was almost dark, but when I pulled back the curtains, the last light of the long day came in. I turned to the wardrobe. 'Open sesame,' I whispered, longing for an earlier time. I reached past Lily's dresses and brought out the polished box. It smelled of beeswax, recently applied. I opened it and strummed the letters with my funny fingers, as if they were strings on a harp. I wanted Lily to speak. To give me the words that would convince Da to keep me. But she was silent.

My strumming stopped. The envelopes at the end were out of tune, not blue or white but the cheap undyed brown of Cauldshiels. I took out the last and moved to the window to read what I had written.

I remembered every word. How could I not? I had written them over and over and over again. They were not the words I had chosen. Those words had been torn up. Your father will only worry, said Miss McKinnon. Then she dictated something appropriate. Again, she said, as she tore the new pages. Neater, or he'll think you are not improving, not trying. *They are a jolly group of girls … a wonderful excursion … perhaps I will become a teacher … I managed an A on my history test.* My marks were the only truth. Again, she said. Don't slouch. The other girls had gone to bed. I sat in that cold room until the clock struck midnight. You have been spoiled, Miss Nicoll. Your father knows this as well as anyone. Complaining about mild discomforts will only prove the point. Then she laid out the last three attempts and asked me to choose the one that showed the best penmanship. Not the last. It was almost illegible. My funny fingers were bent as if still holding a pen. The pain of moving them was unbearable. That one, Miss McKinnon. Yes, dear, I think so too. Now off to bed.

And here it was. Treasured, as Lily's letters were treasured. False words giving false comfort to a man forced to be mother and father both. Perhaps I *was* a burden.

There was one letter for every week I had been away. I took them all from the box and removed the pages. There was nothing of me in any of them. How could Da have believed them? When I returned the envelopes to the box, they were empty of words – but never more meaningful.

❧

I slept badly. Resentments and confusion about Ditte and Cauldshiels – and even Da – gathered strength in the dark. Eventually I gave up trying to silence them.

Da was snoring, a predictable rumble that had always comforted me when I woke in the night. It comforted me now; it meant he wouldn't wake. I got out of bed and dressed, took a candle and matches from my bedside table and put them in my pocket. Then I slipped out of my room, down the stairs and into the night.

The sky was clear and the moon almost full. The black of night only played around the edges of things. When I arrived at Sunnyside, the Murray house stood dark and still, and I thought I could hear the collected breath of the family's slumber.

I pushed on the gate. The house stretched towards the sky, as if suddenly alert, but no light flickered in the windows. I slipped through the gap and left the gate ajar then skirted the boundary, keeping to the deep dark under the trees, until I was looking at the Scriptorium.

In the moonlight it looked like any other shed, and I was annoyed I'd thought it was more. As I got closer, I could see its frailty; gutters laced with rust, paint peeling from the window frames – a wad of paper stopping the draught where the timber was rotted.

The door opened as it always did, and I stood on the threshold waiting for my eyes to adjust. Moonlight through dirty windows cast long shadows around the room. I could smell the words before I could see them, and memories tumbled over themselves; I used to think this place was the inside of a genie's lamp.

I took Ditte's letter from my pocket. It was still crumpled, so I found a space on the sorting table and smoothed it out as best I could. I lit the candle and felt the small thrill of defiance. Draughts competed to bat the flame this way and that, but none were strong enough to blow it out. I made a space on the sorting table and dripped some wax to hold the candle. I made sure it stuck fast.

The word I wanted was already published, but I knew where to find the slips. I ran my finger along a row of pigeon-holes until I came to 'A to Ant'. My birthday words. If the Dictionary was a person, Da told me once, 'A to Ant' would be its first tentative steps.

I pulled a small pile of slips from the pigeon-hole and unpinned them from their top-slip.

Abandon.

The earliest example was more than six hundred years old, and the words that made it were malformed and difficult. As I read through the slips the quotations got easier, and when I was almost at the bottom of the pile I found one I liked. The quotation was not much older than me, and it was written by a Miss Braddon.

I found myself abandoned and alone in the world.

I pinned the slip to Ditte's letter, then read it again. *Alone in the world.*

Alone had a pigeon-hole all to itself, with bundles of slips piled one on top of the other. I took out the topmost and untied its string. The slips had been separated into various senses, each with a top-slip showing the definition. I knew that if I got *A and B* off the shelf, I would find the definitions on the top-slips transcribed into columns, their quotations below.

It was Da who had written the definition I settled on. I read his tight script: *Quite by oneself, unaccompanied, solitary.*

I wondered briefly if he had spoken to Lily about all the ways to be alone. Lily would never have sent me to school.

I unpinned the top-slip from its quotation slips – its job was done, after all – and put the quotations back into their pigeon-hole. Then I returned to the sorting table and pinned Da's definition to Ditte's letter.

Then a sound. A long note in the quiet. It was the gate: its unoiled hinge.

I looked around the Scriptorium for somewhere I might hide. I felt the galloping beat of panic. I couldn't have the words taken from me. They explained me. I reached under my skirt and shoved the letter with its attached slips into the waistband of my drawers. Then I took up the candle from the table.

The door opened and moonlight flooded in.

'Esme?'

It was Da. Relief and anger rose.

'Esme, put the candle down.'

It tilted. Wax dripped onto proofs spread across the sorting table, sealing them together. I saw what he saw. Imagined what he imagined. Wondered if I could actually do it.

'I would never—'

'Give me the candle, Esme.'

'But you don't understand, I was just …'

He blew out the candle and collapsed into a chair. I watched the wisp of smoke wobble upward.

I turned out my pockets and there was nothing, not a single word. I thought he might ask to check my socks, my sleeves, and I looked at him as if I had nothing to hide. He just sighed and turned to leave the

Scriptorium. I followed. When he whispered to close the door quietly, I did as I was told.

Morning was only beginning to colour the garden. The house was still dark, except for a single wavering light in the topmost window above the kitchen. If Lizzie looked out, she would see me. I could almost feel the weight of the trunk as I dragged it from under her bed.

But Lizzie and the trunk were as far away as Scotland. Not seeing them before I left would be my punishment.

April 1898

Da visited Cauldshiels during the Easter break. He'd had a letter from his sister, my real aunt. She was concerned about me. Had I always been so reserved? She remembered me differently, full of questions. She was sorry she had not visited earlier – it was difficult – but she'd noticed bruises across the backs of my hands, both of them. Hockey, I'd said. *Rubbish*, she wrote to Da.

He told me all this on the train back to Oxford. We ate chocolate, and I told him I never played hockey. I looked over his shoulder at my reflection in the darkened window of the carriage. I looked older, I thought.

Da was holding both my hands in his, and his thumbs were circling my knuckles. The bruises on my good hand had faded to a sickly yellow, barely visible, but there was a red welt across the back of my right hand. The puckered skin always took longer to heal. He kissed them and held them against his wet cheek. Would Da keep me? I was too scared to ask. Your mother would know exactly what to do, he'd say, and then he'd write to Ditte.

I took my hands from his, then lay down along the carriage seat. I didn't care that I was as tall as an adult. I felt as small as a child, and

I was so tired. I pulled my knees up to my chest and hugged them. Da draped his coat over me. Pipe tobacco, darkly sweet. I closed my eyes and inhaled. I hadn't known I'd been missing it. I pulled the coat closer, buried my face in its scratchy wool. Beneath the sweet was sour. The smell of old paper. I dreamed I was under the sorting table. When I woke, we were in Oxford.

❧

Da didn't wake me the next day, and it was late afternoon when I finally came down the stairs. I thought to spend the hours before dinner in the warmth of the sitting room, but when I opened the door I saw Ditte. She and Da were seated on either side of the hearth, and their conversation froze when they saw me. Da repacked his pipe and Ditte came over to where I stood. Without any hesitation she wrapped her heavy arms around me, trying to fold my gangly frame into her stout one. As if she still could. I was rigid. She let go.

'I've made enquiries at the Oxford High School for Girls,' Ditte said.

I wanted to scream and cry and rail at her, but I did none of these. I looked to Da.

'We should have sent you there in the first place,' he said sadly.

I returned to bed and only came down again when I heard Ditte leave.

❧

Ditte wrote to me every week after that. I let her letters sit on the sideboard by the front door, unopened, and when three or four had gathered Da would take them away. After a while, Ditte included her pages to me in her letters to Da. He would leave them on the sideboard, unfolded, begging to be read. I'd glance at the writing, absorb a few lines without meaning to, then grab the pages in my fist and crumple them into a ball to be thrown into a dustbin or fire.

The Oxford High School for Girls was on the Banbury Road. Neither Da nor I mentioned how close it was to the Scriptorium. I was welcomed by the few girls from St Barnabas who had gone there, but I limped through the rest of the school year. The headmistress called Da to her office to inform him that I had failed my exams. I sat in a chair outside the closed door and heard her say, 'I can't recommend she continue.'

'What will we do with you?' Da said, as we walked back towards Jericho.

I shrugged. All I wanted to do was sleep.

When we arrived home there was a letter for Da from Ditte. He opened it and began reading. I saw his cheeks colour and his jaw clench, then he went into the sitting room and closed the door. I stood in the hall, waiting for bad news. When he came out, he had the pages Ditte had written for me in one hand. With the other he stroked the length of my arm until our hands were clutching. 'Can you ever forgive me,' he said. He put the pages on the sideboard. 'I think you should read this one.' Then he went into the kitchen to fill the kettle.

I picked up the letter.

28th July 1898

My dear Esme,

Harry writes that you are still not yourself. He skirts the truth of it, of course, but he described you as 'distant', 'preoccupied' and 'tired' in a single paragraph. Most alarming, he reports that you avoid the Scrippy and spend all day in your room.

I was hoping things would be different for you once you were away from Cauldshiels and home with your father, but it's been three months. Now that the summer is here, I'm hoping your mood may lift by degrees.

Are you eating, Esme? You were so thin when I saw you last. I asked Mrs Ballard to spoil you with treats and, until Harry informed me you'd barely left the house, it was some comfort to imagine you sitting on your stool in her kitchen while she baked you a cake. In my mind you are younger, wearing a yellow polka-dot apron tied right up across your chest. That's how I found you once when I visited Oxford. Were you nine, or ten? I can't recall.

Something was happening at Cauldshiels, wasn't it, Esme? The thing is, your letters never said. But your letters, now that I think about it, were too perfect. When I read them now, I see they could have been written by anyone; and yet they are in your distinctive hand.

The other day I re-read how you had walked to the Roman fort of Trimontium, written a poem in the Romantic style of Wordsworth and done satisfactorily in a mathematics test. I wondered whether you had enjoyed the hike and been proud of your poem. The absence of words was the clue, but I didn't see it.

I should have paid more attention to what was missing in your letters, Esme. I should have visited. I would have, if not for Beth's illness. When that passed, the headmistress advised against it. Too disruptive mid-term, she said. I took her word.

Harry wanted you home much sooner (truth be told, Harry never wanted you to leave). It was me, my dear Esme, who suggested his concerns were unfounded, that boarding school would take a while to get used to for a child accustomed to the local parish school and lunchtimes spent in the Scriptorium. I told him to give it another year, that things might change for the better.

After collecting you at Easter, Harry sent me the most direct letter of his life. You wouldn't be going back, he said, whatever my opinion on the subject. You remember I travelled to Oxford the next day. When I saw you, I found no quarrel with his decision.

We barely spoke, you and I. I had hoped that time would restore you, but it seems you need more. You are in my heart, dear girl, even if I have been dislodged from yours. I hope it is not permanent.

I have enclosed a news clipping that I thought might be important to you. I do not want to presume but have found it difficult not to. Please forgive my blind eye.

Yours, with deepest love always,

Ditte

I folded the pages around the tiny news clipping and put them in my pocket. For the first time in a long time I would have something to put in the trunk when I visited Lizzie's room.

❧

'What've you got there, Essy?' said Lizzie, coming into her room and pulling her dirty pinny up over her head.

I looked at the tiny article clipped from the paper. It was just a single sentence, no more than a quotation. *A teacher has been dismissed from Cauldshiels School for Young Ladies following the admission of a student to hospital.*

'Just words, Lizzie,' I said.

'There's no "just words" for you, Essymay, 'specially if they end up in the trunk. What do they say?'

'They say I wasn't alone.'

September 1898

During the day I helped Mrs Ballard in the kitchen, and I only ventured towards the Scriptorium in the late afternoon, when almost everyone had left. I'd hesitate in the doorway, like Lizzie used to do, and watch Hilda moving around the pigeon-holes. She filed slips and removed them; she wrote letters and corrected proofs. All the while, Dr Murray sat like a wise owl at his high desk. Sometimes he would invite me in and sometimes he wouldn't.

'It isn't because he disapproves,' whispered Mr Sweatman once. 'It's because he's so single-minded. When he's puzzling over an entry, his beard could be alight and he'd fail to notice.'

One afternoon I approached Da at the sorting table. 'Could I be your assistant?' I asked.

He put a line through something on the proof he was working on and wrote a note beside it. Then he looked up.

'But you're Mrs Ballard's assistant.'

'I don't want to be a cook; I want to be an editor.'

The words were a surprise, to Da and to me.

'Well, not an editor, but an assistant maybe, like Hilda …'

'Mrs Ballard isn't training you to *be* a cook, just how to cook. It will come in useful when you're married,' said Da.

'But I'm not going to get married.'

'Well, not right away.'

'If I get married, I can't be an assistant,' I said.

'What makes you think that?'

'Because I'll have to look after babies and cook all day.'

Da was silenced. He looked to Mr Sweatman for some support.

'If you're not going to get married, then why *not* aim to become an editor?' Mr Sweatman asked.

'I'm a girl,' I said, annoyed at his teasing.

'Should that matter?'

I blushed and didn't answer. Mr Sweatman cocked his head and raised his eyebrows as if to say, 'Well?'

'Quite right, Fred,' said Da, then he looked at me to judge the seriousness of my statement. 'An assistant is exactly what I need, Essy,' he said. 'And I'm sure Mr Sweatman could do with a hand every now and then.'

Mr Sweatman nodded his head in agreement.

They were true to their word, and I began to look forward to my afternoons in the Scriptorium. Usually I was asked to make polite replies to letters congratulating Dr Murray on the latest fascicle. When my back began to ache or my hand needed a rest, I would return books and manuscripts. There were shelves of old dictionaries and books in the Scriptorium, but the assistants needed to borrow all kinds of texts from scholars or from college libraries to investigate the origins of words. When the weather was fine, it hardly counted as a chore. Most of the good college libraries were near the centre of town. I would ride down Parks Road until I got to Broad Street, then I'd dismount and walk among the bustling crowds between Blackwell's Bookshop and the Old Ashmolean. It was my favourite part of Oxford, where town and gown struck an unusual alliance. Both were superior, in their own minds, to the visitors trying to get a glimpse of the gardens in the grounds of Trinity College, or gain entry to the Sheldonian. Am I town or gown? I sometimes wondered. I didn't fit snugly with either.

'A nice morning for a bicycle ride,' Dr Murray said one day. He was coming in through the gates of Sunnyside when I was going out. 'Where do you take yourself?'

'The colleges, sir. I return the books.'

'The books?'

'When the assistants have finished with them, I take them back to where they belong,' I said.

'Is that right?' he said, then made a noise I couldn't interpret. When he'd gone on his way, I became nervous.

The following morning, Dr Murray called me over.

'I'd like you to come with me to the Bodleian, Esme.'

I looked over to Da. He smiled and nodded. Dr Murray put on his black gown and ushered me out of the Scriptorium.

We rode side by side down the Banbury Road and, following my usual route, Dr Murray turned onto Parks Road.

'A far more pleasant ride,' he said. 'More trees.'

His gown billowed, and his long white beard was swept back over one shoulder. I had no idea why we were going to the Bodleian Library, and I was too stunned to ask. When we turned onto Broad Street, Dr Murray dismounted. Town, gown and visitor all seemed to fall back as he made his way towards the Sheldonian Theatre. As he passed into the courtyard, I imagined the guard of stone emperors along the perimeter nodding to acknowledge the Editor's presence. I followed like a disciple until we came to a halt at the entrance of the Bodleian.

'Ordinarily, it would not be possible for you to become a reader, Esme. You are neither a scholar nor a student. But it is my intention to convince Mr Nicholson that the Dictionary will be realised far sooner if you are permitted to come here and check quotations on our behalf.'

'We can't just borrow the books, Dr Murray?'

He turned and looked at me above his spectacles. 'Not even the Queen is permitted to borrow from the Bodleian. Now, come.'

Mr Nicholson was not immediately convinced. I sat on a bench watching students pass and heard Dr Murray's voice begin to rise.

'No, she is not a student, surely that is obvious,' he said.

Mr Nicholson peered at me, then quietly presented another argument to Dr Murray.

The Editor's response was louder again. 'Neither her sex nor her age disqualifies her, Mr Nicholson. As long as she is employed in scholarship – and I assure you, she is – she has grounds for becoming a reader.'

Dr Murray called me over. Mr Nicholson passed me a card.

'Recite this,' said Mr Nicholson, with obvious reluctance.

I looked at the card. Then I looked around at all the young men in their short gowns and the older men in their long gowns. The words would scarcely come.

'Louder, please.'

A woman walked past: a student in a short gown. She slowed and smiled and nodded. I straightened up, looked Mr Nicholson in the eye and recited.

'*I hereby undertake not to remove from the Library, or to mark, deface, or injure in any way, any volume, document, or other object belonging to it or in its custody; not to bring into the Library or kindle therein any fire or flame, and not to smoke in the Library; and I promise to obey all the rules of the Library.*'

౸

A few days later there was a note on top of the pile of books waiting to be returned to scholars and college libraries.

You would be doing me a service if you could visit the Bodleian and check the date
for this quotation for flounder. It is in a poem by Thomas Hood, published in the
Literary Souvenir:

> *'Or are you where the flounders keep,*
> *Some dozen briny fathoms deep.'*
> *Thomas Hood, Stanzas to Tom Woodgate, 18__*
> *J.M.*

My mood did improve by degrees. As the number of tasks and
errands increased, I began to visit the Scriptorium earlier and earlier
in the afternoon. By the end of the summer of 1899 I was a regular
visitor to many of the college libraries as well as to a number of scholars
who were happy to make their collections available to the Dictionary
project. Then Dr Murray started asking me to deliver notes to the
Oxford University Press in Walton Street.

'If you leave now, you'll catch Mr Hart with Mr Bradley,' Dr
Murray said, hurriedly writing out the note. 'I left them arguing
about the word *forgo*. Hart is right, of course; there is no rationale
for an e. But Bradley needs to be convinced. This should help, though
Bradley won't thank me for it.' He handed me the note and, seeing my
bewilderment added, 'The prefix is *for-*, as in *for*get, not *fore*gone. Do
you understand?'

I nodded, though I wasn't sure I understood at all.

'Of course you do. It's straight*forward*.' Then he looked at me over
his spectacles, one corner of his mouth turning up in a rare smile.
'That's *forward*, without an e, by the way. Is it any wonder Bradley's
sections are so slow to materialise?'

Mr Bradley had been appointed by the Delegates as a second editor
nearly a decade earlier, but Dr Murray was in the habit of putting him
in his place. Da once said it was his way of reminding people who
the engine-driver was and that it was best to let such comments go

unanswered. I smiled, and Dr Murray turned towards his desk. When I was outside the Scriptorium, I read the note.

Common use should not override etymological logic. Forego is absurd. I regret its inclusion in the Dictionary as an alternative spelling and would be happy for Hart's Rules *to discourage it.*

J.M.

I knew about *Hart's Rules*; Da always had a copy to hand. 'Consensus is not always possible, Esme,' he once told me, 'but consistency is, and Hart's little book of rules has been the final arbiter of many an argument about how a word should be spelled or whether a hyphen is required.'

When I was a child, Da would sometimes take me with him to the Press if he had reason to speak with Mr Hart. Mr Hart was known as the Controller. He was in charge of every part of the printing process of the Dictionary. The first time I walked through the stone gateway into the quadrangle, I was awed by its size. There was a great pond in the centre with trees and flower gardens all around. The stone buildings rose two and three storeys high on all sides, and I'd asked Da why the Press needed to be so much bigger than the Scriptorium. 'They don't just print the Dictionary, Esme. They print the Bible, and books of every kind.' I took that to mean that every book in the world came from that place. The grandeur suddenly made perfect sense, and I'd imagined the Controller to be a bit like God.

I dismounted under the imposing stone arch. The quadrangle was crowded with people who clearly belonged there. Boys in white aprons pulled trolleys loaded with reams of paper, some printed and cut down to size, others blank and as large as tablecloths. Men in ink-stained aprons walked in small groups, smoking. Other men, without aprons, scanned books or proofs instead of the path ahead, and one mumbled an apology when he bumped my arm, though he never looked up. In pairs they talked and gestured towards loose sheets of paper, the contents apparently flawed. How many problems of language were solved as they traversed this square? I wondered. Then I noticed two women, a little older than me. They walked across the quad as though they did it every day, and I realised they must work at the Press. But as we drew close, I could see their talk was not like that of the men: they were leaning in, and one had her hand up near her mouth. The other listened then laughed a little. They had nothing in their hands to distract them, no problems to solve. Their day was over and they were glad to be going home. They nodded as I passed.

A hundred bicycles lined one side of the quad. I left mine a little apart so I would find it easily on my way out.

Mr Hart didn't answer when I knocked at his office door, so I wandered down the hall. Da said the Controller never left the building before dinnertime, and never without taking leave of the compositors and making an inspection of the presses.

The composing room was close to Mr Hart's office. I pushed on the door and looked around. Mr Hart was on the other side of the room, talking to Mr Bradley and one of the compositors. The Controller's large moustache was what I remembered most from my visits with Da. Over the years, it had grown whiter, but it had lost none of its volume. It was like a landmark now, guiding me along the rows of compositors' benches, their slanted surfaces crowded with trays of type. I felt I might be trespassing.

Mr Hart glanced at me as I approached, but didn't pause in his conversation with Mr Bradley. The conversation turned out to be a debate, and I had the feeling it would continue until Mr Hart prevailed. He did not have the stature of the second editor, and his suit was not of the same quality, but his face was stern where Mr Bradley's was kindly. It was only a matter of time. The compositor caught my eye and smiled, as if apologising for the older men. He was a good deal taller than both of them, lean and clean-shaven. His hair was almost black, his eyes almost violet. I recognised him then. A boy from St Barnabas. I'd spent a lot of time watching the boys play in their yard when none of the girls would play with me in ours. I could tell he didn't recognise me.

'May I ask how *you* spell forgo?' he asked, leaning towards me.

'Really, they're still talking about that?' I whispered. 'That's why I'm here.'

His brow creased, but before he could ask anything else, Mr Hart addressed me.

'Esme, how is your father?'

'Very well, sir.'

'Is he here?'

'No, Dr Murray sent me.' I handed over the note, a little crushed by my nervous hand.

Mr Hart read it and nodded slowly in agreement. I noticed the twirled ends of his moustache turn up a little. He passed the note to Mr Bradley.

'This should settle things, Henry,' he said.

Mr Bradley read the note and the ends of his moustache remained still. He conceded the argument about *forgo* with a gentlemanly nod of the head.

'Now, Gareth. If you could show Mr Bradley the mats for *get*,' said Mr Hart, while he shook the editor's hand.

'Yes, sir,' the compositor said. Then to me, 'Nice to meet you, miss.'

But we haven't really met, I thought.

He turned towards his bench, and Mr Bradley followed.

I went to say goodbye to Mr Hart, but he had already moved on to another bench and was checking an older man's work. I would have liked to follow him, to understand what each man was working on. Most were setting type from manuscripts: in each case, the piles of uniform pages were in a single hand. Just one author. I looked towards the bench where Mr Bradley now stood with the young compositor. There were three piles of slips tied with string. Another pile was unbound, half the words already in type and the other half waiting.

'Miss Nicoll.'

I turned and saw Mr Hart holding open the door. I wove back through the rows of benches.

Over the next few months, Dr Murray gave me several notes to deliver to the Controller. I took them gladly, hoping for another opportunity to visit the composing room. But every time I knocked on Mr Hart's office door, he would answer.

He only asked me to stay if an immediate reply had been sought from Dr Murray, and on those occasions I was not invited to sit. I thought this an oversight rather than a preference on Mr Hart's part, because he always seemed harried. He would rather be in the composing room too, I thought.

In the mornings I belonged to Mrs Ballard, but I showed little aptitude. 'There's more to it than licking the bowl clean,' she said every time another cake sank or was found, on tasting, to be missing some key ingredient. It was a relief to both of us that my time in the kitchen was being curtailed by errands for the Dictionary. Since becoming Dr Murray's occasional delivery girl, I felt more comfortable in the Scriptorium. My misdemeanours may not have been forgotten, but at least my usefulness was being noticed.

'By the time you return with that book I will have two entries written that would not have been written otherwise,' Mr Sweatman said once. 'Keep this up and we'll be done before the century is out.'

❧

My chores for Mrs Ballard completed, I took off my apron and hung it on the hook of the pantry door.

'You're happier,' Lizzie said, pausing over the vegetables she was preparing.

'Time,' I said.

'It's the Scrippy,' she said, with a cautious look that confused me. 'The longer you spend over there the more you seem like your old self.'

'That's a good thing, isn't it?'

'For sure, it's a good thing.' She pushed a pile of chopped carrots into a bowl then began slicing parsnips in half. 'I just don't want you to be tempted,' she said.

'Tempted?'

'By the words.'

I realised then that there had been no words. There had been errands of all kinds, books and notes and verbal messages, but no words. No proofs. I hadn't been trusted with a single slip.

I had an errands basket by the door of the Scriptorium. Every day there were books to return to various places, and a list for borrowing. There were quotations to check at the Bodleian, letters to post, and notes to deliver to Mr Hart and sometimes to scholars at the colleges.

On one particular day, there were three letters set aside for Mr Bradley. They often turned up at the Scriptorium, and it was my job to deliver them to him in his Dictionary Room at the Press. This room was nothing like the Scriptorium: it was just an ordinary office, not much bigger than Mr Hart's, even though Mr Bradley had three assistants working with him. One of them was his daughter, Eleanor. She was about twenty-three, the same age as Hilda Murray, but she already looked matronly. Whenever I visited, she offered me tea and a biscuit.

On this day, we sat at the small table at the back of the room. It held the tea things, and there was barely enough room for the two of us, but Eleanor didn't like to eat or drink at her desk in case something spilled. She took a bite of her biscuit, and crumbs fell across her skirt. She didn't seem to notice. Then she leaned towards me.

'There's a rumour the Press Delegates will appoint a third editor soon.' Her eyes grew larger behind their wire-rimmed spectacles. 'It seems we are not progressing as fast as they would like. More fascicles means more money back in the coffers of the Press.'

'Where will he go?' I looked around the cramped office. 'I can't imagine Dr Murray sharing the Scriptorium.'

'No one can imagine that,' said Eleanor. 'Thankfully, there is another rumour that we will be moving to the Old Ashmolean. Father was out there last week taking measurements.'

'On Broad Street? I've always loved that building, but isn't it a museum?'

'They're moving most of the collections to the Museum of Natural History on Parks Road, and giving us the big space on the first floor. They'll still have lectures upstairs and the laboratory downstairs.' She looked around. 'It will be quite a change, but I think we'll get used to it.'

'Would Mr Bradley mind sharing his Dictionary Room with another editor, do you think?'

'If it speeds things up, I don't think he'll mind at all. And we'll be next door to the Bodleian. Half the books in England might be printed here at the Press, but copies of *all* the books in England are stored in the Bodleian. What a perfect neighbour.'

I sipped my milky tea. 'What words are you working on, Eleanor?'

'We have embarked on the verb *go*,' Eleanor said. 'And I suspect it will consume me for months.' She drained her teacup. 'Come with me.'

I'd never seen her desk up close. It was covered in papers and books and narrow boxes filled with hundreds of slips.

'Behold, *go*,' she said with a grand gesture of her hand.

I felt an urge to touch them, followed by a rush of shame.

When I left, I walked the bicycle across the busy quad of the Press and under the archway out into Walton Street. Eleanor's slips were the first I'd been close to since returning to the Scriptorium. Had there been a discussion about it? Had Dr Murray agreed to my return as long as I was kept away from the words?

❧

'Maybe I could help sort slips,' I said to Da as we walked home that night. He said nothing, but his hand found the coins in his pocket and I heard them jangle against each other as he moved them between his fingers.

We walked in silence for several minutes, every question in my head finding an uncomfortable answer. Halfway down St Margaret's Road, he said, 'I'll ask James when he returns from London.'

'You never used to ask Dr Murray,' I said.

I heard the coins shift in his pocket. He looked at the pavement and said nothing.

A few days later, when Dr Murray asked me to visit Mr Hart, it was to deliver the slips for *grade* and *graded*. He held the bundles towards me. There were several tied with string, and each slip and top-slip was numbered in case the order was disturbed. I grasped them in my funny fingers, but Dr Murray did not let go. He looked over his spectacles.

'Until they are set in type, Esme, these are the only copies,' he said. 'Every one of them is precious.' He let go and turned back to his desk before I could fashion a reply.

I opened my satchel and took care to place the bundles snugly into the bottom. Precious, every one, and yet there were so many ways they could be lost. I remembered the piles of words on the compositor's bench and imagined a breeze or a clumsy visitor; slips falling to the floor, one riding a wave of air and landing where no one but a child would discover it.

I'd been forbidden to touch them, and now I was given the role of protector. I wanted to tell someone. If anyone had been in the garden just then, I would have found a way to show them the slips, to say that Dr Murray had entrusted them to me. I collected the bicycle from behind the Scriptorium and rode through the gates of Sunnyside and along the Banbury Road. As I turned into St Margaret's Road, tears began to course down my cheeks. They were warm and welcome.

The building on Walton Street greeted me differently, its wide entrance no longer an intimidation but instead a welcoming gesture – I was on important Dictionary business.

When I was in the building, I took one bundle of slips from my satchel and released the bow that held them. Each sense of the word *grade* was defined on a top-slip and followed by the quotations that illustrated it. I scanned the various meanings and found one wanting. I thought to tell Da, or perhaps Dr Murray, and my arrogance made me laugh. Then someone bumped me, or I bumped them, and my funny fingers lost their hold. Slips fell to the ground like litter. When I looked to see where they had landed all I saw were hurrying feet. I felt the blood rush from my face.

'No harm done,' a man said, bending to pick up what had fallen. 'They're numbered for a reason.'

He handed me the slips. My hand shook as I reached for them.

'Goodness, are you all right?' He took my elbow. 'You need to sit down before you faint.' He opened the nearest door and sat me on a chair just inside it. 'I hope the noise doesn't bother you, miss. Take a minute and I'll be right back with a glass of water.'

It was the printing room, and it was, indeed, noisy. But there were rhythms on top of rhythms, and trying to separate them settled my panic. I checked the slips: one, two, three … I counted to thirty. None were missing. I secured their string and put them back in the satchel. When the man returned, I had my face in my hands, all the emotion of the past hour risen to the surface and hard to contain.

'Here, have this,' he said, crouching and offering the glass of water.

'Thank you,' I said. 'I'm not sure what came over me.'

He gave me his hand and helped me up from the chair. His gaze lingered on my funny fingers, and I withdrew them.

'Do you work in here?' I asked, looking beyond him into the printing room.

'Only if a machine needs some tinkering,' he said. 'Mostly I set the type. I'm a compositor.'

'You make the words real,' I said, finally looking at him. His eyes were almost violet. It was the young compositor who'd been standing with Mr Hart and Mr Bradley on my first visit.

He tilted his head, and I thought he might not understand what I meant. But then he smiled. 'I prefer to say that I give them substance – a real word is one that is said out loud and means something to someone. Not all of them will find their way to a page. There are words I've heard all my life that I've never set in type.'

What words? I wanted to ask. What do they mean? Who says them? But my tongue had become tied.

'I should go,' I finally managed. 'I have to deliver these slips to Mr Hart.'

'Well, it was nice to bump into you, Esme,' he said, smiling. 'It is Esme, isn't it? We were never actually introduced.'

I remembered his eyes but not his name. I stood stupid and mute.

'Gareth,' he said, holding out his hand, again. 'Very pleased to meet you.'

I hesitated, then returned my hand to his. He had long tapered fingers and a strangely bulbous thumb. My gaze lingered.

'Pleased to meet you too,' I said.

He opened the door and saw me into the hallway.

'You know the way?'

'Yes.'

'Right then. Go carefully.'

I turned and headed to the Controller's office. It was a relief to hand over the bundles of slips.

⁓

A new century started, and although there was a feeling that anything might happen, I never thought I'd see Dr Murray come to the kitchen door. When Mrs Ballard saw him striding across the lawn, she brushed down her apron and fixed the hair that had come loose from her cap. She unlatched the top door, and Dr Murray leaned in, his long beard wafting on the warm breath coming from the hearth.

'And where is Lizzie?' he asked, glancing at where I stood by the bench, stirring the batter of a cake.

'I sent her to fetch a few things, Dr Murray, sir,' said Mrs Ballard. 'She'll be back in no time, and then Esme will help her with hanging laundry in the drying cupboard. She's a great help to us, is Esme.'

'Well, that may be so, but I'd like Esme to come with me to the Scriptorium.'

Instinctively, I checked my pockets. Mrs Ballard looked at me. I shook my head as if to say, *I've done nothing, I promise.*

'Off you go now, Esme. Follow Dr Murray to the Scrippy.'

I took off my apron and walked, as if through treacle, to the kitchen door.

When I came into the Scriptorium, Da was there, smiling. He had many kinds of smiles, but his 'caged smile' was my favourite. It struggled to be released from behind pursed lips and twitching eyebrows. My fingers unfurled from the fists they'd been making.

Da took my hand, and the three of us walked to the back of the Scriptorium.

'This, Essy, is for you,' Da said, freeing his smile.

Behind a shelf of old dictionaries was a wooden desk. It was the kind I'd sat at in a cold room at Cauldshiels. My fingers twitched remembering the pain of the lid being brought down. A whispered taunt that my fingers were already good for nothing echoed in my head. I began to shake, but Da's hand on my shoulder brought me back to the Scriptorium. When Dr Murray lifted the lid, it revealed new pencils and blank slips, and two books that I immediately recognised.

'They belong to Elsie,' I heard myself say to Dr Murray, wanting to clarify that I hadn't taken them.

'Elsie has read them, Esme. She'd like you to have them. Consider them a late Christmas gift – or, better still, a gift for the new century.'

Then I noticed that the underside of the lid had been pasted with an offcut of wallpaper – a pale green with tiny yellow roses. It was the same paper that covered the walls of the sitting room in the Murray house. The desk was different from those at Cauldshiels in other ways too: it was bigger, with polished wood and hinges that caught the light, and the seat was separate.

Dr Murray closed the lid and stood a little awkwardly. 'Well, then,' he said. 'This is where you'll sit, and your father will employ you to do whatever is useful.'

With that, he gave Da a curt nod and returned to his own desk.

I threw my arms around Da and realised, for the first time, that I had to bend for my cheek to rest against his.

The next morning, I dressed more carefully than usual. I noticed the creases in the skirt that I'd left on the floor and so chose a clean one from the wardrobe. I spent half an hour trying to tame my hair into a tight plait, as Lizzie had once done, but ended with a messy bun, as usual. I spat on my shoes and gave them a rub with the corner of my bedspread. Then I went into Da's room to look in Lily's mirror.

'You can have that in your room, if you like,' said Da, startling me. 'Your mother wasn't a vain woman, but she loved that mirror.'

I blushed, shy of my own reflection and conscious of being examined, and compared. Lily had been tall and slender, like me, and

I had her clear skin and brown eyes. But instead of her flaxen tresses, Da's flame-red curls crowned my head. I saw him in the glass and wondered what he saw.

'She would be proud,' he said.

At Sunnyside, Da checked the morning post, and instead of joining Lizzie and Mrs Ballard in the kitchen I walked with him to the Scriptorium. He turned on the new electric lights and tended the coals until they glowed. The temperature barely shifted, but there was an illusion of warmth. I stood by the sorting table, nervous and awaiting instruction.

Da passed me the bundle of letters. 'This will be your job from now on, Essy,' he said. 'Collect and sort the letters as you've seen me do it. You're lucky Dr Murray no longer makes appeals for words; we used to get sack-loads. But you still need to open everything to check for slips.' He opened one of the envelopes. 'This is a letter, so it gets pinned to the envelope and left for whomever it is intended – you know where everyone sits?'

I nodded. Of course I knew.

I took the letters to the back of the Scriptorium. My desk sat in the alcove made by two shelves of old dictionaries and the only visible section of wall. I imagined it as a large pigeon-hole, built especially for my dimensions. From it, I could see the assistants at the sorting table and Dr Murray at his high desk. To see me, they would have to turn and crane their necks.

It was a relief to realise I could still observe without being observed, but my presence was not accidental. I had a desk, and the assistants would not be instructed to ignore me. I would serve the words as they served the words. And Dr Murray said he would pay me £1. 5s. per month. It was barely a quarter of what Da earned, and it was even less than Lizzie's wage, but it would be enough to buy flowers every week and have curtains made for the sitting room. And

I wouldn't have to ask Da for money when I wanted a new dress.

❧

I looked forward to the daily ritual of sorting the post, and the predictable responses of the assistants when I delivered it. They each had a manner and script that defined them, just as their shoes and socks had once defined them.

Mr Maling was the first on my rounds. '*Dankon*,' he would say, with a little bow of his upper body. Mr Balk rarely looked up and always called me Miss Murray. Hilda had left the year before to take up a lectureship at Royal Holloway College, in Surrey, and Elsie had taken her place beside their father's desk. Mr Balk seemed unable to tell us all apart, despite my height and hair. Da simply said thank you, looking up or not, depending on the complexity of his work.

Only with Mr Sweatman would I linger. He would put down his pencil and twist in his chair. 'What intelligence do you have from Mrs B's kitchen, Esme?' he always asked.

'She has promised a sponge for afternoon tea,' I might say.

'Excellent. You may proceed.'

Most of the letters were for Dr Murray.

'The post, Dr Murray.'

'Is it worth reading?' he would say, looking at me over his spectacles.

'I couldn't say.'

Then he would take the letters and reorder them according to the agreeability of the senders. Certain gentlemen from the Philological Society would be shifted back, but letters from the Press Delegates always ended up on the bottom.

My post round over, I would return to my desk to attend to any small task I might have been given, but the bulk of my day was spent sorting through piles of slips for particular words beginning with M and putting them in order, from oldest quotation to most recent.

The days when the post brought slips were my favourite. I would examine each in the hope of being the one to share a new word with Da or Dr Murray. Every word, no matter where in the alphabet it fell, would have to be checked against the words that had already been collected. The quotation might show a slightly different meaning, or it could pre-date the quotations already collected. When there were slips in the post, I could spend hours among the pigeon-holes and barely notice the time turning.

August 1901

I worked hard, and another year passed. Each day followed the same pattern, though the words coloured them differently. There was the post, the slips, replies to letters. In the afternoon I still delivered books and checked quotations at the Bodleian. I was never restless or bored. Not even the passing of Queen Victoria could depress me; I wore black, like everybody else, but I was the happiest I'd been since my days beneath the sorting table.

When winter passed into spring, Mr Bradley moved from the Press into his new Dictionary Room at the Old Ashmolean, and the third editor, Mr Craigie, joined him with two assistants. Dr Murray did not approve of the new editor and responded by pushing his own team to produce words more quickly. It was as if he wanted to prove the new editor unnecessary, although we all knew the Dictionary was already a decade overdue.

By the summer of 1901, Mr Balk had finally started calling me Miss Nicoll.

❧

'It will be hot in the Scrippy today,' said Lizzie, when I popped my head into the kitchen to say good morning.

'Will you make up some lemonade for us?' I asked.

'I've already been to the market.' She tilted her head towards a bowl of bright-yellow lemons.

I blew her a kiss and walked to the Scriptorium, sifting through the post as I went.

I'd developed a habit of guessing what was in the envelopes before opening them. As I made my way across the garden, I shuffled through the pile for a cursory assessment. A small number were addressed *To the Editor*, some so flimsy they were sure to contain nothing other than a slip. For me, I thought. There were several letters to *Dr James Murray* – most from the general public (their handwriting and return addresses unfamiliar), a few from gentlemen of the Philological Society, and one in the familiar envelope of the Press Delegates. This last was likely to be a caution about funds; if it suggested Dr Murray trim the contents of the Dictionary to speed progress, we would all suffer his bad mood. I placed it at the bottom of the pile so he could start his day with the compliments of strangers.

There were one or two letters for each of the assistants, and then, at the bottom of the bundle, there was a letter addressed to me.

Miss Esme Nicoll, Junior Assistant
Sunnyside, Scriptorium
Banbury Road
Oxford

It was the first letter I'd ever received at the Scriptorium, and the first time I'd been acknowledged as an assistant. My whole body tingled with the thrill, but the sensation dulled when I recognised the handwriting as Ditte's. It had been three years, but I still couldn't think of her without thinking of Cauldshiels, and I didn't want to think of that place.

Already the day was warm, and the air around my desk was still and stifling. Ditte's letter sat separate from the other piles; one page and a single slip. She asked after my health and how I was getting on at the Scriptorium. She'd had good reports from more than one source, she wrote, and I blushed with pride.

The slip was for a common word. I didn't want to be moved by it, but I was. When I searched the pigeon-holes I found no equivalent quotation. It belonged with a large bundle that had already been sorted and sub-edited into twenty variant senses. Instead of putting it in its place, I took it back to my desk.

I traced the writing as I might have done with Da before I learned to read. Ditte had fashioned the slip from heavy parchment and embellished the edges with scrolls. I brought it up to my face and breathed in the familiar scent of lavender. Did she spray the slip, I wondered, or hold it close before putting it in the envelope?

Silence was all I'd had to punish her with, and then I hadn't been able to find the right words to breach it. How I missed her.

I took a blank slip from my desk and copied onto it every word from Ditte's.

LOVE
'Love doth move the mynde to merci.'

The Babees' Book, 1557

I returned to the pigeon-holes and pinned the copy to the most relevant top-slip. Ditte's original slip went into the pocket of my skirt. The first in a long time – it was a relief.

❧

I lost an hour to thoughts of Ditte, to the words I might use to end my silence. When I finally did return to the post, I pulled another slip from its envelope. This one was unadorned, though not uninteresting. There were some words I'd never heard uttered and could hardly imagine using, yet they made their way into the Dictionary because someone great had written them down. Relics, I used to think, when I came across them.

Misbode was one of them. The quotation was from Chaucer's *The Knight's Tale*.

'*Who hath yow misboden, or offended?*' it said.

It was at least five hundred years old. I checked the slip was complete, then searched for the relevant pigeon-hole. There was a small pile, no top-slip. I added Chaucer's quotation. It wouldn't be long before M words needed to be defined. K was almost completed. I returned to my desk, then took up the next envelope to relieve it of its contents. When all the letters were checked and sorted, I made my way around the desks, delivering them to the men in exchange for errands. When I approached Dr Murray's desk, he handed me a pile of letters that had arrived during the previous week.

'Minor enquiries,' he said. 'You know more than enough to respond.'

'Thank you, Dr Murray.'

He nodded and returned to the copy he was editing.

For an hour or so, the rustle of work was only disturbed by the men removing their jackets and loosening their ties. The Scriptorium moaned when the sun found its iron roof. Mr Sweatman opened the door to let in a breeze, but there was no breeze to be had.

I read a letter asking why *Jew* had been split across two fascicles. Splitting a word across two publications had been the focus of more than one argument between Dr Murray and the Press Delegates. It was a question of revenue the Delegates had insisted, when Dr Murray informed them there would be a delay in the next fascicle – variants of *Jew* required more detailed research, he said. Publish what you've got, he was told.

It took six months before *Jew* was reconciled, and every week he received at least three letters from the public asking him to explain. I drafted a reply that suggested the requirements of printing insisted on certain page numbers for each fascicle and that the English language could not be edited to fit such limitations. There were times when a word would need to be split, but the meanings of *Jew* would be reunited when the next volume, *H to K*, was published.

I read what I had written, and was pleased. I looked up to where Dr Murray sat and wondered if I should ask him to review it before I sealed the envelope and attached a stamp.

Dr Murray would be having lunch at Christ Church and was already in academic dress, sitting at his high desk facing the sorting table. His mortar board was firmly in place; his gown was like the great black wings of a mythical bird. From my corner at the back, he looked like a judge presiding over a jury.

Just as I was gathering the courage to approach the bench and ask for my work to be reviewed, Dr Murray pushed back his chair. It scraped across the floorboards in a way that would attract reproach if anyone else had done it. The men all looked up and saw the Editor begin to fume.

Dr Murray had a letter in his hand. His head moved from side to side, a slow denial of whatever he had read. The Scriptorium fell silent. Dr Murray turned and pulled *A and B* from the shelf.

I felt the thump of it landing on the sorting table like a blow to my chest.

He opened to the middle, turned page after page, then took a deep breath when he found the right place. His eyes scanned the columns, and the assistants began to shift. Even Da was nervous, his hand reaching into his pocket to worry the coins he kept there. Dr Murray scanned the page again, returned to the top, then looked more closely. His finger traced the length of a column. He was searching for a word.

We waited. A minute seemed an hour. Whatever word he was looking for was not there.

He looked up, his face volcanic. Then he paused, as if he was about to deliver a sentence. Dr Murray looked at us, each in turn, his eyes narrowed and nostrils flaring above his long silver beard. His gaze was stern and steady, as if searching for the truth in our hearts. Only when it came to me did it flicker. His head tilted and his eyebrows raised. He was remembering my years beneath the sorting table. As was I.

Who hath yow misboden? I imagined him thinking.

Da was the first to follow Dr Murray's gaze to where I sat. Then Mr Sweatman. All of the assistants craned their necks to look at me, though the newest assistants were confused. I had never felt so visible as I did in that moment, and I surprised myself by sitting up straighter. I did not fidget or look down.

If Dr Murray had thought to accuse me, he made a decision not to. Instead, he picked up the letter again and re-read it, then he glanced at the open volume; there was no use searching it a fourth time. He put the letter between its pages and left the Scriptorium without a word. Elsie followed close behind.

The assistants breathed out. Da wiped his brow with a handkerchief. When they were sure Dr Murray had gone into the house, a few men ventured into the garden to seek a breeze.

Mr Sweatman got up and went to the volume of words on Dr Murray's desk. *A and B.* He picked up the letter and read it through. When he looked at me there was sympathy in his eyes, but also the hint of a grin. Da joined him and scanned the letter, then read aloud.

Dear sir,

I write to thank you for your excellent Dictionary. I subscribe to receive the fascicles as they are published and have all four volumes so far bound. They occupy a book case made especially for them, and I hope, one day, to see it filled, though it may be a satisfaction I leave to my son. I am in my sixth decade and not in full health.

It is my habit, since you have furnished the means, to reflect on certain words and understand their history. I had cause to refer to your dictionary while reading The Lord of the Isles. *The word I sought in this instance was 'bondmaid'. It is not an obscure word, but Scott uses a hyphen where I thought it was not needed. Its male equivalent was adequately referenced, but bondmaid was not there.*

I must admit I was perplexed. Your Dictionary *has taken on the status of unquestionable authority in my mind. I realise it is unfair to burden any work of Man with the expectation of perfection, and I can only conclude that you, like me, are fallible, and it was an accidental omission.*

I enlighten you, sir, with good intentions and all due respect.

Yours, etc.

⁓

I walked as slowly as I could across the lawn and past the assistants stretched on the grass, each with a tall glass of lemonade in his hand. As I started up the stairs to Lizzie's room, Mrs Ballard emerged from the pantry, two eggs in each hand.

'Not like you to pass through my kitchen without a by-your-leave,' she said.

'Is Lizzie around, Mrs B?'

'Well, good morning to you too, young lady.' She peered at me above her spectacles.

'I'm sorry, Mrs B. There's been an upset in the Scriptorium and we're all taking a minute. I was hoping Lizzie would be around, maybe I could just …'

'An upset, you say?' She continued to the kitchen bench, and began cracking the eggs on the rim of a bowl. She looked at me to respond.

'They've lost a word,' I said. 'Dr Murray is furious.'

She shook her head and smiled. 'Do they think we'll stop speaking it if it's not in their dictionary? Can't be the first word they've lost.'

'I think Dr Murray believes that it is.'

Mrs Ballard shrugged and transferred the bowl to her hip. She beat the eggs till her hand was a blur and the kitchen filled with a comforting thrum.

'I'll wait for Lizzie in her room,' I said.

Lizzie came in just as I was reaching for the trunk. 'Esme, what on earth are you doing?'

'It's filthy under here, Lizzie,' I said, my head under her small bed, my hands searching the void. 'It's not at all what I would expect from the most accomplished housemaid in Oxford.'

'Come out from under there, Essymay. You'll soil your dress.'

I crawled backwards, dragging the trunk with me.

'I thought you'd forgotten all about that trunk.'

I thought about the news clipping Ditte had sent. It would be on top of all the other words in the trunk. I hadn't been able to face it for a long time.

The trunk was covered in a film of dust. 'Did you keep it safe on purpose, Lizzie, when I went to school? Or just by accident?'

Lizzie sat on the bed and watched me. 'There seemed no reason to mention it to anyone.'

'Was I really such a bad child?' I asked.

'No, just a motherless one, like so many of us.'

'But that's not why they sent me away.'

'They only sent you to school. And it probably was 'cos you'd no mother to care for you. They thought it best.'

'But it wasn't best.'

'I know that. And they came to know that. They brought you home.' Lizzie tucked a lock of my unruly hair back into its pin. 'What's made you remember it now?'

'Ditte sent me a slip.' I showed it to her. As I read the quotation, I saw her relief.

Then I looked at her sheepishly. 'There is another reason,' I said.

'Which is?'

'Dr Murray thinks a word is missing from the Dictionary.'

Lizzie looked at the trunk, and her hand sought her crucifix. I thought she might start fretting, but she didn't.

'Open it slowly,' she said. 'In case something has made a home of it and is startled by the light.'

❧

I sat all afternoon with my Dictionary of Lost Words. Lizzie came and went more than once, bringing sandwiches and milk, and reluctantly relaying a message to Da that I was feeling poorly. When she came into her room for the third time, she turned on the lamp.

'I'm knackered,' she said, sitting heavily on the bed and disturbing the slips spread across it. She moved her hand through them like she was moving it through leaves. 'Did you find it?' she asked.

'Find what?'

'The lost word.'

The look on Dr Murray's face came back to me.

'Oh, yes,' I said. 'I did find it, eventually.'

I reached over to Lizzie's bedside table and picked up the slip. There was no question of me giving it to Dr Murray. Even if he wasn't in a temper, I couldn't think of a single scenario that would make the word's presence in my hand acceptable.

'Do you remember it, Lizzie?' I said, holding it out to her.

'Why would I remember it?'

'It was the very first. I wasn't sure, but when I took everything out of the trunk, there it was, right at the bottom. Do you remember? It had looked so lonely.'

She thought for a bit, then her face brightened. 'Oh, I do remember. You found my mother's hat pin.'

I looked at the engraving on the inside of the trunk, *The Dictionary of Lost Words*. I blushed.

'Stop that now,' she said, then nodded towards the word I was still holding in my hand. 'How could Dr Murray know that word was missing? Does he count them? There'd be so many.'

'He got a letter. From a man who expected to find it in the volume with all the A and B words, but didn't.'

'People can't expect every word to be in there,' Lizzie said.

'Oh, but they do. And sometimes Dr Murray has to write to tell them why a word has not been included. There are all sorts of good reasons, Da tells me, but this time was different.' I was excited, recalling the drama of the morning. Against all common sense, I couldn't help a feeling of accomplishment. I had been the cause of something that seemed to really matter.

I saw concern on Lizzie's face.

'What is it, then?' she asked. 'What is the word?'

'*Bondmaid*,' I said, deliberate and slow, feeling it in my throat and on my lips. 'The word is *bondmaid*.'

Lizzie tried it: '*Bondmaid*. What does it mean?'

I looked at the scrap of paper. It was a top-slip, and I recognised Da's hand. I could see where the pin once joined it to all the quotation slips, or maybe a proof. If I'd known it had come from Da, would I have kept it?

'Well, what does it mean?'

There were three definitions.

'*A slave girl*,' I said. 'Or *a bonded servant*, or *someone who is bound to serve till death*.'

Lizzie thought on it for a while. 'That's what I am,' she said. 'I reckon I'm bound to serve the Murrays till the day I die.'

'Oh, I don't think it describes you, Lizzie.'

'Well enough,' she said. 'Don't look so stricken, Essymay. I'm glad

I'm in the Dictionary; or would have been, if not for you.' She smiled. 'I wonder what else is in there about me?'

I thought about the words in the trunk. Some I hadn't heard or read until I saw them on a slip. Most were commonplace, but something about the slip or handwriting had endeared them to me. There were clumsy words with poorly transcribed quotations that would never end up in the Dictionary, and there were words that existed for one sentence and no other: fledglings, nonce words that never made it. I loved them all.

Bondmaid was no fledgling word, and its meaning disturbed me. Lizzie was right; it referred to her as it referred to a Roman slave girl.

Dr Murray's rage came back to me then and I felt mine rising to meet it. It should not be, this word, I thought. It shouldn't exist. Its meaning should be obscure and unthinkable. It should be a relic, and yet it was as easily understood now as at any time in history. The joy of telling the story faded.

'I'm glad it isn't in the Dictionary, Lizzie. It's a horrible word.'

'That it may be, but it's a true word. Dictionary or no, bondmaids will always exist.'

Lizzie went to her wardrobe to select a clean pinny. 'Mrs B has left me to get dinner on, Essymay. I have to go. You can stay, if you like.'

'I will if you don't mind, Lizzie. I need to write to Ditte. I'd like the letter to make the morning post.'

'It's about time.'

16th August 1901

My dear Esme,

I have waited so long for your letter. I thought of it as my penance, and justly deserved. Nevertheless, it has been a hard sentence, and I am glad for it to be over.

I have not been in solitary confinement and am well aware of all that can be reported of a factual nature. You have grown like a 'sapling willow' according to a rare flourish from James when describing the garden party for 'H to K'. Your father complains that you now tower over him but is wistful about your growing resemblance to Lily.

I know enough to be satisfied that you are reading well and learning one or two domestic skills considered desirable in a young lady. All these details I have gratefully received, but what I have longed for these past years is something of you, Esme. Your thoughts and desires. Your developing opinions and curiosities.

In this respect, your letter has been a balm. I have read and re-read it, noticing on each pass some further evidence of your keen mind. The recent fuss about a missing word has certainly piqued your interest and, while it was not intentionally excluded, 'bondmaid' joins a number of fine words that should have been included in Volume I but were not (do not, for instance, mention 'Africa' to Dr Murray: it is a sore point).

What is clear to me is that during your time under the sorting table you absorbed more than most who have sat before a blackboard for six years. It was a mistake for any of us to assume the Scriptorium was not a suitable place to grow and learn. Our thinking was limited by convention (the most subtle but oppressive dictator). Please forgive our lack of imagination.

And so, to your main enquiry.

Unfortunately, there is no capacity for the Dictionary to contain words that have no textual source. Every word must have been written down, and you are right to assume they largely come from books written by men, but this is not always the case. Many quotations have been penned by women, though they are, of course, in the minority. You might be surprised to learn that some words take their provenance from nothing more substantial than a technical manual or a pamphlet. I know of at least one word that was found on the label of a medicine bottle.

You are correct in your observation that words in common use that are not written down would necessarily be excluded. Your concern that some types of words, or words used by some types of people, will be lost to the future is really quite perceptive. I can think of no solution, however. Consider the alternative: the inclusion of all these words, words that come and go in a year or two, words that *do not stick to our tongue through generations. They would clog the Dictionary. All words are not equal (and as I write this, I think I see your concern more clearly: if the words of one group are considered worthier of preservation than those of another ... well, you have given me pause for thought).*

Early ambitions that the Dictionary be a complete record of the meaning and history of all English words has proved quite impossible, but let me reassure you that there are many fine words recorded in literary texts that also do not pass the tests laid down by Dr Murray and the Philological Society. I am enclosing one such word.

'Forgiven-ness.'

It is from a novel by Adeline Whitney called Sights and Insights. *Beth read it soon after it was published. She wasn't at all complimentary (Mrs Whitney is overt in her opinion that a woman should restrict her activities to the home and her words to the domestic), but she found this word interesting and wrote the slip out herself. Years later, I was asked to write the entry, though it never got past the first draft.*

For reasons I'm sure I don't need to explain, I have had cause to think of it lately. I was never very diligent in returning rejected words to the Scriptorium, and so here it is — an offering and a request. If you accept it, my soul would feel blessedly its own redemption and forgiven-ness (to quote Mrs Whitney).

Yours, with love,

Ditte

PART THREE

1902–1907

Lap–Nywe

May 1902

Two years after I received my first pay packet, Dr Murray asked me to show Rosfrith the process of sorting slips and checking senses and anything else that would help her settle in as the newest assistant. After half an hour, it was clear there was no need for my instruction. Like all her siblings, Rosfrith had been sorting slips since she was a child. She may not have hidden beneath the sorting table, but she knew her way around the Scriptorium.

'I am superfluous to need,' I said, and Rosfrith grinned. She was so like Elsie, though a little slimmer, a little taller, a little fairer. She had the same fine-featured face, the same downward slant to her eyes. They would have made her look sad if she didn't smile so much. I left her at the desk she would share with her sister, just to the left of Dr Murray's, and returned to my own. Slips for words beginning with L sat in neat piles along the edge. When I sat down, I wondered what it would feel like to divide the task of sorting them with someone who looked a little like me.

Normally, I would take my time over the words I sorted. If the word was familiar, I would check my understanding of it against the example provided by the volunteer. If it was unfamiliar, I would commit its meaning to memory. These new words became the focus of my walk home with Da. If he did not know the word then I would explain it to him, and we would shuttle it back and forth in ever more elaborate sentences.

But *listless* started me yawning. It had thirteen slips of unvaried meaning, and it was easy to let my mind wander beyond the confines of the Scriptorium. I thought of what Ditte had said about the need for words to have a textual history. Well, *listless* certainly had that. The earliest quotation was from a book written in 1440, so its inclusion was assured, but it wasn't nearly as interesting as Lizzie's word, *knackered*. Lizzie had never once said she felt listless, but she was knackered all the time.

I pinned all the *listless* slips together, from oldest quotation to most recent. One was only partially completed: *listless* was in the top-left corner, and there was a quotation, but it had no date, book title or author. It would have been discarded, but my heart still raced as I put it in my pocket.

Mrs Ballard was already sitting at the table when I came into the kitchen, and Lizzie was making ham sandwiches for their lunch. There were three teacups already out.

'What does *knackered* mean, Lizzie?'

Mrs Ballard scoffed. 'You could ask anyone in service that question, Esme. We'd all have an answer.'

Lizzie poured the tea and sat down. 'It means you're tired.'

'Why don't you just say tired, then?'

She thought about it. 'It's not just tired from lack of sleep; it's tired from work – physical work. I get up before dawn to make sure everyone in the big house will be warm and fed when they wake, and I don't go to sleep till they is snoring. I feel knackered half the time, like a worn-out horse. No good for nothing.'

I took the slip from my pocket and looked at the word. *Listless* wasn't quite like *knackered*. It was lazier. I looked at Lizzie and understood why she would never have cause to use it.

'Do you have a pencil, Mrs B?'

Mrs Ballard hesitated. 'I don't much like the look of that slip of paper in your hand, Esme.'

I showed it to her. 'It's incomplete, see? It's scrap. I'm going to reuse it.'

She nodded. 'Lizzie, love, there's a pencil just inside the pantry, near my shopping list. Would you get it for Esme?'

I put a line through *listless* and turned the slip over. It was blank, but I wavered. I'd never written a slip before. I'd been taking words for years – reading them, remembering them, rescuing them. I turned to them for explanation. But when the Dictionary words let me down, I'd never imagined I could add to them.

As Lizzie and Mrs Ballard watched on, I wrote:

KNACKERED

'I get up before dawn to make sure everyone in the big house will be warm and fed when they wake, and I don't go to sleep till they is snoring. I feel knackered half the time, like a worn-out horse. No good for nothing.'

Lizzie Lester, 1902

'Don't reckon Dr Murray will think that a proper quotation,' said Mrs Ballard. 'But it's good to see it written down. Lizzie's not wrong. It wears you out, being on your feet all day.'

'What did you write?' Lizzie asked.

I read it to her and she reached for her crucifix. I wondered if I'd upset her.

'Nothing I ever said has been written down,' she finally said. Then she got up and cleared the table.

I looked at my slip. It would have been at home in one of the pigeon-holes, I thought, and I wondered what Lizzie would think of her name and her words nestled against the likes of Wordsworth and Swift. I decided to create a top-slip and pin it to Lizzie's word; then I remembered that all the K words were already published.

I left Lizzie and Mrs Ballard to their lunch and took the stairs two at a time. The trunk under Lizzie's bed was more than half full. I placed *knackered* on top of the pile.

This would be the first, I thought. It was unique because it hadn't come from a book. But against all the rest, there was nothing to distinguish it. I pulled the ribbon from my hair and tied it around the slip. It looked forlorn on its own, but I could imagine others.

Da once told me that it was Dr Murray's idea to make the slips the size they were. At first he sent prepared slips to volunteers, but after a while it was enough to simply instruct people to provide their words and sentences on pieces of paper six by four inches. Blank paper was not always available to some of the volunteers, and when I was small, Da would search for me under the sorting table to show me the slips cut from newspaper, old shopping lists, used butcher's paper (a brown stain of blood blooming across the words) and even pages torn from books. I found these last shocking and suggested Dr Murray dismiss volunteers who ruined books. Da laughed. The worst offender, he said, was Frederick Furnivall. Dr Murray might think of dismissing him occasionally, but Frederick Furnivall was secretary of the Philological Society. The Dictionary was his idea.

Dr Murray's slips were ingenious, Da said. Simple and efficient, their value increasing as the Scriptorium filled with words and storage became more and more limited. Dr Murray designed them to fit the pigeon-holes exactly. Not an inch of space had been wasted.

Each slip had its own personality, and while it was being sorted there was a chance the word it contained would be understood. At the very least, it would be picked up and read. Some slips were passed from hand to hand, others were the subject of long debate and sometimes a row. For a while, every word was as important as the one before it and the one after it, no matter what its slip had been cut from. If it was complete, it would be stored in a pigeon-hole, pinned or tied with other slips, their conformity highlighted by the oversized and colourful few that were cut to their own design.

I often wondered what kind of slip I would be written on if I was a word. Something too long, certainly. Probably the wrong colour. A scrap of paper that didn't quite fit. I worried that perhaps I would never find my place in the pigeon-holes at all.

My slips would be no different from Dr Murray's, I decided, and I began collecting all sorts of paper to cut to the right size. My favourite slips were cut from the blue bond paper Lily once used. I'd taken a few sheets from the drawer of Da's writing desk. I would save these for beautiful words. The rest were a mixture of ordinary and extraordinary: a pile of original blank slips from the Scriptorium, forgotten in a dusty corner and surely missed by no one; slips cut from school essays and algebra exercises; a few postcards bought by Da but never sent (almost the right size, but not quite); and wallpaper offcuts, a little thick but beautifully patterned on one side.

I began to carry them around, hoping to capture more words like *knackered*.

Lizzie was a great source. In a week, I recorded seven words I was sure weren't in the pigeon-holes. When I checked, five of them were. I threw my doubles away and put the remaining two in the trunk with *knackered*, tying them together with my ribbon.

The Scriptorium was not so fruitful. Every now and then Dr Murray said something interesting in his Scottish brogue, usually under his breath. *Glaikit* was a common utterance in response to incompetency or slow work, and I dared not ask him to repeat it, though I wrote a slip and defined it as *idiot or nincompoop*. When I searched the volume with F and G, I was surprised to find it was already there. The other assistants spoke nothing other than words they read in well-written books. I doubted any of them had ever spent much time listening to what was said in Mrs Ballard's kitchen or what flew between the traders of the Covered Market.

I didn't have to help in the kitchen any more, but sometimes I did. I preferred it to going home alone when Da worked late. The new curtains and fresh flowers brightened up our house, but during the long summer evenings I preferred to stay talking with Lizzie. Then when it was cold, it seemed a waste to use the coal for just one person.

'Could I ask you to do something for me, Lizzie?' We were standing side by side at the sink.

'Anything, Essymay. You know that.'

'I'm wondering if you'd help me collect words,' I said, looking at her sideways to gauge her reaction. Her jaw clenched. 'Not from the Scriptorium,' I quickly added.

'Where would I find words?' she asked, not taking her eyes off the potato she was peeling.

'Everywhere you go.'

'The world ain't like the Scrippy, Essy. Words don't lie around waiting for some light-fingered girl to pick them up.' She turned and gave me a reassuring smile.

'That's just the point, Lizzie. I'm sure there are plenty of wonderful words flying around that have never been written on a slip of paper. I want to record them.'

'Whatever for?'

'Because I think they're just as important as the words Dr Murray and Da collect,' I said.

''Course they's—' She stopped, corrected herself. 'What I mean to say is, of course they *are* not. They're just words we use 'cos we don't know anything better.'

'I don't think so. I think sometimes the proper words mustn't be quite right, and so people make new words up, or use old words differently.'

Lizzie gave a little laugh. 'The people I talk to at the Covered Market have no idea what the proper words are. Most of them can't hardly read, and they stand all bewildered whenever a gentleman stops to chat.'

We finished peeling the potatoes, and Lizzie started cutting them in half and adding them to a large pot. I dried my hands on the warm towel hanging by the range.

'Besides,' Lizzie continued, 'it ain't right for a woman in service to be dawdling around them that like to use colourful language. It would reflect badly on the Murrays if I was seen to be engaging in the wrong sort of talk once I've finished my errands.'

I'd imagined a pile of words so big I'd need a new trunk to store them all in, but if Lizzie wouldn't help I'd barely collect enough to strain my ribbon.

'Oh, please, Lizzie. I can't wander around Oxford alone with no purpose. If you don't do this for me, I might as well give it up.'

She finished cutting the last few potatoes, then turned to look at me. 'Even if I did hang around eavesdropping, I'd only be welcome with the women. Men, even the sort that work the barges, would tame their talk for the likes of me.'

Another idea began to form. 'Do you think there are some words that only women use, or that apply to women specifically?'

'I 'spose so,' she said.

'Would you tell me what they are?' I asked.

'Pass me the salt,' she said, lifting the lid off the potatoes.

'Well, will you?'

'I don't think I could,' she said.

'Why not?'

'There's some I won't say and others I can't explain.'

'Maybe I could come with you on your errands. I could be the one eavesdropping. I won't get in your way or make you dawdle. I'll just listen, and if I hear an interesting word I'll write it down.'

'Maybe,' she said.

&

I began to rise early on Saturdays to accompany Lizzie to the Covered Market. I filled my pockets with slips and two pencils, and followed Lizzie like Mary's lamb. We would start with the fruit and vegetables – the freshest were had first thing. Then the butcher's stall or the fishmonger's, the bakery and the grocer. We would go down one alley and up the other, looking in the windows of the little shops selling chocolates or hats or wooden toys. Then we'd go into the tiny haberdashery. Lizzie sometimes came home with a new thread or needles. More often than not, I came home disappointed. The stallholders were friendly and polite, and every word they said was familiar.

'They want you to spend your money,' Lizzie said. 'They ain't about to risk offending your delicate ears.'

Sometimes I caught a word as we passed the fishmonger's or a group of men unloading carts piled with vegetables. But Lizzie wouldn't ask them what it meant and she wouldn't let me anywhere near them.

'I'll never collect any words at this rate, Lizzie.'

She shrugged and continued on her well-worn path around the market.

'Maybe I'll just have to go back to saving words from the Scriptorium.' That stopped her, as I knew it would.

'You wouldn't …?' she said.

'I might not be able to help myself.'

She contemplated me for a moment. 'Let's see what old Mabel's peddling today.'

❧

Mabel O'Shaughnessy repelled and attracted like two ends of a magnet. Hers was the smallest stall in the Covered Market: two wooden crates pushed side by side, their contents of found objects displayed on top. Lizzie usually steered us in a different direction, and for a long time Mabel had been nothing more to me than a passing image of sharp bones ready to tear through papery skin, and a tattered hat that barely covered patches of naked scalp.

When we approached, it was clear that Lizzie and Mabel were well acquainted.

'You eaten today, Mabel?' Lizzie said.

'Ain't sold enough to buy a stale bun.'

Lizzie reached into our groceries and handed her a roll.

'Who's this then?' Mabel said, her mouth full of bread.

'Esme, this is Mabel. Mabel, this is Esme. Her father works for Dr Murray.' She looked at me apologetically. 'Esme works for the Dictionary too.'

Mabel held out her hand: long, grime-covered fingers protruded from the scraps of fingerless gloves. I didn't shake hands, ordinarily, and instinctively wiped my funny fingers against the fabric of my skirt, as if to rid them of something distasteful. When I offered my hand, the old woman laughed.

'No amount of wipin' will fix that,' she said. Then she took my hand in both of hers and examined it like only the doctor ever had. Her filthy fingers held each of mine in turn, testing the joints and gently straightening them. Hers were as straight and nimble as mine were bent and stiff.

'Do they work?' she asked.

I nodded. She seemed satisfied and let go. Then she motioned to the contents of her stall. 'Nothin' stoppin' you then.'

I started picking through her offerings. No wonder she hadn't eaten: everything she sold was flotsam, broken things dragged out of the river. The only colour came from a cup and saucer, both chipped but otherwise functional. She'd put one on top of the other as if they belonged together, though they never had. No one with the coin to spare would ever drink their tea from that cup, I thought, but to be polite I picked it up and examined the delicate pattern of roses.

'China that is. The saucer too,' said Mabel. ''Old 'em up to the light.'

She was right. Fine china, both. I put the roses back on the bluebell saucer, and there was something joyous about the combination among the silty browns of everything else. We shared a smile.

But it wasn't enough. Mabel nodded again towards her wares, so I touched and turned and picked up one or two. There was a stick, no longer than a pencil but twisted along its length. I expected it to be rough, but it was as smooth as marble. When I brought it close to peer at its knotty end, an ancient face peered back. The cares of a lifetime had been carved into the old man's expression, and his beard was wrapped around the twist of the stick. I felt a butterfly in my chest as I imagined it on Da's desk.

I looked at Mabel. She'd been waiting, and now she offered me a gummy grin and an outstretched hand.

I took a coin from my purse. 'It's remarkable.'

'Naught else to do with me 'ands now no one wants 'em round their shaft.' I wasn't sure I understood, and when I failed to react the way she'd expected, she looked to Lizzie. 'She dumb?' she asked.

'No, Mabel, she just don't have an ear for your particular form of English.'

When we were back at Sunnyside, I took out a slip and a pencil. Lizzie refused to tell me the meaning of *shaft*, but she nodded or shook her head in response to my guesses. The colour in her face told me when I got it right.

We became regular visitors to Mabel's stall. My vocabulary swelled, and Da delighted in the occasional whittling. They leaned against his pens and pencils in the old dice cup that had always sat on his desk.

Mabel was coughing and clearing her throat of great gobs of phlegm every few words or so. I'd been visiting her with Lizzie for the best part of a year and never known her to be silent, but I thought the cough might impede her. It didn't; it only made her harder to decipher. When she coughed again, I offered my handkerchief, hoping it would stop her spitting on the flagstones beside her stool. She looked at it, but made no move to take it.

'Nah, I's right, lass,' she said. Then she leaned sideways and hawked what had accumulated in her mouth onto the ground. I flinched. She was pleased.

While I inspected her whittling, Mabel prattled on about the criminal, financial and sexual frailties of her neighbouring stallholders, her commentary barely interrupted to tell me the price of something.

Among her rheumy words was one I thought I'd heard before – one Lizzie had denied any knowledge of, though it had been clear from her reddening face that she was lying.

'Cunt,' Mabel said, when I asked her to repeat it.

'Come on, Esme,' Lizzie said, taking my arm with uncharacteristic urgency.

'Cunt,' Mabel said, a little louder.

'Esme, we should go. We have a lot to do.'

'What does it mean?' I asked Mabel.

'It means she's a cunt: a fuckin' nasty bitch.' Mabel glanced towards the flower stall.

'Mabel, lower your voice,' Lizzie whispered. 'They'll have you out of here for that language, you know that.' She was still trying to pull me away.

'But what does it actually mean?' I asked Mabel again.

She looked at me, all gums. She loved it when I asked her to explain a word. 'You got yer pencil and paper, lass? Yer goin' ta wan' ta write this one down.'

I shook Lizzie's hand from my arm. 'You go, Lizzie. I'll catch up.'

'Esme, if anyone overhears you talking like that … well, Mrs Ballard will know before we're even home.'

'It's all right, Lizzie. Mabel and I are going to whisper,' I said, turning to look sternly at the old woman. 'Aren't we, Mabel?'

She nodded like a waif waiting for a bowl of soup. She wanted her words written down.

I took a blank slip from my pocket and wrote *Cunt* in the top-left corner.

'It's yer quim,' Mabel said.

I looked at her, hoping the sense of what she'd just said would find me, as it sometimes did after a second or two, but I was stumped.

'Mabel, that doesn't help.' I took another slip and wrote *Quim* in the top-left corner. 'Put *cunt* in a sentence for me,' I said.

'I got an itchy cunt,' she said, scratching the front of her skirts.

It helped, but I didn't write it down. 'Is it the same as crotch?' I whispered.

'You is dim, lass,' said Mabel. 'You got a cunt, I got a cunt, Lizzie got a cunt, but old Ned over there, he ain't got a cunt. Get it?'

I leaned in a little closer, holding my breath against Mabel's stink. 'Is it the vagina?' I whispered.

'Fuck, yer a genius, you are.'

I pulled back, but not before the full force of her exhaled laugh hit me in the face. Tobacco and gum disease.

I wrote: *Woman's vagina; insult.* Then I crossed out *Woman's.*

'Mabel, I need a sentence that makes it crystal clear what it means,' I said.

She thought, went to say something, stopped, thought some more. Then she looked at me, a childish joy spreading across the complicated landscape of her face.

'You ready, lass?' she asked. I leaned against her crate and wrote her words: *There was a young harlot from Kew, who filled her cunt up with glue. She said with a grin, if they pay to get in, they'll pay to get out of it too.*

Her laughter spawned a violent fit of coughing, which required a few swift slaps on the back to ease.

When she was recovered, I wrote, *Mabel O'Shaughnessy, 1902,* beneath the quotation.

'And *quim*?' I asked. 'Does it mean the same thing?'

She looked up at me, still amused. ''Tis the juices, lass.' She flicked her tongue in and out against her cracked lips. 'Mine ain't sweet no more, but once –' she rubbed her thumb against two fingers '– I'd eat well 'cos of me juices. The men loves to think they got you goin'.'

I thought I understood. I wrote: *Vaginal discharge during intimate relations.*

'Is it also an insult?' I asked.

''Course,' Mabel said. 'Quim's just proof of yer shame. The likes of us use it just the same as we use cunt.' Then she looked towards the flower stall. 'She and 'er old man are fuckin' quims, and there's no doubt about it.'

I added: *Insult.*

'Thanks, Mabel,' I said, putting the slips back in my pocket.

'You don't want a sentence?'

'You've given me plenty. I'll choose the best when I get home,' I said.

'So long as me name goes on it,' she said.

'It will. No one else would want to claim it.'

She gave another gummy grin and presented me with one of her whittled sticks. 'A mermaid.'

Da would love it. I took two coins from my purse.

'Worth an extra penny, I reckon,' said Mabel.

I gave her two more, one for each word, then went to find Lizzie.

'And what did Mabel have to say for herself?' asked Lizzie on the walk back to Sunnyside.

'Quite a lot, actually. I ran out of slips.'

I waited for Lizzie to ask more questions, but she had learned not to. When we arrived at Sunnyside, she invited me in for tea.

'I need to check something in the Scriptorium,' I said.

'You won't put your new words in the trunk?'

'Not yet. I want to check to see how *cunt* was defined for the Dictionary.'

'Esme.' Lizzie looked desperate. 'You can't say that word out loud.'

'So you know it?'

'No. Well, I know *of* it. I know it's not a word for polite society. You mustn't say it, Essymay.'

'All right,' I said, delighted at the effect the word had. 'Let's just call it the *C-word*.'

'Let's not call it anything. There is no reason it ever needs to be used.'

'Mabel says it's a very old word. So it should be in the volume for C. I want to see how close I came to defining it.'

The Scrippy was empty, though Da's and Mr Sweatman's jackets were still on the backs of their chairs. I went to the shelf behind Mr Murray's desk and took down the second volume of words. *C* was even bigger than *A and B*; it had taken half my childhood to compile. When

I searched its pages, Mabel's word was not there.

I returned the volume and began searching the pigeon-holes for C. They were dusty from lack of attention.

'Looking for something in particular?' It was Mr Sweatman.

I folded Mabel's slips into my hand and turned. 'Nothing that can't wait until Monday,' I said. 'Is Da with you?'

Mr Sweatman took his jacket off the back of his chair. 'Stopped by the house to have a quick word with Dr Murray. He should be here any minute.'

'I'll wait for him in the garden,' I said.

'Righto. I'll see you on Monday.'

I lifted the lid of my desk and placed the slips between the pages of a book.

❧

I began going to the Covered Market alone. Whenever my work took me to the Bodleian or the Old Ashmolean, I would make a detour through the crowded alleyways of stalls and shops. I wandered slowly; I loitered at the window of the milliner so I could eavesdrop on the grocer and his boy standing on the street; I took my time choosing fish on Fridays in the hope of catching an unfamiliar word passed between the fishmonger and his wife.

'Why won't Dr Murray include words that aren't written down?' I asked Da as we walked to the Scriptorium one morning. I had three new slips in my pocket.

'If it's not written down, we can't verify the meaning.'

'What if it's in common use? I hear the same words over and over at the Covered Market.'

'They may be commonly spoken, but if they are not commonly written they will not be included. A quotation from Mr Smith the greengrocer is simply not adequate.'

'But some nonsense from Mr Dickens the author is?'

Da looked at me sideways.

I smiled. '*Jog-trotty*, remember?'

Jog-trotty had caused considerable debate around the sorting table a few years earlier. It had seventeen slips, but they all contained the same quotation. It was the only quotation, as far as Mr Maling could ascertain.

It's rather jog-trotty and humdrum.

'But it's Dickens,' said one assistant. 'It's nonsense,' said another. 'It's for an editor to decide,' said Mr Maling. And as Dr Murray was away, it fell to the newest editor, Mr Craigie. He must have admired Dickens, because it was included in *H to K*.

'Touché,' said Da. 'So, give me an example of a word you've heard at the market.'

'*Latch-keyed*,' I said, remembering the way Mrs Stiles at the flower stall had said it to a customer, and her glance in my direction.

'You know, that word sounds familiar.' He looked pleased. 'I think you might find that there's already an entry.'

Da's pace increased, and when we arrived at the Scriptorium he went straight to the shelf that held the fascicles. He removed 'Lap to Leisurely' and began leafing through it, repeating 'latch-keyed' under his breath.

'Well, a *latch-key* is used to unlock a night gate, but *latch-keyed* isn't here.' He moved to the pigeon-holes, and I followed.

Except for us, the Scriptorium was empty. I felt like a child again. *Latch-keyed* would be in the middle somewhere, I thought. Not too high and not too low.

'Here it is.' Da took a small pile of slips to the sorting table. 'Ah, I remember now – I wrote the entry. *Latch-keyed* means *to be furnished with a latch-key*.'

'So, someone who's *latch-keyed* can come and go as they please?'

'That is the suggestion.'

I looked over his shoulder and read the top-slip. There were various definitions in Da's writing.

Unchaperoned; undisciplined; referring to a young woman with no domestic constraint.

'All the quotations are from the *Daily Telegraph*,' said Da, passing me one.

'And why should that matter?'

'Believe it or not, Dr Murray has asked that very same question.'

'Of whom?'

'Of the Press Delegates when they want to cut costs. Cutting costs means cutting words. According to them, the *Daily Telegraph* is not a credible source, and its words are expendable.'

'I suppose the *Times* is a credible source?'

Da nodded.

I looked at the slip he'd given me.

LATCH-KEYED

'All latch-keyed daughters and knicker-bockerred maidens, and discontented people generally.'

Daily Telegraph, 1895

'It isn't a compliment, then?'

'That depends on whether you think young ladies should always be chaperoned, disciplined and under domestic constraint.' He smiled, then became serious. 'In general, I think it would be used to criticise.'

'I'll put them away,' I said.

I gathered up the slips. As I walked back to the pigeon-holes, I put *latch-keyed daughters* in the sleeve of my dress. Superfluous to need, I thought.

☙

By the end of 1902 I'd become confident collecting my own words, but at the Scriptorium, I was still running errands and adding new quotations to piles of slips that had already been sorted years earlier by volunteers. I found myself becoming frustrated by the definitions that some words were given. I was tempted to draw a line through so many, but it was not my place. Temptation, though, can only be resisted for so long.

'Esme, is this your handiwork?'

Da pushed a proof across the breakfast table and pointed to a scrap of paper pinned to its edge. The handwriting was mine. There was nothing in his tone that indicated my edit was good or bad. I stayed silent.

'When did you do it?' he asked

'This morning,' I said, not looking up from my bowl of porridge. 'You left it out when you went to bed last night.'

Da sat reading what I'd penned.

MADCAP

Often applied playfully to young women of lively or impulsive temperament.
'On the boards, she was the merriest, gayest, madcap in the world.'

Mabel Collins, *The Prettiest Woman in Warsaw*, 1885

I looked up. Da was waiting for an explanation. 'It captures a sense that wasn't there,' I said. 'I've taken the quotation from another sense that it wasn't at all suited to. I often think the volunteers have got it quite wrong.'

'As do we,' Da said. 'Which is why we spend so long rewriting them.'

I blushed, realising Da had left the proof out because he was still working on it. 'You'll come up with something better, but I thought I might save you a little time if I drafted it,' I said.

'No. I'd finished with it. I thought my definitions were adequate.'

'Oh.'

'I was wrong.' He took the proof and folded it. For a moment, we were silent.

'Perhaps I could make more suggestions?'

Da raised his eyebrows.

'About the meanings given to words,' I said. 'When I'm sorting them and adding new slips, perhaps I could write suggestions on any top-slips that I think are …' I paused, unable to criticise.

'Inadequate?' Da said. 'Subjective? Judgemental? Pompous? Incorrect?'

We laughed.

'Perhaps you could,' he said.

❧

My request hung in the air while Dr Murray considered me over his spectacles.

'Of course you can,' he said, finally. 'I look forward to seeing what you come up with.'

I'd had a speech ready in case he denied me, and so I was caught short by his easy agreement. I stood, stunned, in front of his desk.

'Whatever you suggest is likely to be refined,' he said. 'Your perspective, however, will be grist to the mill of our endeavour to define the English language.' He leaned forward then, and his whiskers twitched at the edges of his mouth. 'My own daughters are fond of pointing out the inherent biases of our elderly volunteers. I'm sure they will be glad to have you on their side.'

From then on I did not feel superfluous, and the task of sorting slips took on a new challenge. Da would inform me whenever one of my suggestions made it into a fascicle. The proportion increased with my confidence, and I kept a tally on the inside of my desk: a little notch for every meaning penned and accepted. As the years passed, the inside of my desk became pitted with small achievements.

May 1906

I enjoyed the freedom of having a salary, and I became familiar with a number of the traders at the Covered Market. I continued to join Lizzie on Saturday mornings, but with my own basket to fill, and an allowance from Da for groceries. When we were done with the food shopping, I would take her into the draper's shop. Bit by bit I was replacing everything in our house that was worn out or depressingly functional. I enjoyed spending my money in this way, although Da only sometimes noticed. The last shop we'd go into was always the haberdashery, and it was my greatest joy to buy Lizzie a new thread.

On other days, when Lizzie wasn't with me, I'd visit certain stallholders who I knew had a way with words. They spoke with accents from far up north or the south-west corner of England. Some were Gypsy or travelling Irish, and they came and went. They were mostly women, old and young, and few of them could read the words they'd given me once I wrote them down. But they loved to share them. Over a few years I'd managed to collect more than a hundred. Some words, I discovered, were already in the pigeon-holes, but so many were not. When I was feeling in the mood for something salacious, I would always visit Mabel.

A woman I'd never seen before was picking through Mabel's wares in the same distracted way I usually did. They were deep in conversation, and I was reluctant to interrupt. I hung back among the buckets of flowers at Mrs Stiles' stall.

I bought flowers from Mrs Stiles every week, but my association with Mabel over the past few years had been noted, and the florist was not friendly. This made lingering all the more awkward.

'Have you decided what you want?' Mrs Stiles had come from behind her counter to straighten flowers that didn't need straightening.

I heard Mabel snort at something the woman said. Looking over, I glimpsed pale skin and a rouged cheek as the woman averted her face, just slightly, to avoid the rank breath that I knew assailed her. I wondered why she was still there; pity only required a moment. I had an uncanny sense I was watching myself, as others might have watched me – as Mrs Stiles must surely have watched me.

The florist was waiting for some kind of response, so I drifted towards the bucket of carnations. Their pastel symmetry was bland and somehow repellent, but they were well placed to see Mabel's visitor more clearly. I bent slightly, as if inspecting the bunches, and felt Mrs Stiles' barely restrained disapproval. Petals fell from some lilac blooms she was adjusting with too much vigour.

'For you, Mabel,' I said a few minutes later, handing over a small posy of lilacs, their scent an obvious relief to Mabel's new acquaintance. I dared not look back at the florist, but Mabel was shameless. She took the posy and critically inspected its wrapping of brown paper and simple white ribbon. 'It's the flowers that matter,' she said too loudly, then held them to her nose with exaggerated delight.

'How do they smell?' asked the young woman.

'Couldn't tell you. 'Aven't smelled nothin' for years.' Mabel handed her the blooms, and the woman buried her face in them, sucking in their scent.

With her eyes closed, I could take her in. She was tall, though not as tall as me, and her figure curved like that of a woman in a Pears' soap advertisement. Above a high lace collar, her skin was pale and without blemish. Honey-blonde hair hung in a loose plait down her back, and she wore no hat.

She laid the flowers down between a barnacled bell that was unlikely to ever ring again and the whittled face of an angel.

I picked up the whittling. 'I haven't seen this one before, Mabel.'

'Finished this mornin'.'

'Is she someone you know?' I asked.

'Me before I lost me teeth.' Mabel laughed.

The woman made no move to leave, and I wondered if I'd interrupted some private conversation they were waiting to resume. I took my purse from my pocket and searched for the right coins.

'Thought you'd like 'er,' Mabel said. At first I thought she was talking about the young woman, but she picked up the whittled angel and accepted my coins.

'My name's Tilda,' the woman said, offering her hand.

I hesitated.

'She don't like shakin' 'ands,' said Mabel. 'Scared you might flinch.'

Tilda looked at my fingers then straight in my eyes. 'Not much makes me flinch,' she said. Her grip was firm. I was grateful.

'Esme,' I said. 'Are you a friend of Mabel's?'

'No, we've just met.'

'Kindred spirits, I reckon,' said Mabel.

Tilda leaned in. 'She insists I'm a dollymop.'

I didn't understand.

'Look at 'er face. Never 'eard of a dollymop.' Mabel was not so discreet, and Mrs Stiles made it known she'd taken offence with a scraping of buckets and a mumbled protest. 'Come on, girl,' Mabel said to me. 'Take out yer slips.'

Tilda cocked her head.

'She collects words,' said Mabel.

'What kinds of words?'

'Women's words. Dirty ones.'

I stood dumb, caught with no adequate explanation. It was as though Da had asked me to turn out my pockets.

But Tilda was interested, not appalled. 'Really?' she said, taking in the loose fit of my jacket and the daisy chain Lizzie had embroidered around the edge of the sleeves. 'Dirty words?'

'No. Well, sometimes. Dirty words are Mabel's speciality.'

I took out my bundle of blank slips and a pencil.

'*Are* you a dollymop?' I asked, not sure how offensive it might be but curious to try the word out.

'An actress, though to some it's the same thing.' She smiled at Mabel. 'Our friend tells me that treading the boards was how she got into her particular line of work.'

I began to understand and wrote *dollymop* in the top-left corner of a slip I'd cut from a discarded proof. These slips were becoming favourites, though the pleasure I took in crossing out the legitimate words and recording one of Mabel's on the other side was never without an echo of shame.

'Can you put it in a sentence?' I asked.

Tilda looked at the slip, then at me. 'You're quite serious, aren't you?' she said.

Heat flushed my cheeks. I imagined the slip through her eyes, the futility of it. How odd I must have seemed.

'Give 'er a sentence,' Mabel urged.

Tilda waited for me to look up. 'On one condition,' she said, smiling with anticipated satisfaction. 'We're putting on a production of *A Doll's House* at New Theatre. You must come to the matinee this afternoon and join us after, for tea.'

'She will, she will. Now give 'er a sentence.'

Tilda took a lungful of air and straightened. Her gaze fell just beyond my shoulder and she delivered her sentence with a working-class accent I'd not detected before. 'A coin for the dollymop will keep your lap warm.'

'That's experience talkin' if you ask me,' Mabel said, laughing.

'No one asked you, Mabel,' I said. I wrote the sentence in the middle of the slip.

'Is it the same as *prostitute*?' I asked Tilda.

'I suppose. Though a dollymop is more opportunistic and far less experienced.'

Tilda watched as I fashioned a definition.

'That sums it up perfectly,' she said.

'Your last name?' My pencil hovered.

'Taylor.'

Mabel tapped her whittling knife on the crate to get our attention. 'Read it to me, then.'

I looked around at all the market-goers.

Tilda held out her hand for the slip. 'I promise not to project.'

I gave it to her.

DOLLYMOP

A woman who is paid for sexual favours on an occasional basis.
'A coin for the dollymop will keep your lap warm.'

Tilda Taylor, 1906

A good word, I thought, as I put the slip back in my pocket. And a good source.

'I must get on,' Tilda said. 'Costume call in an hour.' She reached into her purse and pulled out a programme.

'I play Nora,' she said. 'Curtain goes up at two.'

❧

When Da came home from the Scriptorium, I had lunch ready: pork pies from the market and boiled green beans. A fresh vase of flowers was on the kitchen table.

'I've been invited to the matinee of *A Doll's House* at New Theatre,' I said when we were eating.

Da looked up, surprised but smiling. 'Oh? And who has invited you?'

'Someone I met at the Covered Market.' Da's smile turned to a frown, and I quickly continued. 'A woman. An actress. She's in the play. Would you like to join me?'

'Today?'

'I'm happy to go alone.'

He looked relieved. 'I was quite looking forward to an afternoon with the newspapers.'

After lunch, I walked down Walton Street towards town. At the Press, a crowd of people at the end of their working week spilled through the archway, the long afternoon ahead animating their conversations. Most headed the way I had just come, back to their homes in Jericho, but small groups of men and a few young couples started walking towards the centre of Oxford. I followed and wondered if any would be going to New Theatre.

On George Street, the small caravan of people I'd been walking behind peeled off to pubs and tea shops. None entered the theatre.

I was early, but the emptiness of the theatre was still a surprise. It looked bigger than I remembered it. There were seats for hundreds of people, but there were barely thirty there. I struggled to decide where to sit.

Tilda trotted up the carpeted stair from the stage to where I stood. 'Bill said he saw the most striking woman come into the theatre and I knew it would be you.' Tilda took my hand and pulled me towards the front row, where a single person sat.

'Bill, you were right. This is Esme.'

Bill stood and made a little theatrical bow.

'Esme, this is my brother, Bill. You must sit with him in the front row, so I can see you. Obviously, you will be lost in the crowd if you sit anywhere else.' Tilda kissed her brother on the cheek and left us.

'When you sit in the front you can imagine the theatre is full and that you have the best seats to a sold-out show,' said Bill when we were both seated.

'Is that something you have to do often?'

'Not usually, but it's been useful for this show.'

It was easy sitting there with Bill, though I knew I should probably feel uncomfortable. He lacked the formality that I was used to in the men who came and went from the Scriptorium. He was more town than gown, of course, but there was something else about him I couldn't articulate. Bill was younger than Tilda by ten years, he said, which made him twenty-two. Just two years younger than me. He was tall enough to look me in the eye, and had Tilda's fine nose and full lips, but they were hidden among a riot of freckles. He shared his sister's green eyes, but not her honeyed hair: Bill's was darker, like treacle.

I listened to him talk while we waited for the play to start. He talked mostly about Tilda. She'd cared for him when no one else would, he told me. Did they have no parents? I asked.

'No. Not dead, though,' Bill said. 'Just absent. So I follow her wherever the theatre calls her.' Then the lights went down and the curtain went up.

Tilda was mesmerising, but the rest of the performers were not.

'I'm not sure tea will be sufficient this afternoon,' said Tilda when we finally left the theatre. 'Do you know where we can get a drink, Esme? Somewhere the rest of the cast won't go.'

I had only ever been to pubs with Da for Sunday lunch – never just for a drink. We mostly stayed in Jericho, but we'd once gone to a tiny pub near Christ Church. I led the way to St Aldate's.

'Is Old Tom the owner?' asked Bill when we were standing outside the pub.

'It's named for Great Tom, the bell in Tom Tower.' I pointed to the belltower down St Aldate's Road. I was ready to tell them more, but Tilda turned and walked inside.

It was five o'clock and Old Tom was beginning to fill, but Bill and Tilda were a striking pair. They cut through the crowd like a warm knife through butter. I followed, slightly bent, my eyes down. It was the wrong time of day for a meal, and I could count the women present on one hand. I imagined Lizzie grabbing her crucifix when I told her how I'd spent my afternoon.

'How kind,' I heard Tilda say as three men got up from their table and offered it to her.

Bill held her chair as she sat, then did the same for me. 'What would you like?' he asked.

I really wasn't sure. 'Lemonade,' I said, in a way that begged approval.

The bar was only a few feet away, and Bill shouted his order above the heads of the other men. At first there were grumbles, but when Bill pointed to where we sat, suddenly our refreshment became everyone's priority.

Tilda drained her whiskey. 'Did you enjoy the play, Esme?'

'You were quite wonderful.'

'Thank you for saying, but you have skilfully avoided the question.'

'It was mediocre,' said Bill, saving me.

'That may be the nicest thing anyone has said about it, Bill.' She put her hand on his arm. 'It is also the reason our season has been cut. Effective immediately.'

'Fuck.'

I was startled. Not by the word, but by his easy use of it.

Bill turned. 'Sorry,' he said.

'Don't apologise, Bill. Esme is a collector of words. If you're lucky she'll write that one down on one of her little scraps of paper.' Tilda held up her empty glass.

'Sorry, old girl, our recent unemployment does not extend to two whiskeys.'

'But I haven't told you the good news.' Tilda smiled. 'As Esme said, *I* was quite wonderful. A couple of the Oxford University players thought so too. They made up the majority of today's audience, and they've asked me to join them in *Much Ado About Nothing*. I'm to play Beatrice. Their original has come down with chickenpox.' She paused to let Bill take it in. 'They have a terrific reputation, and the first few nights are nearly fully booked. I arranged a cut of the box office.'

Bill slapped the table so all the glasses jumped. 'That is fucking brilliant. Is there a job for me?'

'Of course; we are a package, after all. You will dress and undress and occasionally feed lines. They'll be fighting over you, Bill.'

Bill returned to the bar and I took out a slip. Mabel had only ever used *fuck* in the negative.

'You might need more than one,' said Tilda. 'I can't think of many words more versatile.'

❧

Fuck was not in *F and G*.

146

'Looking for something in particular, Essy?' asked Da as I put the volume back on the shelf.

'I am, but you won't want me to say it out loud.'

He smiled. 'I see. Try the pigeon-holes. If it's been written down, it'll be there.'

'If it's been written down, shouldn't it be in the Dictionary?'

'Not necessarily. It has to have a legitimate history in the English language. And even then ...' he paused '... put it this way: if you don't want to say it out loud, it may have fallen foul of someone's sense of decorum.'

I searched the pigeon-holes. *Fuck* had more slips than most, and the pile was divided into even more variant meanings than Bill and Tilda could provide. The oldest was from the sixteenth century.

The Scriptorium door opened, and Mr Maling came in with Mr Yockney, our newest, smallest and baldest assistant. I put the slips back and went to my desk to sort the post.

At eleven o'clock, I went to sit with Lizzie in the kitchen.

'Mabel says you made a new friend on Saturday,' she said as she poured my tea.

'Two friends, actually.'

'Are you going to tell me about them?'

Lizzie said almost nothing as I recounted my day. When I mentioned Old Tom, her hand sought the crucifix. I didn't tell her about Tilda's whiskey, but I made sure to say I drank lemonade.

'They'll be in rehearsals for a few weeks,' I said. 'I thought we could go together when the play opens.'

'We'll see,' said Lizzie. Then she cleared the table.

Before going back to the Scriptorium, I climbed the stairs to her room and added Bill and Tilda's words to the trunk.

❧

The Bodleian Library was just minutes from New Theatre, so every request to find a word or verify a quotation became an opportunity to visit Bill and Tilda in rehearsals. My enthusiasm for these errands did not go unnoticed.

'Where to this morning, Esme?' Mr Sweatman was walking his bicycle towards the Scriptorium as I was getting ready to ride off.

'The Bodleian.'

'But this is the third time in as many days.'

'Dr Murray is in search of a quotation, and it is my job to hunt it down,' I said. 'It is also my pleasure – I love the Library.'

Mr Sweatman looked at the iron walls of the Scriptorium. 'Yes, I can see why you would. And what is the word, may I ask?'

'*Suffrage*,' I said.

'An important word.'

I smiled. 'They are all important, Mr Sweatman.'

'Of course, but some mean more than we might imagine,' he said. 'I sometimes fear the Dictionary will fall short.'

'How could it not?' I forgot I was in a hurry. 'Words are like stories, don't you think, Mr Sweatman? They change as they are passed from mouth to mouth; their meanings stretch or truncate to fit what needs to be said. The Dictionary can't possibly capture every variation, especially since so many have never been written down—' I stopped, suddenly shy.

Mr Sweatman's smile was broad, but not mocking. 'You have an excellent point, Esme. And if you don't mind me saying, you are beginning to sound like a lexicographer.'

I rode as fast as I could along Parks Road and arrived at the Bodleian in record time. Blackstone's *Commentaries on the Laws of England* was easy to find. I took it to the nearest desk and looked at the three slips Dr Murray wanted me to check. They each had the same quotation, more or less (it is the *more or less* that I need you to verify, Dr Murray had said).

I found the page, scanned it, ran my finger along the sentence and checked each quotation against it. They were each missing a word or two. A good day at the Library, I thought, as I drew a line through what the volunteers had written. As much as I wanted to be on my way, I took care to transcribe the correct quotation onto a clean slip.

In all democracies therefore it is of the utmost importance to regulate by whom, and in what manner, the suffrages are to be given.

I read the quotation again, double-checked its accuracy. Looked for the publication date: 1765. I wondered to whom Blackstone thought the suffrages should be given. I wrote the word *correction* in the bottom-left corner of the slip and added my initials, *E.N.* Then I pinned it to the three other slips.

I took the longer route back to the Scriptorium, stopping in at New Theatre.

Inside, it took a moment for my eyes to adjust to the dark. The players were onstage, paused mid-scene. A few people were seated in the middle rows.

'I was wondering if I'd see you today,' said Bill when I sat beside him.

'I have ten minutes,' I said. 'I wanted to see them in their costumes.'

It was a dress rehearsal. Opening night was just three days away.

'Why do you come every day?' asked Bill.

I had to think. 'It's about seeing something before it's fully formed. Watching it evolve. I imagine sitting here on opening night and appreciating every scene all the more because I understand what has led to it.'

Bill laughed.

'What's so funny?'

'Nothing. It's just that you don't speak often, but when you do it's perfect.'

I looked down and rubbed my hands together.

'And I love that you never talk about hats,' Bill said.

'Hats? Why would I talk about hats?'

'Women like to talk about hats.'

'Do they?'

'The fact you don't know that is what will make me fall in love with you.'

Suddenly, every word I ever knew evaporated.

❧

31st May 1906

My dear Esme,

Your new friends sound like an interesting pair. By interesting, I mean unconventional, which is generally a good thing, though not always. I trust you can judge the difference.

As to the inclusion of vulgar words in the Dictionary, Dr Murray's formula should be the sole arbiter. It is quite scientific, and strict application insists on certain types of evidence. If the evidence exists, the word should be included. It is brilliant because it removes emotion. When used correctly the formula does exactly what it was designed to do. When put aside, it is useless. There have been times when it has been put aside (even by its inventor), so that personal opinion can be exercised. Vulgar words, as you call them, are the usual casualties. No matter the evidence for their inclusion, there are some who would wish such words away.

For my part, I think they add colour. A vulgar word, well placed and said with just enough vigour, can express far more than its polite equivalent.

If you have started to collect such words, Esme, may I suggest you refrain from saying them in public — it would do you no good at all. If you do feel like expressing them, you may like to ask Mr Maling for their translation into Esperanto. You'll be surprised at how versatile that language is, and how liberal Mr Maling can be when it comes to vulgarities.

Yours, with love,

Ditte

June 1906

Much Ado About Nothing opened at New Theatre on the 9th of June. Bill's function on opening night was to help the actors with stays, stockings and wigs. Malfunctions were frequent, and so I sat with him in the wings and watched from the side.

'Are you ever tempted?' I asked, as we watched Tilda become Beatrice.

'I couldn't act to save my life,' Bill said. 'Which is why I'm so good at dressmaking.'

'Really?'

'And carpentry and front-of-house and anything else that may be required.' His hand brushed against mine. 'And you? Have you ever been tempted?'

I shook my head. Bill's fingers flirted with mine, and I didn't move them away.

'Can you feel it?' he asked, stroking the scarred skin.

'Yes, but it's far away, as if you were touching me through a glove.'

It was a poor explanation. His touch was like a whisper in my ear, the breath of it spreading through my whole body and making me shudder.

'Does it hurt?'

'Not at all.'

'How did it happen?'

When I was little, the answer had been a complicated knot of emotion in the middle of my chest – I'd had no words to explain it. But Bill's hand was steady around mine, and I craved its warmth.

'There was a slip …' I began.

'A word?'

'I thought it was important.'

Bill listened.

Time in the Scriptorium had always stretched and contracted to fit my moods, but it had rarely dragged. Since meeting Tilda and Bill, I had found myself looking at the clock more often.

For weeks, every performance of *Much Ado About Nothing* was played to a full theatre. I'd been to three Saturday matinees and taken Da to an evening performance. As I sat at my desk, the hands of the clock seemed stuck on half-three.

Dr Murray returned from a meeting with the Press Delegates and spent a full half-hour translating *his* dressing-down into a dressing-down of the assistants. 'Three years into the letter M and we've only published up to *mesnalty*,' he boomed. I tried to recall what *mesnalty* meant: a legal term, the kind Da and I rarely played with. But its root was *mesne,* which reminded me of *mense*, meaning generous, kind, tactful. Da had spent longer than usual collating quotations and fashioning definitions. In the end, Dr Murray had drawn a line through several of them. I looked to where Da was sitting and knew he didn't regret a minute spent with that lovely word.

When the lecture was over, the silence was profound. The clock showed four. Dr Murray sat at his high desk reading proofs with more agitation than usual. The assistants barely straightened from their work; none spoke. No one dared leave before five o'clock.

When the hour struck, there was a collective tilt of heads towards Dr Murray, but he remained as he was and the work continued. At half-five, another turning of heads. From where I sat, it looked choreographed. I let out a small sound, and Da turned. *As quiet as a mouse*, his look cautioned. Still Dr Murray sat, his pencil poised to correct and excise.

At six o'clock, Dr Murray put the proofs he'd been working on in an envelope and rose from his desk. He walked towards the door of the Scriptorium and placed the envelope in the tray, ready to be taken to the Press in the morning. He looked back at the sorting table where the heads of all seven assistants were still bent, their pencils paused in hopeful anticipation of release.

'Do you not have homes to go to?' Dr Murray asked.

We relaxed. The storm was over.

'Do you have a word for me, Essy?' Da asked as he closed the door to the Scriptorium.

'Not tonight. I'm taking Lizzie to the theatre, remember?'

'Again?'

'Lizzie's never been.'

He looked at me. '*Much Ado About Nothing*, I suppose?'

'I think she'll find it funny.'

'Has she been to a play before?'

'Not that she's told me.'

'You don't think the language will …'

'Da, what a thing to say.' I kissed him on the forehead and walked towards the kitchen, a flutter of uncertainty rising.

Lizzie had been adjusting her one good dress for years. It had never been fashionable, but I'd always thought its shamrock green made her look lighter. As we walked along Magdalen Street, I thought it made her look pale. Lizzie crossed herself as we passed the church.

'Oh, Lizzie, there's a stain.' I touched a greasy patch above her waist.

'Mrs B needed help with the basting,' she said. 'She's not so steady as she used to be, and it splashed as she took it from the oven.'

'Could you not wipe it clean?'

'Best to soak it, and there was no time. I figured it was only you and me and no one would pay it any mind.'

It was too late to change plans – Tilda and Bill would be waiting at Old Tom. I looked at Lizzie through their eyes. She was thirty-two, a month older than Tilda, but her face was lined and her hair hung lank, grey already mixing with the brown. Rather than reminding me of a Pears' soap advertisement, her shape was tending towards that of Mrs Ballard. I'd barely noticed before.

'Shouldn't we turn down George Street?' Lizzie said, as I continued straight into Cornmarket.

'Actually, Lizzie, I thought you might like to meet my new friends. We've arranged a drink at Old Tom before the play.'

'The pub on St Aldate's?' she said.

Her arm was in mine, and I felt her stiffen.

❧

Bill's smile was wide, and Tilda gave a wave as we entered Old Tom. Lizzie hesitated in the doorway as I'd seen her hesitate on the threshold of the Scriptorium.

'You don't need an invitation, Lizzie,' I said.

She followed me, and I had the feeling that I was the elder and she was the child.

'This must be the famous Lizzie,' said Bill, bowing and taking the hand that hung limply at her side. 'How do you do?'

Lizzie stuttered something and pulled her hand away a little too soon, rubbing it as if it had been slapped. Bill pretended he didn't notice and shifted attention to Tilda.

'Tilda, the bar is three-deep. Use your charms to get us a round.' He looked to Lizzie. 'Watch them part to let her through. She's like Moses.'

Lizzie leaned in to me. 'I won't be needing a drink, Esme.'

'Just lemonade for Lizzie, Bill,' I said.

Tilda was nodding and smiling her way through the tight crowd of men waiting to order drinks. Bill had to shout, 'Lemonade plus our usuals, sis.'

Tilda raised an arm in acknowledgement. When I turned to Lizzie, I caught her looking at me as though we'd just met and she was taking stock of who I might be.

'I told them I needed to be in wardrobe at seven,' said Tilda a few minutes later, four drinks expertly held between her hands. 'One offered to dress me and three promised to see the play. I should be on commission, the number of tickets I sell.'

Lizzie took the glass Tilda offered, her eyes dropping to the low cut of Tilda's dress, the swell of her bosom. I looked from one to the other, seeing each in the other's eyes. An old maid and a harlot.

'Here's to you, Lizzie,' Tilda said, raising her whiskey. 'Between Esme and old Mabel I feel I already know you.' Then she tilted her head back and emptied the glass. 'I must go and dress. Will I see you after the play?'

'Of course,' I said, but Lizzie shifted beside me. 'Perhaps.'

'I'll let you convince them, Bill. It's what you do best.'

Tilda worked her way through the crowd, drawing one kind of look from the men, another from the women.

❧

The following Monday, Lizzie poured tea from the large pot on the range and passed the cup to Da.

'Did you enjoy the play, Lizzie?' he asked.

She continued to pour another cup and didn't look up. 'I only understood half, but I liked the look of it, Mr Nicoll. It was very good of Esme to take me.'

'And did you meet Esme's new friends? I was impressed by Miss Taylor's performance when I saw her, but I'm afraid I have to rely on you to vouch for them.'

The next cup was for me, and Lizzie took her time to add the sugar she knew I liked.

'I can't say I've met people like them before, Mr Nicoll. They have a confidence I'm not used to, but they was polite to me, and kind to Esme.'

'So, you approve?'

'It's not my place to approve, sir.'

'But you'll go again, to the theatre?'

'I know I should like it more, Mr Nicoll, but I'm not sure it's for me. I was dreadful tired the next day and the fires still needed to be set, and breakfast made.'

'Would I approve?' Da asked later as we walked across the garden to the Scriptorium.

Did I want him to? I wondered.

'You would like them. And I daresay you'd take Tilda's side in an argument.' I hesitated, picturing Tilda in Old Tom after the show, a cigar in one hand, a whiskey in the other, mimicking Arthur Balfour. She deepened her voice and rounded her vowels and mocked his resignation the year before as Prime Minister. All to the general merriment of everyone gathered, Liberal and Conservative alike. 'Though I'm not sure you would approve,' I finished.

He opened the door of the Scriptorium. Instead of going in, he turned and looked up at me. I knew this look and waited for him to invoke Lily's greater wisdom. She would know what to do, he would say, without offering his own encouragement or warning – at least until a letter from Ditte arrived with words he could repeat. But this time he did not prevaricate.

'I find that the more I define, the less I know. I spend my days trying to understand how words were used by men long dead, in order to draft a meaning that will suffice not just for our times but for the future.' He took my hands in his and stroked the scars, as if Lily was still imprinted in them. 'The Dictionary is a history book, Esme. If it has taught me anything, it is that the way we conceive of things now will most certainly change. How will they change? Well, I can only hope and speculate, but I do know that your future will be different from the one your mother might have looked forward to at your age. If your new friends have something to teach you about it, I suggest you listen. But trust your judgement, Essy, about what ideas and experiences should be included, and what should not. I will always give you my opinion, if you ask for it, but you are a grown woman. While some would disagree, I believe it is your right to make your own choices, and I can't insist on approving.' He brought my funny fingers to his lips and kissed them, then he held them to his cheek. It had the emotion of a farewell.

We stepped into the Scriptorium, and I inhaled its Monday-morning smell. I went to my desk.

There was a pile of slips to sort into pigeon-holes, a few letters needing simple responses and a proof page with a note from Dr Murray: *make sure each quote is in its proper chronological order.* It was hardly going to be a taxing day.

The Scriptorium began to fill. The men bent to their words; the challenge of articulating meaning creased their brows and sparked quiet debates. I put quotations from the fifteenth century before those of the sixteenth century and no one asked my opinion.

Just before lunch, Da let me know that a suggestion I had made for one sense of *mess* would be in the next fascicle, with minor adjustments. I lifted the lid of my desk and added a notch to the scarred wood. It brought none of the satisfaction it once had. It felt like a conciliation. I looked towards Dr Murray. He was sitting straight-backed, his head tilted towards his papers; proofs or letters, I couldn't tell. His face was relaxed, and the movement of his pen was smooth. It was as good a time as any to approach. I rose from my desk and walked with more confidence than I felt to the front of the Scriptorium.

'Dr Murray, sir?' I placed the letters I'd drafted on his desk. He didn't look up from his work.

'I'm sure they are fine, Esme. Please add them to the post.'

'I was wondering ...'

'Yes?' Still, he worked on, the task absorbing.

'I was wondering if I could do more?'

'The afternoon post is bound to bring more enquiries about the timing of the next fascicle,' he said. 'I wish they would stop, but I'm glad you enjoy replying. Elsie refuses to endure the tedium.'

'I meant that I would like to do more with the words. Some research, perhaps. Of course, I would still attend to correspondence, but I'd like to contribute more meaningfully.'

Dr Murray's pencil paused, and I heard a rare chuckle. He looked at me over his spectacles, assessing me as if I were a niece he hadn't seen in a while. Then he pushed some papers around on his desk, found what he was looking for and read it silently. He held the note up. 'This is from Miss Thompson, your godmother. I asked her to research a variant of *pencil*. Perhaps I should have asked you.' He handed me the note. 'Follow it up. Find indicative quotations and draft a definition of the sense.

4th July 1906
Dear Dr Murray,

I feel I have imperilled my character by going about getting these things. The hairdresser's is the place for them. When I asked for an eye-pencil, they offered

*brown, chestnut, black and also a reddish-brown. They did not recognise the term
'lip-pencil'.*

Yours,

Edith Thompson

❧

The stalls were filling and Tilda had not arrived. Bill was being shouted at by the young man playing Benedick.

'She's your sister; why don't you know where she is?'

'I'm not her keeper,' said Bill.

The actor looked at Bill, incredulous. 'Of course you are.' Then he stormed off, his wig askew and runnels of sweat lining his painted face.

Bill turned to me. 'I'm really not her keeper, you know. She's mine.' He glanced towards the stage door.

'If she's not here soon you may have to play Beatrice,' I said. 'You must know every line.'

'She went to London,' he said.

'London?'

'"The business", she calls it.'

'What is that?'

'Women's suffrage. She's thrown her lot in with the Pankhursts.'

The stage door opened and Tilda rushed in. There was a huge smile on her face and a large package in her arms.

'Look after this, Bill. I have to dress.'

'Watch out for Benedick,' I said.

'I shall tell him a lie he will want to believe.'

Beatrice outwitted Benedick that night. When Tilda took her bow, the applause went on for so long that Benedick walked offstage before it was over.

Afterwards, instead of heading towards Old Tom, Tilda led us in the opposite direction, to the Eagle and Child on St Giles' Street.

One of the two front rooms was already full, and Tilda manoeuvred her way into it. I hung back in the narrow doorway with Bill, trying to make sense of the gathering. I counted twelve women in various dress. Some were well-to-do, but most were what Da would call *middle class*: women not so different from me.

Tilda paused in her greetings and called back to where we stood, 'The parcel, Bill. Can you pass it over?'

Bill gave the parcel to a short, round woman who thanked him by saying, 'Good man, we need more like you.'

'I'm not such a rare bird,' he said, seeming to know what she meant. I felt as though I had arrived in the middle of a conversation.

'Your usual?' Bill asked.

'Will it help me understand what's going on?'

'You'll understand soon enough.' He walked down the narrow hall to the bar.

'Sisters,' Tilda began, 'thank you for joining the fight. Mrs Pankhurst promised you would be here and here you are.' The women, all twelve, looked pleased with themselves, like students who had received the teacher's favour.

'I've brought the leaflets, and there is a map showing where each of us is to deliver them.' Tilda opened the parcel and let the leaflets be passed around. They showed a woman in academic dress sharing a cell with a convict and a lunatic.

'A degree from Oxford University would be a fine thing,' I heard one woman say.

'Add it to the list,' said another.

'Esme,' Tilda called above the din. 'Could you spread the map on the other table?' She held a folded map above the heads of the women in front of her. I hesitated, not knowing what else I might be agreeing to. She seemed to understand and held the map, and my gaze, patiently. I nodded, and moved into the room with the other women.

I sat with my back to the window that faced the street, my hand on one corner of the map to stop it from sliding off the table under the women's excited scrutiny. The chatter was exhilarating; women discussed tactics and swapped routes to suit their own addresses – some wanted to deliver leaflets where no one would know them, others wanted the convenience of their own street so they could make a hasty return if challenged.

Most of the women agreed that the leaflets should be delivered in the night. Others, fearful of the dark or of disapproving husbands, devised a plan to wrap each pamphlet in a temperance meeting notice. The idea was congratulated, but the work of putting the decoy together was for those women who chose it.

When the details were settled, Tilda gave each woman a small packet of leaflets, and they began to leave the Eagle and Child in excited pairs.

Three women hung back, and when the others were gone, Tilda ushered them over to the map. I moved to the other end of the tiny room while they made further plans. I took out a slip.

SISTERS
Women bonded by a shared political goal; comrades.
'Sisters, thank you for joining the fight.'

Tilda Taylor, 1906

The women left with their leaflets and another, larger package. Bill came back as Tilda was folding the map.

'Are you ready for that drink now?' he said, proffering a whiskey and the shandy I had developed a taste for.

'Perfect timing, Bill,' said Tilda, taking her glass and looking at me. 'It's exciting, isn't it?'

I didn't know if it was or not. I felt flushed and curious, and my pulse raced, but it might have been anxiety. I wasn't at all sure if this was an experience I should embrace or reject.

'Drink up,' Tilda said. 'We still have work to do.'

We left the Eagle and Child and turned towards the Banbury Road. Tilda handed me my own packet of leaflets, wrapped in brown paper and tied with string. It could have been a pile of proofs, newly arrived from the Press.

'I'm not sure I should,' I said, holding them uncomfortably.

'Of course you should,' she said. Bill walked just in front, deliberately keeping out of our conversation.

'I'm not like you, Tilda. I'm not like any of those women back there.'

'You have a womb, don't you? A cunt? A brain capable of making a decision between bloody Balfour and Campbell-Bannerman? You're exactly like those women back there.'

I held the package away from my body, as if it contained something corrosive.

'Don't be a coward,' she said. 'All we're doing is putting pieces of paper in letter boxes. At worst they will be thrown in the fire; at best they will be read and a mind might change. Anyone would think I was asking you to plant a bomb.'

'If Dr Murray found out …'

'If you really think he'd care then make sure he doesn't. Now, this is your route. There are enough for both sides of Banbury, between Bevington and St Margaret's Road.'

The route included Sunnyside. I continued to hesitate.

'You live in Jericho, don't you?'

I nodded.

'It's not that far out of your way,' she said. 'Bill, go with her.'

'What about you?' I asked.

'No one will be surprised to see me taking the night air without a chaperone, but you need a man on your arm. More's the pity.'

There were few people to greet as we walked up St Giles': one other couple and a band of drunken gowns, ostentatiously polite as they split to move around us. As St Giles' turned into Banbury, the way ahead was deserted. My anxiety fell back, and regret about my reluctance rose to take its place.

'Shall I do it?' Bill asked as we approached the first letter box beyond Bevington Road.

Bill knew what I knew – that I *was* different from those women. That I might agree with them but did not have the guts to stand in the midst of them. I shook my head as he reached for the package. He transferred his hand to the small of my back, and I was grateful for the strength of it. I pulled on the bow Tilda had tied and let the paper wrapping fall back from the leaflets. An image of an imprisoned woman accused me of apathy.

By the time we reached Sunnyside, my pile was much diminished. I'd set a fast pace, and Bill had granted me an ungrudging silence after I sniped that his banter might wake people and have them look out of their windows. At the sight of the red pillar box, I slowed. When I was small, I'd thought Dr Murray must have been very important to have his own pillar box. I'd loved to think of it full of letters that talked of nothing but words. When I'd learned the alphabet, Da had let me write my own letters, with made-up words and made-up meanings and silly sentences that meant nothing to anyone except him and me. He would give me an envelope and a stamp, and I would address my letter to him at the Scriptorium, Banbury Road, Oxford. I would walk by myself through the garden and out of the gates, and post my letter in Dr Murray's pillar box. For the next few days, I would watch Da's face as he opened the post that was delivered to Sunnyside, sorting the slips into their piles and reviewing the letters. When he finally came to my letter, he'd regard it with the same seriousness with which he regarded all the others. He'd read it through, nod his head as if agreeing with an important argument then call me over to seek my opinion. Even when I giggled, he'd keep a straight face. I still felt a particular thrill posting Scriptorium letters in the pillar box.

'Seventy-eight,' Bill said into the silence.

'The Scriptorium.'

'You can skip it, if you like.'

I took a quick step towards the letter box on the gate and dropped the pamphlet in. It fell to the bottom with a gentle swish.

The next morning, Da held the umbrella while I emptied the letter box at Sunnyside. The leaflet was at the bottom of the pile, exposed and vulnerable without an envelope. I could see the edge of it and was suddenly concerned that I might be expected to discard it; whose pile, after all, would I put it in? Its significance had grown after I had put it in the letter box, and my anxiety with it. But in the morning light, and among all those letters from learned men and clever women, the leaflet had lost its strength.

I was disappointed. I had feared what it might do, and now I feared it would do nothing.

'Da, I promised Dr Murray I would include some new quotations in a pile of slips he is sending to Ditte for sub-editing,' I said. 'Can the post wait this morning?'

'Give it to me. It will be an easy start to the day.'

I was grateful for his predictable response.

Da's profile was clear from where I sat at my desk. Instead of sorting slips, I watched for a change in expression as he went through the post. When he got to the bottom of the pile, he picked up the leaflet. I held my breath.

He looked it over, read the caption and considered it for a minute with a serious face. Then he relaxed into a smile, his head nodding in comprehension of the cartoon – the cleverness, perhaps? Or the argument? Instead of screwing it up, he put it in one of his piles. He rose from the sorting table and delivered each pile to its place.

'This should interest you, Essy,' Da said, as he placed a small pile of slips on my desk. 'It came with the post.'

He watched me as I took the leaflet from him and looked it over as if I'd never seen it before.

'Something worth discussing with your young friends,' Da said, before walking away.

Tilda was right; I was a coward. I put the leaflet in my desk and took my newest slip from my pocket.

Sisters. I searched the pigeon-holes. *Sisters* had plenty of slips, and already they had been sorted and top-slips written for different senses, but *comrades* was not one of them.

❧

Lizzie was spending more and more time in the kitchen since Mrs Ballard began having her turns. The doctor had cautioned against standing for long periods, so Mrs Ballard had taken to sitting at the kitchen table with a pot of tea, issuing instructions. When I came in, she was turning the pages of the *Oxford Chronicle* and reminding Lizzie to salt the bird that had just been delivered.

'Don't be mean with it, now,' she said. 'It needs a goodly amount to make it tender. The longer it sits, the better.'

Lizzie rolled her eyes but kept her smile. 'You've had me salting the birds since I was twelve, Mrs B. I reckon I know what to do.'

'Been some trouble in town, they say,' said Mrs Ballard, ignoring Lizzie. 'Some suffragettes caught painting slogans on the Town Hall. It says here they was chased down St Aldate's and they might have got away except one of them fell and the other two stopped to help her up.'

'Suffragettes?' said Lizzie. 'I've never heard that before.'

'That's what it says.' Mrs Ballard read through the article. 'It's what they're calling Mrs Pankhurst's women.'

'Just slogans?' I said. I'd expected arson.

'It says here that they used red paint to write *Women: No more rights than a convict.*'

'Didn't your leaflet say that, Esme?' asked Lizzie, her hands in the bird, her eyes on me.

'The one who fell is married to the magistrate,' Mrs Ballard continued. 'And the other two are from Somerville College. All educated ladies. How shaming.'

'It wasn't my leaflet, Lizzie. It came in the post.'

'Any idea who delivered it?' she asked, without looking away.

I felt a crimson flush rise up my neck and engulf my face. She had my answer and returned to the bird, her movements a little rougher.

I moved to read the article over Mrs Ballard's shoulder. Three arrests. No convictions, so no trial. I wondered if Tilda and Mrs Pankhurst would be disappointed.

In the Scriptorium, I searched the pigeon-holes. *Suffrage* was there, and so was *suffragist*. *Suffragette* wasn't. I dug out recent copies of the *Times of London*, the *Oxford Times* and the *Oxford Chronicle* and took them to my desk. Each had articles mentioning *suffragettes*, one referred to *suffragents*, and another used the word *suffragetting* as a verb. I cut them out, underlined the quotations and stuck each to its own slip. Then I put all of them in the pigeon-hole they belonged to.

The performance was over for another night, and Bill and I were helping Tilda change into her street clothes.

'You're too comfortable, Esme,' Tilda said as she stepped out of Beatrice's bloomers.

'But I live here, Tilda.'

'So do the magistrate's wife and the women from Somerville College.'

An hour later, we were at the Eagle and Child again. I felt dull against the energy of the women who had gathered to help. The new leaflet urged them to join Emmeline Pankhurst at a march in London, and already they were making travel plans. I wanted their resolve to infect me, but by the time we had spilled onto the street I had convinced myself I wouldn't be joining them.

'You're scared, that's all,' Tilda said, her hand on my cheek like I was a child. She gave a bundle of leaflets to Bill and began to walk backwards. 'Problem is, Esme, you're scared of the wrong thing. Without the vote nothing we say matters, and that should terrify you.'

❧

Lizzie was at the kitchen table, her sewing basket and a small pile of clothes in front of her. I looked towards the pantry for Mrs Ballard.

'In the house, with Mrs Murray,' Lizzie said. Then she handed me three crumpled leaflets. 'I found them in your coat pocket. I wasn't snooping, just checking the seams 'cos I was fixing the hem.'

I stood dumb. I had a familiar feeling that I deserved to be in trouble, but didn't quite understand why.

'I've seen them here and there, fallen out of letter boxes and stuck up at the Covered Market. I've been told what they say. Even been asked if I was going.' She scoffed. 'As if I could go to London for the day. She'll lead you astray, Essymay, if you let her.'

'Who?'

'You know very well.'

'I know my own mind, Lizzie.'

'That may be, but you've never been any good at knowing what's good for you.'

'It's not just about me; it's about all women.'

'So, you did deliver them?'

Lizzie was thirty-two years old and looked forty-five. I suddenly understood why. 'You do everyone's bidding, Lizzie, but you have no say,' I said. 'That's what these pamphlets are all about. It's time we were given the right to speak for ourselves.'

'It's just a lot of rich ladies wanting even more than they already have,' she said.

'They want more for all of us.' My voice was rising. 'If you're not going to stand up for yourself then you should be glad someone else will.'

'I will be glad if you stay out of the papers,' she said, as calm as ever.

'It's apathy that keeps the vote from women.'

'*Apathy*.' Lizzie scoffed. 'I reckon it's more than that.'

I stormed out then, forgetting my coat.

When I returned to the kitchen just before lunch, Mrs Ballard was sat at the table, a cup of tea steaming in front of her.

'Only three for sandwiches today, Mrs B,' I said, looking around for Lizzie.

'Too late for that.' She nodded towards the plate on the bench, piled with sandwiches, just as Lizzie appeared at the bottom of the stairs that led to her room.

I looked over and smiled, but Lizzie only nodded.

'Dr Murray has a meeting with the Press Delegates, and Da and Mr Balk have gone off to see Mr Hart,' I continued, wanting to pretend we were not in a quarrel. 'Spelling errors, apparently. Da said they'd be gone for hours.'

'It will be sandwiches for our tea then, Lizzie,' said Mrs Ballard.

'No good wasting them,' Lizzie replied as she crossed to the bench and began removing some of the sandwiches to a smaller plate.

'I can do that,' I said.

'Will you be going to the theatre tonight, Esme?' Lizzie was not so keen to pretend.

'I suppose I will.'

'You must know the lines by heart.'

It was a rebuke I had no answer for. It was true, and Bill liked to tease when he caught me mouthing Tilda's words. 'You could be her understudy,' he'd said.

'Would you like to come?' I asked Lizzie.

'No. I was obliged the first time, Esme, but once is enough.'

She might have stopped there if my relief hadn't been so transparent. She sighed and lowered her voice. 'You're not so worldly as them, Essymay.'

'I'm hardly a child.'

Mrs Ballard scraped back her chair and took the herb basket out to the garden.

'Maybe it's about time I became "more worldly", as you put it. Things are changing. Women don't have to live lives determined by others. They have choices, and I choose not to live the rest of my days doing as I'm told and worrying about what people will think. That's no life at all.'

Lizzie took a clean cloth from the drawer and spread it over the plate of sandwiches she and Mrs Ballard would eat later that day. She straightened and took a deep breath, her hand finding the crucifix around her neck.

'Oh, Lizzie. I didn't mean—'

'Choice would be a fine thing, but from where I stand things look much the same as they always have. If you've got choices, Esme, choose well.'

❧

The final performance was sold out. They had three curtain calls and a standing ovation, and the performers were drunk on it before they'd even raised a glass. Tilda led them from New Theatre to Old Tom, each arm entwined with that of an actor, both of whom leaned in with an intimacy that turned the heads of the evening crowd.

I walked behind with Bill. It was our usual position in this weekly procession, and as usual he found my hand and encouraged me to rest it on his forearm, bringing us close. But the mood was different. His own hand rested on mine, his fingers tracing an intricate pattern on my bare skin. He spoke very little and was less intent on keeping up.

'They're jubilant,' I said.

'It's always like this on the last night.'

'What will happen?' I leaned in closer, as if conspiring.

'There will be at least one arrest, one dunking in the Cherwell, and …' He looked at me.

'And?'

'Tilda will find her way into the bed of one of those two – whichever is able to sneak her into their rooms.'

'How can you know that?'

'It's her habit,' he said, clearly trying to gauge my reaction. 'She denies them all season – fucking is bad for the play, she says – then she lets them have her.'

I knew it already; Tilda had said as much. At the time I'd blushed, and Tilda had said, 'If the gander can do it, why not the goose?' She'd refused my arguments, and I'd begun to hear them as borrowed and not truly my own.

'You know, Esme,' she'd said, 'women are designed to like it.'

Then she'd told me how.

'What is it called?' I'd asked the next day, the memory of my fumbling and the exquisite pleasure of it still fresh.

Tilda laughed. 'You managed to find it, then?'

'Find *what*?'

'Your nub. Your *clitoris*. I'll spell it for you, if you want to write it down.' I took a slip and a stub of pencil from my pocket. Tilda spelled it out. 'A medical student told me what it was called, though he had little understanding of it.'

'What do you mean?' I asked.

'Well, *he* described it as a remnant cock – proof we were of Adam,' he said. 'But, like you, he had no idea what it could do. Or if he did, he thought it irrelevant.' She smiled. 'It brings a woman pleasure, Esme. That's its only function. Knowing that changes everything, don't you think?'

I shook my head, not understanding.

'We're designed to enjoy it,' Tilda had said. 'Not avoid it or endure it. Enjoy it, just like them.'

As we followed Tilda and her entourage, Bill seemed shy for the first time since I'd met him.

'She won't come home tonight,' he said.

An appropriate response rested on my tongue, but I said nothing.

'She made sure I knew that.'

His words travelled through me, to the place I now had a word for. I knew what would happen if I went with him. I longed for it.

'I can't be late,' I said.

'You won't be.'

࿊

A few days later, Bill, Tilda and I met for tea at the station. Bill kissed my cheek. Anyone watching would have guessed old friends, cousins, perhaps. They wouldn't have noticed his gentle breath in my ear, or the shiver that met it. Over three evenings, he had explored me. Found seams of pleasure I didn't know existed. Should he stay in Oxford? he'd asked. If you have to ask, I'd said, then probably not.

Tilda handed me a paper bag.

'Don't worry, they're not leaflets.' She smiled.

I opened the bag.

'A lip-pencil, eye-pencil and eyebrow-pencil,' said Tilda. 'Easily obtained, though perhaps not from the hairdresser your godmother goes to. I also bought you some lipstick. Red, to go with that hair of yours. You'll need a new dress to make it work.'

I took out a slip. 'Put *lip-pencil* in a sentence.'

'The lip-pencil followed the contours of her ruby lips like an artist's brush.'

'She's been practising that,' said Bill.

'I can't write that on a slip.'

'If this is for the real Dictionary, doesn't it need to come from a book?' Bill asked.

'It's supposed to, but even Dr Murray has been known to make up a quotation when those that exist don't do justice to the sense.'

'That's my sentence, take it or leave it,' said Tilda.

I took it. Bill poured more tea.

'Do you have a play already lined up in Manchester?' I asked.

'It's not theatre work that's taking us to Manchester, Essy,' said Bill. 'Tilda's joined the WSPU.

'Which is?'

'The Women's Social and Political Union,' said Tilda.

'Mrs Pankhurst thinks her stage skills will be useful,' said Bill.

'I can project my voice.'

'And make it sound posh.' Bill looked at his sister with such pride. I couldn't imagine him ever leaving her.

December 1906

Elsie Murray made her way around the Scriptorium, her hand full of envelopes. I watched as each of the assistants received one, variations in thickness indicating seniority, education, gender. Da's envelope was thick. Mine, like Rosfrith's and Elsie's, looked almost empty. She stopped by her sister's chair, and as they spoke Elsie re-pinned a lock of fair hair that had escaped Rosfrith's bun. Satisfied it would stay, Elsie continued towards my desk.

'Thank you, Elsie,' I said as she handed me my wage.

She smiled and put an even larger envelope on my desk. 'You've been looking a bit bored these past few day days, Esme.'

'No, not at all.'

'You're being polite. I've done my fair share of sorting and letter-writing. I know how tedious it can be.' She opened the envelope, pulled out a page of proofs and slid it towards me. 'Father thought you might like to try your hand at copy-editing.'

It wasn't a cure for the mood that had descended on me, but it was welcome. 'Oh, Elsie, thank you.'

She nodded, pleased. I waited for her usual questions.

'A new play will be starting at New Theatre tonight,' she said.

'Yes.'

'Will you be going?'

I had been getting an envelope every Friday for six years, and every Friday Elsie would enquire about what treat I would buy myself. It had always been something to brighten our house, but since meeting Tilda my answer had barely wavered: I would take myself to the theatre. 'What is so fascinating about *Much Ado About Nothing*?' she'd asked once. Bill came to mind, his thigh against mine in the darkness beyond the stage, our eyes on Tilda.

'I don't think I'll be going to the theatre tonight,' I said.

She regarded me for a moment. Her dark eyes seemed sympathetic.

'Plenty of time. I read it was popular in London, and they're expecting a long season.'

But I couldn't imagine another troupe or another play, and the thought of sitting in the stalls with someone other than Bill brought me close to tears.

'Must get on,' Elsie said, touching my shoulder briefly before walking away.

When she was gone, I looked at the proofs she had given me. It was the first page of the next fascicle, and a slip was pinned to the edge with an additional example for *misbode*.

Dr Murray's scrawled instructions were to *edit the page to make it fit*. I recalled the word coming out of an envelope years before; a lady's neat script and a line from Chaucer. Da and I had played with it for a week. This new sentence made me pause. *Her misboding sorrow for his absence has almost made her frantic.*

I missed them. It was as if they had written a play and constructed the set, and whenever I was with them I had a part to perform. I fell into it so easily: a secondary character, someone ordinary against whom the leads could shine. Now that they had packed up and left, I felt I had forgotten my lines.

But did Bill's absence make me frantic?

He'd given me something I'd wanted since the first time he took my hand. It wasn't love; nothing like it. It was knowledge. Bill took words I'd written on slips and turned them into places on my body. He introduced me to sensations that no fine sentence could come close to defining. Near its end, I'd heard the pleasure of it exhaled on my breath, felt my back arch and my neck stretch to expose its pulse. It was a surrender, but not to him. Like an alchemist, Bill had turned Mabel's vulgarities and Tilda's practicalities into something beautiful. I was grateful, but I was not in love.

It was Tilda I missed the most; her absence that left a misboding sorrow. She had ideas I wanted to understand and she said things I could not. She cared more for what mattered and less for what didn't. When I was with her I felt I might do something extraordinary. With her gone, I feared I never would.

'Poorly again, Essy?' Lizzie asked, when I came into the kitchen for a glass of water. 'You're looking a bit pale, that's for sure.'

Mrs Ballard was checking the Christmas pudding she'd made a few months earlier and drizzling over some brandy. She looked at me through narrowed eyes, and a frown deepened the lines of her face. Lizzie poured me some water from the jug on the kitchen table, then went to the pantry and brought out a packet of digestives.

'Shop-bought biscuits, Mrs B!' I said. 'Did you know these were lurking in your pantry?'

She blinked, and her face relaxed. 'Dr Murray insists on McVitie's. Reminds him of Scotland, he says.'

Lizzie passed me a biscuit. 'It'll settle your stomach,' she said.

Food was the last thing I wanted, but Lizzie insisted. I sat at the kitchen table and nibbled at the biscuit while Mrs Ballard and Lizzie busied themselves around me. They got little done. When Lizzie wiped down the range for the third time, I finally asked if something was wrong.

'No, no, pet,' Mrs Ballard was quick to say. 'I'm sure everything will be all right.' But the frown returned to her face.

'Esme,' Lizzie said, finally putting down her cloth. 'Will you come upstairs a minute?'

I looked at Mrs Ballard, who nodded for me to follow Lizzie. Something *was* wrong, and for a moment I thought I might be sick. I took a deep breath and it passed, then I followed Lizzie up the stairs to her room.

We sat on her bed. She looked at her hands, uncomfortable in her lap. It was me who reached out and took them in mine. She had bad news, I thought. She was ill, or maybe all my talk of choices had caused her to seek a better position. Before she said a word, my eyes had welled.

'Do you know how far gone you are?' Lizzie said.

I stared at her, trying to match the words to something I might understand.

She tried again. 'How long have you been …' she looked at my stomach and then met my eyes, '… expecting?'

I understood her then. I pulled my hands from hers and stood up.

'Don't be ridiculous, Lizzie,' I said. 'It's not possible.'

'Oh, Essymay, you silly duffer.' She stood to take my hands again. 'You didn't know?'

I shook my head. 'How can *you*?'

'Ma was always in the family way. It was all I knew before I came here. The sickness of it should be over soon,' she said.

I looked at her like she was mad. 'I can't have a baby, Lizzie.'

❧

Expect. Expectant. Expecting.

It means *to wait.* For an invitation, a person, an event. But never for a baby. Not a single quotation in *D and E* mentioned a baby. Lizzie calculated that I'd been 'expecting' for ten weeks, but I'd been oblivious.

The next day, I stayed in bed instead of joining Da for breakfast. A headache, I told him, and he agreed that I looked pale. As soon as he left for the Scriptorium, I went to his room and stood in front of Lily's mirror.

I was a little pale, yes, but in my nightdress I could see no change. I loosened the ribbon around my neck and let the nightdress fall to the floor. I remembered Bill tracing his finger from my head to my toes. Naming every part of me. My gaze retraced his path; gooseflesh rose as it had each time we'd been together. I stopped at my belly, at the hint of roundness that could easily be a big meal or wind or the heaviness before my monthly bleed. But it was none of those things, and the body I had so recently learned to read was suddenly incomprehensible.

I pulled the nightdress back up and tied the ribbon tight. I returned to bed and pulled the covers up to my neck. I lay there for hours, barely moving, not wanting to feel what might be going on inside me.

I was waiting, but not for a baby. I was waiting for a solution.

I slept badly that night. In the morning, I felt worse for the lack of sleep, but I insisted on going to the Scriptorium. I kept a packet of McVitie's in my desk and nibbled them through the morning post and while sorting slips. I tried to improve on the top-slip meanings suggested by volunteers, but nothing better would come to mind.

I looked over to the sorting table. Da sat where he had always sat, as did Mr Sweatman and Mr Maling. Mr Yockney sat where Mr Mitchell used to, and I suddenly wondered what kind of shoes he wore and whether his socks matched. Would another child be welcomed beneath the sorting table? Or would new assistants complain and chastise and accuse? Da coughed, brought out his handkerchief and blew his nose.

He had a cold, that was all, but I suddenly realised that he was older, greyer, fleshier. Would he have the energy to be mother and father, grandmother and grandfather? Would it be fair to ask it of him?

At lunchtime, I joined Mrs Ballard and Lizzie in the kitchen and suffered their anxiety.

'You must tell your father, Essymay. And Bill should be made to do the right thing,' Lizzie said.

'I won't be telling Bill,' I said. Lizzie stared at me, her face full of fear.

'At least write to Miss Thompson. She'll help you tell your father. She'll know what to do,' suggested Mrs Ballard.

'There's time yet,' I said, not knowing if there was or there wasn't. Lizzie and Mrs Ballard looked at each other but said nothing more. The kitchen became unbearably silent. When Lizzie asked if I'd be going with her to the Covered Market on Saturday, I said I would.

∽

The market was crowded. It was a relief. I hovered beside Lizzie as she went from stall to stall, testing the firmness of one fruit, the give of another. The banter was familiar and reassuring; no one made a point of asking how I felt or of telling me I looked pale.

Eventually, we made our way to Mabel's stall. It had been weeks since I'd seen her. She looked smaller, the unnatural curve of her back more pronounced. As we got closer I could see that she was whittling. Closer still, and the movement of her hands was mesmerising, their dexterity a contradiction to her wretched body.

Mabel was so absorbed that she didn't notice we were standing by her stall until Lizzie put an orange on the crate in front of her. Her craggy face barely registered the gift, but she put down the knife and whisked the orange into the folds of her rags. Then she picked up her knife and resumed her whittling.

'You'll like this, when it's done,' she said, looking at me.

'What is it?' asked Lizzie.

Mabel turned to Lizzie for a moment and passed her the figure.

'It's Taliesin the bard. Or maybe Merlin the wizard. I reckon Miss Words-Worth 'ere will like it for 'er da.' She looked back to me, expecting praise for her wordplay. I gave a wan smile.

'It must be one or the other,' said Lizzie.

'One and the same,' said Mabel, her eyes shifting over me and narrowing slightly. 'Just the name keeps changin'.'

Lizzie handed back the whittling, and Mabel took it without looking away from my face. I shifted uncomfortably and she leaned forward.

'Yer showin',' she whispered. 'In yer face. If you took off that coat, I reckon I'd see it.'

The shouts of stallholders, the clatter of carts, the competing conversations; all the sounds of the market were sucked into a single piercing note. Instinct made me look around, made me do up the undone buttons of my coat.

Mabel smiled and sat back. She was pleased with herself. I began to shake.

Until that moment, my anxiety had been all about telling Da. I hadn't thought about what anyone else might think, or what the consequences of them knowing might be. I looked around again and felt like some small creature with nowhere to run.

'Ain't 'eard of no wedding,' Mabel said.

'Enough, Mabel,' Lizzie whispered.

Their words cut through the ringing in my ears, and the sounds of the market came flooding back. There was a moment of relief when I realised that nobody seemed to have noticed. But it didn't last. I had to lean on Mabel's crate to stop from falling.

'Don't worry, lass,' Mabel said. 'Got a few weeks yet. Most people don't notice what they don't expect to see.'

Lizzie spoke for me, a measure of my fear apparent in her voice.

'But if *you* can tell, Mabel …'

'Ain't no one 'ere with my particular – what should I call it – *expertise.*'

'You have children?' I could barely hear my own voice ask the question.

Mabel laughed, her blackened gums ugly and mocking. 'I ain't so stupid as that,' she said. Then she lowered her voice even more. 'There are ways not to 'ave 'em.'

Lizzie coughed and started picking up various objects on Mabel's table, showing me one and then another and asking if I liked them. Her voice was louder than it needed to be.

Mabel held my gaze. Then, in a voice that carried to the flower stall and beyond, she said, 'What can I interest you in, lass?'

I played along, picking up the unfinished figure of Taliesin and turning it over in my shaking hand. I barely saw it.

'One of me best, that one. But it ain't quite done,' Mabel said, reaching for it. 'Reckon I'll 'ave it finished after lunch, if you want to come back.'

'Time to go, Esme.' Lizzie took my arm.

'I'll keep it tucked away so no one else buys it,' Mabel said as we turned to leave.

I nodded. Mabel nodded back. Then Lizzie and I left the market without finishing the shopping.

'Will you come in for tea?' Lizzie asked when we got to Sunnyside. The senior assistants all worked a half-day on Saturday, and I'd often kept Lizzie company in the kitchen while I waited for Da.

'Not today, Lizzie. I thought I'd go home and hang a few decorations as a surprise for Da.'

When I got home, I climbed the stairs to Da's room and again stood in front of Lily's mirror. It wasn't my belly that Mabel had noticed; it was my face. I peered into the glass, trying to see what she had seen, but the face that stared back was as it had always been.

How was that possible? It must have changed year to year, and yet I could not see it. I looked away from the mirror then glanced back quickly, trying to catch a glimpse of myself as a stranger might. I saw a woman's face, older than I expected, her eyes wide and brown and frightened. But I saw nothing that told me she was pregnant.

I went back downstairs and wrote Da a note. I was dress shopping, it said. I'd be home around three with pastries for afternoon tea.

I cycled back to the Covered Market. When I arrived, I was out of breath – more than usual. A familiar boy came to where I stood and offered to lean my bicycle against the nearest wall. He'd keep an eye on it, he said. His mother nodded from her stall, and I nodded back. Did she see something in my face? Is that why she told her boy to help? I looked in at the market – the clamour only added to the chaos in my head.

As I walked among the shops and stalls, I felt I was drawing every eye. I needed to act normally. I went from one stall to another, recalling Tilda and the others as they practised backstage; the rehearsal was never as convincing as the performance. I wondered if I was convincing anyone.

By the time I arrived at Mabel's stall, my basket was full. I handed her an apple.

'You need to eat more fruit, Mabel,' I said. 'Keep the catarrh out of your chest.'

She exaggerated her rotten smile so I could see the deficit of teeth. 'I ain't eaten an apple since I was a lass 'bout your age,' she said.

I put the apple back in my basket and pulled out a ripe pear. She took it and pressed her thumb into the flesh. If she rejected it, there would be a bruise by the time I got it home.

But she didn't reject it. 'A treat indeed,' she said, wrapping her gums around it and letting the juice run down her chin. She wiped it with the back of a rag-wrapped hand, removing days of grime from one small area of skin.

'Mabel,' I began, but the words wouldn't come.

Mabel's cracked lips softened as they sucked on the flesh of the pear. I felt myself flush, and the nausea I thought was over returned in a sickening wave that made me lean against the edge of Mabel's crate.

'That Lizzie won't approve of what yer plannin',' she said, her voice low.

It was a truth I'd been arguing with for days. Lizzie refused to hear me when I said I couldn't have a child. The plainer my words, the more she would handle the crucifix around her neck. Like her faith, it was always there, hidden and quiet and personal. But in the past week, she hung on to it like it was the only thing keeping her from Hell.

It judged me, that crucifix, and I hated it. I imagined it twisting my words and whispering its translation in her ear. We were in some kind of tug of war, with Lizzie in the middle. It was not a contest I wanted to lose.

'I reckon Mrs Smyth might still be in the trade,' Mabel whispered, while picking up random objects as if to show me their worth. 'She was an apprentice, so to speak, when I was in need. Be an old hag and good at it by now, I'd wager.'

A trembling began in my hands and worked its way along my limbs until my body was shivering with it.

'Breathe normal, lass,' Mabel said, holding my gaze with hers.

I held on to the crate and tried to stop taking the air in gulps, but the shivering continued.

'You got yer pencil and one of them slips?' she said.

'What?'

'Take 'em out of yer pocket.'

I shook my head. It didn't make sense.

Mabel leaned forward. 'Do it,' she said, then a little louder, 'I just gave you a word and you'll forget it if you don't write it down.'

I reached into my pocket for a slip and a pencil. By the time I was poised to write, the trembling had subsided.

'*Trade*,' Mabel said, leaning back a little but not taking her eyes off my face.

I wrote *trade* in the top-left corner. Below that I wrote *Mrs Smyth might still be in the trade.*

'You feelin' better now?' Mabel asked.

I nodded.

'Fear hates the ordinary,' she said. 'When yer feared, you need to think ordinary thoughts, do ordinary things. You 'ear me? The fear'll back off, for a time at least.'

I nodded again and looked at the slip. *Trade* was such a common word.

'Where did you say Mrs Smyth lived?' I asked.

Mabel told me, and I wrote it on the bottom of the slip.

Before I left, Mabel retrieved something from within the many folds of cloth that kept her warm. 'For you,' she said, handing me a disc of pale wood into which she'd carved a shamrock. 'Thanks for the pear.'

I folded the slip around it and put it in my pocket.

It was an ordinary terraced house with identical terraced houses either side. A Christmas wreath still hung on the door despite the arrival of a new year. I checked the address again then looked along the length of the street. It was empty. I knocked.

The woman who answered the door might have been old, but she was straight-backed and well-dressed and could almost look me in the eye. I assumed I had the wrong house after all and began to stammer an apology, but she cut in.

'Lovely to see you, my dear,' she said, rather loudly. 'How is your mother?'

I stared at her, confused, but she kept the smile on her face and took my arm to draw me into the house.

'Keeping up appearances,' she said when the door was closed. 'The neighbours are all busybodies.' She looked at me then, like Mabel had, searched my face and glanced down the length of my body. 'I assume you wouldn't want them all knowing your business.'

I couldn't find the words for a reply, and Mrs Smyth didn't seem to require one. She took my coat and hung it on a coat stand by the door, then she walked down the narrow hall, and I followed. She ushered me into a small sitting room, walls lined with books, a fire burning low in the hearth. I could see where she'd been sitting before I knocked: a velvet sofa, midnight blue with large, soft cushions of various patterns scattered across the back. It was big enough for two, but only at one end was the velvet worn and the seat depressed from years of being favoured. A book was splayed open on the table beside it, the spine strained. As Mrs Smyth stoked the fire, I moved closer to the book. *In Mary's Reign*, by Baroness Orczy. I'd bought it years before, from Blackwell's bookshop. For a moment I forgot why I was there and regretted the disturbance I had caused.

'I like to read,' Mrs Smyth said, when she caught me looking at the book. 'Do you like to read?'

I nodded, but my mouth was too dry to speak. She went to her sideboard and poured a glass of water.

'Take a sip, don't gulp it,' she said, handing it to me. I did as she instructed.

'Good,' she said, taking the glass from me. 'Now, may I ask who recommended me?'

'Mabel O'Shaughnessy,' I whispered.

'You can speak up,' she said. 'No one can hear us in here.'

'Mabel O'Shaughnessy,' I said again.

Mrs Smyth did not immediately recognise Mabel's name, and it was little help to describe the way she looked. But when I told her what I knew of her past, and mentioned her Irish lilt, Mrs Smyth began to nod.

'She was a repeat customer,' she said, unsmiling. 'A stall in the Covered Market, you say?'

I nodded, looked down at my feet. The floor of the sitting room was covered in a richly patterned carpet.

'I didn't think she'd survive the game,' she said.

I looked up. 'The game?'

'Clearly it's not why you're here.'

'I beg your pardon?'

'I get two types of women knocking on my door,' she said. 'Those who get around too much and those who get around too little.' She looked me up and down, took in every article of clothing. 'You are the latter.'

'And the *game*?' I asked again, my hand going to my pocket to check I had a slip and pencil.

'The game is whoring,' she said, as if nothing worse than *whist* or *draughts* had crossed her lips. 'There are players, like any game, though the dice are always loaded. When you lose you end up in gaol, the cemetery or here.'

She put her hand on my belly, and I jumped. When she began digging her fingers in, I tried to move away.

'Stay still,' she said, putting one hand in the small of my back so she could get purchase with the other. '*Mrs Warren's profession*, some call it, because of the play by Bernard Shaw. Do you like the theatre?' she asked, but didn't wait for an answer. 'I was invited to the opening night of that one. Whores aren't the only women who find their way to my door. I get my fair share of actresses too.' She stopped prodding and took a step back.

'I'm not …'

'I can see that you're neither a whore nor an actress,' she said.

Then we stood there, silent. She was thinking, weighing something up. Finally, she let out a long breath.

'It's quickening,' she said.

'What does that mean?' I asked.

'Quickening is the fluttering in your belly which means the baby has decided to stay.'

I stared at her.

'It means you've come to me too late.'

Thank God, I thought.

❧

GAME

Prostitution.

'The game is whoring. There are players, like any game, though the dice are always loaded.'

Mrs Smyth, 1907

QUICKENING

Stirrings of life.

'Quickening is the fluttering in your belly which means the baby has decided to stay.'

Mrs Smyth, 1907

❧

Sunnyside was quiet when I walked my bicycle through the gates. The afternoon was getting on; it was dusky and the Scriptorium was dark. Everyone had gone home. I could see Lizzie through the kitchen window, and I watched her for a while. She moved back and forth between the range and the table, no doubt preparing dinner for the Murrays. Once, when I was little, she told me she didn't much like cooking.

'What do you like?' I'd asked.

'I like sewing and I like looking after you, Essymay.'

I was shivering. I leaned the bicycle against the ash and walked towards the kitchen.

Inside, I stood on the threshold, the door closed behind me, the heat of the range warming my face. But the shivering didn't stop.

Lizzie looked at me. Her hand hovered at her chest. She had questions she didn't ask.

The shivering got worse, and she was there. Her thick arms around me, guiding me to a chair. She put a cup in my hands; it was almost too hot, but not quite. She told me to drink. I drank.

'I couldn't have done it,' I said, looking up into her face. She held me against her belly and stroked my hair.

When she spoke, she was slow and careful, as if I were a stray cat she was afraid would run off before it could be helped. 'He seemed like a nice enough man, that Bill. You could tell him,' she said.

She held me a little tighter as she said it, and I didn't move away. I'd thought about it. I'd imagined it. In my heart I was certain that Bill would do the right thing if he knew. That Tilda would make sure of it. I spoke as slowly and carefully as Lizzie just had.

'I don't love him, though. And I don't want to be married.'

She stiffened slightly, and I felt her take a breath. Then she pulled a chair close to mine and sat opposite me, our hands clasped.

'Every woman wants to be married, Essymay.'

'If that's true, then why isn't Ditte married, or her sister? Why not Elsie or Rosfrith or Eleanor Bradley? Why not you?'

'Not all women get the chance. And some … well, some are just brought up with too many books and too many ideas, and they can't settle to it.'

'I don't think *I* could settle to it, Lizzie.'

'You'd get used to it.'

'But I don't want to get used to it.'

'What do you want?'

'I want things to stay as they are. I want to keep sorting words and understanding what they mean. I want to get better at it and be given more responsibility, and I want to keep earning my own money. I feel as though I've only begun to understand who I am. Being a wife or a mother just doesn't fit.' It all came out in a rush and ended in sobbing.

By the time the sobbing stopped I knew what I had to do. I asked Lizzie to find some notepaper and a pen. I would write to Ditte.

11th February 1907
My dear, dear Esme,

Of course you must come, and I will help arrange what must be arranged. But there is the question of your father, and of the way things might look. I will come to Oxford this Friday. I will arrive at 11.30am and would like you to meet me at the station. We will go straight to the Queens Lane Coffee House — it's a long way from Jericho, and we're unlikely to bump into anyone we know. Leave Lizzie to her duties at Sunnyside, but assure her that we three shall speak before I leave.

Your situation is not as rare as you might think. Many a young lady of means or education has found herself similarly inconvenienced. It is the oldest dilemma in history — the Virgin Mary, indeed! (Please don't read this aloud to Lizzie, I know she would not approve.) But you see my point. You are in good company, though that is unlikely to soothe you. I'm just grateful you had the good sense to confide in me before you had a chance to consider alternative solutions. From down that alley many a young lady has not returned.

I have a proposition for you, Esme. If you are going to come and live with Beth and me, I would like you to be my research assistant. My History of England *is in need of updating, and I have been contemplating a biography of my grandfather for some years. He was a parliamentarian, you know. A very interesting man, with ideas before his time — I daresay your friend Tilda would have liked him very much. I will, of course, require your services at the earliest convenience. We can discuss the details when we have tea on Friday.*

Do you understand me, Esme? You will be doing me a great service, and when the work is done, you will return to Oxford and continue with your role in the Scriptorium. Your path, whatever you want it to be, need not be diverted.

I will put all that is relevant in a letter to Dr Murray, and I am confident he will consider my offer an opportunity that will only increase your value to him on your return.

Now, to your father. I have written to tell him of my trip, using 'nag' as my excuse (if the current quotations are our guide to its meaning, then it will be recorded that women are the only perpetrators of this particular form of harassment). My plan at this stage is to arrange to see Harry at home, prime him for the news, calm his worst fears (which will all be for your current and future welfare) and make it clear we have it all in hand. Then you must tell him everything – within reason. He is a good man, Esme. He is not a prude or a zealot or a conservative, but he is a father and he loves you very much. You must remember that he wakes every day to a photograph of you in your infant smock. This news will be a shock. He will need time and understanding, and perhaps the opportunity to rant and rave. Allow him this.

Beyond that, there are other things we must discuss, but I think it best to leave them until we sit across from each other with a good pot of tea between us.

So, I will see you this Friday, 11.30am. Don't be late.

Yours,

Ditte

❧

It was raining – not heavily, but the people walking up and down High Street were opening umbrellas and turning their collars up against the damp. I watched them as Ditte talked. She was scripting the lies and half-truths that would make my absence from the Scriptorium reasonable.

We drank two large pots of tea at the coffee house. When we came out onto the street, the rain had stopped and a weak sun was shining on the damp pavement. I blinked away the glare.

March 1907

Two weeks later, Da stood with me on the platform waiting for the train that would take me towards Bath. I thought about every conversation we had had since Ditte emerged from our sitting room and gave me the nod to go in and speak with him. We had said so little. Gestures and sighs had punctuated our interactions. He had touched my face and held my funny fingers whenever words failed him. I knew how much he wished that Lily was there and how he thought that if she had been, things would be different. I knew he thought he had failed me, rather than me failing him. But he said none of it, and so I could only return his affection with a touch of my own.

When the train came, he carried my trunk into the second-class carriage and settled me in a seat by the door. He might have said something then, but there were three others already seated around me. He kissed my forehead and stepped out into the corridor, but he didn't leave immediately. He smiled a sad smile, and I suddenly realised that I would come home completely changed; that contrary to what Ditte had promised, my path, whatever it was, had already been diverted. I stood up then and wrapped my arms around him. He held me until the whistle blew.

Beth was to meet me off the train at Bath, but when I scanned the platform, there was no sign. I disembarked and waited where the porter had left my trunk.

A woman waved. She was taller, slimmer and far more fashionable than Ditte, but there was something similar in the shape of her nose. I smiled as she approached.

'It's criminal that this is the first time I've met you,' she said, taking me in an unexpected hug that nearly toppled me.

'Of course, I know all about you,' Beth said when we were seated in the back of the cab.

I flushed and looked down at my lap.

'Oh, not just that,' she said, as if *that* was trivial. 'You are Edith's favourite topic of conversation, and I never tire of hearing about you.' She leaned in. 'You must forgive us, Esme. We are a couple of spinsters without a dog; we must discuss something.'

Ditte and Beth lived between Bath Station and Royal Victoria Park, so the cab ride was short. We stopped in front of a three-storey terraced house, identical in every way to the terraced houses that stretched left and right. Beth saw me staring up at the attic windows.

'It was left to us,' she said, 'so we'd never have to marry. It's far too big, of course, but we have a lot of guests, and a woman comes every morning to clean. Mrs Travis insists we keep the rooms on the top floor closed. Saves on dusting, she says. She has very little aptitude for dusting, so we've agreed.'

All those rooms, I thought. I would have dusted my own if they'd invited me when I was fourteen.

Beth was younger than Ditte and her opposite in almost every way, yet there seemed to be no tension or argument between them. I'd always thought that Ditte was like the trunk of a great tree: anchored securely to what she knew to be true. After just a few days in Bath, I began to think of Beth as the canopy. In mind and body, she responded to whatever forces came her way. Despite her fifty years she shimmered, and I was mesmerised.

I had a week's grace – 'to settle in,' Beth said – then she began inviting visitors for afternoon tea. 'We can't talk about you all of the time,' she teased.

On the day our first visitors were due to arrive, the sisters called me downstairs to lay a tray in preparation. 'Mrs Travis is an ordinary housekeeper,' Ditte said, as she transferred the cake from a cooling rack to a plate, 'but her Madeira is unrivalled.'

'Perhaps I'll stay in my room,' I said.

'Nonsense,' said Beth, coming into the kitchen. 'It will play out perfectly. We will talk about Edith's revision of her English history and then her employment of you will make perfect sense to everyone.' She leaned in and said in a conspiratorial tone, 'You are not without a reputation of your own, you know.'

My hand went to my belly, still hidden, and I blushed scarlet. Beth made no effort to calm my fears.

'Don't tease her, Beth,' said Ditte.

'But it's so easy,' she said, smiling. 'You have a reputation, Esme, as a natural scholar. According to Dr Murray you are the equal of any Oxford graduate. He is particularly fond of telling the story of you camping all day beneath the sorting table. He claims his lenience has allowed the development of a particular affinity for words.'

Horror turned to gratitude, and the heat stayed in my face.

'He would not approve of me telling you this, of course,' said Beth. 'Praise dulls the intellect, in his opinion.'

There was a knock at the door.

'Always on time,' Beth said to Ditte. Then she turned to me. 'Just keep your hand from hovering above your belly and no one will notice a thing.'

Three gentlemen. All scholars, all residing in Somerset when they weren't expected to teach. Professor Leyton Chisholm was an historian at the University of Wales and a contemporary of the sisters. He was so comfortable in their company that he helped himself to cake without it being offered and sat unasked in the most comfortable chair. Mr Philip Brooks was also a friend, but not old enough to take such liberties. He had to stoop to avoid hitting his head on the doorway, and Beth made a game of standing on tip-toe to kiss him on the cheek. Mr Brooks taught geology at University College, Bristol, as did Mr Shaw-Smith, the youngest of the three. He was a stranger to the sisters but had come along at the insistence of Mr Brooks. His youthful face was eager but could not yet support a beard. He stumbled through the introductions.

'In time you will get used to us, Mr Shaw-Smith,' said Beth, and I wondered if she was referring to us three, or to the whole of womankind.

When the men were seated, Ditte and I arranged ourselves at either end of the settee. Beth poured the tea and nodded for me to pass the cake. When everyone was served and compliments about the Madeira had been given, I sat back and waited for Beth to ask some provocative question that would give the men their cue. I expected gentlemen's anecdotes and hubris, intellectual disagreements argued on ever-diminishing points of logic. I expected the occasional entreaty for an opinion (out of courtesy), and I was already anticipating my disappointment at the automatic taming of language that would be observed due to the fact we three wore skirts.

But that was not how the afternoon proceeded. These gentlemen had come to listen, to test their ideas and be persuaded otherwise – not by each other, but by the sisters. The men's gaze fell comfortably on Beth, following her as she moved to turn on a lamp, watching her hands as she checked the level in the teapot and poured them each another cup. When she spoke, they leaned in, asked her to clarify, took it in turns to play with her ideas and combine them with their own. They argued with her, inviting her to defend her position. She often smiled before delivering a withering rebuke for sloppy reasoning. If they came around to her way of thinking, which they often did, it was never to be polite. I was astonished.

Ditte spoke far less, but she frequently bent towards Professor Chisholm to quietly discuss some point the younger men were debating with Beth. When Ditte was asked for her opinion, the company would fall silent. On points of history, she was clearly the authority, and her words were treated with a respect I had only ever seen given to Dr Murray.

'It is that exact question that Edith intends to explore in the revision of her *History*,' said Beth at one point. 'Which is why we have invited Esme to stay for a while. She is to be Edith's research assistant.'

'Isn't that your job, Beth?' said Professor Chisholm.

'Usually, yes, but as you know I have a writing project of my own.' She gave him a cheeky smile.

'And what would that be, Miss Thompson?' said Mr Shaw-Smith.

Beth turned her whole body towards the question and paused before speaking.

'Well,' she said. 'It's scandalous, really. I've been writing a novel, of the very worst kind, and by some miracle it's going to be published.'

I noticed a smile flit across Ditte's face as she reached for another slice of Madeira.

'What is it called?' he asked.

'*A Dragoon's Wife*,' Beth said with pride. 'It's set in the seventeenth century, and my task over the next few months is to add a little more *steam* to the narrative.'

'Steam?'

'Yes, *steam*, Mr Shaw-Smith. And I can't tell you how much fun I'm having.'

The young man finally understood and took refuge in his teacup. I reached into my pocket to feel the stub of a pencil and the edge of a slip.

'Gestures are important, of course,' Beth continued. '*He* might offer his hand; *she* might take it. But arousal is a bodily function, wouldn't you agree, Mr Shaw-Smith?'

He was speechless.

'Of course you do,' she said. 'If you want a bit of steam in a novel, the skin must flush and the pulse must race – for characters, and for readers, in my opinion.'

'You're saying that desire should be exposed,' said Mr Brooks.

'Of course,' she said. 'More tea, anyone?'

I excused myself and the men all stood. Mr Shaw-Smith seemed grateful for the disturbance. I wanted to write down Beth's words before the exact quotation faded.

When I returned, there was another visitor.

'Esme, this is Mrs Brooks.'

Mrs Brooks stood up to greet me. She barely came to my shoulder.

'Don't you dare call me Mrs Brooks,' she said, holding out her hand. 'I only answer to Sarah. I'm Philip's wife and chauffeur.'

Her grip was firm and her shake efficient. I suspected there was nothing small about her character.

'It's true,' said Mr Brooks. 'My wife has learned to drive and I have not. Feel free to be amused – most of our friends are – but it is an arrangement that suits us quite well.' He looked at Sarah. 'I do not fit easily behind the steering wheel, do I, dear?'

'You do not fit easily anywhere, Philip,' Sarah said, laughing. 'And the motorcar was not made for my stature either, but how I love it.'

Another pot of tea was drained, and barely a crumb of cake remained on the plate when Sarah insisted it was time to go.

'I must deliver these gentlemen to their homes before dark,' she said.

We all rose. But as each gentleman bade Beth farewell, she'd engage him in some small aside. After ten minutes Sarah was forced to clap her hands like a schoolmistress to get them to follow her out the door.

❧

The sisters enjoyed hosting afternoon teas, and over the next month I became acquainted with more people than I had in all my years at the Scriptorium. Mr Shaw-Smith was never seen again, but Professor Chisholm was a frequent caller.

'He magically appears on our doorstep whenever Mrs Travis bakes her Madeira,' whispered Beth one day. 'It's extraordinary, really.'

Philip Brooks joined him once, and on another occasion Philip and Sarah came alone. Mrs Brooks was quite plain to look at, and when she spoke she was often blunt. I suspected her intellect paled against those of the sisters, but she had a way of saying things that somehow highlighted the truth. She reminded me of Tilda.

When my belly became too difficult to hide, I began organising outings to coincide with afternoon teas. At first it was to Victoria Park or the Baths, and when it rained I would shelter in the Abbey and listen to the choirboys practising. But Ditte soon put a stop to this.

'You have an historian's aptitude for investigation, Esme,' she said one evening over dinner. 'Rather than having you wander aimlessly around Victoria Park tomorrow, I'd like you to visit the archives at Guildhall.'

'Edith, don't forget the ring,' said Beth, taking another slice of beef and drowning it in gravy.

Ditte took off the gold band that she wore on her little finger and gave it to me. I knew what it was meant to do, so I slipped it on. The fit was perfect.

'I've never been able to wear it on that finger,' said Ditte.

'You've never wanted to,' said Beth. 'But it suits Esme.'

The next time the sisters had visitors I was in London, searching the archives of the British Museum and spending a few days with Da. The time after that I was in Cambridge, staying with a sympathetic friend of Beth's who never once enquired after my husband.

I took my research seriously, and my skill grew with my belly. Rather than restricting me, Ditte had given me a kind of freedom. She'd paved the way with letters of introduction. She wrote that I was her niece and gave me her last name. She was careful not to associate me with the Scriptorium. Wherever I went, I was expected – my entry to archives and reading rooms was automatic; the documents I needed were organised in advance and waiting for me to scrutinise.

At first, I was sure I convinced no one. I stumbled around and apologised too much, and I was far too grateful when admittance was given. At the entrance to the Old Schools reading room at Cambridge, I saw an attendant double-check Ditte's letter, and my heart ached at the thought I might be expelled before I'd had the chance to breathe in that heady combination of aged stone, leather and wood. When he noticed the band of gold on my hand, the belly beneath it became of little consequence. He let me pass, and I stood on the threshold a moment too long.

'Are you all right, madam?' the attendant asked.

'I could not be better,' I said.

I made my way with steady steps towards a table at the far end of the room. The wooden floor announced me to the bent heads and absorbed readers; the architects of that great room had not considered the clip-clop of a lady's shoe. I acknowledged the curiosity of every gentleman scholar with a straightening of my aching back and a curt nod of my head. By the time I sat down, I was exhausted from the effort.

I never thought anywhere could rival Oxford for its history and beauty, but every time I ventured out on my own I was forced to reflect on how little I knew. Oxford and the Scriptorium had always been enough. Our visits to family in Scotland had always seemed a little too long, and the one time I'd been away on my own had made me wary of ever leaving again. Despite myself, I began to enjoy this new adventure – though the reason for it was becoming harder to ignore.

The sisters were not only complicit in my predicament, but seemed to delight in it. At breakfast they would quiz me about the quality of my sleep, about my appetite and desire for strange foods (none, which was a particular disappointment for Beth). My weight and sleeping patterns were recorded in a small notebook, and one day Beth asked, with uncharacteristic shyness, if I would allow her to see my body naked.

'I would like to draw it,' she said.

I had become used to standing naked in front of the mirror, tracing my curves from breast to pubis. I was trying to commit them to memory. I agreed.

While Beth drew, I stood beside the window in my bedroom and looked out at the garden. It was a mess of colour and overgrown edges. The apple tree was full of life, and its blossom littered the ground beneath. It was beautiful, I thought, in its unpruned neglect. Sunlight fell across my belly, and its heat was proof of my nakedness. But I felt no shame or embarrassment. Beth sat on the bed, and I could hear the scratching of her charcoal against the paper.

When she asked me to lay one hand above and one below the bloom of my belly, I complied. My skin was warm, and I pressed against it. Then there it was: a movement beneath the tightening skin. A response. Against all reason, I caressed the growing thing inside me and whispered a few words of greeting.

I didn't notice when Beth put the sketchbook down. She draped a dressing gown over my shoulders and went to the door to invite Ditte in.

'Beautiful,' Ditte said, looking at the sketch, but she struggled to look up at me. She left as quietly as she had come, but I saw her wipe her eyes.

❧

'Sarah Brooks will be coming for afternoon tea today,' said Ditte while we were eating lunch. Normally she would have told me the day before.

'I'll go for a walk around Victoria Park. It's a lovely day.'

Ditte looked at Beth, then back at me. 'Actually, we'd like you to stay.'

I looked down at my belly, now huge and undeniable, then I looked quizzically at Ditte.

'They're good people,' she said.

At first, I didn't understand. I'd been deprived of any company other than that of the sisters since April, when Da visited for my twenty-fifth birthday. It was almost June; I was huge.

Beth rose from the kitchen table and began to busy herself with the coffeepot. 'They have been unable to have a baby of their own, Esme,' she said. 'They would make good parents for yours.'

The words were falling into place as Ditte reached her hand across the table to take hold of mine. I didn't pull it away, but I couldn't return the gesture of her gentle squeeze. I was winded, unable to speak from the vacuum that had just been created in my chest. It wasn't just a lack of breath; it was an inadequacy of words. I had a feeling that I understood precisely, but had no words for.

On the periphery of that feeling, I could see Beth turn from the stove, coffeepot in one hand, her features uncomfortable with the smile they were trying to support. What did she see to make her face collapse and her hand shake? A little coffee spilled on the floor, but she made no move to clean it up. Instead, she looked to her sister. I'd never seen her so unsure.

I couldn't settle on what to wear, though my choices were few. The last time I'd seen Sarah, I'd thought my belly well hidden. Now, I wondered if she had known all along. The idea made me uncomfortable, annoyed. I put on a dress that accentuated my bosom and sat too tightly around my middle, then I stood in front of the mirror. There was something obscene about it, and something wonderful. I traced my funny fingers over the curve of my breast, over my nipple, over the swell of baby beneath the tightened skin. I felt it move and saw the undulation beneath the fabric of the dress.

I changed into a blouse and skirt, both borrowed from Ditte. I wore a housecoat over the top.

As soon as I came into the sitting room, Sarah stood up. The sisters wanted the afternoon to be more comfortable than it could possibly be, so they remained seated and threw out casual phrases of welcome that sounded forced and overly cheerful: 'Here you are'; 'You'll have tea, won't you, Esme?'; 'We were just commenting on how warm it is'; 'A slice of Madeira, Sarah?'

Sarah ignored them and came straight over to where I stood. She took both my hands in hers. 'Esme, if you would prefer this not to happen, I understand. This will be far harder for you than for anyone. You must take your time, and you must be sure.'

It was regret and sorrow and loss. It was hope and relief. And it was other things that had no name, but I felt them in my gut and could taste their bitterness. The frustration of not being able to articulate any of it came in a flood of tears.

Sarah caught me, wrapped her strong arms around me and let me sob on her shoulder. She felt solid and unafraid.

When Beth finally poured the tea, we were all blowing our noses.

We drank tea and ate cake, and I watched a crumb stick steadfastly to the corner of Sarah's mouth. I noticed how she listened to everything Beth said, never interrupting but not always agreeing when she had a chance to reply. I listened to the sound of her voice and was reminded of how easily she laughed. I wondered if she could sing.

I had avoided thinking about what would happen when the pregnancy was over. I didn't ask questions and the sisters had only ever hinted at it. Was this always the plan? I thought.

Of course it was.

Did it need to be?

Of course it did.

The baby was a girl. This I knew, though I couldn't say how. And I'd begun to love her.

'Esme?' Beth said.

All three women were waiting for me to reply to something I'd not heard.

'Esme,' Sarah said, 'would it be all right with you if I visited again?'

I looked to Ditte. When the review of her *History* was complete, I would return to Oxford and resume my work at the Scriptorium. She'd said this, and I'd agreed.

There should have been a word for what I felt right then, but despite all my years in the Scriptorium I couldn't recall a single one.

I nodded.

The warm weather held, and I grew enormous. Ditte was happy with the research I had done, and insisted I spend long hours reclining on the couch and proofreading the edits she'd been making to her *History*. Sarah came for tea each Tuesday afternoon, and I sat quietly observant. I found something else to like about her every time, but they were uncomfortable hours, and my ambivalence didn't shift. So much needed to be said, but the pouring of tea and handing around of Madeira cake kept getting in the way.

Then, one Tuesday, I waddled into the sitting room to find Sarah still wearing her hat and driving gloves.

'I thought I'd take you out,' she said.

It was an unexpected relief, and I took a deep breath as if I was already in the fresh air.

'Just the two of us,' she continued, turning to the sisters, who nodded in unison.

I was surprised when she opened the passenger door of a Daimler and helped me in. I'd rarely travelled in a private motorcar, and never one driven by a woman. Sarah had short legs and short arms, and her whole body was engaged in making the car move. She kept leaning forward to shift the gears, back to press the pedals. It was as if her arms and legs were being worked by a puppeteer. I coughed to disguise a laugh.

'Are you poorly?' she asked.

'Not at all,' I said.

Sarah never insisted on conversation and was unusually clumsy with small talk – she once responded to a comment on the weather by explaining the relationship between barometric pressure and rain – so our journey was silent except for the crunch of gears and the occasional disparaging comment about other people's driving.

By the time we arrived at the Bath Recreation Ground, I had filled three slips with various quotations for *damn-dunderhead*. They looked as though they had been written in a fit of palsy.

'Somerset are playing Lancashire for the championship,' Sarah said, helping me down from my seat and craning to see the scoreboard. 'Lancashire are chasing 181 runs, not a difficult target, so Philip has his work cut out. Do you like cricket, Esme?'

'I'm not sure. I've never sat to watch a whole game played.'

'You're too polite to say that it goes for too long and that watching grass grow would be more exciting. No, don't deny it, I can see it in your face.' She put her arm through mine, adjusting with ease to my height, and we started walking around the perimeter of the oval. 'By the end of the afternoon, you will be astonished you could ever think such a thing.'

Mr Brooks was already on the pitch, and I wondered if Sarah had been deliberate in her timing. Since their intentions had been made clear, he had not joined his wife for tea at the sisters'. I had assumed he felt that this whole business was best kept to the women. It wasn't until I saw him deliver his first ball that I thought 'this business' may not be finalised. I was being courted, I realised, and at some point I would have to accept or reject what was being offered. He'd given his hat to the umpire, and the sun shone off his bald head. He was as tall as Sarah was short, and he loped towards the pitch on long thin legs, releasing the ball from a windmill of arms.

'It was Philip's idea,' Sarah said after his second wide delivery.

'What was?'

'To bring you to the match. Oh, that was short. It's going to go all the way to the boundary.'

There was applause from one section of the crowd sitting on the other side of the oval.

'Our lot won't be happy. I daresay he's distracted. Poor man, he so wanted to impress you.'

'Me?'

'Yes; as I said, it was his idea. He's been desperate to come to tea, but I kept putting him off. It was uncomfortable, don't you think?'

I just looked down.

'I think he was hoping to demonstrate his credentials for fatherhood by putting on a good show in the middle.'

Though I liked it, her directness still took me by surprise.

'Well, that's him done. Fifteen runs off the over. He'll be glad it's tea.'

I watched as the cricketers walked from the pitch towards the club rooms. When Philip looked in our direction, Sarah waved. Instead of following his team-mates, he made his way across the ground to join us. Long strides, a slight stoop.

'Please tell me you've only just arrived,' he said, as he drew close. He might have been blushing or sunburned, I couldn't tell.

'Can't do that I'm afraid, darling. We arrived just as Sharp came out to bat.' Sarah stood on tip-toe to kiss him, and I couldn't help wondering whether Philip's stoop was an adjustment to marriage.

He looked at the scoreboard. 'I'll be fielding from now on, I expect,' he said. Then he turned to me, his hazel eyes shining.

'Esme,' he said. 'It's so lovely to see you again.'

I wasn't sure what I should say. I offered a nod, but barely a smile. When he held out his large hand, I gave him mine. He saw my funny fingers and didn't flinch, but I still expected his grip to be limp from the fear of crushing what looked so fragile. Instead, his grip was firm enough to keep my hand from slipping free. When he let go, it was at just the right moment. You can tell a lot from the way a man takes your hand, Da once told me.

❧

It was Tuesday, and Mrs Travis had left for the day. Sarah was due for afternoon tea, and the sisters were in the kitchen getting the tray ready. When I came in, Ditte was arranging slices of cake on a plate, and Beth was heating the teapot. I was about to ask if I could help when I felt a trickle down the inside of my leg. Before I could register what it was, I felt it gush out. I gasped and the sisters turned.

'I think it's my waters,' I said.

Ditte held a slice of cake and Beth the kettle. For a few seconds they hardly moved. Then suddenly they were flapping around like chickens in fright: turning this way and that and speaking over each other. They debated whether I should eat or avoid eating, continue with the raspberry-leaf tea or stop drinking it. Lie down or have a bath.

'I'm sure the doctor said *not* to let her have a bath,' said Beth.

'But I remember Mrs Murray saying that a bath was such a relief, and she's had hundreds of babies,' said Ditte, with none of her usual calm and precision.

I didn't feel like eating, drinking or bathing, but neither of them thought to ask.

'I think I just need to change into something dry,' I interrupted. I was still standing in the puddle that had sent the sisters into such a flurry.

'Have the pains started?' asked Beth.

'No. I feel just as I did ten minutes ago, only damper.'

I hoped my response would calm them down, but they looked at me, bewildered. When they heard a knock at the door, they both rushed to answer it, leaving me alone in the kitchen.

'Where is she?' Sarah's voice.

All three came into the kitchen, Sarah in the lead, an enormous smile on her freckled face.

'This is all perfectly normal,' she said, holding my gaze until she was sure I understood. Then she turned to the sisters and said it more sternly: 'Perfectly normal.' Noticing the cake on the kitchen table and steam rising from the pot, she said, 'Ah, excellent. Tea will be just the thing. Esme and I will join you in ten minutes.' She took my arm and led me up the stairs.

In my bedroom, Sarah kneeled on the floor in front of where I stood; she removed one shoe, then the other. Without comment, she reached under my skirt and unclipped my stockings. I felt her fingers walk the length of each leg as she rolled the stocking down. Gooseflesh followed in their wake. Sarah did not ask if she could care for me; she just did it.

'*Is* it normal?' I asked.

'Your waters broke, Esme. And they flowed clear. It is *perfectly* normal.'

'But Dr Scanlan said the pains would start straight after. I feel no different.'

She looked up, her hand stroking my calf absent-mindedly.

'The pain will come,' she said. 'In five minutes or five hours. And when it does, it will hurt like the devil.'

I knew this to be true, but had hoped there might be exceptions. I felt my face pale. She winked.

'I advise swearing. It will relieve the pain when it is at its worst, though you have to be convincing. Nothing half-hearted or under your breath. Shout it out. Childbirth is the only time you can get away with it.'

'How do you know?' I asked.

She stood.

'Where do you keep your nightclothes?'

I pointed to the bureau. 'Bottom drawer.'

'I've birthed two babies,' Sarah said as she took out a clean nightdress. 'Unfortunately, their waters did not run clear.'

She helped lift my dress over my head, then the slip. She kneeled again and used the slip to pat my legs dry. She removed my drawers, checking every inch of the damp cloth before finally bringing them to her nose.

I recoiled.

'Smells as it should,' she said, grinning at me. 'I've also helped my sister birth five of her littluns. Her bloomers all smelled like this and each of those babes was born squalling.'

She threw the bloomers on the pile of other garments. There was nothing else to remove. I was as naked as I'd ever been.

'Will you stay?' I asked.

'If you want me to.'

'Do women usually swear when they have their babies?'

She dropped the nightdress over my head. It billowed, then settled against my skin like a breeze. She helped me find the arm holes.

'If they know the right words, they can hardly help it.'

'I know some quite bad words. I collect them from an old woman at the market in Oxford.'

'Well, it's one thing to hear them in the market and quite another to have them roll around inside your mouth.' She took my dressing gown from the back of the door and helped me into it. 'Some words are more than letters on a page, don't you think?' she said, tying the sash around my belly as best she could. 'They have shape and texture. They are like bullets, full of energy, and when you give one breath you can feel its sharp edge against your lip. It can be quite cathartic in the right context.'

'Like when someone cuts in front of you on the way to the cricket?' I said.

She laughed. 'Oh dear. Philip calls it my motormouth. I hope you weren't offended.'

'A bit surprised, but I think that's when I started to really like you.'

No words then; Sarah just stood on her toes and kissed me on the cheek. I bent slightly to meet her.

❧

ATTEND
To direct one's care to; to take care or charge of, to look after, tend, guard.

TRAVAIL
Of a woman: to suffer the pains of childbirth.

DELIVERED
Set free; disburdened of offspring; handed over; surrendered.

RESTLESS
Deprived of rest; finding no rest; esp. uneasy in mind or spirit.

SQUALL
A small or insignificant person.
A sudden and violent gust, a blast or short storm.
To scream loudly or discordantly.

❧

Light edged the curtains. The room was empty of its earlier crowd. The mess had been returned to order. Lavender masked the smell of blood and shit.

Shit. I'd said that word aloud, over and over. And I'd said others that Mabel had taught me. My throat was hoarse with them. I hadn't dreamed it.

Though I did dream. And in the dream, a baby cried.

It was crying still. My breasts ached from the sound.

❧

Their conversation was whispered, but I heard it.

'Better off not seeing it, else she changes her mind.' The midwife.

'It needs a feed.' Sarah.

'To keep a lie-child condemns her and it. I'll fetch a wet-nurse.' The midwife.

❧

I threw back the covers and swung my legs over the side of the bed. Unfamiliar muscles moaned from their ordeal. A terrible sting made me squeal. I had a memory of that pain, blurred by ether.

I tried to rise, but my head throbbed and the sharp sounds of a moment before became dull, as if I'd just slipped below the water in a bath. I sat back down and closed my eyes. In the darkness behind my lids was the negative of a face, two points of unwavering light seared onto my retina. When I finally stood, I felt my insides slip out. I reached down to stop the flow, but there was no need; someone had fitted a belt and padded it with a towel.

'Back to bed, sweet girl.' It was Sarah. She was still there, her freckles in full colour, her eyes holding me, still unwavering.

'I should nurse it.'

'Her,' she said.

Her, I thought.

'I should nurse Her.'

❧

NURSE
Of a woman: to suckle, and otherwise attend to, or simply to take care, or charge of an infant.

❧

They were all there: Ditte and Beth, Sarah and the midwife. They watched as I nursed. They heard Her suckling as I heard Her suckling, but they couldn't feel the strength of Her suck or the weight of Her against my belly. They were oblivious to Her smell. For half an hour, Her little noises were the only sound in the room. No one gave voice to their hopes or their fears.

'Tears are quite normal,' said the midwife.

How long had I been weeping?

❧

How many times did I nurse Her? I couldn't count, though I'd meant to. Time became an elastic thing, and the boundary between dreams and waking was blurred. They took it in turns to sit with us, never leaving us alone. I wanted to bury my face in that sweet place below the shell of Her ear, breathe in the warm biscuity smell of Her. 'I could eat you up,' I wanted to say. I wanted to undress Her and trace every chubby crease, kiss Her from head to toe and whisper my love into the pores of her skin.

Several weeks passed. I did none of these things.

❧

Sarah sat on the bed, her large, freckled hand stroking the golden down on our baby's head. 'You can change your mind.'

I'd tried to imagine it a hundred different ways.

'It's not just *my* mind that would need to change,' I said.

She knew this. As she looked at me, I saw relief wrestle with a shadow of regret. She was glad, I think, that I'd said it out loud. She turned from me, took longer than usual to fold a new napkin.

'Shall I take her?' Sarah asked.

I could think of no way to answer. I looked down and noticed milk had pooled at the edge of Her sleeping mouth. I moved a little and watched it dribble down Her chin. I felt the weight of Her, so much heavier than when I'd first held Her. I tried to think of a word that could match Her beauty.

There was none. There are none. There never would be a word to match Her.

I gave Her to Sarah. A few months later, Sarah and Philip emigrated to South Australia.

PART FOUR

1907–1913

Polygenous—Sorrow

September 1907

There was no end to the words. No end to what they meant, or the ways they had been used. Some words' histories stretched so far back that our modern understanding of them was nothing more than an echo of the original, a distortion. I used to think it was the other way round, that the misshapen words of the past were clumsy drafts of what they would become; that the words formed on our tongues, in our time, were true and complete. But I was realising that, in fact, everything that comes after that first utterance is a corruption.

I had forgotten, already, the exact shape of Her ear, the particular blue of Her eyes. They got darker in the weeks I nursed Her; they may have got darker still. I woke every night to Her phantom cry and knew I would never hear a single word wrapped in the music of Her voice. She was perfect when I held Her. Unambiguous. The texture of Her skin, Her smell and the gentle sound of Her sucking could be nothing other than what they were. I had understood Her perfectly.

With every breaking dawn, I recreated the detail of Her. I would start with the translucent nails on Her tiny toes and work my way up through chubby limbs and creamy skin to golden lashes, barely there.

But then I would struggle to recall some little thing, and I understood that as the days and months and years went on my memory of Her would fade.

Lie-child. That's what the midwife had called her. But it wasn't in 'Leisureness to Lief'. I searched the pigeon-holes: five slips, pinned to a top-slip. It had been defined. *A child born out of wedlock; a bastard.* It had been excluded. A note had been written on the top-slip: *Same as love-child – excise.*

But was it? Did I love Bill? Did I miss him?

No. I'd just lain with him.

But I loved Her. I missed Her.

She couldn't be defined by any of the words I found, and eventually I stopped looking.

I worked. I sat at my desk in the Scriptorium and filled the spaces of my mind with other words.

20th September 1907

Dear Harry,

Tucked into your many pages of news about the Dictionary and life in the Scrippy were a few words that have been worrying me. You are not one to exaggerate, and in my opinion you are prone to optimism when none is warranted, so I can only assume your concern for Esme is appropriate.

I have heard of such moods in women who have been through what she has, and we must consider the possibility that she is grieving. Her situation is not uncommon. (The past year has been quite an education in these matters, and you would be surprised at how many young women find themselves in trouble. Some of the stories I've heard are chilling, and I will not repeat them. Suffice to say, our dear Esme is lucky to have such a loving father.) And so, let us continue to care for her until she returns to herself.

We are quite lost without her. As Beth says, her constant enquiring kept us honest. One might have expected her to grow out of it, and there were times, I must confess, when I wished she would just accept the wisdom of others. But she requires convincing, and I am sure my History will be the better for it.

But now you tell me she has fallen quiet, so I have taken the liberty of making a few enquiries.

I have a friend with a small cottage in Shropshire. It is nestled into the hills and has views across to Wales (on a good day, of course). The tenant has recently passed on, and so the cottage is empty. Beth and I spent a week there not so long ago. Beth will vouch for the walking: it is superb, with many steep paths to test the heart and distract the mind. It is just what Esme needs. I can vouch for the comfort: it would not suit some young ladies, but Esme is not fussy.

I have secured the cottage for the month of October. I have also written to James and Ada Murray, and they have agreed that Lizzie should accompany Esme on the trip. Before you protest, Harry, I was very discreet, though I did need a ruse. I said that I'd heard Esme was having trouble recovering from a cold she contracted while staying in Bath. James immediately agreed she should build her strength. He is firmly of the belief that a good walk can cure anything and was keen to point out that he doesn't agree with wrapping people up and sitting them in lounge chairs by the sea the moment they start to cough. I thought he might object to Lizzie being gone for so long, but he admitted she'd had no more than a few days off in years and deserved a holiday. I sent my agreement in the afternoon post of the same day (along with a few words he wasn't expecting for another week, just to ensure he wouldn't change his mind).

My dear Harry, I hope these arrangements suit you, and of course I hope they suit Esme. I'm sure we shall have no problem convincing her. The train journey from Oxford to Shrewsbury is straightforward, and my friend assures me of the cooperation of their neighbour Mr Lloyd. He is paid a small retainer to keep the cottage in good order. He will collect the girls and settle them in.

Yours, etc.

Edith

❧

We arrived at Cobblers Dingle as the sun was setting and the mild day was giving way to a chill. Mr Lloyd insisted he get the fire started in the stove before leaving. As he bent to the job, he informed us he would pop in or send his lad to check the stove and set the fire in the bedroom each afternoon, though the shed was full of cut wood and kindling if the need arose earlier.

Lizzie stood when he bid us farewell. His slight bow was offered to her, and although it was my place, she was forced to respond.

'Thank you, Mr Lloyd,' she said. 'We're most grateful.'

'Anything you need, Miss Lester, I'm but ten minutes up the lane.'

When he'd gone, Lizzie became industrious. As I stood in the doorway, watching Mr Lloyd's buggy recede down the long carriageway into the lane, I heard her opening drawers and cupboards, taking a mental inventory of supplies and kitchen utensils. She found the kettle full and put it on the stove, then she prepared a pot for tea.

'We can be grateful for a well-stocked pantry,' she said, replacing the lid on a tin of tea leaves and pouring the boiled water into the pot before turning towards me. I was still standing in the doorway.

'Come and sit, Essymay.' Lizzie took my arm and led me to a chair at the small kitchen table. After she put the steaming cup in front of me, she touched my arm and sought my gaze. 'It's hot, mind,' she said, as if I were five years old. She had cause for such caution.

Lizzie seemed taller, straighter. It wasn't just that Cobblers Dingle was small. Without the authority of Mrs Murray and the instruction of Mrs Ballard, she took on an air of assurance I'd rarely seen in her. She explored every nook and cranny of the cottage and sought to understand its many idiosyncrasies. She is mistress of this place, I thought on our second morning, the idea breaking through the fog of my mind like a shaft of light, but quickly retreating from the effort of further contemplation.

I sat where she placed me and watched her perpetual motion around me. If I roused, it was because she propelled me. I never resisted, but I was incapable of initiating anything.

A few days after we arrived, Mr Lloyd came to the kitchen door with a cake from Mrs Lloyd and a basket of eggs. Lizzie was forced, once again, to talk with him. She managed three sentences instead of her previous two.

The day after that, Mr Lloyd sent his son, Tommy, to tend the fires. Lizzie insisted he join us for tea and proceeded to interrogate him about the opportunities for walking in the area.

'There's a path that goes right up the hill to the copse of beech trees,' he said, his mouth full of his mother's cake. 'It's steep, but the view is good. From there you choose to go where you like, just mind you shut the gates.'

⁓

Lizzie bent to tie the laces of my boots. It was a familiar gesture from years before. Her head was uncovered, and grey hair grew like wire from her crown. She's growing old, I thought. But she was only eight years my senior. It had always seemed more. I wondered if she wished for a different life, if she imagined Cobblers Dingle as her own little house. I wondered if she pined for a baby she would probably never have.

Mr Lloyd had doffed his hat and looked her in the eyes when he spoke. *Anything you need, Miss Lester.* And she'd blushed, as if it was the first time a man had gone out of his way for her. But she was too old now, I thought. Too old to do anything other than what she had been doing since she was eleven. Bending to tie my laces. Bending to one task after another at someone else's behest. One or two of my tears fell into the nest of her hair, but she didn't notice.

By the time we reached the path, our skirt hems were damp from crossing the small field beside the cottage, and I was already out of breath. Lizzie was diligent about securing the gate, so I had time to assess the route. It was as steep and uneven as Tommy had warned, and the top of the hill – who knew how far up – was hidden by a meandering line of trees. Twisted, moss-covered branches encroached onto the path here and there, and I realised the route must have rarely been used by anything taller than a sheep. More than anything, I wanted to turn back.

'This will help,' said Lizzie, coming up beside me. She held out a sturdy stick.

I tried to fashion a sentence that would convince her to let me return to the cottage, but she shook her head. She pushed the stick into my hand, and I noticed her cheeks were red from exertion and her eyes were bright. She held on to the stick until she was sure I wouldn't drop it, as if passing the baton in a relay. I tightened my grip, and she released hers. Then she turned and led the way up the narrow path.

It was a relief when the path veered away from the trees. It cut a wobbly and fathomless trail across the hill, as if the sheep who made it were trying to reduce the incline. Lizzie trusted it to lead her in the right direction, and I found my tread falling rhythmically behind hers. We walked in silence until Lizzie saw a stile.

'This way,' she said.

Lizzie tried to pull up her skirts to climb the wooden structure, but as she released one hand to steady herself, the fabric dropped and caught on the weathered timber. I hadn't thought to bring a split skirt, and neither had she. I should have known better – I'd spent a year in Scotland, where walking was the only relief from that dreadful school, and shorter split skirts were part of the uniform. But Lizzie had never left Oxford, and she had packed for both of us.

Lizzie began to laugh. 'We'll wear trousers tomorrow,' she said.

'We can't wear trousers.'

'We have no choice. All the clothes in that wardrobe at the cottage belong to a man,' she said. 'I'm sure no one will mind if we borrow them.'

The next day, Lizzie laid two pairs of trousers on the bed for us to change into after breakfast.

'Have you ever worn trousers, Lizzie?' I asked when I joined her in the kitchen.

'Never in my life,' she said, smiling as if she knew the pleasure that awaited.

Lizzie had cooked oats overnight in the low heat of the range. She drizzled them with fresh cream from the Lloyds and topped them with apples she had stewed before I woke.

'Everything aches,' I said, holding the edges of the chair to lower myself into it.

'I know,' Lizzie said. 'But it's a wholesome ache, not a knackered ache.'

'An ache is an ache.'

'I can't recall a day when I haven't had an ache in some part of my body. This is the first time I've thought it might be a sign of good, not ill.'

I took up my spoon and stirred the apple and cream into the porridge. There was an ache in the centre of me that I couldn't shift, but that morning I did feel it a little less urgently.

After breakfast, Lizzie pulled on a large pair of trousers and an oversized shirt.

'They're too big, Lizzie.'

'Nothing a belt won't fix,' she said, searching the wardrobe for one. 'And who's around to judge?'

'Mr Lloyd could pop in at any time.'

She coloured a little, but shrugged. 'He don't seem the type to judge.'

My trousers were made for a smaller man, or perhaps the same man when he was young. They were short in the leg but a better fit around the waist. Lizzie insisted I too wear an oversized shirt so she wouldn't have to wash my blouses each day.

'There's a pair of thick socks in the drawer,' Lizzie said. 'They'll keep your ankles from getting scratched.'

Down in the kitchen, Lizzie bent to my boots then to her own. She found hats on a hook at the back of the pantry door and placed them on our heads. Then she took the walking stick she'd saved from the day before and put it in my hand.

We stood opposite each other, fully dressed, and Lizzie took me in. 'You look like a wanderer,' she said, then she looked down at her own attire and turned round so I could admire the full effect. She chuckled, and the chuckle became a laugh, and the laugh overwhelmed her until her eyes streamed and her nose ran. She was right. I imagined the townsfolk of Oxford throwing bread ends and coppers into our hats. I didn't laugh, but I couldn't stop a smile.

We walked after breakfast and every afternoon. I kept the stick, but needed it less as I began to feel stronger. I hadn't known, exactly, that I'd been weak, but the walking and Lizzie's porridge and Mrs Lloyd's cakes were reviving something in me. I slept less and noticed more.

Lizzie no longer blushed when Mr Lloyd spoke to her. She met his eye and, if he asked, she gave him her opinion without looking down. After a week, Mrs Lloyd began bringing her cakes in person. She would accompany Mr Lloyd or Tommy in the afternoon and stay after they had set the fires. It became Lizzie's habit to bake biscuits every morning and to lay the kitchen table for tea every afternoon. She laid it for four, though Mr Lloyd always declined. 'I'd only stop you ladies talking of what you will,' he said one day, backing out of the kitchen with his hat pressed against his belly, a slight bend to his back as if he were taking leave of the king.

As soon as he was gone, Lizzie would arrange a plate with biscuits and generous slices of Mrs Lloyd's cake. Then she would put the kettle on to boil and busy herself with tea leaves and pot. Mrs Lloyd, already seated in the chair facing the stove, would start up the conversation wherever they had left off the day before. Their banter always went back and forth like a game of badminton, as if they'd known each other their entire lives. I felt I was seeing Lizzie as she might have been.

I caught myself wondering why Mrs Lloyd never stood to lend a hand – I had plenty of time to ponder, as my reserve had deflected all polite attempts at inclusion. I rejected all the obvious reasons: rudeness, laziness, fatigue from tending her own hearth and four boys. In the end, I decided it was kindness. There was nothing demanding about Mrs Lloyd's manner, and she didn't watch the tea being poured in order to judge its strength. She was simply acknowledging that this was Lizzie's kitchen, Lizzie's little cottage, and she was her guest. I'd been watching Lizzie make tea my whole life, but it was always for the Murrays, Mrs Ballard (who always watched the tea being poured) or for me: her mistress, her boss or her charge. The thought shocked me. I'd never once seen Lizzie with a friend.

I started making my excuses. With little protest, Lizzie began to lay the table for two.

Shropshire had been organised as a kind of treatment for my depression. I couldn't have thought about it so clearly before, but as the heaviness of living without Her began to lift I realised I might have thrown myself into the Cherwell if I'd had the wherewithal to think of it.

The hill demanded payment, and I knew I would never reach the top without the pain of the climb in my lungs and legs, no matter how fit I became. I'd complained about it those first few days – sat down and cried for lack of breath, and other things. I didn't want to be there. But Lizzie had never let me turn back.

'It's the kind of pain that achieves something,' she said.

'What does it achieve?' I moaned.

'Time will tell,' she said, pulling me to my feet.

Then one afternoon I made it to the top without tears or complaint.

I stood with my hands on my hips, breathing in the cooling air and looking beyond the valley towards Wales. I'd seen the view every day for weeks, but it was the first time I'd cared for it.

'I wonder what those hills are called,' I said.

'Wenlock Edge, according to Mr Lloyd,' said Lizzie.

I looked at her in surprise. What else did she know?

She stopped watching me so closely after that, and sometimes, when she and Mrs Lloyd had more anecdotes than one pot of tea could accommodate, she let me walk the hills alone.

'I'm a bondmaid to the Dictionary,' I heard Lizzie say to Mrs Lloyd one afternoon as I pulled on my boots.

'And you say young Esme is one of them that finds the words?' said Mrs Lloyd.

Lizzie laughed and I threw her a look. 'You could say that,' she said, giving me a wink.

'I can't think of anything more boring,' said Mrs Lloyd. 'Do you remember having to write the same word over and over till all the letters slanted the same way? Numbers made more sense to me. Their meaning never changes.'

'I never did make all the letters slant the same way,' said Lizzie.

'There's many that don't,' said Mrs Lloyd, taking another biscuit.

I picked up the walking stick that now leaned by the door.

'Will you be all right?' said Lizzie. Her voice was light, but her gaze was watchful.

'I will,' I said. 'Enjoy your tea.'

As I climbed the hill, I wondered what Lizzie and Mrs Lloyd were talking about. It was the first time I'd cared to think about it, and I was shocked that I'd been so self-absorbed. Sheep scattered from the path as I walked along, but they didn't go far. They watched me pass, and I was reminded of the scrutiny of scholars when I walked into the reading room at Cambridge. It wasn't an uncomfortable thought.

I'd felt a little triumphant then, and I felt a little triumphant now. As though perhaps I'd achieved something.

❧

Lizzie climbed out of the buggy, and Tommy climbed out after her. 'I'll get that, Miss Lester,' he said, reaching for the basket of provisions in the back.

'Thank you, Tommy,' said Lizzie. She watched him take the basket into the kitchen then looked up at Mrs Lloyd. 'Lovely morning, Natasha. For sure, I'll miss our outings.'

Natasha. What an exotic name for a farmer's wife. I continued to watch them through the open window of the bedroom. Mrs Lloyd shimmied across the front seat of the buggy and leaned down to rest her hand on Lizzie's upturned cheek. '*Bostin*,' I heard her say. I didn't know what it meant, but Lizzie seemed to. She covered Mrs Lloyd's hand with hers as if she were grateful for the comment. They carried on their farewell in quieter tones. When I saw Tommy heading back to the buggy, I hurried down the stairs to say my own goodbye and wave them off.

As soon as we were back in the house, I turned to Lizzie. 'What did Mrs Lloyd mean when she said *bostin*?'

Lizzie turned towards the stove, intent on getting the kettle on to boil.

'Oh, it's just an endearment.'

'But I've never heard it before.'

'Nor me,' Lizzie said, taking our teacups from beside the basin, where I'd left them to dry that morning. 'Natasha said it once or twice, and other people besides. I thought it was a foreign word so I asked where it was from.'

'What did she say?' I searched my pockets, but they were empty. Lizzie poured hot water into the pot to warm it. She opened the tin of tea in readiness.

'The word's from here – not foreign at all.'

I looked around the kitchen, but there was nothing to write on or with.

'There's a notebook and pencils in the top drawer beside your bed,' Lizzie said, picking up the pot and rotating it to warm the sides. 'You fetch them first.'

Lizzie was sitting at the table when I came back down; our cups were steaming, and there were a plate of biscuits and a pair of scissors beside the pot. 'To cut the page down to size,' Lizzie said.

When I was ready, she began. I was reminded of old Mabel, and the reverence she gave to this process. What was it that made them sit up straighter and check their thoughts before they spoke? Why did they care so much?

'*Bostin*,' Lizzie said, pronouncing the *n* with care. 'It means *lovely*.' She blushed.

'Can you put it in a sentence?'

'I can, but you must write Natasha's name below it.'

'Of course.'

'Lizzie Lester, my *bostin mairt*.'

I wrote out the slip, then cut another.

'And *mairt*? What does that mean?'

'Friend,' said Lizzie. 'Natasha is my friend, my *mairt*.'

I guessed at the spelling, and looked forward to adding these new words to my trunk. It had been a while since I had thought about it.

Tomorrow we would be gone from Cobblers Dingle. I was going to miss the waves of green hills. I would miss the silence. When we first came, I found it too quiet, my thoughts too loud. But the silence had turned out not to be complete: the valley hummed and sang and bleated. When my thoughts had been heard and argued with, and when some kind of peace had been struck, I'd begun to listen to the valley like some would listen to music or a holy chant. There was solace in its rhythm, and it slowed the beat of my heart.

I seemed better, according to Ditte. Her letters had been regular, even if mine, in the beginning, had not. I had recently regained the habit of writing to her, and apparently this was one sign of my improving health. Another, Ditte wrote, was an unexpected letter from Lizzie.

Mrs Lloyd penned it. How brave of Lizzie to ask. She wrote that 'Everything is high or deep or endless — there's no shortage of places to do yourself in, yet Essy comes home every time with no sign of trying.' If only everyone was as straight-speaking as her.

Was I better? Before Shropshire I'd felt broken, as though I would fall should the scaffold of my work be removed. I didn't feel that now, but there was a fine crack through the middle of me, and I suspected it might never mend. I remembered Lizzie apologising to Mrs Lloyd the first time she stayed to chat, for the chip in the cup.

'A chip doesn't stop it from holding tea,' Mrs Lloyd had said.

As our final day ended, the sky blushed pink – a parting gift, I thought. Lizzie had made a picnic of cheese, bread and Mrs Lloyd's sweet cucumber pickle. She laid it on the lawn beside the cottage.

'God is in this place,' she said, without shifting her gaze from Wenlock Edge.

'Do you think so, Lizzie?'

'Oh, yes. I feel him more here than I ever have in church. Out here it's like we're stripped of all our clothes, of the callouses on our hands that tell our place, of our accents and words. He cares for none of it. All that matters is who you are in your heart. I've never loved him as much as I should, but here I do.'

'Why is that?' I asked.

'I reckon it's the first time he's noticed me.'

For a very long time, neither of us spoke. The sun broke through a long brushstroke of cloud and came down over Wenlock Edge and the Long Mynd behind it – one was like a shadow of the other.

'Do you think he'll forgive me, Lizzie?' It was barely more than a thought, but I knew I'd spoken the words.

Lizzie stayed silent, and the Long Mynd finally made a memory of the setting sun, leaving a landscape of blue hills. When she got up and went into the cottage, I realised it was not God's forgiveness I cared about; it was hers. I imagined her dilemma. She wanted to reassure me, but couldn't lie with God's face turned on her.

The drone that had been filling my ears since She was born, the shade that had been drawn over my eyes, the dull feeling in my arms and legs and breasts – they lifted all at once. I could hear and see and feel with an intensity that stole my breath and frightened me. I shivered, suddenly cold. There was the faintest smell of coal smoke and the sounds of birds calling their own to roost, their songs as clear and distinct as church bells. My face was wet with loss and love and regret. And woven through it all there was a thread of shameful relief.

Lizzie came out with a rug, crocheted in all the colours of an autumn wood. She wrapped it around my shoulders and weighed it down with her solid arms.

'It's not his place to forgive you, Essymay,' she whispered into my ear. 'It's no one's but yours.'

November 1907

Lizzie and I stepped from the train. We put our cases down and pulled the collars of our coats higher against the November chill. Shropshire had been our Indian summer, and Oxford felt like winter. As we waited for a cab to take us to Sunnyside, I had to remind myself that behind the hard stone of all the buildings, a river flowed.

At Sunnyside, scarlet leaves still clung to the ash between the Scriptorium and the kitchen. Lizzie and I stood beneath it to say our goodbyes. It had a heaviness about it, this farewell, as if we were leaving to travel in different directions, when in fact we were back on shared and familiar ground. But something had shifted. Lizzie was different, or perhaps it was just that now I saw her differently, as a woman who existed beyond my need for her. When we'd left Oxford I'd been her charge, as always. Now we embraced as friends, comfort going in both directions. In Shropshire, we had each found something we'd longed for, but as I held her, I feared Lizzie's new confidence would be too fragile to survive who she had to be in Oxford. She had her own concerns for me, and she voiced them into the quiet space of our embrace.

'It's not about forgiveness, Essymay. We can't always make the choices we'd like, but we can try to make the best of what we must settle for. Take care not to dwell.'

She searched my face, but I couldn't give her the assurance she wanted. I hugged her a little tighter, but promised nothing.

Mrs Ballard was leaning on a walking stick and holding the kitchen door for Lizzie. I turned towards the Scriptorium. It was time to return to our lives.

Every time I came home, the Scriptorium seemed smaller. I'd been grateful for it when I returned from Ditte's: it had wrapped around me, and as long as I'd stayed within its word-lined walls I'd felt protected. This time was different. I stood in the doorway, my travelling bag still heavy in my hand, and wondered how I would fit.

There were three new assistants. Two had joined the sorting table, and the other was set up at a new desk a little too close to my own. Da saw me hovering, and his face broke into a smile that threatened to overwhelm me. He pushed back his chair in such haste that it toppled. As he tried to catch it, the papers he was working with went flying. I dropped my bag and went to help, bending to reach beneath the sorting table for a stray slip. I handed it to Da, who took my hand and held it to his lips. Then he searched my face, as Lizzie had just done.

I nodded, gave a small smile. He was satisfied, but there was so much to say and too many people looking on. Work around the sorting table was suspended, and I felt stupid for coming straight to the Scriptorium instead of going home. But I'd known Da would be working, and I was afraid of an empty house.

He hooked my arm through his and turned me towards the new assistants.

'Mr Cushing, Mr Pope, this is my daughter, Esme.'

Mr Cushing and Mr Pope both stood. One was tall and fair, the other short and dark, and each offered a hand in greeting then pulled it back to allow the other to go first. My own hand hung awkwardly, unshaken, between us. If they weren't so preoccupied with each other I might have wondered if they were avoiding the touch of melted skin, but they laughed. Then each urged the other to proceed, and the farce continued.

'Just bow to the young lady and try not to bang your heads,' said Mr Sweatman from the other side of the sorting table. 'You see what happens when you leave us, Esme? We must make do with music-hall comedians.'

Mr Cushing, the taller, bowed, which gave Mr Pope the opportunity to take my hand.

'Well, that's cheating,' said Mr Cushing.

'Opportunistic, my friend. Fortune favours the bold.'

They began addressing me in turns. They were pleased to meet me, had heard so much about my work on the Dictionary, were delighted when Da told them about my research for Miss Thompson – they had studied her history of England at school. They hoped my lungs had felt the benefit of my time in Shropshire. I blushed at the thought I'd been the topic of conversation, at the truth and lies of it.

'Dr Murray will be glad for the sight of you, Miss Nicoll,' said Mr Cushing. 'Only yesterday, he mentioned in passing that we take up twice the room but produce half the copy of the young woman who works at the back of the Scriptorium. I presume that is you, and it is a pleasure.' Again, he bowed.

'We weren't offended,' Mr Pope was quick to say. 'We're blow-ins. Here for the semester. Our reward for studying philology. I think I've learned more this past month than I would in a year at Balliol. I also take my hat off to you, Miss Nicoll.'

There was an audible sigh from the back of the Scriptorium.

'You are disturbing the peace, Mr Pope,' Da said with a smile.

'Quite,' said Mr Pope, and he and Mr Cushing nodded towards me and lowered themselves back into their chairs.

Da took my elbow and led me to the back of the Scriptorium.

'Mr Dankworth, may I introduce my daughter, Esme.'

Mr Dankworth finished the edit he was making, rose from his chair and offered a curt nod. 'Miss Nicoll.'

I returned the nod and the greeting, and he resumed his seat. His attention was back on the pages in front of him before Da and I had turned to leave.

'Not a blow-in,' Da said, when we were out of earshot.

The next day, the Scriptorium was even more crowded. Dr Murray was sitting at his high desk, and Elsie and Rosfrith Murray were moving about the shelves as they so often did when their father was at work. They each greeted me with an embrace, the warmth of which was unprecedented but not unwelcome.

'I hope you are quite well now, Esme,' Elsie said quietly, and I wondered what story she had been told. But before there was any more conversation, Dr Murray interrupted.

'Ah, good,' he said, when he saw me standing with his daughters. He came over with a sheet of paper in one hand and a pile of slips in the other. 'The etymology of *prophesy* has caused Mr Cushing some concern. It is obvious where he has strayed.' Mr Cushing caught my eye and nodded in agreement. 'Perhaps you could review his efforts and make the necessary corrections? They will need to be ready for typesetting in a week.' Dr Murray handed me the materials. Then, as an afterthought, he said, 'A good walk. It does one the world of good, don't you agree?'

'Yes, sir,' I said.

He looked at me as if trying to judge the truth of my answer, then he turned and went back to his work.

I made my way around the sorting table, said good morning to

Mr Sweatman and *bonan matenon* to Mr Maling, and rested my hand on Da's shoulder for just a moment. He patted my hand, and when he turned to look towards the back of the Scriptorium, I realised it was a conciliatory gesture. I could barely see my cherished workspace beyond the bulk of Mr Dankworth, whose desk had been placed perpendicular to mine.

When I was closer, I saw that the surface of my desk was piled with books and papers that I knew I hadn't left there a month ago. I remembered the stray slips with women's words sitting inside it, waiting to join the others in the trunk under Lizzie's bed. Anxiety fluttered in my chest.

Mr Dankworth must have heard me approach, but he didn't turn round. I stood beside him for a moment, taking him in. He was large, not fat, and everything about him was as neat as a pin. His dark hair was short and parted in a straight line, right down the middle. He had no beard and no moustache, and his fingernails were as well kept as a woman's. He must have chosen to sit with his back to everyone.

'Good morning, Mr Dankworth,' I said.

He glanced at me. 'Good morning, Miss Nicoll.'

'Please, call me Esme.'

He nodded and looked back to his work.

'Mr Dankworth, I was wondering if I could reclaim my desk?' There was no indication he'd heard me. 'Mr Dankworth, I—'

'Yes, Miss Nicoll, I heard you. If I could finish this entry, I'll attend to it.'

'Oh, of course.' I stood, waiting for permission to proceed. How easily I was put in my place.

He continued to bend over his proofs. From where I stood, I could see ruler-straight lines through unwanted copy and neat corrections noted in margins. His left elbow rested on the desk, and his hand massaged his temple as if coaxing the words out of his brain. I recognised something of my own attitude in this posture, and my first impression of him, not at all charitable, moved a little towards the positive.

A minute passed. Then another.

'Mr Dankworth?'

His hand fell with a thump against the desk, and his head jerked up. I saw his shoulders lift with a deep breath and imagined his eyes rolled towards the heavens. He pushed his chair back and moved between his desk and mine. There was barely room for him.

'Let me help you,' I said, picking up a book from my desk and trying to catch his eye.

He took it from me, his eyes averted. 'No need; there's an order. I'll do it.'

He removed the last book, and I waited, fingertips kneading my skirt, to see if he would turn back to my desk and lift the lid. For a moment, I was back at school, lined up with all the other girls ready for inspection. The insides of our desks, our stockings, our drawers. I never understood why they mattered. Mr Dankworth returned to his chair, and the sound of its protest brought me back to the Scriptorium. He'd finished. My desk was bare. But there was now a wall of books along the front and side edge of Mr Dankworth's desk. An effective screen.

I sat down and spread out the pile of slips for *prophesy*. I ordered them by date, then referred to the notes Mr Cushing had prepared.

A week went by, and the Scriptorium felt like an old friend I had to reacquaint myself with. Mr Pope and Mr Cushing rose from their chairs every time Elsie, Rosfrith or I entered, and competed to help or pay the nicest compliments. Their loquaciousness was an irritation to almost everyone except Da, who rewarded their attentions to me with small smiles and nods. Dr Murray was not so encouraging.

'Gentlemen, the more words you employ to flatter the ladies the fewer you define. Your constant use of the English language is, in fact, doing it a disservice.' They quickly turned to their work.

Mr Dankworth was a different matter altogether. The only words that passed between us were related to the inevitable inconvenience of me having to pass by his desk to get to mine. 'Excuse me, Mr Dankworth'; 'My apologies, Mr Dankworth'; 'Your satchel, Mr Dankworth, perhaps you could keep it under your desk so I don't have to keep stepping over it?'

'He's very good at what he does,' Da said one evening as I was preparing dinner. A maid now came four afternoons a week, which left three dinners for us to cook ourselves. *Mrs Beeton's Book of Household Management* was stained with my efforts, but I wasn't improving.

'He has an eagle-eye for inconsistency and redundancy, and he rarely makes mistakes.'

'But he's odd, don't you think?' I brought the hashed cod to the table. It sat like a stagnant pool within its mashed potato border.

'We're all a bit odd, Esme, though perhaps lexicographers are odder than most.'

'I don't think he likes me very much.' I served Da and then myself.

'I don't think he likes people very much; doesn't understand them. You mustn't take it personally.' Da took a sip of water and cleared his throat. 'And what about Mr Pope and Mr Cushing? How do you find them?'

'Oh, very pleasant. And funny, in a fumbling way.' The cod was overcooked and under-salted. Da seemed not to notice.

'Yes. Nice young men. Is there one you prefer? Good families I'm told, both of them.' He took another sip of water. 'I wonder, Essy. Do you ... I mean, would you consider ...'

I put down my knife and fork and looked at him. Beads of perspiration were gathering at his temples. He loosened his tie.

'Da, what are you trying to say?'

He took his handkerchief and wiped his brow. 'Lily would have had all this in hand.'

'Had what in hand?'

'Your future. Your security. Marriage and such.'

'*Marriage and such*?'

'It never occurred to me that it was something I should arrange. Ditte would normally … but it doesn't seem to have occurred to her either.'

'Arrange?'

'Well, not arrange. *Facilitate*.' He looked down at his food then back up at me. 'I failed you, Essy. I wasn't paying attention; I wasn't really sure what I should be paying attention *to*, and now …'

'And now, what?'

He hesitated. 'And now you're twenty-five.'

I stared him down. He looked away. We ate in silence for a while.

'What exactly *is* a good family, Da?'

I could see he was relieved the subject had shifted a little.

'Well, I suppose for some it's about reputation. Others, money. For others it might be education or good works.'

'But what does it mean for you?'

He wiped his mouth with a napkin, then placed his knife and fork on the empty plate.

'Well?'

He came round to my side of the table and sat beside me. 'Love, Essy. A good family is one where there is love.'

I nodded. 'Thank goodness for that, because I have neither education nor money, and my reputation relies on secrets and lies.' I pushed my own plate away in frustration. The fish was inedible.

'Oh, my dear, dear girl. I know I've let you down, but I don't know how to fix things.'

'Do you still love me, after everything that has happened?'

'Of course I do.'

'Then you have not let me down.' I took up his hand and stroked the freckled skin on the back. It was dry, but the palm of his hand and the pads of his fingers were as smooth as silk. They always had been, and I'd always found it curious. 'I have made mistakes, Da, and I have made choices. One of those choices was not to seek a marriage.'

'Would it have been possible?' he asked.

'Yes, I think so. But it was not what I wanted.'

'But, Essy, life is hard for women who aren't married.'

'Ditte seems to cope. Eleanor Bradley seems happy; Rosfrith and Elsie aren't engaged, as far as I know.'

He searched my face, trying to understand what I was saying, what it meant. He was editing the future he thought I would have, excising the wedding, the son-in-law, the grandchildren. A sadness clouded his eyes. I thought of Her.

'Oh, Da.' Tears fell, and neither of us wiped our cheeks. 'I have to think that I've made the right decisions. Please, please, just keep loving me. It's what you do best.'

He nodded.

'And promise me.'

'Anything.'

'Don't try to fix things. You are a brilliant lexicographer but not a matchmaker.'

He smiled. 'I promise.'

The Scriptorium was an uncomfortable place for a while. Though I demurred, and Da stopped encouraging their efforts to impress me, Mr Pope and Mr Cushing were slow to understand. 'They are a bit slow with everything,' Da commented with an apologetic smile.

But the source of most of my discomfort was Mr Dankworth. Before he arrived, my desk had the perfect amount of privacy and perspective.

I could do my work without interference, and when I paused I needed only to lean a fraction to my right to have a view of the sorting table and of Dr Murray on his perch. If I leaned a fraction further, I could see who came and went through the Scriptorium door. Now, when I looked to my right, my view was the bulk of Mr Dankworth's hunched shoulders and the perfect part of his hair. I felt imprisoned.

Then he began scrutinising my work.

I was the least qualified assistant in the Scriptorium; even Rosfrith outranked me, having finished her schooling. But no one brought it to my attention quite like Mr Dankworth. He had a particular way of interacting with each and every person in the Scriptorium based on where he thought they sat in the hierarchy. He practically bowed in front of Dr Murray. He deferred to Da and Mr Sweatman, and he ignored Mr Cushing and Mr Pope on the grounds, I suppose, that they were 'blow-ins'. He had a strange reaction to Elsie and Rosfrith – I'm not sure he knew one from the other, having never met either's eye, but he skirted around them both as if they represented a ledge from which he might fall. He never corrected them or questioned them, though, and I came to think their father's name protected them from his scrutiny and disdain. Those, he reserved chiefly for me.

'This is not right,' he said one day when I came back from eating my lunch. He was standing by my desk and holding a small square of paper in his large hand. I recognised it as a variant meaning I had pinned to the proof I was editing.

'I beg your pardon?'

'Your syntax is not clear. I have rewritten it.'

I manoeuvred past him and sat at my desk. Sure enough, a new square of paper was pinned to the proof with Mr Dankworth's precise handwriting. It said what it should say, and I tried to figure out how it was different from what I had written.

'Mr Dankworth, may I have my original?'

He didn't answer, and when I looked up I could see it was too late. He was by the grate, watching it burn.

～

Christmas still hung from trees, inside and out. As we walked towards Sunnyside, Da pointed out every decorated version he spied through the windows of sitting rooms along St Margaret's Road. We'd made a game of this once, searching these private spaces for the grandest or most charming tree, trying to guess what gifts were underneath and the nature of the children who would rush to unwrap them. It wasn't a game I wanted to play now. I hadn't counted Christmas among my losses, but it became clear that I'd given it away when I'd given Her away. As Da tried to pull me out of the reflective mood I'd settled into, I wondered what else I had forfeited.

The Scriptorium was empty when we arrived. We would have it to ourselves, Da said, until Mr Sweatman, Mr Pope and Mr Cushing returned on Wednesday. The Murrays were in Scotland until the new year, and the other assistants would trickle in towards the end of the week.

'And Mr Dankworth?' I asked.

'First Monday of the new year,' Da said. 'You have a whole week without him looking over your shoulder.'

The relief must have been plain on my face. He smiled. 'Not every gift is wrapped and under the tree.'

The next few days passed in a nostalgic blur. Each morning we collected the post, which I sorted and reviewed and delivered to the desk of the intended recipient. If there were slips, they became my morning's work.

When Mr Sweatman returned, he spent a few minutes pacing the room and casting his eye over the sorting table and the smaller desks. 'It may look as if Cushing and Pope have just stepped out for lunch, but I am reliably informed that by mutual agreement they will not be returning,' he said at last. 'Murray calculated their contribution in the negative and suggested they pursue careers in banking. Jolly good advice, Pope said, and they all shook hands.'

Their places at the sorting table were strewn with papers and books.

'I'll tidy up then, shall I?' I opened the covers of one or two books to identify their owners.

'An excellent idea,' said Mr Sweatman. 'And when it's cleared, it should suit Mr Dankworth perfectly, don't you think?'

I looked at him. 'Do you think he'll prefer it?'

'It was always Murray's intention that Dankworth sit with the rest of us, but Cushing and Pope needed supervision and there wasn't the room. I have no doubt your peace will be restored before we've all acquired the habit of writing 1908 instead of 1907.'

My peace was not restored. Mr Dankworth said that he had established ways of working that would be disturbed if he moved to the sorting table. Of course, I thought. It would be far harder to review my corrections if he moved.

Mr Sweatman made the suggestion regularly, but Mr Dankworth was consistent in his reply that he was comfortable with the current arrangement, thank you very much, curt nod.

As the days lengthened towards spring, my mood lightened. I looked forward to errands outside the Scriptorium and I wore a triangular path between Sunnyside, the Press and the Bodleian Library.

I was taking books from the basket by the door and putting them in the crate attached to the back of the bicycle when Dr Murray came up to me.

'Corrected proofs for Mr Hart, and the slips for *romanity*.' He handed me three pages with editing marks all over them and a small bundle of slips, ordered and numbered and tied with string. As I was putting them in my satchel, one of the corrections caught my eye. It would have to wait. I walked my bicycle out onto the Banbury Road and headed towards Little Clarendon Street.

Little Clarendon was just round the corner from the Press and always crowded with people. Leaving my bike near the window of a tea shop, I took a table inside, waited for the waitress to bring me a pot of tea, then took the proofs from my satchel. There were seven double pages: three from Da, three from Mr Dankworth and one from Ditte. Ditte's was creased from its confinement in an ordinary envelope, but just like the others it was winged with comments and new entries written in her familiar hand. Dr Murray had made additional notes against hers, agreeing or disagreeing – his opinion would always be the final edit.

The correction I was looking for was one of Da's, an additional entry pinned to the proof's edge. There was a ruler-straight line through every word and Mr Dankworth had rewritten it. When? I wondered. And did Da know? I unpinned it from the proof.

I checked the pockets of my skirt and was pleased to find a small number of blank slips and the stub of a pencil. Like the skirt, neither had been used in a long while. I took a slip and rewrote the entry exactly as Da had composed it, then I pinned it where the original had been. I looked carefully at the rest of Da's proofs and found two, three, four other occasions when Mr Dankworth had interfered.

I began to rewrite Da's original edits, my confidence increasing with every word, but when I came to the last, my hand froze. It was an entry for *mother*. The proof already gave the first meaning as *A female parent,* but to this Mr Dankworth had added, *A woman who has given birth to a child.*

I left it.

November 1908

Lizzie looked up from where she was kneading dough at the kitchen table.

'There's a troubled face if ever I saw one,' she said.

'I've made three mistakes this morning,' I said. 'He makes me so nervous.' I slumped into a chair.

'Let me guess. Mr Sweatman? Mr Maling? Or could it be that you're talking about Mr Dankworth?'

Lizzie had been hearing versions of this complaint since we'd returned home from Shropshire a year before. I'd been escaping to her kitchen as often as I could. Usually she would work around me, but if there was a letter from Mrs Lloyd she'd brew a fresh pot and place a plate of biscuits, morning-baked, between us as I read aloud. She was recreating her Shropshire mornings, and I was always careful not to insert myself between her and her friend. I'd read carefully, without comment or pause, and when I was done I would take a pen and paper from the kitchen drawer and wait for Lizzie to compose her response. *My dearest Natasha*, she would always start.

Today there was no letter and there were no biscuits. I took a sandwich from the plate on the kitchen table. 'He watches me,' I said, taking a bite.

Lizzie looked up with raised eyebrows.

'Not in that way. *Definitely* not in that way. He can't say good morning, but he has no trouble telling me where I've gone wrong with grammar or style. This morning he told me I'd taken liberties with a variant meaning of *psychotic*. In his opinion, females are prone to overstatement, and for that reason should not be employed where precision is needed.'

'Had you taken liberties?' she teased.

'It would never occur to me,' I replied, smiling.

Lizzie kept kneading.

'When I came back from lunch yesterday, he'd left a copy of *Hart's Rules* on my desk. He'd pinned notes to my edits with the page numbers I should refer to in order to improve my corrections.'

'Are *Hart's Rules* important?'

'They're mainly for compositors and readers at the Press, but they help to make sure that everyone working on the Dictionary is writing in the same way, using the same spelling.'

'You mean there are different ways of writing and spelling?'

'I know it sounds like codswallop but there are, and the smallest thing can cause the biggest arguments.'

Lizzie smiled. 'And what would the *Rules* say about *codswallop*?'

'Nothing; it's not a valid word.'

'But you've written it on a slip. I remember you doing it, right here at this table.'

'That's because it's an excellent word.'

'Did it help? Him giving you the *Rules*?'

'No. It just makes me question myself at every turn. Things I knew for sure are suddenly confusing. I'm working more slowly and making more errors than ever.'

Lizzie shaped the dough and put it in a tin, then she dusted it with flour. She was assured in this, as she was with everything that needed doing in the kitchen. Since her last fall, Mrs Ballard only came in to cook Sunday roast and write the lists for the weekly orders. Lizzie did everything else, though there were fewer Murrays to feed as the children were all grown and most had left. An occasional maid came most days to help in the house.

'Will you come with me to the market on Saturday?' Lizzie asked carefully. 'Old Mabel's been asking after you.'

Mabel. I hadn't seen her since … The thought wouldn't configure itself. Since what? Since I'd asked for her help? Since I'd gone to Ditte's? Since Her. This was what happened every time I thought about my last visit to Mabel. It marked a moment in time, and thinking about it caused me to think of Her. I wondered how Sarah and Philip might have celebrated Her first birthday. What gift they would give Her for Christmas. I imagined Her walking and wished I'd heard Her first word.

'She has a word for you,' Lizzie said, and I looked up, startled. For a moment I wasn't sure who she was talking about. 'Says she's been saving it. I wouldn't ask, but I don't reckon Mabel's long for this place.'

I rose early and dressed with unnecessary care. I was nervous about seeing Mabel. Ashamed it had taken me so long. When the morning post fell through the slot in the door, I was glad for the distraction. It was one of Tilda's sporadic postcards. The picture on the front was of the Houses of Parliament in Westminster.

2nd November 1908

My dear Esme,

You told me once that you wished our slogan was 'Words not Deeds' instead of 'Deeds not Words', and I laughed at your naivety. So, when I heard about Muriel Matters chaining herself to the grille in the Ladies' Gallery in the House of Commons, I could not help but think of you.

It was an ingenious act of attention-seeking (I'm sure Mrs Pankhurst wishes she had thought of it), but it will be her words that move minds. She is the first woman to speak in the House of Commons, and her words were intelligent and eloquently spoken. Hansard may not record them, but the newspapers have. She is Australian, apparently. Perhaps it is the right to speak in her own Parliament that gives her the confidence to speak in ours.

'We have sat behind this insulting grille for too long,' she said. 'It is time that the women of England were given a voice in legislation which affects them as much as it affects men. We demand the vote.'

'Hear, hear!' we must all shout.

With fondness,

Tilda

Australia, I thought. She will be able to vote. I put the postcard in my pocket and hoped the thought of Her having a better life on the other side of the world would protect me from regret.

∾

Lizzie and I paused amid the morning crowd jostling in front of the fruit stall.

'I have a long list,' said Lizzie. 'I'll join you soon.'

She left, but for a moment I stayed where I was. I could see Mabel's stall, pathetic in its poverty, its lack of custom. Mrs Stiles' flower-filled buckets were a cruel contrast.

I approached, and Mabel acknowledged me with a bob of her head, as if she'd only seen me the day before. She was skeletal in her rags, and her voice was an echo of itself. What breath she had gurgled in her chest, damp and dangerous. When I leaned in to hear what she had to say, her decay was overpowering. All that was left on her crate were a few broken things and three whittled sticks. One I recognised from the last time I'd seen her, more than a year before. It was the head of a crone, finely carved.

I picked it up. 'Is this you, Mabel?'

'In better days,' she whispered.

The other two sticks were poor attempts at carving, made by hands that could barely hold a knife. I picked them up and turned them round and felt all the grief of knowing they were her last.

'Still a penny?'

A cough wracked her and she spat into a rag. 'Not worth a penny,' she managed to say.

I took three coins from my purse and put them on the crate.

'Lizzie says you have a word for me.'

She nodded. As I reached for my slips and pencil, she reached into the folds of her clothes. Mabel brought out a fistful of paper slips and put them on the crate between us. Then she turned her face up to mine and made a sound that made me think she was going to spit again. But it was a laugh, and her rheumy eyes were smiling.

'She 'elped,' Mabel said looking over at Mrs Stiles, who was straightening her flower buckets. 'Told 'er I'd shut me gob whenever there was ladies sniffin' 'round 'er flowers. Better for business, I told 'er. She 'ad to agree.' Again, her drowning laugh.

I picked up the slips, crushed and grubby from where they'd been stored. They were the right size, with the contents more or less as I would write them.

'When?' I asked.

'When you went away. Thought you'd need cheerin' on yer return. Whatever 'appened.' She reached into her clothes again. 'I saved this for you, too.'

Another carving, exquisite in its detail. Familiar.

'Taliesin,' Mabel said. 'Merlin. Me 'ands gave up after that.'

I took more coins from my purse.

'Na, lass,' Mabel said, waving the coins away. 'A gift.'

I had been avoiding Mabel, but now the state of her, this kindness and the reason for it, ambushed me. I felt paralysed, unable to raise a defence against memory. Like a vessel, I filled with sadness until I could no longer hold it, and it spilled, soaking my face.

'I 'eard you got the morbs,' Mabel said, refusing to look away. 'Only natural.'

Lizzie was there then, at my side, a pocket handkerchief in her hand, an arm around my shoulders. 'Mabel will be all right,' she said, misunderstanding. 'Won't you, Mabel?'

Mabel held my gaze a moment longer, then brought her hand to her chin and struck the thinker's pose. After a moment, she said, 'Nah, I don't reckon I will.' And as if to emphasise her point, the last word turned into a phlegmy cough so violent I thought it would shake her bones loose. It was enough to bring me back to myself.

'Enough joking,' Lizzie said, her hand gentle on Mabel's back.

When Mabel's coughing stopped and my tears dried, I asked, '*Morbs*, Mabel? What does it mean?'

'It's a sadness that comes and goes,' she said, pausing for breath. 'I get the morbs, you get the morbs, even Miss Lizzie 'ere gets the morbs, though she'd never let on. A woman's lot, I reckon.'

'It must derive from *morbid*,' I said to myself as I began to write out the slip.

'I reckon it *derives* from grief,' said Mabel. 'From what we've lost and what we've never 'ad and never will. As I said, a woman's lot. It should be in your dictionary. It's too common not to be understood.'

Lizzie and I left the covered market, each with our own thoughts. Mabel's state had been a shock.

'Where does she live?' I was ashamed I'd never thought about it before.

'Workhouse Infirmary on Cowley Road,' said Lizzie. 'A wretched place full of wretched people.'

'You've been?'

'Took her there myself. Found her sleeping on the street, a pile of rags draped across that crate of hers. Thought she was dead.'

'What can I do?'

'Keep buying her whittling and writing down her words. You can't change what is.'

'Do you really believe that, Lizzie?'

She looked at me, wary of the question.

'Surely things could change if enough people wanted them to,' I continued. I told her about Muriel Matters speaking in Parliament.

'I can't see nothing changing for the likes of Mabel. All that ruckus the suffragettes make, it isn't for women like her and me. It's for ladies with means, and such ladies will always want someone else to scrub their floors and empty their pots.' There was an edge to her voice I'd rarely heard. 'If they get the vote, I'll still be Mrs Murray's bondmaid.'

Bondmaid. If I hadn't found it and explained what it meant would Lizzie see herself differently?

'Yet it sounds as though you'd change things, if you could,' I said.

Lizzie shrugged, then paused to put down her bags. She rubbed her hands where the handles had left red grooves. My own bag was lighter, but I did the same.

'You know,' she said, when we were on our way again, 'Mabel thinks her words will end up in the Dictionary, with her name against them. I heard her bragging to Mrs Stiles, and I didn't have the heart to right her.'

'Why does she think that?'

'Why wouldn't she? You never told her otherwise.'

Our pace was slow, and despite the cold day, a trickle of sweat ran down the side of Lizzie's face. I thought about all the words I'd collected from Mabel and from Lizzie and from other women: women who gutted fish or cut cloth or cleaned the ladies' public convenience on Magdalen Street. They spoke their minds in words that suited them, and were reverent as I wrote their words on slips. These slips were precious to me, and I hid them in the trunk to keep them safe. But from what? Did I fear they would be scrutinised and found deficient? Or were those fears I had for myself?

I never dreamed the givers had any hopes for their words beyond my slips, but it was suddenly clear that no one but me would ever read them. The women's names, so carefully written, would never be set in type. Their words and their names would be lost as soon as I began to forget them.

My Dictionary of Lost Words was no better than the grille in the Ladies' Gallery of the House of Commons: it hid what should be seen and silenced what should be heard. When Mabel was gone and I was gone, the trunk would be no more than a coffin.

❧

Later, in Lizzie's room, I opened the trunk and nestled Mabel's words among Mr Dankworth's clandestine corrections. I was surprised by how many I had collected.

Since discovering Mr Dankworth's unauthorised corrections, I'd made a habit of checking proofs before delivering them to Mr Hart, though I only unpinned the corrections if I thought they added nothing to the original edit.

I began watching him. I watched him searching the shelves for slips or books, conferring with Dr Murray or sitting down at the sorting table to ask one of the other assistants a question. I saw him tilting his gaze towards their work, but I never saw him mark it with his pencil. Then, one morning, Mr Dankworth arrived early at the Scriptorium as I was finishing my cup of tea with Lizzie. Da had joined Dr Murray for an early meeting with the other editors at the Old Ashmolean.

I saw Mr Dankworth go into the Scriptorium and begin riffling through the edited proofs waiting in the basket by the door. 'Lizzie, look,' I said, and she came to the kitchen window. We watched as Mr

Dankworth removed a proof from the pile and took a pencil from his breast pocket.

'So, you're not the only one with Scrippy secrets,' said Lizzie.

I'd decided to keep Mr Dankworth's secret – despite myself, I liked him a little more because of it.

Now I looked into the trunk and saw Mabel's words resting against Mr Dankworth's neat hand. She'd like that, I thought. He wouldn't. I read random slips, his and hers. *Not quite*, he'd written on a top-slip I recognised as one of Mr Sweatman's – it seemed Dr Murray's were the only edits that escaped his fastidious attentions. Mr Dankworth had drawn a line through the definition and rewritten it, no more accurately in my mind, though two words shorter. I'd rewritten Mr Sweatman's original and pocketed Mr Dankworth's correction. It was such a contrast to Mabel's poorly spelled and childishly written slips. Their production had obviously been an effort for Mrs Stiles, making the favour all the more generous.

I re-read the meaning I'd written for *morbs*. Not quite, I thought. Mabel wasn't morbid and nor was I. Sad, yes, but not always. I took a pencil from my pocket and made the correction.

MORBS

A temporary sadness.
'I get the morbs, you get the morbs, even Miss Lizzie 'ere gets the morbs … A woman's lot, I reckon.'

Mabel O'Shaughnessy, 1908

I put the slip in the trunk and rested Taliesin on top.

～

The following Saturday, I joined Lizzie again for her trip to the Covered Market. As always, it was crowded, but we pushed through.

'Dead.' Mrs Stiles called from her stall when she saw us coming. 'Carted her off yesterday.'

Mrs Stiles momentarily looked me in the eye, then bent to arrange a bucket of carnations. Lizzie and I turned to look for Mabel.

'She'd stopped coughing, you see. Blessed silence, I thought. But then it was a bit too quiet.' She paused in her arranging and took a deep breath that stretched the fabric across her bent back. She stood to face us. 'Poor love. She'd been dead for hours.' Mrs Stiles looked from me to Lizzie and back again, her hands smoothing down her apron again and again, her mouth tight around the slightest quiver. 'I should have noticed sooner.'

The space that Mabel had occupied was already gone; the neighbouring stalls had expanded to fill it. I stood there for a minute or an hour, I don't know which, and struggled to imagine how Mabel and her crate of whittled sticks had ever fitted there. No one who passed seemed to notice her absence.

May 1909

When Mr Dankworth moved to the sorting table, it felt as though a too-tight corset had finally been unhooked. It was Elsie who made it happen.

'You know, Esme,' she said one morning, when I tried to suggest a particular word might need a more skilled eye than mine, 'everyone who contributes copy to the Dictionary will leave a trace of themselves, no matter how uniform Father, or Mr Dankworth, would like it to be. Try to take Mr Dankworth's comments as suggestion, not dictum.'

A week later, I overheard her commenting that it was hard to access some of the shelves with Mr Dankworth's desk in such close proximity. That afternoon, Dr Murray had a word with Mr Dankworth, and when I came in the next day Mr Dankworth was sitting at the sorting table opposite Mr Sweatman, a border of stacked books set up between them.

'Good morning, Mr Sweatman, Mr Dankworth,' I said.

A smile from one, a nod from the other. Mr Dankworth still couldn't look me in the eye. Already his desk had been removed, and mine was just visible beyond one of the shelves.

I sat and lifted the lid. The paper that lined the inside was curling at the edges, but the roses were as yellow as they'd always been. As I ran my fingers over the flowers, I counted back the years to the first time I'd sat at the desk. Was it nine years or ten? So much had happened, and yet I hadn't moved an inch.

'Well, that looks familiar,' said Elsie. 'I remember pasting it on. A long time ago now.'

For a moment we were both silent, as if Elsie too was suddenly aware of time moving past her. I'd never thought much about her life beyond the Scriptorium, or Rosfrith's. They had grown out of their perfect plaits and become their father's helpers. I envied them, as I always had, but now I wondered if this was what they had hoped for, or whether it was just what they had accepted.

'How are your studies going, Elsie?' I asked.

'I've finished. Sat my exams last June.' Her face was bright with the pride of it.

'Oh, congratulations!' I said. Remembering that She had turned one last June. 'I didn't know.'

'No graduation, of course. No degree. But it's satisfying to know I would have achieved both if I wore trousers.'

'But you can have it conferred somewhere else, can't you?'

'Oh, yes, but there's no hurry. I'm not going anywhere.' She looked down at the proofs in her hand as if trying to remember what they were. Then she held them out. 'From Father. A quick proofread. He wants them at the Press tomorrow morning.'

I took the proofs. 'Of course.' I looked towards the space where Mr Dankworth's desk had been. 'And thank you.'

'A small thing.'

'That all depends on your perspective.'

She nodded, then made her way past the sorting table to Dr Murray's desk and the pile of letters awaiting her drafted replies.

The lid of my desk was still open. Everything I needed to do my work was there: notepaper, blank slips, pencils, pens. *Hart's Rules*. Beneath *Hart's Rules* were things I didn't require to do my work: a letter from Ditte, postcards from Tilda, blank slips made from pretty paper, and a novel. When I picked it up, three slips fell out. Seeing Mabel's name made my eyes well up. It was enough to bring on the morbs, I thought. And then I smiled.

Each slip had the same word but a variation on the meaning. I remembered the shock of hearing it, then Mabel's delight and the racing of my heart when I first wrote it down. *Cunt* was as old as the hills, Mabel had said, but it wasn't in the Dictionary. I'd checked.

The slips for *C* had been boxed up, but words for a supplement were stored in the shelves closest to my desk. Dr Murray had started collecting them as soon as the fascicle for 'A to Ant' was published. 'Dr Murray has already anticipated that the English language will evolve faster than we can define it,' Da told me. 'When the Dictionary is finally published, we'll go back to A and fill in the gaps.'

The pigeon-holes were almost full of slips for supplementary words. They were meticulously ordered, and it didn't take me long to find the thick pile of slips with quotations from books dating back to 1325. The word was as old as Mabel had said it was. If Dr Murray's formula had been applied, it would certainly have been included in the thick volume behind his desk.

I looked at the top-slip. Instead of the usual information, there was a note in Dr Murray's hand saying simply, *Exclude. Obscene.* Below that, someone had transcribed a series of comments, presumably from correspondence. It looked like Elsie Murray's handwriting, but I couldn't be sure:

'The thing itself is not obscene!'
— James Dixon

'A thoroughly old word with a very ancient history.'
                    — Robinson Ellis

'The mere fact of its being used in a vulgar way does not ban it from the
English language.'
                    — John Hamilton

I looked at the top-slip again; there was no definition. I put the slips back in their place and returned to my desk. On a blank slip, I wrote:

CUNT

1. Slang for vagina.

2. An insult based on the premise that a woman's vagina is vulgar.

I gathered Mabel's words into a small pile and pinned my definitions to it. Then I rummaged around for other slips. There was a handful, all meant for the trunk under Lizzie's bed, but hastily hidden at one time or another, then half forgotten. I gathered them up and put them between the pages of the novel for safekeeping.

I spent the rest of the afternoon on the proofs Elsie had given me, every now and then looking up to watch her. She moved about the Scriptorium in her diligent way, always ready to do her father's bidding. Had they argued about the word? Or had she found it missing and then searched for reasons why? Did Dr Murray even know she'd transcribed the arguments for the word's inclusion on his top-slip, or that she'd included it with supplementary words? No, of course not. She lived between the lines of the Dictionary as much as I did.

'Ready to go?' Da said.

I was surprised to realise how late it was. 'I'd like to finish this proof,' I said. 'Then I'll pop in on Lizzie. You go ahead.'

'What on earth are you doing?' Lizzie said, coming into her room and seeing me on the floor, bent over the trunk. 'You look like you're bobbing for apples.'

'Can you smell it, Lizzie?'

'I certainly can,' she said. 'I've often wondered if something might have crawled in and died.'

'It doesn't smell bad, it smells of … well, I don't really know how to describe it.' I bent forward again, hoping the smell would identify itself.

'It smells like something that should've got a regular airing has been locked away too long,' said Lizzie.

Then I realised. My trunk was beginning to smell like the old slips in the Scriptorium.

Lizzie removed her apron. It was splattered with roasting juices, and she was changing it for a clean one just as Mrs Ballard used to do before she took a roast to table. As if evidence of their toil was offensive. Before Lizzie could put on her clean apron, I had her in a hug.

'You're exactly right.'

She extracted herself and held me at arm's length. 'You'd think after all these years I'd understand you, Essymay, but I got no clue what you're talking about.'

'These words,' I said, reaching into the trunk and pulling out a handful. 'They weren't given to me to hide away. They need an airing. They should be read, shared, understood. Rejected, maybe, but given a chance. Just like all the words in the Scriptorium.'

Lizzie laughed and put the clean apron over her head. 'You thinking of making a dictionary of your own, then?'

'That's exactly what I'm thinking, Lizzie. A dictionary of women's words. Words they use and words that refer to them. Words that won't make it into Dr Murray's dictionary. What do you think?'

Her face fell. 'You can't. Some of them isn't fit.'

I couldn't help smiling. Lizzie would be delighted if *cunt* disappeared from the English language.

'You have more in common with Dr Murray than you could ever know.'

'But what's the point?' she said, picking a slip out of the trunk and looking at it. 'Half the people who say these words will never be able to read them.'

'Maybe not,' I said, heaving the trunk onto her bed. 'But their words are important.'

We looked at the mess of slips inside the trunk. I remembered all the times I'd searched the volumes and the pigeon-holes for just the right word to explain what I was feeling, experiencing. So often, the words chosen by the men of the Dictionary had been inadequate.

'Dr Murray's dictionary leaves things out, Lizzie. Sometimes a word, sometimes a meaning. If it isn't written down, it doesn't even get considered.' I placed Mabel's first slips in a pile on the bed. 'Wouldn't it be good if the words these women use were treated the same as any other?'

I started sifting through slips and papers in the trunk, pulling out women's words and putting them to one side. Some words began to pile up, with different quotations from different women. I had no idea I'd collected so many.

Lizzie reached under her bed and pulled out her sewing basket. 'You'll be needing these if you're going to keep all that in order.' She put her pincushion in front of me; it was hedgehog-full.

When I'd finished sorting all the words in the trunk it was dark outside. Both of us had sore fingers from pinning slips together.

'Keep it,' Lizzie said, when I handed back the pincushion. 'For new words.'

There was a tiny hole in the wall of the Scriptorium, just above my desk. I'd noticed it when the chill of the previous winter had pricked the back of my hand like a needle. I'd tried to block it with a ball of paper, but the paper kept falling out. Then I realised I had a view: I caught fragments of people as they smoked their cigarettes; of Da and Mr Balk as they packed their pipes and exchanged Dictionary gossip. *Gossipiania*, I always thought, when titbits found my ear. An entry had been written for the word, but it was struck through in the final proof. I recognised all the assistants from what I could see of their clothes, and I had the uncanny feeling I was under the sorting table again.

The slight shaft of light had been moving across my page like a sundial, so I noticed when it disappeared. There was the clang of a bicycle being propped against the Scriptorium, and I leaned towards the hole. I saw unfamiliar trousers and an unfamiliar shirt, sleeves rolled up to the elbows. Ink-stained fingers unbuckled an ink-stained satchel. The fingers were long, but the thumb spread oddly at the end. The man was checking the contents, as I would check the contents of my own satchel just before going through the gates of the Press. I tilted my gaze upward, a slightly awkward manoeuvre, in an attempt to see his face. It wasn't possible.

I pulled back from the hole and leaned a little to my right so I would have a view of the Scriptorium door.

He stood on the threshold. Tall and lean. Clean-shaven. Dark hair, curling. He saw me peering around the bookshelf and smiled. I was too far away to see his eyes, but I knew them to be evening blue, almost violet.

I'd forgotten his name, even though I remembered him telling it to me once, the first time I delivered words to the Press. I was barely more than a girl, and he'd been kind.

Since then, I'd only seen him from a distance when I went searching for Mr Hart in the Press. The compositor always stood at a bench at the far end of the composing room, practically obscured by the tray that held all the type. He would sometimes look up when I came through the door. He would always smile, but he'd never waved me over. I'd never known him to come to Sunnyside.

The only other person in the Scriptorium, besides me, was Mr Dankworth. I watched his head jerk up, attentive to who had come in. He took a second to make his judgement.

'Yes?' he said, in the tone he reserved for men with dirty fingernails. My fist closed tightly around my pencil.

'I have Dr Murray's proofs. *Si* to *simple*.'

'I'll take them,' said Mr Dankworth, holding out his hand but not getting up.

'And you are?' the compositor asked.

'I beg your pardon?'

'The Controller would like to know who takes receipt of the proofs, if it isn't Dr Murray himself.'

Mr Dankworth rose from the sorting table and approached the compositor. 'You can tell the Controller that Mr Dankworth took receipt of the proofs.' He took the pages before they were proffered.

In my place at the back of the room, I held my breath, irritation and embarrassment rising. I wanted to intervene, to welcome the compositor into the Scriptorium, but without his name I would look foolish.

'I'll be sure to do that, Mr Dankworth,' the compositor said, looking Mr Dankworth square in the face. 'My name is Gareth, by the way. It's a pleasure to meet you.' He held out his ink-stained hand, but Mr Dankworth just stared at it and rubbed his own hand up and down on the side of his trousers. Gareth lowered his arm and offered a slight nod instead. He glanced quickly to where I sat, then turned and left the Scriptorium.

I took a blank slip from my desk and wrote:

GARETH
Compositor.

❧

I was standing just inside the door of the Scriptorium, reading an article in the *Oxford Chronicle* while Dr Murray finished off some correspondence he wanted me to take to Mr Bradley.

It was a small piece, buried in the middle pages.

Three suffragettes, arrested after a rooftop protest against Prime Minister Herbert Asquith, have been forcibly fed in Winson Green Gaol after several days on hunger strike. The women were gaoled for civil disobedience and criminal damage after throwing tiles at police from the roof of Bingley Hall in Birmingham, where Mr Asquith was holding a public budget meeting. Women were barred from attending.

My throat began to constrict. 'How do you force-feed a grown woman?' I said, to no one in particular. I skimmed the column of words, but there was no explanation of the procedure, and the women weren't named. I thought of Tilda. Her last postcard had been from Birmingham, where, she'd written, *women were willing to do more than just sign petitions.*

'Something for Mr Hart at the Press,' said Dr Murray, startling me. 'But visit the Old Ashmolean first; Mr Bradley is waiting on this.' He handed me a letter with *Bradley* written on the envelope along with the first proofs for the letter T.

The Old Ashmolean was as grand as the Scriptorium was humble. It was stone instead of tin, and the entrance was flanked by the busts of men who had achieved something – I don't know what. When I'd first seen them, I'd felt small and out of place, but after a while they'd encouraged a defiant ambition, and I'd imagined walking into that place and taking my seat at the Editor's desk. But if women could be barred from a public budget meeting, I had no right to that ambition. I thought about Tilda, her hunger for the fight. And I thought about the women who had gone to gaol. Could I starve myself? I wondered. If I thought it would help me become an editor?

I climbed the stairs to large double doors that opened into the Dictionary Room. It was airy and light, with stone walls and a high ceiling held up by Grecian stone pillars. The Dictionary deserved this space, and when I first saw it I'd wondered why Mr Bradley and Mr Craigie had been given the honour of occupying it instead of Dr Murray. 'He is a martyr to the Dictionary,' Da said, when I asked. 'The Scrippy suits him perfectly.'

I looked around the vast room, trying to work out which assistants were behind the mess of papers that covered every table. Eleanor Bradley looked above her parapet of books and waved.

She cleared some papers off a chair, and I sat down. 'I have a letter for your father,' I said.

'Oh, good. He's hoping for Dr Murray's agreement on a question that he and Mr Craigie have been discussing.'

'Discussing?' I raised an eyebrow.

'Well, they are polite, but each is hoping for a nod in their direction from the chief.' She looked at the envelope in my hand. 'Pa will be glad to have it resolved one way or another.'

'Is it about a particular word?'

'A whole language.' Eleanor leaned in, her wire-framed eyes huge with the gossip. She spoke quietly: 'Mr Craigie is wanting to take another trip to Scandinavia and the Netherlands. Apparently, he's thrown his support behind a campaign to recognise Frisian.'

'I've never heard of it.'

'It's Germanic.'

'Of course,' I said, remembering a one-way conversation I'd had with Mr Craigie at the picnic for *O and P*. The subject of the Germanic language had animated him for over an hour.

'Pa thinks it's outside the scope of an editor of our *English* dictionary. He fears R will never be completed if Mr Craigie keeps pursuing other goals.'

'If that's his argument, I'm sure he'll have Dr Murray's support,' I said.

I stood up to go, then hesitated. 'Eleanor, have you read about the suffragettes in gaol in Birmingham? They're being force-fed.'

She coloured and clenched her jaw. 'I have,' she said. 'It's shameful. Like the Dictionary, the vote seems inevitable. Why we have to suffer so much and for so long I cannot fathom.'

'Do you think we will live to enjoy it?' I asked.

She smiled. 'On that question, I am more optimistic than Pa and Sir James. I am sure we will.'

I wasn't so sure, but before I could say any more, Mr Bradley approached.

I pedalled as fast as I could between the Old Ashmolean and Walton Street. It wasn't so much the darkening sky that spurred me on as my fears for Tilda and women like her – and fears for all of us if their efforts should fail. The exertion didn't quiet my worries.

When I arrived at the Press, I shoved my bicycle between two others, angry that there was never enough room to park it easily. I strode across the quad, scowling at the men and searching the women's faces; if they knew about the force-feeding, it didn't show. I wondered how many of them felt as useless as I did.

Instead of going to Mr Hart's office, I walked to the composing room. The slip with the compositor's name was in my pocket. I took it out and looked it over, though there was no need for a reminder. By the time I reached the room my steps had slowed.

Gareth was setting type. He didn't look up as I came in, but I didn't feel like waiting for an invitation. I took a deep breath and began to walk between the benches of type.

The men nodded and I nodded back, my anger dissipating with each friendly gesture.

'Hello, miss. You looking for Mr Hart?' said someone familiar whose name I didn't know.

'Actually, I wanted to say hello to Gareth,' I said. I barely recognised the confident voice as my own.

It didn't seem to matter to anyone that I was wandering around the composing room, and it occurred to me that the intimidation I always felt might have been of my own creation. By the time I was at Gareth's bench, the emotion that had propelled me was exhausted, my confidence spent.

He looked up, his face still set in concentration. Then a smile broke through. 'Well, this is a nice surprise. Esme, isn't it?'

I nodded, suddenly aware I'd prepared nothing to say.

'Do you mind if I just finish setting this section? My stick is nearly full.'

Gareth held the 'stick' in his left hand. It was a kind of tray that held lines of metal type. He kept it all in place by pressing his thumb tight against it. His right hand flew around the bench in front of him, gathering more type from small compartments that reminded me of Dr Murray's pigeon-holes on a tiny scale; each was dedicated to a single letter instead of bundles of words. Before I knew it, his stick was full.

His eyes flicked up, and he noticed my interest. 'The next step is to turn it out into the forme,' he said, indicating a wooden frame beside his bench. 'Does it look familiar?'

I looked at the forme. Except for a gap where the new type would go, it was the size and shape of a page of words – but what page of words, I could not tell. 'It looks like a different language.'

'It's back to front, but it will be a page in the next Dictionary fascicle, as soon as I've made this correction.'

He put the stick down very carefully and rubbed his thumb.

'Compositor's thumb,' he said, holding it up for me to have a closer look.

'I should know better than to stare.'

'You're welcome to stare. It's a mark of my trade, that's all.' He stepped down from his stool. 'We all have one. But I'm sure you didn't come here to talk about thumbs.'

I'd come into the composing room in defiance of some perceived bar. Now, I felt foolish.

'Mr Hart,' I fumbled. 'I thought I might find him here.' I looked around as if he might be hiding behind one of the benches.

'I'll see if I can find out where he is.' Gareth dusted the seat of his stool with a white cloth. 'You can sit here if you like, while you wait.'

I nodded and let him push the stool beneath me. I looked at the type still held on the stick. It was almost impossible to decipher; not just because the letters were back to front, but because there was so little differentiation from the background. It was all gun-metal grey.

If the other compositors had been interested in the strange woman talking to Gareth, they no longer were. I picked up a bit of type from the nearest compartment.

It was like a tiny stamp, the letter slightly raised on the end of a piece of metal about an inch long and not much wider than a toothpick. I pressed it against the tip of my finger – it left the imprint of a lower-case *e*.

I looked at the stick again. He said it would fit into a page of the Dictionary. It took a while, but the words finally started to make sense. When they did, I felt a rising panic.

b. Common scold: a woman who disturbs the peace of the neighbourhood by her constant scolding.

Was that what they were, those women in Winson Green? I looked at the proofs beside the forme. It appeared this type wasn't being set for the first time; rather, Gareth was attending to edits. There was a note from Dr Murray pinned to the edge of an entry.

No need to define SCOLD'S BRIDLE; simply cross-reference to the relevant entry for BRANKS.

I read the entry that would be edited.

c. scold's bit, bridle: an instrument of punishment used in the case of scolds etc., consisting of a kind of iron framework to enclose the head, having a sharp metal gag or bit which entered the mouth and restrained the tongue.

I imagined them being held down, their mouths forced open, a tube shoved in, their cries muted. What damage must it do to the sensitive membrane of their lips and mouths and throats? When the procedure was over, would they even be able to speak?

I searched the bench and picked each letter from a different compartment: the *s*, the *c*, the *o*, the *l*, the *d*. They had a weight, these letters. I rolled them about in my hand. My skin prickled with their sharp edges and was marked by the ink of forgotten pages.

The door of the composing room opened, and Gareth walked in with Mr Hart. I put the type in my pocket and pushed back the stool.

'The first corrections for the letter T,' I said, handing the proofs to Mr Hart.

He took them, blind to the smudges of ink on my fingers. I quickly put my hand in my pocket. Gareth was not so distracted, and from the corner of my eye I saw him check the type he had been setting. He found nothing missing, and his gaze swept over the tray. I clutched at the type, felt their sharp edges and held them so tight they hurt.

'Excellent,' said Mr Hart as he looked over the pages. 'We inch forward.' Then he turned to Gareth. 'We will review these tomorrow. Come and see me at nine.'

'Yes, sir,' said Gareth.

Mr Hart headed towards his office, still looking through the proofs.

'I must be off,' I said, walking away from Gareth without looking at him.

'I hope you visit again,' I heard him say.

When I walked my bicycle out of the Press, the sky was darker. Before I reached the Banbury Road, it had split apart. By the time I arrived at the Scriptorium, I was dripping wet and shivering.

'Stop!' Mr Dankworth shouted when I opened the Scriptorium door.

I stopped, and only then realised what a sight I must be. Everyone was looking in my direction.

Rosfrith stood up from where she was sitting at her father's desk. 'Mr Dankworth, are you proposing that Esme stand out in the rain all afternoon?'

'She'll drip all over our papers,' he said more quietly, then he bent to his work as if uninterested in what happened next. I stayed where I was. My teeth began to chatter.

'Father should never have sent you out. Anyone could see it was going to rain.' Rosfrith took an umbrella out of the stand and then took my arm. 'Come with me; he and your father are due back soon, and they'll both be upset if they see you in this state.'

Rosfrith held the umbrella over us both as we crossed the garden to the front of the house. I was rarely invited into the main part of the Murray home, and could count on one hand the number of times I'd walked through the front door. In that moment, I imagined I was feeling a little of what Lizzie must have felt every day of her life.

'Wait here,' Rosfrith said when the front door was closed behind us. She went towards the kitchen, and I could hear her calling to Lizzie. A minute later, Lizzie was in front of me, patting me down with a towel warm from the linen press.

'Why didn't you just wait it out at the Press?' Lizzie asked as she kneeled to undo my shoes and remove my soaked stockings.

'Thank you, Lizzie, I'll take it from here.' Rosfrith took the towel and led me up the stairs to her bedroom.

I was older than Rosfrith by almost two years, and yet I'd always felt younger. As she searched through her wardrobe for clothes that might fit me, I saw in her the self-assured practicality of her mother. Mrs Murray was as entitled to a damehood as Dr Murray was to a knighthood, Da had said. 'Without her, the Dictionary would have faltered long ago.'

How reassuring it must be to know how you should act: like having a definition of yourself written clearly in black type.

'You're taller, and thinner, but I think these will fit.' Rosfrith laid a skirt, blouse, cardigan and undergarments on her bed, then left me to change.

Before I stepped out of my own skirt, I searched the pockets. In one, there was a handkerchief, a pencil and a wad of damp blank slips. I went to throw the wad in the wastepaper basket and couldn't help but look at the papers on Rosfrith's desk. Everything was neatly arranged. There was a photograph of her father after receiving his knighthood, and one of the whole family in the garden of Sunnyside. There were proofs and letters at various stages of completion. I recognised the recipient of the letter she'd been working on most recently. It was the governor of Winson Green Gaol. *Dear Sir*, it said. *I wish to object*. That was as far as she had gone. Beside it was a copy of the *Times of London*.

From my other pocket, I pulled out the type I'd stolen from Gareth, and the slip with his name on it. It was almost translucent from the rain, but his name was still visible.

After I'd changed into Rosfrith's clothes, I wrapped the type in my damp handkerchief and put it in one of the skirt pockets. I picked up the slip with Gareth's name on it. He knew I'd taken the type. I'd be too ashamed to visit him again. I dropped the slip in the wastepaper basket.

Then I turned again to Rosfrith's desk. The *Times of London* gave the women in Winson Green more column space. Tilda wasn't one of them; not this time, I thought. Charlotte Marsh was the daughter of artist Arthur Hardwick Marsh. Laura Ainsworth's father was a respected school inspector. Mary Leigh was the wife of a builder. This was how the women were defined.

Bondmaid. It came back to me then, and I realised that the words most often used to define us were words that described our function in relation to others. Even the most benign words – *maiden*, *wife*, *mother* – told the world whether we were virgins or not. What was the male equivalent of *maiden*? I could not think of it. What was the male equivalent of *Mrs*, of *whore*, of *common scold*? I looked out of the window towards the Scriptorium, the place where the definitions of all these words were being bedded down. Which words would define me?

Which would be used to judge or contain? I was no *maiden*, yet I was no man's *wife*. And I had no desire to be.

As I read how the 'treatment' was administered, I felt the ghost of a gag reflex and the pain of a tube scraping membrane from cheek to throat to stomach. It was a kind of rape. The weight of bodies holding you down, restraining your clawing hands and kicking feet. Forcing you open. At that moment, I wasn't sure whose humanity was more compromised: the women's or the authorities'. If the authorities', then the shame was all of ours. What, after all, had I done to help the cause since Tilda left Oxford?

Rosfrith returned and we descended the stairs together. 'Are you a suffragette, Rosfrith?' I asked.

'I don't sneak out at night and smash windows, if that's what you're asking. I would prefer to call myself a suffragist.'

'I don't think I could do what some women do.'

'Starve yourself or be a public nuisance?'

'Neither.'

Rosfrith paused on the staircase and turned to me. 'I don't think I could, either. And I can't imagine … well, you've read the papers. But militancy isn't the only way, Esme.'

Rosfrith resumed her descent and I followed, two steps behind. There was so much I wanted to ask her, but despite us both having grown up in the shadow of the Dictionary, I felt we were worlds apart.

We lingered a while in the kitchen doorway, watching the rain. 'I'd best make a run for it,' Rosfrith said eventually. 'But you've been wet enough for one day – wait here in the warm till it's passed. We certainly can't have you catching cold.' She opened her umbrella and trotted the distance between kitchen and Scriptorium.

Lizzie was crouched in front of the range. 'Look at your face, Essymay. What on earth is wrong?'

'The papers, Lizzie. You'd be shocked to know what is going on.'

'No need to read the papers; the market serves just as well.' She shovelled coal onto the rising flames and shut the heavy cast-iron door with a bang. She looked stiff as she pulled herself up to standing.

'And are they talking about what's happening to the suffragettes in Birmingham?' I said.

'Yes. They're talking about it.'

'Are they angry? About the hunger strikes and the forced feeding?'

'Some are,' she said as she began slicing vegetables and putting them in a large pot. 'Others think they're going about things all wrong. That you catch more flies with honey.'

'But do they think they deserve what's happening to them? It's torture.'

'Some think they can't be left to starve to death.'

'And what do *you* think, Lizzie?'

She looked up, her eyes rimmed red and watering from the onions. 'I wouldn't be that brave,' she said.

It wasn't an answer, but I might have said the same thing if I'd been honest with myself.

∿

11th April 1910

Happy birthday, my dear Esme,

I can't believe you are twenty-eight. It makes me feel quite old. This year, in light of your continued concerns, I have enclosed a book by Emily Davies. Emily was a friend of my mother's and has been involved in the suffrage movement for half a century. She has quite a different approach to Mrs Pankhurst and is a firm believer in the equalising effect of women's education — her arguments are quite compelling. I am hoping that if you read Thoughts on Some Questions Relating to Women *you might give some thought to taking a degree yourself. Which leads me to your letter.*

I read it aloud over breakfast. Beth and I are at one with your concerns, though we do not feel as impotent as you seem to.

This is not a new fight, and while the actions of Emmeline Pankhurst's army of women will certainly draw attention to the cause, they may not hasten a satisfactory resolution. We will get the vote sooner or later, but that will not be the end of it. The fight will go on, and it cannot rely solely on women prepared to starve themselves.

Our grandfather was outspoken on the topic of women's right to vote back when 'universal suffrage' was the political argument of the day. I wonder how our dictionary will define universal. Back then, it meant all adults, regardless of race, income or property. But it did not mean women, and against this our grandfather railed. It would be a long campaign, he was heard to say, and to be successful it would have to be fought on many fronts.

You are not a coward, Esme. It pains me to think that any young woman would think such a thing because she is not being brutalised for her convictions. If Tilda is campaigning for the WSPU, it suits her completely. She is an actress and knows how to provoke an audience. If you want to be useful, keep doing what you have always done. You once made the observation that some words were considered more important than others simply because they were written down. You were arguing that by default the words of educated men were more important than the words of the uneducated classes, women among them. Do what you are good at, my dear Esme: keep considering the words we use and record. Once the question of women's political suffrage has been dealt with, less obvious inequalities will need to be exposed. Without realising it, you are already working for this cause. As grandfather said, it will be a long game. Play a position you are good at, and let others play theirs.

Now, to other news. I have thought long and hard about whether silence is best, but Beth has convinced me that silence is a void filled with anxieties. Sarah writes that they have settled comfortably in Adelaide and that little Megan is thriving. There is more I could share on that topic, but I will wait to be asked.

Not unrelated to your enquiries, Sarah has just voted in her first election! Isn't it wonderful? Women in South Australia have been exercising this right for the past fifteen years. As far as I can glean, none have had to smash any windows or starve themselves for the privilege. You are no doubt aware that a few of those good women have travelled to England to support the cause. Do you recall the young woman who chained herself to the grille in the Ladies' Gallery and spoke in the House of Commons? Well, she is a local Adelaide girl. From all accounts, South Australia is none the worse for women's suffrage. To the contrary, Sarah writes that it is quite a pleasant place once you get used to the heat. Society does not seem to have broken down in any way. It is only a matter of time before it happens here.

Before I sign off, Beth wants me to tell you that A Dragoon's Wife *has just been reprinted. It seems the fight for suffrage is not incompatible with the romance of being swept off one's feet. We are a complicated species.*

Yours,

Ditte

Megan. Meg. MeggyMay.

She had a name and She was thriving. That was all I needed to know. All I could hold without bursting.

Two more birthdays passed. Megan turned three, then four. An account of Her became part of Ditte's annual gift, as Lily's story had once been. She would send a book, a letter, Her first steps, Her first words. The book was always put aside, and Ditte's news soon forgotten. I struggled to recall the motion of my days.

December 1912

Time marked the Scriptorium in subtle ways from one year to the next. Books piled higher and pigeon-holes were built for more slips, the shelving creating a nook for an old chair that Rosfrith brought over from the house. It became a favourite retreat for Mr Maling when he had need to study a foreign text. The beards around the sorting table were greyer, and Dr Murray's grew ever longer.

It was never a noisy place, but the Scriptorium had an ensemble of sounds that combined to create a comforting hum. I was used to the shuffling of papers, the scraping of pens and the sounds of frustration that identified each person like a fingerprint. If a word was troubling him, Dr Murray would grunt and get down from his chair to take a lungful of air from the doorway. Mr Dankworth would make a metronome of his pencil, a slow tap marking the rhythm of his thought. Da would cease to make any sound at all. He would remove his spectacles and rub the bridge of his nose. Then he'd rest his chin on his hand and raise his eyes to the ceiling, just as he would if our dinner conversation had stumped him.

Elsie and Rosfrith had their own accompanying sounds, and I loved to hear the hems of their skirts sweep the floor, catching slips that had been carelessly dropped (such windfall, I sometimes thought, and I would watch to see where they ended up so I could collect them if no one else did). The Murray girls – I still thought of them this way, though we had all passed thirty – would also disturb the air with lavender and rose. I would breathe it in as a tonic against the sometimes careless hygiene of the men.

Once in a while, the Scriptorium would be stilled and silent and all mine. It was usually just before the publication of a fascicle: the editors and their senior assistants would meet at the Old Ashmolean to settle last-minute arguments, and Elsie and Rosfrith would take the opportunity to be somewhere else.

Normally, with the Scriptorium to myself, I would wend my way among the tables and shelves, looking for small slips of treasure. But on this particular day, I was in a hurry. I'd spent my morning tea break in Lizzie's room, sorting through more slips from the trunk, and now I had a small bundle of women's words I wanted to catalogue.

I lifted the lid of my desk and took out the shoebox I was using as a pigeon-hole for my words. It was half full of small bundles of slips, each representing a word, with meanings and quotations from various women pinned together. I spread the new slips across my desk. Some belonged with words I'd already defined; others were new and needed a top-slip. This was what I enjoyed most: considering all the variants of a word and deciding which would be the headword, then fashioning a definition to suit it. I was never alone in this process; without fail, I would be guided by the voice of the woman who used it. When it was Mabel, I would linger a little longer, making sure I got the meaning just right, and imagining her gummy grin when I did.

Lizzie's pincushion lived in my desk now, and I took a pin to secure quotations for *git*. Tilda was the first to give me a quotation, but Mabel liked to use it whenever she spoke about a man she did not like. Even Lizzie used it from time to time. So it was an insult, but not vulgar;

and Mabel had never used it to refer to Mrs Stiles, so it could only refer to men. I stuck the pin through one corner of the slips and began composing a top-slip in my head.

'What's this?'

The pin pricked my thumb and made me gasp. I looked up. Mr Dankworth was beside me, peering at the mess of slips spread across my desk. They were exposed and vulnerable. Clearly not the words I was supposed to be working on.

'Nothing of any consequence,' I said, trying to bundle the slips back into a pile and smiling up at him, conscious of how stupid I must look: a grown woman squashed behind a school desk.

He leaned over a little to get a closer look at the words. I tried to push back my chair, but found that I couldn't. For the moment, I remained stuck while he continued his inspection.

'If it's of no consequence, why are you doing it?' he asked, reaching over me so that I had to bend to avoid him. He picked up the pile of slips.

A sudden memory asserted itself, one I'd thought buried under time and kindness. I was smaller, the desk was similar, but the feeling that I had no control over what would happen next was so strong. I felt winded. I'd allowed myself to imagine my life unfolding differently to that of so many of the women I observed. But at that moment, I felt as constrained and powerless as any of them.

And then I felt furious.

'It will be of no consequence to *you*,' I said. 'Though it is important.' I pushed with more force against the chair until Mr Dankworth was obliged to move out of the way.

I stood close to him, as close as we might have been just before a kiss. His forehead was creased as if in permanent concentration, and wiry white hairs sprang from the slick black either side of his perfect part. They were unruly, and I was surprised he hadn't pulled them out.

273

He stumbled back. I put my hand out for the slips, but he held on to them.

He turned towards the sorting table, taking my slips with him. He spread them out like they were a pack of cards. Then he fingered them, moved them about. *Manhandling*, I thought. I would write a slip for it when he was done.

Mr Dankworth stopped to read one or two words as if considering their value. I could tell when the philologist in him was intrigued: his forehead softened and the purse of his lips relaxed. I was reminded of those rare times I thought we might have something in common. The longer he considered my words, the more I wondered whether I had overreacted.

My shoulders dropped, and my jaw relaxed. How I longed to talk with someone about women's words, their place in the Dictionary, the flaws in method that might have meant they were being left out. In that moment, I imagined Mr Dankworth and I as allies.

Suddenly he swept the slips together, unconcerned with their order. 'You were right and you were wrong, Miss Nicoll,' he said. 'Your project is of no consequence to me, but it is also of no importance.'

I was too stunned to respond. When he handed me the pile of slips, my hand shook so much that I dropped them.

Mr Dankworth looked at the slips strewn across the dusty floor and made no move to help pick them up. Instead, he turned back to the sorting table and searched his own papers, found whatever he had come for, and left.

The shake in my hand travelled into every part of my body. I kneeled to gather the slips but could not place them in any kind of order. I couldn't focus, and they seemed meaningless. When I heard the Scriptorium door open again, I closed my eyes against the dread it might be Mr Dankworth – the humiliation of him seeing me on my knees.

Someone bent down beside me and began picking up slips. He had long, beautiful fingers, but the thumb on his left hand was misshapen. Gareth, the compositor. I had a vague memory of this happening before. He picked up one slip after another, dusting each off before handing it to me.

'You'll be able to sort them later,' he said. 'For now, it's best to just get them, and you, off this cold floor.'

'It was my fault,' I heard myself say.

Gareth didn't respond, he just continued to hand me the slips. It had been years since I stole his type, and despite his friendliness I had managed to discourage anything more than a polite acquaintance.

'It's just a hobby. They don't really belong here,' I said.

Gareth paused for a moment, but still said nothing. Then he gathered up the last slip, traced his finger over it and read the word out loud: '*Pillock*.' He looked up, smiling; lines fanning out from around his eyes.

'There's an example of how it is used,' I said, leaning closer to point out the quotation on the slip.

'Seems about right,' he said, reading it. 'And who's Tilda Taylor?'

'She's the woman who used the word.'

'These aren't in the Dictionary, then?'

I stiffened. 'No. None of them are.'

'But some are quite common,' he said, sifting through them.

'Among the people who use them, they are. But common isn't a prerequisite for the Dictionary.'

'Who uses them?'

I was ready now to have the fight I'd shied from just minutes earlier. 'The poor. People who work at the Covered Market. Women. Which is why they're not written down and why they've been excluded. Though sometimes they *have* been written down, but they're still left out because they are not used in *polite society*.' I felt exhausted, but defiant.

My hands were still shaking, but I was ready to go on. I looked him in the eye. 'They're important.'

'You better keep them safe, then,' said Gareth, standing as he passed me the last slip. Then he offered his hand and helped me off the floor.

I took the slips back to my desk and put them beneath the lid. Then I turned to Gareth. 'Why are you actually here?' I asked.

He opened his satchel and pulled out proofs for the latest fascicle. '"Sleep to Sniggle",' he said, holding them in the air. 'If there aren't too many edits, we could go to print before Christmas.' He smiled, nodded, then delivered the proofs to Dr Murray's desk before leaving the Scriptorium. I thought he might turn and smile again, but he didn't. If he had, I would have told him there were likely to be plenty of edits.

Everyone returned to the Scriptorium after lunch, and I waited for Mr Dankworth to betray me. I was too old to be sent away, but there was enough time and silence for me to imagine a dozen other punishments. All of them began with the humiliation of my pockets being turned out, and ended with me never returning to the Scriptorium.

But Mr Dankworth never mentioned my words to Dr Murray. For days, I watched him, holding my breath every time he had cause to consult the Editor, but they never looked in my direction. I realised that not only were my words of no consequence to Mr Dankworth, but the fact I was spending time on them when I should have been doing Dictionary work was also of no concern.

I was responding to a spelling enquiry, one that had become all too common since the publication of 'Ribaldric to Romanite'. *Why*, asked the writer, *does the new Dictionary prefer* rime *when* rhyme *is so ubiquitous? Habit and good sense insist on the latter. Am I to be*

judged an illiterate? It was a thankless task as there was no reasonable response. The familiar sound of Gareth's bicycle was reason enough to leave it unfinished. I put down my pen and looked towards the door.

This was his third visit to the Scriptorium since he had helped pick my words off the floor a few weeks earlier.

'A nice young man,' Da had said the first time he noticed Gareth saying hello.

'As nice as Mr Pope and Mr Cushing?' I'd asked.

'I'm sure I don't know what you mean,' Da had said. 'He's a foreman. One of the few people Mr Hart trusts to convey concerns about style.' He'd looked at me then and raised his eyebrows. 'But usually those conversations occur at the Press.'

When the door opened, a pale daylight shone in. The assistants looked up, and Da nodded a greeting before glancing in my direction. Dr Murray stepped down from his stool.

I was too far away to hear what they said, but Gareth was pointing to a section of proof and explaining something to Dr Murray. I could see that Dr Murray agreed: he asked a question, listened, nodded, then he invited Gareth to come over to his desk, and together they examined some of the other pages. Mr Dankworth, I noticed, diligently ignored the entire interaction.

Gareth waited as Dr Murray wrote a quick note to Mr Hart. When it was written, and Gareth had put it in his satchel, the young man and the old walked together into the garden.

I saw them just beyond the door. Dr Murray stretched as he sometimes did when he'd been bent over proofs all morning. Their demeanour changed, became more intimate. Mr Hart was ill with exhaustion, Da had told me, and I guessed a mutual concern.

Dr Murray came back into the Scriptorium alone. I was surprised by the heaviness of the breath that escaped my lungs. He left the door open, and the fresh December air began circulating among the tables.

Two of the assistants put on their jackets; Rosfrith pulled a shawl around her shoulders. I did not normally hold with Dr Murray's idea that fresh air kept the mind sharp, but I had become too warm to think straight, and for once I was glad of it. I returned to the task of justifying *rime*.

'This is for you.' It was Gareth.

For a moment, it was impossible to look up. All the heat that had been in my body was now in my face.

'It's a word for your collection. One of my ma's. She used to use it this way all the time, but I couldn't find it in the fascicles we keep at the Press.' He spoke quietly, but I heard every word. Still I didn't look up; I had no confidence that I would be able to speak. Instead, I focused on the slip of paper Gareth had placed in front of me. He must have taken it from the pile of blanks kept on the shelf nearest the door. It was the commonest of words, but the meaning was different. I recognised it from when I was a little girl.

CABBAGE

'Come here, my little cabbage, and give me a hug.'

Deryth Owen

Deryth, what a beautiful name. The sentence was more or less as Lizzie would have said it.

'Mothers have a vocabulary all their own, don't you think?' he said.

'Actually, I wouldn't know.' I looked over at Da. 'I never knew my mother.'

Gareth looked stricken. 'Oh, I'm sorry.'

'Please, don't be. As you can imagine, my father has his own way with words.'

He laughed. 'Well, yes, he would.'

'And your father?' I asked. 'Does he work at the Press?'

'It was Ma who worked at the Press. She was a bindery girl. Organised my apprenticeship when I was fourteen.'

'But your father?'

'It was just my ma and me,' he said.

I looked at the slip in my hand and tried to imagine the woman who called this man her little cabbage. 'Thank you for the slip,' I said.

'I hope you don't mind me seeking you out.'

I looked at the sorting table. There were one or two furtive glances towards my desk and a strange smile on Da's face, though his eyes were steadfastly on his work.

'I'm very glad you did,' I said, looking into his face then quickly back at the slip.

'Well, I'll be sure to do it again.'

When he was gone, I opened the lid of my desk and sorted through my shoebox of slips until I found where Gareth's belonged.

January 1913

There was a crowd gathering around the Martyrs' Memorial when I rode towards the Bodleian. I could have avoided it by going down Parks Road as I usually did, but instead I rode the length of the Banbury Road until the crowd diverted me.

Notices had been posted all over Oxford. Leaflets littered the streets, and all the newspapers had run stories in support and against. The suffrage societies of Oxford were coming together for a peaceful procession from St Clement's to the Martyrs' Memorial. It would be hours before they started, but things were being set up and there was already an expectation, an excitement. It might have been a fair, but with the crackle of a looming thunderstorm in the air.

There were fewer people in the Bodleian than usual. I took my time searching the shelves of Arts End. The books Dr Murray wanted me to check were old, the quotations almost foreign on the page and easy to get wrong. I sat at a bench worn smooth by long-dead generations of scholars and wondered how many had been women.

I rode back the way I had come. The procession had arrived, and the crowd had swelled. Women outnumbered men by three to one, but I was surprised by the men who were there: all sorts. Men with ties and men without. Men on the arms of women. Men standing alone. Men huddled in small groups, capped and collarless, their arms folded in front of them, their legs pegged wide.

I leaned my bicycle against the railing of the tiny cemetery beside St Mary Magdalen, then I stood on the edge of the crowd.

When I'd read about the procession, I'd hoped Tilda might return to Oxford for it. I'd written to her and included a leaflet: *I'll wait by the little church near the Martyrs' Memorial.*

She'd sent a postcard back.

We shall see. The WSPU has not been invited (Mrs Pankhurst's methods are not embraced by many of the educated ladies of Oxford). But I'm glad you have joined the sisterhood and will be adding your voice to the cry — it's about time.

A woman was speaking on a platform set up by the Martyrs' Memorial, though from where I stood it was difficult to see whom, and I could barely hear what she said above the jeering. The leaflets had instructed us to *PAY NO ATTENTION* to those who wanted to disrupt, and for the most part the women and men who supported the speaker were doing just that. But the detractors were many, and they shouted from all corners of the crowd. Music began to blare from a gramophone placed in an open window of St John's College. A cloud of pipe-smoke rose from a group of men beside the speakers' platform. Another group began singing so loud that it was impossible to hear anything else. On the edge of the crowd, I felt strangely vulnerable.

The crowd around the Martyrs' Memorial churned. I stood on my toes to see what was happening and saw the disturbance move out through the sea of people. It came towards me, but I only realised what it meant when two men emerged in front of me, their arms locked around each other, each throwing punches. The man wearing a collar and tie was larger, but his arms flailed and his fists kept missing their target. The other man was more accurate. He wasn't wearing a jacket despite the cold, and his shirtsleeves were rolled up above his elbows. I moved back, but Magdalen Street was still congested and I was pushed up against the bicycles leaning against the railings of the church cemetery.

I saw police on horseback wade through the mass. The horses frightened the crowd, which split. People began to run, half the crowd towards Broad Street, half towards St Giles'. I took a step and was knocked from my feet. Women's shoes and men's; dress hems splashed with dirt. I was pulled up, knocked down again. Two women I didn't know yanked me up and told me to go home, but I stood, paralysed.

'Bitch!'

A rough red face, almost touching mine; the nose broken years before and never straightened. Then a gob of spit. I could barely breathe. I brought both arms up to protect myself, but the blow I expected never came.

'Hey! Leave off.'

A woman's voice. Loud. Ferocious ... Then gentle. 'They're cowards,' she said. The words and tone were familiar. I let my arms drop, opened my eyes. It was Tilda. She pulled me away and wiped the spit from my cheek. 'Scared their wives will stop doing their bidding.' She threw her handkerchief on the ground then took a step back.

'Esme. More beautiful than ever.' Tilda laughed at the look on my face.

Another scuffle started up beside us, and for a moment I was glad of the distraction. Then I saw who was involved.

'Gareth?'

He turned and the other man took his chance. A rough fist caught Gareth's lip, and a smirk spread over the stranger's face. I recognised the assailant's broken nose. Gareth managed to stay on his feet, but the man ran off before there was a chance to retaliate.

'Your lip is bleeding,' I said when Gareth was standing closer. He touched it and flinched, then smiled when he saw my concern, and flinched again.

'I'll live,' he said. 'What did you do to make that bloke so angry? He was making a beeline for the two of you.'

'Bastard,' said Tilda. Gareth's head swung her way. 'Oh, not you. You are our knight in shining armour.' She curtsied theatrically, her smile mocking. Gareth saw it for what it was and looked awkward.

'Tilda,' I said, taking her arm. 'This is Gareth. He works at the Press. He's a friend of mine.'

'A friend?' she said, raising her eyebrows.

I ignored her but couldn't look Gareth in the eye. 'Gareth, this is Tilda. We met years ago, when her theatre troupe came to Oxford.'

'Nice to meet you, Tilda,' Gareth said. 'Are you here for a play or for this?' He surveyed the confusion.

'Esme invited me, and Mrs Pankhurst thought it an opportunity to raise awareness, so here I am.'

There was so much shouting, and a siren. Women were being chased down Broad Street. 'I think we should go,' I said.

Tilda hugged me. 'You go – I think you're in good hands,' she said. 'But come to Old Tom on Friday evening. We have so much to catch up on.' Then she turned to Gareth. 'And you must come too. Promise me you will.'

Gareth looked to me for direction. Tilda watched on, waiting to see how I would respond. It was as if no time had passed since last I'd seen her. Daring and fear battled it out inside me. I did not want fear to win.

'Of course,' I said, looking back at Gareth. 'Perhaps, we could go together?'

His grin split the fragile seal of his cut lip, which started bleeding again. I reached into the pocket of my dress but found I had no handkerchief.

'A bit of paper would do the trick,' he said, trying to keep the smile in his eyes from spreading to his lips. 'It's little worse than a shaving cut.'

I extracted a blank slip and tore the corner off it. He dabbed at his lip with the sleeve of his shirt, then I placed the bit of paper on the cut. It stained red immediately, but held.

'I'll see you both on Friday,' Tilda said, winking at me. Then she turned towards Broad Street, where the fray seemed to be concentrating.

Gareth and I turned in the opposite direction.

❧

'Esme! Good Lord, what happened?' Rosfrith saw us as we walked in through the gates of Sunnyside. She looked to Gareth for an explanation.

'The procession to the Martyrs' Memorial got out of hand,' he said.

Gareth and I had barely spoken on our walk up the Banbury Road. Tilda had unsettled us and rendered us both shy.

'This happened at the procession?' said Rosfrith. She looked me up and down. My skirt was torn and soiled, my hair had come loose, my cheek smarted from where I'd continued to rub it to remove the filth of that man's hatred. 'Oh dear,' she continued. 'Mamma was there with Hilda and Gwyneth. It was wise of you to go together, though it doesn't seem to have helped you,' she said.

I found my tongue. 'Oh, no, we met quite by accident. I don't know how Gareth came to be there.'

She looked from Gareth to me, sceptical.

I was unable to hold her gaze and turned to Gareth. 'Why *were* you there?'

'Same reason you were,' he said.

'I'm not sure why *I* was there,' I said, as much to myself as to him.

Just then, Mrs Murray walked in through the gates with her eldest and youngest daughters. All three were unscathed and excited. Rosfrith ran to them.

Gareth walked with me to the kitchen and I introduced him to Lizzie. He helped explain what had happened.

'Let me give you something for that lip.' Lizzie dampened a clean cloth and passed it to him.

He removed the scrap of paper and held it up for us both to see. 'Stopped me bleeding to death, this did.'

'What on earth is it?' asked Lizzie, peering at it.

'The edge of a slip,' Gareth said, smiling in my direction.

'I really am grateful, you know,' I said. 'That man was terrifying. It was unfair of Tilda to mock you.'

'She was just testing me.'

'What do you mean?'

'Making sure I was on the right side.'

I smiled. 'And *are* you on the right side?'

He smiled back. 'Yes, I am.'

He seemed more sure than I was, and part of me felt ashamed. 'Sometimes I think there may be more than two sides,' I said.

'You'd do well not to take the side of the suffragettes,' Lizzie said. 'They're slowing things down with all their mischief.' She handed Gareth a glass of water.

'Thank you, Miss Lester,' he said.

'You call me Lizzie. I don't answer to anything else.'

We watched as he drank it down. When he finished, he took the glass to the sink and rinsed it. Lizzie looked at me in astonishment.

'People have always taken different roads to get to the same place,' Gareth said when he turned back to face us. 'Women's suffrage won't be any different.'

When Gareth left, Lizzie sat me down and washed my face. She brushed out my hair and rolled it back into a bun.

'Never met a man like him,' she said. 'Except maybe your da. He also rinses his cup.'

She had the same look on her face that Da did whenever Gareth visited the Scriptorium. I ignored her.

'You never did say why you was there,' she said.

I couldn't tell her about Tilda. It was the one topic we avoided, and the events of the day wouldn't help to elevate her in Lizzie's eyes. 'I was coming home from the Bodleian,' I said.

'Would have been quicker to come along Parks Road.'

'There was so much anger, Lizzie.'

'Well, I'm just glad you weren't badly hurt, or arrested.'

'What are they so scared of?'

Lizzie sighed. 'All of them are scared of losing something; but for the likes of him that spat in your face, they don't want their wives thinking they deserve more than they've got. Makes me glad to be in service when I think that men like that might be the alternative.'

The day was almost over when I returned to the Scriptorium. Tilda's postcard was sitting on top. I read it again then wrote a new slip, in duplicate.

SISTERHOOD
'I'm glad you have joined the sisterhood and will be adding your voice to the cry.'

Tilda Taylor, 1912

I searched the fascicles. *Sisterhood* was already published. The main sense referred, in one way or another, to the sisterhood experienced by nuns. Tilda's quotation belonged with the second sense: *Used loosely to denote a number of females having some common aim, characteristic or calling. Often in a bad sense.*

I went to the pigeon-holes and found the original slips. Newspaper clippings made up most of the quotations. In a clipping about females who agitate on questions they know nothing about, a volunteer had underlined *the shrieking sisterhood.* The most recent slip, from an article written in 1909, described women of the suffragette type as *a highly educated, screeching, childless, and husbandless sisterhood.*

They were all insulting, and I was heartened to think that Dr Murray had rejected them. Even so, I rewrote the published definition on a new slip, leaving off *in a bad sense*, and pinned a copy of Tilda's quotation in front of it. Then I put them in the pigeon-holes reserved for supplementary words.

When I turned away from the shelves, Da was watching me.

'What do *you* think of newspapers as a source of meaning?' he asked.

'What else did you see?'

He smiled, but it seemed an effort. 'I don't mind what you *add* to the pigeon-holes, Essy. Even if your quotations don't come from a text, they might encourage the search for something similar. The closest we can get to understanding new words is newspaper articles. James spends quite a bit of his time these days arguing for their validity.'

I thought about the clippings I'd just read. 'I'm not sure,' I said. 'They often seem no better than opinion, and if you want opinion to define what something means then you should at least consider all sides. Not all sides have a newspaper to speak for them.'

'It's a good thing, then, that some of them have you.'

Da and I sat together in the sitting room, both of us trying to make conversation and failing; both of us trying not to let the other see our eagerness for the knock on the door. It was already six o'clock. Da was facing the window onto the street. Whenever his eyes registered someone passing, I held my breath for the sound of the gate then released it when the gate did not sing.

Da looked more animated than he had in a while. When I'd told him Gareth had offered to accompany me to Old Tom, Da had smiled as if relieved, but I couldn't interpret it. Was he glad I had a chaperone for my meeting with Tilda, or was he glad I had a gentleman caller? He must have thought the latter would never happen. Whichever it was, it was the first time in weeks that the lines on his forehead had relaxed.

'You've been looking tired lately, Da.'

'It's the letter S. Four years and we're not even halfway through. It's sapping, stupefying, soporific …' He paused to think of another word.

'Slumberous, somnolent, somniferous,' I offered.

'Excellent,' he said, with a smile that took me back to our word games of years ago. Then he looked past me, through the window. His smile widened. The gate sang. I felt the tingle of perspiration under my arms and was glad when Da rose to answer the knock. He and Gareth stood talking in the hall for a few minutes. I stood up and checked my face in the mirror above the fireplace. I pinched my cheeks.

I hadn't been inside Old Tom since Tilda was last in Oxford. As Gareth and I approached, I was ambushed by memories of Bill. Then memories of Her.

'Is everything all right, Esme?'

I looked up at the sign hanging above the door of the small pub; a drawing of the Christ Church belltower.

'Quite all right,' I said. Gareth opened the door for me to step in.

Old Tom was as crowded as it had always been, and at first I thought Tilda may not have come. Then I saw her, at a table with three other women right at the back. She must have caused the usual fuss when she walked in, but she wasn't encouraging it the way she had seven years before: we had to push ourselves past small groups of men to reach her, but none appeared to be throwing flattery her way. It didn't feel as welcoming as it once had.

Tilda rose and embraced me. 'Ladies, this is Esme. We became fast friends the last time I was in Oxford.'

'You live here?' one of the women asked.

'She does,' said Tilda, her arm pulling me close. 'Though she hides herself away in a shed.'

The woman frowned. Tilda turned to me.

'How is your dictionary progressing, Esme?'

'We're up to S.'

'Good God, really? How can you stand going so slow?' She let me go and sat back down.

The other women were all looking up at me for a response. There were no spare chairs.

'We collect words for a few letters at the same time; it's not as tedious as it sounds.' No one said anything for a moment. I felt Gareth shift a little closer and was glad he had come.

'And this is …' Tilda hesitated and made a show of searching her memory. 'Gareth, isn't it?'

'Good to see you again, Miss Taylor,' he said.

'Tilda, please. And these lovely ladies are Shona, Betty and Gert.'

Shona was the youngest of the three, no more than twenty. The other two were a good ten years older than I was.

'I recognise you now,' said Gert. 'You were Tilda's helper that night at the Eagle and Child.' She looked at Tilda. 'Do you remember, Tilds? That was my first real *outing*.'

'The first of many,' Tilda said.

'And there will be many to come, the rate we're going.' Gert looked at me. 'We're no closer to the vote than we were a decade ago.' A few heads turned in our direction. Tilda stared them down.

'And what do you think of it all, Gareth?' Tilda said.

'Women's suffrage?'

'No, the price of pork. Of course, women's suffrage.'

'It affects us all,' he said.

'A supporter, then,' said Betty. Her voice gave away her northern origins, and I wondered if she'd come down from Manchester with Tilda.

'Of course.'

'But how far would you go?' Betty asked.

'What do you mean?'

'Well, it's easy to *say* the right things' – she glanced towards me – 'but words are meaningless without action.'

'And sometimes action can make a lie of good words,' Gareth said.

'And what would you know of our struggle, Gareth?' Tilda leaned back in her chair and sipped her whiskey.

My head turned from one to the other.

'My mother had to bring me up alone while working at the Press,' Gareth said. 'I know quite a lot.'

Gert scoffed. Tilda threw her a silencing glance. Gert raised a glass of sherry to her lips, and I noticed a gold band and a large diamond ring. She was a class or two above Betty. Shona had remained silent throughout the conversation, her head bowed deferentially, and I suddenly had the thought that she might be Gert's maid. My heart started to pound.

'And what do *you* know of our struggle, Gert?' I asked. Shona did her best to conceal a smile.

'I beg your pardon?'

'Well, it seems to me that we are not all struggling in the same way. Isn't it true that Mrs Pankhurst was willing to negotiate for women with property and education to get the vote, but not women like Gareth's mother, for instance?'

Tilda sat open-mouthed, a smile in her eyes. Gert and Betty were appalled, but speechless. Shona looked up for a moment, then back at her lap. The men immediately beside us had gone completely quiet.

'Excellent, Esme,' Tilda said, raising her now empty glass. 'I was wondering when you would join in.'

❧

The January night was cold, and Gareth offered me his coat for the walk back through the Oxford streets to Jericho.

'I'm quite all right,' I said. 'And you'll freeze if you take it off.'

He didn't insist. 'What did Tilda mean about you joining in?' he asked.

'She's always thought I didn't know my own mind when it came to women's suffrage.'

'Your ideas sounded pretty clear to me.'

'Well, that might be the most I've ever said on the subject, but that Gert woman was so awful I couldn't bear to be agreeable.'

'I didn't like what they were hinting at,' Gareth said.

'What do you mean?'

'*Deeds not words.*' He was thoughtful for a minute. 'Essy, do you know why Tilda is in Oxford?'

Essy. Gareth had never called me anything except Miss Nicoll, or Esme. A shiver went through me.

'You *are* cold,' he said, and he took off his coat and placed it over my shoulders. His hand brushed my neck as he straightened out the collar. I tried to remember what he'd asked me a moment before.

'She's here for the procession,' I said, pulling his coat around me. The warmth of him was still in it. 'And me. We were quite good friends for a while.'

We slowed on Walton Street, passed the back of Somerville College and stopped when we came to the Press. It was completely dark except for the orange glow from an office above the archway.

'Hart,' Gareth said.

'Does he never go home?'

'The Press *is* his home. He lives on the grounds with his wife.'

'And where do you live?'

'Near the canal. Same workers' cottage I grew up in with Ma. When she died, they let me stay. It's too small and too damp for a family.'

'Do you like working at the Press?' I asked.

Gareth leaned against the iron railing. 'It's all I know. It's not really a matter of liking.'

'Do you ever imagine a different life?'

He looked at me, cocked his head a little. 'You don't ask the usual questions, do you?'

I didn't know what to say.

'The usual questions are usually very uninteresting,' he continued. 'I sometimes imagine travelling, to France or Germany. I've learned to read both languages.'

'Only read?'

'That's all that's required for my job. I've been learning since I was an apprentice. It's Hart's doing. He set up the Clarendon Institute to educate his ignorant workforce. And to give the band a place to practise.'

'There's a band?'

'Of course. And a choir.'

When we started walking again there was less distance between us, but we fell silent as we turned onto Observatory Street. I was wondering if Gareth would ask me to walk out with him again. I was hoping he was thinking of it and wondering if I'd say yes. As we came to the house, I noticed Da in the sitting room. He was facing the window as he had earlier in the evening. He opened the door before I had a chance to knock. Gareth and I could only say goodnight.

❧

Tilda stayed in Oxford.

'I'm bunking in with a friend,' she told me. 'She has a narrowboat on the Castle Mill Stream. I can see the belltower of St Barnabas through the window beside my bed.'

'Is it comfortable?'

'Comfortable enough. And warm. She lives there with her sister, so it can be a bit tight. We have to take it in turns to dress.' She smiled wide.

I wrote my address on a slip and gave it to her. 'Just in case,' I said.

∾

Winter passed into spring. When I asked why Tilda was still in Oxford, she said she was gathering members for the WSPU. When I pressed her, she changed the subject.

'I thought I'd see more of you while I was here,' she said one afternoon as we walked along the towpath of the Castle Mill Stream, 'but you seem to spend all your free time with Gareth.'

'That's not true. We only have lunch together in Jericho now and then. And he's taken me to the theatre a few times.'

'You did always *love* the theatre,' Tilda said. 'Oh, Esme, you blush like a schoolgirl.' She took my arm in hers. 'I bet you're still a virgin.'

I blushed deeper and dropped my head. If she noticed she chose not to say anything, and we walked for a while without talking. The surface of the stream was alive, and I felt the bite of a mosquito on the back of my neck. 'How is the narrowboat, Till, now the weather has warmed?'

'Oh, God. It feels like living in a sardine tin left out in the sun. We're all a bit off.'

'You're welcome to stay with us, you know. I'm sure Da won't mind the extra company.' I offered, knowing she would turn me down again.

'It won't be for much longer,' she said. 'My deployment is almost over.'

'You make it sound like you're in an army.'

'Oh, but I am, Esme. Mrs Pankhurst's army.' She made a mock salute. 'The WSPU.'

'I've started going along to some of the local suffrage meetings Mrs Murray and her daughters attend,' I said. 'And there are a number of men, though the women do most of the talking.'

'Talk is all they do,' Tilda said.

'I don't think that's true,' I said. 'They produce a journal, and they organise all kinds of events.'

'It's all talk though, isn't it? The same words over and over again, and what's changed?'

I remembered Gareth asking why Tilda was really in Oxford. I'd long worked out that it wasn't for me, but I thought maybe it was for her friend in the narrowboat. Now I realised it was something else altogether. But I didn't want to know what.

'How is Bill?' I asked, not looking at her.

Tilda had mentioned Bill now and then. It was always fleeting and I was always grateful. But she would be leaving Oxford soon and I suddenly needed to know how he was.

'Bill? That rogue. He broke my heart. He got some silly girl knapped and stopped being at my beck and call. I was furious.'

'Knapped?'

She grinned. 'I know that look. Do you still carry those slips of paper around in your pockets?'

I nodded.

'Get one out then.'

We stopped walking, and Tilda laid her shawl on the grass beside the path. We sat.

'This is nice,' she said as I readied the slip and pencil. 'It's like before.'

I felt it too, but I knew that nothing would ever be like before. '*Knapped*,' I said as I wrote it on the slip. 'Put it in a sentence.'

She leaned back on her elbows and raised her face to the first day of summer. She took her time as she used to, wanting to get the quotation just right.

'Bill got some silly girl knapped and now he's a daddy, working all day and half the night to feed his squalling babe.'

It should have been obvious what *knapped* meant the first time she'd said it, but the newness of the word had made me deaf to the words either side of it. My hand shook a little as I finished the sentence.

'He's a father?' I said, watching Tilda's face. Her eyes remained shut to the sunlight, her jaw didn't twitch.

'Little Billy Bunting, I call him. He's five years old. Cute as a button, loves his aunty Tiddy.' She looked at me then. 'He still calls me that, even though he can talk as well as anyone. He's as bright as Bill was at that age.'

I looked at the slip.

KNAPPED

Pregnant.

'Bill got some silly girl knapped and now he's a daddy, working all day and half the night to feed his squalling babe.'

Tilda Taylor, 1913

Bill hadn't told her about us. He had neither bragged nor confessed. It wasn't the first time since giving Her away that I wished I had been able to love him.

Dr Murray called me over. 'Esme, I anticipate your workload and responsibilities will increase over the next few months,' he said.

I nodded, as if it were nothing, but I longed for more responsibility.

'Mr Dankworth will be leaving us at the end of the day and starting with Mr Craigie's team tomorrow,' Dr Murray continued. 'I believe he will be a great asset to our third editor. You know, better than most, how exacting he is.' A twitch of whiskers and slightly raised brows. 'Such qualities will go a long way to speeding up Craigie's sections.'

Two pieces of good news in one conversation; I hardly knew how to respond.

'Well, what have you to say? Is it acceptable?'

'Yes, Dr Murray. Of course. I'll do my best to fill the gap.'

'Your best is more than good enough, Esme.' He turned his attention back to the papers on his desk.

I was dismissed, but I didn't leave. I chewed my lip and wrung my hands. I spoke in a rush before I could censor myself.

'Dr Murray?'

'Yes.' He didn't look up.

'If I am to do more, will that be reflected in my wage?'

'Yes, yes. Of course. Starting next month.'

It was clear that Mr Dankworth would have preferred to leave without any acknowledgement, but Mr Sweatman wasn't going to let him. At the end of the day, he rose from his chair and began the farewells. The other assistants followed suit, each repeating general niceties and comments about Mr Dankworth's eagle-eye. No one really knew enough about Mr Dankworth to say anything particular.

Mr Dankworth suffered our good wishes and handshakes, wiping his hand repeatedly on the leg of his trousers.

'Thank you, Mr Dankworth,' I said, sparing him the discomfort of shaking another hand and offering a small tilt of my head instead. He appeared relieved. 'I've learned a great deal from you.' Now he was confused. 'I'm sorry I didn't always show gratitude.'

Mr Sweatman tried to hide his grin. He coughed and returned to his place at the sorting table. The others peeled away. I tried to hold Mr Dankworth's gaze, but he focused just beyond my right shoulder.

'You're welcome, Miss Nicoll.' Then he turned and left the Scriptorium.

Soon after, Gareth arrived. He handed Dr Murray some proofs he'd been waiting for, acknowledged Da and Mr Sweatman, then made his way to me.

'Sorry I'm late,' he said. 'Mr Hart chose this afternoon to remind us all about the rules.'

'The rules in his booklet?'

Gareth laughed. 'They're only the tip of the iceberg, Es. Every room in the Press has its own rules – surely you've seen them on the wall as you come in?'

I shrugged apologetically.

'Well, the Controller thinks we've all been blind to them and made sure every one of us read them aloud before leaving this afternoon.' He smiled. 'As the new manager, I had to go last.'

'Manager? Oh, Gareth, congratulations.' Without a thought, I jumped up and hugged him.

'If I'd known this would be your reaction, I would have asked for a promotion sooner,' Gareth said.

Da and Mr Sweatman turned to see what the excitement was about, and I pulled away before Gareth's arms could encircle me.

Flustered, I gathered my bag and fastened my hat. I went over to Da and kissed him on the head. 'I might be home late tonight, Da. Mrs Murray said it could be a long meeting.'

'I won't wait up, if that's all right, Essy,' he said. 'But I trust Gareth will see you home safe.' His smile nudged fatigue aside.

As we walked down the Banbury Road, I told Gareth about my own promotion.

'Well, not a promotion really – I'm still hovering on the bottom rung with Rosfrith – but it's an acknowledgement.'

'And well deserved,' he said.

'Why do you think men come along to these meetings?' I asked.

'Because the organisers of the Oxford Women's Suffrage Society have invited them.'

'Besides that.'

'Different reasons, I suspect. Some want what their wives and sisters want. Others have been told to be supportive, or else.'

'Which are you?'

He smiled. 'The first, of course.' Then his expression sobered. 'My ma had a hard life, Es. Too hard. And no say over any of it. I go to these meetings for her.'

❧

It was after midnight when the meeting ended. We walked in a tired and comfortable silence back to Observatory Street.

I tried to hush the gate as I opened it, but it still let out a sweet note, disturbing a figure that I hadn't noticed hiding in the dark.

'Tilda, what on earth?'

Gareth took the key from me and opened the door. We ushered Tilda into the kitchen and turned on the light. She was a mess.

'What's happened?' Gareth said.

'You don't want to know, and I'm not going to tell you. But I need your help. I'm so sorry, Esme. I wouldn't have come, but I'm hurt.'

The sleeve of her dress was filthy – no, not just filthy, burned. It hung in charred shreds. One hand was cradled in the other.

'Show me,' I said.

The skin of her hand was mottled, red and black – dirt or burned skin, I couldn't tell. My funny fingers prickled with some kind of memory.

'Why didn't you go straight to a doctor?' said Gareth.

'I couldn't risk it.'

I searched the cupboards for ointments and bandages, but all I found were plasters and cough medicine. Lily would have stocked the cupboards better, I thought. And she would have known what to do.

'Gareth, you have to get Lizzie. Tell her to bring her medicine pouch – something for burns.'

'It's long after midnight, Es. She'll be asleep.'

'Maybe. The kitchen door is always open. Call up the stairs; don't frighten her. She'll come.'

When Gareth had gone, I filled a bowl with cold water and put it on the kitchen table in front of Tilda. 'Will you tell me what happened?'

'No.'

'Why? Do you think I'd disapprove?'

'I *know* you'd disapprove.'

I asked the question I barely wanted the answer to. 'Was anyone else hurt, Till?'

Tilda looked at me. A shadow of doubt, of fear, crossed her face. 'I honestly don't know.'

Pity rose in my chest, but anger overtook it. I turned away and pulled open a drawer, took out a clean tea towel and slammed the drawer shut. 'Whatever it is you've done, what do you think it will achieve?' When I turned back to Tilda, the doubt and fear had left her.

'The government isn't listening to all the eloquent, sensible words of your suffragists. But they can't ignore what we *do.*'

I took a deep breath and tried to focus on her hand. 'Does it hurt?'

'A bit.'

'Mine didn't, so that's probably good.' I lifted her arm so her hand hovered over the bowl of water. When she resisted. I pushed it under. She didn't complain. Giant blisters had deformed her fingers. Her whole hand had started to swell. Below the water, the charred and angry skin was magnified and shocking against the pale slenderness of her wrist.

'I want the same things as you, Till, but this isn't the right way. It can't be.'

'There is no right way, Esme. If there was, we'd have voted in the last election.'

'Are you sure it's the vote you have your eye on, and not the attention?'

She smiled weakly. 'You're not wrong. But if it makes people take notice it might make them think.'

'They might just think you're mad and dangerous. They won't negotiate with that.'

Tilda looked up at me. 'Well, perhaps that's when the sensible words of your suffragists come in.'

The gate sang. I jumped up to open the door. Lizzie stood on the threshold, bewildered. She looked past me into the hall, and I realised it was the first time she had ever been in my home.

'Oh, Lizzie, thank goodness.' I closed the door behind them and ushered them towards the kitchen.

Lizzie barely acknowledged Tilda, but she took her arm gently and lifted her hand from the bowl of water. She laid it on the tea towel and blew the burned skin dry.

'It might look worse than it is,' she finally said. 'Blisters usually mean there's good skin beneath. Try not to pop them too soon.' She took a small bottle of ointment from her leather pouch and removed the stopper. Gareth held the bottle while Lizzie spread the ointment over Tilda's peeling skin, careful to avoid the blisters. Only once did Tilda draw a sharp breath. Lizzie looked to her then, their eyes meeting for the first time. Lizzie's face was full of a concern I recognised.

She wrapped Tilda's hand in gauze. 'I can't promise it won't scar.'

'If it does, I'll be in good company,' Tilda said, looking to me.

'And you should see a doctor.'

Tilda nodded.

'Well, then,' Lizzie said, 'if that's all I'm needed for, I'll be off back to my bed.'

Tilda put her good hand on Lizzie's arm. 'I know you don't approve of me, Lizzie, and I understand why you wouldn't. But I am so very grateful.'

'You're a friend of Esme's.'

'You could have said no,' Tilda said.

'No, I couldn't.' With that, Lizzie stood and let Gareth guide her back to the front door. When I tried to catch her eye, she looked away.

It was three in the morning when Gareth returned from walking Lizzie home.

'Will she forgive me?' I asked.

'Funny, she asked me the same thing about you.' Then he turned to Tilda. 'There's a train to London at 6 a.m. Do you think you should be on it?'

'Yes. I think I should.'

Gareth turned to me. 'Would your father mind if Tilda stayed here until then?

'Da won't know. He's not likely to wake before seven.'

'Do you have much that needs to be collected from the narrowboat?' he asked Tilda.

'Nothing that can't be sent on, if Esme doesn't mind lending me some clean clothes.'

Gareth put on his jacket. 'I'll be back in a couple of hours to walk you to the station.'

'I don't need a chaperone.'

'Yes, you do.'

Gareth left. I tip-toed upstairs and found a dress that I thought Tilda could tolerate. It would be a bit long and barely fashionable for a woman like her, but needs must. When I returned to the lounge, Tilda had fallen asleep.

I put a rug over her and wondered when we would see each other again. I loved her, and I feared for her. I wondered if this was what it felt like to be a sister. Not a comrade – I knew I wasn't that – but a flesh-and-blood sister. Like Rosfrith and Elsie. Like Ditte and Beth. I watched the breath go in and out of her, watched her eyes twitch. I tried to imagine what she was dreaming.

When the day shone pale through the front windows, I heard the gate sing.

❧

The *Oxford Times* ran the story of Rough's Boathouse. The fire brigade could do nothing to stop it burning to the ground and estimated the damage bill to be more than three thousand pounds. No one was hurt, it said, but four women had been seen fleeing: three in a punt, and one on foot. None had been caught, but it was generally suspected they were suffragettes, following the distribution of pamphlets targeting rowing clubs for their objection to women joining the sport. The act of arson signalled an escalation in their campaign. In a show of concern and opposition to militancy, Oxford's established suffrage organisations had already condemned the act and were collecting money for the workmen who had been laid off because of it.

When Mrs Murray came into the Scriptorium the next day with a collection jar, I gave all the change I had.

'Very generous of you, Esme,' she said, shaking the jar. 'An example to the gentlemen of the sorting table.'

Da looked in my direction and smiled, proud and oblivious.

May 1913

I never said goodbye to Da. When they took him from the house, one side of his face had collapsed, and he couldn't speak. I kissed him and said I would follow with pyjamas and the book that was beside his bed. His eyes were desperate as I babbled on.

I changed his sheets and put the vase of yellow roses I'd arranged for my room on his bedside table. I picked up his book, *The Getting of Wisdom*. 'An Australian novel,' Da had said. 'About a bright young woman; it's hard to believe a man wrote it. I think you would like it very much.' We might have talked more, but I couldn't. *Australian*. I'd made an excuse and left the table.

When I arrived at the Radcliffe Infirmary, they told me he was gone. *Gone*, I thought. It was wholly inadequate.

Gareth hauled a mattress up the narrow stairs to Lizzie's room, and I slept there until the funeral. Lizzie collected what I needed from the house so I wouldn't have to face its emptiness, but I couldn't help thinking of her going from room to room, checking all was well. In my mind, I followed her from the front door, saw her collect the post and pause as she wondered what to do with it. I suspected she would protect me from whatever the letters might contain by leaving them on the hall table.

I didn't want to go any further, but Lizzie, I knew, would pop her head into the sitting room, then the dining room that we never used. She would walk through to the kitchen and wash the dirty dishes. She would test that the windows were firmly shut and check the locks on every door. Then she would put her hand on the banister at the bottom of the stairs and cast her eyes to the top. She would take a deep breath and begin her ascent. She got a little heavier every year, and this had become her habit. I'd seen it a thousand times as I followed her up her own staircase.

I wanted it to stop, but I had no more control of my thoughts than of the weather. I imagined her searching my wardrobe for a black dress, and my weeping began. Then I remembered the roses beside Da's bed. Lizzie would find them drooping. She'd pick up the vase to take it downstairs, and she'd wonder whether Da had had the pleasure of seeing them at their best before he was taken to the Radcliffe.

I wanted the flowers to stay. Not to rot, but to stay, slightly wilting, for eternity.

❧

5th May 1913

My dear Esme,

I will arrive in Oxford the day after tomorrow, and I will not leave your side the whole time I am there. We shall hold each other up. You will, of course, have to shake the hands of a lot of well-meaning people and listen to stories of your father's kindness (there will be many), but at the right time I will lead you away from the sandwiches and the well-wishers, and we will wander along Castle Mill Stream until we get to Walton Bridge. Harry loved that spot; it's where he proposed to Lily.

This is no time to be strong, my dear girl. Harry was father and mother to you, and his passing will leave you feeling lost. My own father was very dear to me, and I know a little of how your heart must ache. Let it ache.

My father still echoes in my mind whenever I need good counsel; I suspect yours will do the same in time. In the interim, make the most of that young man you have become so attached to. 'Lily would like him very much,' Harry said in his last letter. Did he ever tell you? There could be no higher blessing.

I expect you are camping in Lizzie's room. I will go straight to Sunnyside from the train.

All my love,
Ditte

❧

As promised, Ditte led me away from all the well-wishers. We didn't say goodbye; we just walked into the garden, past the Scriptorium and out onto the Banbury Road. On St Margaret's Road, I realised Gareth was with us, just a few steps behind. We walked in silence until we got to the towpath along Castle Mill Stream.

'Harry took this walk every Sunday afternoon, Gareth,' Ditte said. Gareth fell into step beside me.

'He came here to discuss the week with Lily. Did you know that, Esme?'

I didn't.

'I say discuss, but it was a meditation, really. He would walk along this path with his head full of the week's concerns, and by the time he arrived at Walton Bridge the most pressing would have asserted itself. He told me he would sit and consider it from Lily's perspective.' She looked to see if she should continue. I hoped she would, but I was mute.

'Of course you were the main topic of conversation, but I was surprised to hear that he would also consult Lily on everything from what to wear to some function to whether he should buy lamb or beef for Sunday lunch – on the few occasions he decided to tackle a roast with all the trimmings.'

I felt the smallest smile, remembering the beef, raw or burnt, and our Sunday strolls into Jericho.

'Truly,' Ditte said, squeezing my arm.

It was a gift, this story. As I listened to Ditte, my memories of life with Da were subtly touched up, like a painter might add a daub of colour to give the impression of morning light. Lily, always so absent, suddenly wasn't.

'There it is,' Ditte said, as we approached the bridge. 'This was their spot.'

I'd walked under it so often, but now it looked completely different. Gareth took my hand, then he led me to the bench at the edge of the path and sat close enough to feel me trembling.

This wasn't how it was supposed to happen, I thought. But was I thinking about Da or Gareth? Gareth had never held my hand before. I'd thought I'd have Da forever.

We sat. The stream barely moved beneath the bridge, but small disturbances broke the surface every now and then. I could easily imagine Da sitting there, letting his thoughts ebb and flow.

'Someone's left flowers,' Gareth said.

I looked to where he was pointing, as did Ditte, and saw a bunch of flowers laid carefully beside the arch of the bridge. They were not fresh, but they hadn't completely expired. Two or three blooms still held some shape and colour.

'Oh, my,' I heard Ditte say with a catch in her voice. 'They're for Lily.'

I was confused. Gareth shifted closer to me.

Tears ran quietly along the creases around Ditte's eyes. 'I was with him the first time, after her funeral. I had no idea he was still bringing her flowers.'

I looked around, half expecting to see him. It had only been a few days, but I was getting used to this trick of grief, and for the first time I was not overcome. The breath that filled my lungs felt easier. Before I let it go, I caught the decaying scent of rush daffodil. Da had never liked them, but he'd told me they were Lily's favourite.

❧

I couldn't escape Da's absence. I felt it when I turned onto Observatory Street, and when I opened the door to our house, I had to force myself to step over the threshold. Lizzie stayed for a few weeks, and the smell of Da's pipe faded beneath the smells of her cooking. In the morning, I rose when she rose and we walked together to Sunnyside. I'd help her in the kitchen for an hour to make up some of the time she lost by staying with me, and when the first person arrived at the Scriptorium I would cross the garden and go in.

There was a space at the sorting table that no one filled. Perhaps it was out of respect for me, but from where I sat I saw the way Mr Sweatman tucked in Da's chair, and how often Mr Maling looked in that direction with a query on his tongue. Dr Murray got older in the weeks and months after Da died. He stared along the length of the sorting table and made no effort to look for a new assistant. I hated the space that Da had left and avoided looking at it whenever I came into the Scriptorium.

Grief was all I could feel. It crowded my thoughts and filled my heart and left no room for anything else. I walked out with Gareth every now and then. If it rained we would have lunch in Jericho, but if the weather was fine we walked along the Cherwell. Hawthorn marked the months since Da's death: berries ripened, then leaves fell. We wondered if the winter might bring snow. I took Gareth's friendship for granted. I needed it to fill the void and couldn't contemplate anything more or less than what it was. When he sought to take my arm in his, I didn't notice until the gesture had been withdrawn.

Christmas loomed, and my aunt insisted I visit her and my

cousins in Scotland. Without Da, they seemed almost like strangers. I made excuses and travelled to Bath instead, where Ditte and Beth administered liberal amounts of good humour, pragmatism and Madeira cake. I returned to Oxford feeling lighter than when I'd left.

❧

I walked into the Scriptorium on the third day of 1914 and there was a new lexicographer sitting where Da had once sat. Mr Rawlings wasn't young and he wasn't old. He was unremarkable and oblivious to who had sat in that spot at the sorting table before him.

It was an enormous relief to us all.

PART FIVE

1914–1915
Speech–Sullen

August 1914

There was a new hum in the Scriptorium. I felt it as an animal might when there is a decrease in air pressure before a storm. The prospect of war had heightened our senses. All over Oxford, young men were getting about with more spring. Their strides were longer and they talked louder – or so it seemed. The students had always raised their voices above the necessary volume in order to impress a pretty girl or intimidate a townie, but in the past the topics had varied. Not any more. Student and townie alike talked of nothing but war, and it seemed that most of them couldn't wait for it to come.

In the Scriptorium, two of the newer assistants began to spend their breaks talking about coming face-to-face with the Kaiser and winning the war before it could start. They were young and pale and thin. They wore spectacles, and if they'd been in any fights at all they would have been awkward scraps over library books or proper grammar. Neither could approach Dr Murray without a hesitant step and a stutter, so I judged them unlikely to persuade the Kaiser to give up Belgium. The older assistants had more sober conversations, their faces darkening in a way that rarely occurred during their disagreements about words. Mr Rawlings had lost a brother in the Boer War, and he told the younger men that there was no glory in killing. They nodded, polite. They didn't notice the waver in his voice, and before he was out of earshot they were talking again about the particulars of joining up, wondering how long they would have to train before they were sent into the fray. Mr Rawlings bent under the weight of it.

'This war is going to slow the Dictionary down,' I heard Mr Maling say to Dr Murray. 'It's a gun they want in their hand, not a pencil.'

From then on, I woke every morning with a dread fear.

～

No one slept on the night of the 3rd of August, even if they took to their beds and tried. Our two young assistants travelled to London and spent the balmy night carousing in Pall Mall, waiting for word that Germany had withdrawn from Belgium. It didn't come. As Big Ben chimed the first hour of a new day, they sang 'God save the King'.

The next day, they returned to the Scriptorium full of a bravado that didn't suit them. They approached Dr Murray together and told him they had volunteered. 'Both of you are short-sighted and unfit,' I heard Dr Murray say. 'You'd do more good for your country if you stayed here.'

It was impossible to concentrate, so I rode to the Press. I'd never known it to be so quiet. In the composing room, only half the benches had a man standing at them.

'Just two?' Gareth said, when I told him what had happened at the Scriptorium. 'Sixty-three men marched out of the Press this morning. Most were volunteers in the Territorial Force, but not all. There would have been sixty-five, except Mr Hart pulled two out by the collars who he knew to be underage. Said he'd give them a hiding after their mothers had.'

Mr Maling was right: the war slowed the Dictionary down. Within a few months, there were only women and old men left in the Scriptorium. Mr Rawlings, who was not quite old, had left because of a nervous complaint, and there was a space at the end of the sorting table once more. No one filled it.

Over at the Old Ashmolean, Mr Bradley's and Mr Craigie's teams were similarly reduced, and Mr Hart was down to half his printing and compositing staff.

I'd never worked so hard.

'You're enjoying this,' Gareth said, as he stood beside my desk one day, waiting for me to finish an entry.

I'd been given more responsibility, and I couldn't deny I was happy about it. He took an envelope out of his satchel.

'No proofs?' I said.

'Just a note for Dr Murray.'

'Are you the errand boy now?'

'My duties have multiplied. The juniors have all signed up.'

'I'm glad you're not a junior, then,' I said.

'I had to fight for this particular errand,' Gareth went on. 'We're also down compositors and printers, and Mr Hart has asked foremen and managers to fill in where possible. He'd glue me to my old bench if he could, but I wanted to see you.'

'I don't suppose Mr Hart is taking the new circumstances in his stride.'

Gareth looked at me like it was an understatement. 'If he's not careful the rest of us will sign up too.'

'Don't say that,' I said. He'd put words to the fear I woke up with.

꩜

The heat and heady excitement of August had given way to a damp autumn. Dr Murray developed a cough, and Mrs Murray insisted he avoid the Scriptorium. 'As cold as an icebox,' she said, and it was barely an exaggeration, even when the grate was ablaze.

'Nonsense,' was his reply, but they must have come to a compromise because from then on Dr Murray arrived at ten every morning and left at two – unless Mrs Murray wasn't home to notice, in which case he would stay until five, his rough and faltering breath an incentive for us all to work harder and longer. He barely spoke of the war except to grumble about the inconvenience to the Dictionary. Despite our efforts, output had slowed and printing was backing up. Years were added to the expected completion date. I probably wasn't the only person wondering if Dr Murray would live to see it.

Ditte and other trusted volunteers were pushed into greater service, and every day brought proofs and new copy from all over Britain. Dr Murray had even begun sending proofs to Dictionary staff fighting in France. 'They'll be grateful for the distraction,' he said.

When I opened the first envelope from across the Channel, I could barely breathe. There were smudges of dirt from its journey. I imagined the route it must have taken, and the hands it must have passed through. I wondered if all the men who had touched it were still alive. I didn't recognise the handwriting, but I knew the name on the back of the envelope. I tried to remember him but could only conjure an image of a small, pale-faced young man hunched over his desk at one end of the Dictionary Room in the Old Ashmolean. He usually worked with Mr Bradley, and Eleanor Bradley had described him as quietly brilliant but socially terrified. His corrections were thorough and needed little from me. Dr Murray was right, I thought. He must have been grateful for the distraction.

The following week, I met Gareth for lunch at a pub in Jericho.

'It's a pity Mr Hart can't send copy to France for printing,' I said. Gareth was quiet, and I was filling the silence with my story. 'I like the idea of giant presses being dragged to the front, and soldiers being equipped with metal type instead of bullets.'

Gareth stared at his pie, poking holes in the pastry with his fork. He looked up and frowned. 'You can't make light of this, Es.'

I felt my face heat, then realised he was on the verge of tears. I reached across the table and took his free hand.

'What's happened?' I asked.

He took a long time to reply, never taking his eyes from mine. 'It just feels pointless.' He looked back down at his food.

'Tell me.'

'I was resetting type for *sorrow*.' He drew a quick breath and looked to the ceiling. I gave up his hand so he could wipe his face.

'Who?' I asked.

'They were apprentices. Been at the Press barely two years.' He paused. 'Started together, left together. Thick as thieves.'

He pushed the pie out of the way and put his elbows on the table, held his head in his hands. He stared at the tablecloth and finished his story. 'Jed's mother came to the composing room looking for Mr Hart. Jed was the younger of the two, not even seventeen. She came to tell Mr Hart that he won't be coming back.' He looked up then. 'She was a wreck, Essy. Deranged. Jed was her only child, and she couldn't stop saying that he was only turning seventeen next week. Over and over, like the fact of it would bring him back because he should never have been there in the first place.' He took a deep breath. I blinked to hold back my own tears. 'Someone found Mr Hart, and he took her to his office. We could hear her wailing as he led her down the hall.'

I pushed my own plate away. Gareth drank half his glass of stout.

'It was impossible to return to that word,' he said. 'It made me sick just looking at the type. The war's only been going a couple of months, and they think it will be years. How many Jeds will there be?'

I had no answer.

He sighed. 'I suddenly couldn't see the point,' he said.

'We have to keep doing what we do, Gareth. No matter what that is. Otherwise we're just waiting.'

'It would be good to feel I was doing something useful. Typesetting *sorrow* won't take the sorrow away. Jed's mother will feel what she feels, no matter what is written in a dictionary.'

'But maybe it will help others to understand what she is feeling.'

Even as I said it, I wasn't convinced. Of some experiences, the Dictionary would only ever provide an approximation. *Sorrow*, I already knew, was one of them.

Barely a week went by that didn't bring another mother to the Controller's door with the news her son would not be returning. The editors at the Scriptorium and Old Ashmolean were not so burdened, but neither were they immune. By virtue of education or connection, the lexicographers became officers, though their learning hardly equipped them to be leaders of men. Staff at the Press were from a broader spectrum – part of the fodder classes, Gareth said. He stopped telling me every time someone from the Press died.

The door to Mr Hart's office was ajar. I knocked and pushed it open a little wider.

'Yes,' he said, without looking up from his papers.

I walked towards his desk, but still he didn't look up. I cleared my throat. 'Last-minute edits, Mr Hart. *Speech* to *spring*.'

He looked up, the creases between his brows deepening as he took the proofs and the note from Dr Murray. He read the note and I saw his jaw clench. Dr Murray wanted another edit – the third or fourth, I wasn't sure. I wondered if the plates had been cast. I dared not ask.

'Illness doesn't make him less pedantic,' Mr Hart said.

It wasn't meant for me, so I remained quiet. He stood and walked towards the door. He didn't ask me to wait, so I followed him.

The composing room was quiet of talk, but there was a percussive clicking of type being placed in sticks then turned out into formes that would hold a whole page of words. I waited by the door as Mr Hart approached the nearest bench. The compositor was young – no longer an apprentice, but too young for the war. He looked nervous as Mr Hart cast an eye over his forme. I wondered how easily mistakes could be noticed when everything was back to front. Mr Hart seemed satisfied and patted the assistant on the back, then he moved towards the next bench. Dr Murray's edits would have to wait.

I remained just inside the door and searched the room. Gareth was at his old bench: despite now being a manager, he was needed to set type for a few hours a day. I watched him like a stranger might. There was something unfamiliar about him. His face was more intent than I'd ever seen it and his body surer. It struck me that we are never fully at ease when we are aware of another's gaze. Perhaps we are never fully ourselves. In the desire to please or impress, to persuade or dominate, our movements become conscious, our features set.

I'd always thought him lean, but watching him work, his shirtsleeves rolled up and the muscles in his forearms taut, I noticed the elegance of his strength. In his concentration and the fluidity of his movements, he looked to me like a painter or a composer, his placement of type as deliberate as notes on a sheet of music.

I felt a pang of guilt. I knew too little of what he did. I'd assumed it was nothing more than mechanical monotony. After all, the words were chosen by the editors, the meanings suggested by writers. All he had to do was transcribe them. But that was not what I saw. He studied a slip then made a selection of type. He placed it, considered it, took a pencil from behind his ear and made notes on the slip. Was he editing? With the surety of having solved a problem, he removed the type and replaced it with a better arrangement.

Only in his sleep would I see him this unguarded. I was surprised to realise that I longed to see him sleep. The thought pierced my heart.

Gareth stood up straight and moved his head from side to side, stretching out his neck. The movements must have caught Mr Hart's eye, because the Controller suggested a correction to the type on the forme he was inspecting, then walked towards his manager. Gareth saw him, and there was the slightest tightening of muscles in his shoulders and face: an adjustment to being observed. I too began to walk towards Gareth. When he saw me, a smile broke across his face and he was entirely familiar again.

'Esme,' he said. His delight warmed every part of me.

Only then did Mr Hart realise I was there. 'Oh, yes, of course.' There was an awkward silence as Mr Hart and I both wondered whether we were getting in the way of the other's conversation with Gareth.

'I'm sorry,' I said. 'Perhaps I should wait in the corridor?'

'Not at all, Miss Nicoll,' said Mr Hart.

'Mr Hart,' said Gareth, bringing us all back to the business we were there for. 'Edits from Sir James?'

'Yes.' Mr Hart approached Gareth at his bench. 'It's as you anticipated. I'm tempted from now on to let you make the change when you notice it; it would save a damn lot of time.' Then, remembering me, he made a grudging apology for his language. Gareth suppressed a grin.

When they'd finished discussing the edits, Gareth asked if he could take his break early.

'Yes, yes. Take an extra quarter-hour,' said Mr Hart.

'You've flustered him,' Gareth said, as Mr Hart walked away. 'I'll just finish setting this line.'

I watched as Gareth selected small bits of metal type from the tray in front of him. His hand moved quickly, and the stick was soon full. He turned it out into the forme and rubbed his thumb.

'Do you think Mr Hart was serious when he said he'd let you make changes to the copy before setting it in type?'

Gareth laughed. 'Good God, no.'

'But you must be tempted,' I said carefully.

'Why do you say that?'

'Well, I'd never thought much about it before, but seeing you here I realise you spend your life with words, putting them in their place. Surely you've developed opinions about what reads well.'

'It's not my job to have opinions, Es.' He wasn't looking at me, but I could see a smile hovering by the edge of his mouth.

'I'm not sure I could like a man without opinions,' I said.

He smiled then. 'Well, in that case, let's just say that I have more opinions about the copy that comes from the Old Ashmolean than I do about the copy that comes from the Scriptorium.' He stood to remove his apron. 'Do you mind if we stop by the printing room?'

The printing room was in full operation, huge sheets of paper coming down like the wings of a giant bird or being rolled off large drums in quick succession; the old way and the new, Gareth said. Each had a rhythm for the ear and the eye, and I found it strangely soothing to see the pages pile up.

Gareth led me to one of the old presses. I felt the air shift as the giant wing descended.

'Harold, I have that part you asked for.' Gareth took a small wheel-like part from his pocket and gave it to the old man. 'If you have trouble fitting it, I can come back this afternoon and do it.'

Harold took the part, and I noticed his hands shaking ever so slightly.

'Esme, may I introduce Harold Fairweather. Harold is a master printer, recently come out of retirement – isn't that right, Harold?'

'I'm doing my bit,' said Harold.

'And this is Miss Esme Nicoll,' Gareth continued. 'Esme works with Dr Murray on the Dictionary.'

Harold smiled. 'Where would the English language be without us?'

I looked at the pages coming off the printer. 'Are you printing the Dictionary?'

'That I am.' He nodded towards a pile of printed sheets.

I picked up the edge of one, held it between my thumb and fingers and rubbed the paper. I was anxious not to touch the words in case the ink was still wet. I had an image of smudging one and the word being erased from the vocabulary of whoever bought the fascicle that the page belonged to.

'These old presses have personalities,' Harold was saying. 'Gareth knows this one as well as anyone.'

I looked at Gareth, 'Is that so?'

'I started on the presses,' he said. 'I was apprenticed to Harold when I was fourteen.'

'When it plays up he's the only one can coax it to behave, even before we lost half the mechanics,' said Harold. 'Don't know how I'll get on without him.'

'I can't imagine why you'd *have* to get on without him,' I said.

'Hypothetical, miss,' he replied quickly.

'You should visit more often,' Gareth said as we walked along Walton Street. 'Hart is in the habit of docking a quarter-hour from our lunch break these days, not adding it.'

'Dr Murray's the same. It's as though the Scriptorium and the Press are their battlegrounds. They have no other contribution to make.' As soon as I said it, I regretted it.

'Hart's always been a hard taskmaster,' Gareth said. 'But if he isn't careful he'll lose more men to his unreasonable demands than to the war.'

We walked into the heart of Jericho. It was crowded with lunchtime activity, and Gareth nodded at every second person. Every family was connected to the Press in some way.

'Will he lose you?' I said.

Gareth paused. 'He's particular, occasionally moody, and he drives himself and his staff harder than necessary, but he and I have a way of working that suits us both. I've grown fond of him over the years, Es. I think it's mutual.'

I'd seen it myself, many times. Gareth had an ease and confidence that softened Mr Hart as it softened Dr Murray.

We turned into Little Clarendon Street and walked towards the tea shop. 'But will he lose you?' I asked again.

Gareth pushed open the door, and the bell above tinkled. I stood on the threshold, waiting for him to reply.

'You heard Harold,' he said. 'Hypothetical.'

He guided me to a table at the back and pulled out the chair for me to sit.

'I saw the look he gave you,' I said, as he pulled out his own chair. 'It was an apology.'

'He knows compliments make me uncomfortable.'

Gareth couldn't look at me. Instead, he looked around for the waitress. He caught her eye and turned back to examine the menu.

'What do you fancy?' he said, without looking up.

I reached my hand across the table and enfolded his. 'I fancy the truth, Gareth. What are you planning?'

He looked up. 'Essy ...' But nothing came after it.

'You're scaring me.'

He reached into his trouser pocket and pulled something out. He held it in his fist between us, and I saw his face flush and his jaw clench.

'What is it?' I asked.

His fingers curled back, revealing the crushed remains of a white feather.

'Put it away,' I said.

'It was tied to the back door at the Press,' Gareth said.

'So, it could be for anyone. Hundreds of people work there.'

'I know that. I don't think it was for me, necessarily. But it makes you think.'

The waitress interrupted, and Gareth ordered.

'You're too old,' I said.

'Thirty-six is not too old. And it's better than being twenty-six, or sixteen, for God's sake. Those boys have barely lived.'

The waitress put the pot of tea between us. I barely breathed as she carefully placed the teacups and milk jug.

As soon as she moved away, I said, 'You sound like you want to go.'

'Only the young or stupid would want to go to war, Essy. No, I don't *want* to go.'

'But you're thinking about it.'

'It's impossible not to.'

'Well, think about me instead.' I heard the child in my voice, the desperate plea. I hadn't asked this of him before, and I'd avoided any sentiment that might encourage more than friendship.

'Oh, Essy. I never stop thinking about you.'

When the sandwiches arrived the waitress didn't fuss over their placement, but our conversation ceased nonetheless. Neither of us was brave enough to resume it, and we spent the next fifteen minutes eating without a word.

After lunch we walked along the towpath of Castle Mill Stream. Snowdrops carpeted the bank as if challenging winter to do a better job.

'I have a word for you,' Gareth said. 'It already exists, but the Dictionary doesn't show it being used like this. I thought it should be in your collection.' He took a slip out of his pocket, a bright white square of paper that I knew had been cut from one of the giant sheets used in the presses. He read it silently to himself, and I wondered if he wanted to change his mind and keep it.

At the next bench, we sat.

'I set the type for this word, a while ago now.' He continued to hang on to it. 'It means so many things, but the way this woman used it made me think something might be missing from the Dictionary.'

'Who was the woman?' But I knew before he answered.

'A mother.'

'And the word?'

'*Loss*,' he said.

The papers were full of it. Since the war had begun, we could have filled a whole volume with quotations containing *loss*. The casualty lists in the *Times of London* kept a count of it, and the Battle of Ypres had overwhelmed its pages. The dead included Oxford men. Press men. Jericho boys Gareth had known since they were small. *Loss* was a useful word, and terrible in its scope.

'Can I see it?'

Gareth looked again at the slip, then passed it to me.

LOSS

'Sorry for your loss, they say. And I want to know what they mean, because it's not just my boys I've lost. I've lost my motherhood, my chance to be a grandmother. I've lost the easy conversation of neighbours and the comfort of family in my old age. Every day I wake to some new loss that I hadn't thought of before, and I know that soon it will be my mind.'

Vivienne Blackman, 1915

Gareth put a hand on my shoulder. It was reassuring. I felt the gentle squeeze, the caress of his thumb. Something more than friendship that I couldn't discourage. But he had no idea.

I've lost my motherhood. The words had forced a memory: kindly eyes in a freckled face; an anchor during pain. Sarah, my baby's mother. Her mother. I tried to recall something of Her, but Her smell lingered only as words I'd once written down and stored in the trunk. When I closed my eyes, I saw nothing of Her face, though I remembered writing that Her skin was *translucent*, Her lashes *barely there*. This woman, Vivienne Blackman, knew something of me. It was something Gareth could not possibly imagine.

'Who is she?' I asked.

'Her three boys worked at the Press. They all joined the 2nd Ox and Bucks in August. And two of them *were* just boys; too young for sense – though sense can make cowards of older men.' He saw his words register on my face and quickly went on. 'Mr Hart was unwell, so she told me.'

'Does she have other children?' I asked.

He shook his head. We said no more.

❧

… I will pray for the safe return of your boys.
Your dearest friend, Lizzie

I gave Lizzie the pages I'd scribed. She folded them carefully and put them in an envelope, then she took her fourth biscuit.

'Tommy will be ever so lonely without his brothers,' she said.

'Do you think he'll sign up?'

'If he does, it'll break Natasha's heart.'

'Lizzie, do you ever wish you could tell Natasha your deepest secrets without having to write them through me?' I asked.

'I got no deep secrets, Essymay.'

'If you did, would you want her to know, even though it might change what she thought of you?'

Lizzie's hand went to her crucifix, and she looked down at the table. She had always given God the credit for any wisdom she gave me. I had long ceased to believe he had anything to do with it.

She lifted her head. 'I reckon I might want her to know, if it was

324

something that mattered to me, or something that explained me somehow.'

Her answer made my stomach churn. 'Would it matter, though, if you kept your secret?'

Lizzie got up to put more hot water in the teapot.

'I don't think he'll judge you,' she said.

I whipped round, but her back was to me. I had no way of reading her face. She might have been talking about God, or she might have been talking about Gareth. I hoped she was talking about both.

A clear night ushered in a blue-sky day and a glittering frost. But the cold morning didn't last, and my coat felt heavy as I pedalled towards the Press with Dr Murray's proof corrections.

Mr Hart's office door was half open. I knocked but there was no reply. I peeked round and saw that he was at his desk, his head in his hands. Another mother, I thought. There had been a small article in the *Oxford Times* about the number of men from the Press who had signed up, the number who had died. The loss of so many staff would delay the publication of some significant books, it said. Including *Shakespeare's England*.

I did not believe it was *Shakespeare's England* bowing the Controller's head, and suddenly the article seemed callous. To name a book but not a single man. I stepped back from the doorway and knocked louder. Mr Hart looked up this time, a little dazed, a little frightened. I handed him the corrected proofs.

Next, I went to find Gareth, but he wasn't in his office. I found him in the composing room, leaning over his old bench.

'Can't stay away from it?' I said.

Gareth looked up from the type. His smile unconvincing. 'Too many empty benches,' he said. 'The printing room is the same. Only the bindery is at full strength now, though a few of the women have signed on to the Voluntary Aid Detachment.' He wiped his hands on his apron.

'Perhaps Mr Hart should think about employing women as printers and compositors.'

'It's been raised, but it's not a popular idea. Inevitable, though, I think.'

'Mr Hart looks awful.'

Gareth took off his apron and we walked together to where other identical aprons hung on individual hooks. 'I think he's falling into one of his depressions,' he said. 'It's understandable. This place is like a village; everyone is related to someone, and each death ripples through it.'

When we crossed the quad, it struck me for the first time just how quiet it really was. Instead of walking towards Jericho, I directed Gareth down Great Clarendon Street. 'It's not too cold,' I said. 'I thought we could walk along the Castle Mill Stream. I've brought sandwiches.'

I could think of nothing ordinary to say as we walked, though Gareth seemed not to notice. We turned into Canal Street and passed St Barnabas Church. It was only as we were on the towpath that he asked if everything was all right. I tried to smile, but was completely unsuccessful.

'You're making me nervous,' he said.

I chose a quiet spot dappled with weak sunshine. Gareth took off his coat and spread it on the ground, and I placed mine beside his. We sat, too close for the acrimony I thought would come. I took the sandwiches out of my satchel and passed him one.

'Say it,' he said.

'Say what?'

'Whatever is on your mind.'

I searched his face. I didn't want anything to change the way he looked at me, but I also wanted him to understand me completely. My mind swirled with images and emotion, and I could not recall a single word of what I had rehearsed. I felt breathless. Got to my feet. Walked beside the stream, gulping air, but still I couldn't breathe. Gareth called after me, but the rushing in my ears made him sound far away.

I would tell him about Her, I knew that. Though I might not be forgiven. I felt sick, but I turned back.

❧

We sat opposite each other. Each on our own coat, Gareth looking down now, stunned and silent. I'd told him everything. I'd said words I'd been afraid of – *virgin, pregnant, confinement, birth, baby, adopted* – and I was calmer. The nausea had gone.

I watched Gareth, detached. I might have lost him, but the loss of Her was certain. He might have been disappointed in me, but I was disappointed in myself.

I rose and started walking away. When I looked back he was still sitting where I'd left him, his hand was stroking the coat I'd left behind.

Along Canal Street, I found the doors to St Barnabas were open. I sat in the Morning Chapel. I don't know how long I'd been there before Gareth found me and put my coat over my shoulders. He sat beside me. When he took my arm sometime later, I let him lead me back out into the winter sunshine.

When we arrived at the Press, I collected my bicycle and insisted I could ride back to the Scriptorium alone.

Gareth looked at me – no acrimony, but there was a sadness.

'It doesn't change anything,' he said.

'How can it not?'

'I don't know. It just doesn't.'

'But it might, over time.'

He shook his head. 'I don't think so. The war has made the present more important than the past, and far more certain than the future.

How I feel right now is all I can rely on. And after all that you've told me, I think I love you more.'

Few words have as many variants as *love*. I felt it resonate deep in my chest and knew it to mean something different from any other version I'd heard or uttered. But the sadness on Gareth's face remained. He took my hand and kissed the scars, then he turned and went into the Press.

❧

When I stirred the next morning, the house felt frigid. I could hardly raise my body from the bed. Gareth's words should have been a relief, but they were tempered by his sadness. He was holding something back from me, as I had from him. I shivered and wished that Lizzie was there.

I dressed quickly and walked in near darkness to Sunnyside.

Lizzie was up to her elbows in suds when I came into the kitchen. The bench was crowded with breakfast things: dirty bowls and teacups; plates with crumbs of toast.

'The range is blazing,' she said. 'Go warm yourself while I finish the dishes.'

'Where's the girl who normally comes in the morning?' I asked. There had been a few, and the name of the current one escaped me.

'Gone. At least the war's good for some people: the factories pay more than the Murrays ever could.'

I removed my coat and took up a tea towel. 'Any chance Mrs Ballard could come out of retirement?'

'She struggles to get out of her chair these days,' said Lizzie.

I cut a thick slice of bread and spread it with jam. 'I made an extra loaf,' said Lizzie. 'Take it with you when you leave tonight.'

'You really don't need to do that,' I said, licking jam from my fingers.

'You're in the Scrippy dawn to dusk and no maid – I really don't know why you let the maid go. Someone needs to look after you.'

When I was warm to my bones and my stomach was full, I walked across the garden to the Scriptorium. I was grateful to find it empty. No one would arrive for an hour at least.

It had barely changed since I'd hidden beneath the sorting table, and for a moment I could imagine my world with Da in it and no war. I trailed my fingers along the shelves; it was a way of remembering.

I sat at my desk and listened to the hush. There was a whisper from the hole in the wall, and I raised my hand to feel the breath of cold air. It was sharp, almost painful, and I thought about those native peoples who mark their skin at moments in life that define them. Words would be inscribed upon me. But which words?

There was a clang against the Scriptorium wall, and the whispering stopped. I pulled my hand back from the hole and looked through. It was Gareth.

He propped his bicycle and straightened, checked inside his satchel and closed it with care. I had spied him a hundred times and come to love how he ushered the words back and forth as if they were fragile and precious.

But I was nervous. I checked myself. Curls had sprung from my bun, and I tucked them in. I pinched my cheeks and bit my lips. I sat with my back uncomfortably straight, expecting Gareth to come through the Scriptorium door. I was afraid of what he might say.

He didn't come. I bent to my work and let the curls fall loose.

A quarter-hour passed before I heard the Scriptorium door open.

'Does Dr Murray know you're here from sparrow's?' he asked.

'I like the solitude,' I replied, searching his face for some clue to his frame of mind. 'But I'm glad for the interruption. I heard you arrive; what took you so long?'

'I thought I'd find you in the kitchen, with Lizzie. I couldn't say no when she offered me tea.'

'She likes you.'

'I like her.'

I looked at Gareth's satchel, supported by his hand. 'It's a bit early to be delivering proofs.'

He didn't answer immediately. Instead he gazed at me as if recalling my confession. I looked down.

'No proofs. Just an invitation for a picnic lunch,' he said. 'It's going to be another beautiful day.'

I could only nod.

'I'll be back at midday, then.' He smiled.

'All right,' I said.

When he left, I took a shuddering breath and leaned my head against the wall. Light from the hole fell across the old scars on my hand. When Gareth approached the back of the Scriptorium to retrieve his bicycle, the light dimmed then brightened. Dimmed again. Morse code, I thought, but I couldn't read it. I felt the weight of his body as he leaned against the iron wall, heard the metal hum through my skull. Did he know how close he was to me? He stayed there a long while.

Just before midday I was sitting at the kitchen table with Lizzie.

'Let me fix that hair of yours,' she said.

'There's no point. It always finds a way of escaping.'

'When *you* do it, it does.' She stood behind me and rearranged the pins. When she was done, I shook my head. The curls stayed put.

Through the kitchen window, we saw Gareth. He strode across the garden towards us, his satchel slung over his shoulder, a picnic basket in one hand. Lizzie jumped up to open the door and usher him in.

Gareth nodded at Lizzie and smiled wide. 'Lizzie,' he said.

'Gareth,' she replied. Her smile a mirror image.

There were whole sentences behind that greeting that I couldn't fathom. Gareth put his picnic basket on the kitchen table, and Lizzie bent to the range to remove a flan she had been warming. She placed it in the bottom of the basket and covered it with a cloth. Then she filled a flask with tea and handed it to Gareth along with a small jar of milk.

'Do you have a rug?' she asked him.

'I do,' he said.

She took her wool shawl off the back of a chair. 'It might be warm for December, but you'll still need this over your coat,' she said, handing it to me.

I took it, bemused by the pleasure this picnic was giving Lizzie. 'Would you like to join us?' I asked.

She laughed. 'Oh, no. Too much to do.'

Gareth lifted the basket off the table. 'Shall we go?'

I gave him my hand and he led me out of the kitchen.

We walked to Castle Mill Stream and along the towpath to Walton Bridge.

'Hard to believe winter has started,' Gareth said as he spread the rug and put the flan in the centre. Steam rose.

He smoothed the spot where he wanted me to sit, then took the flask from the basket and poured tea into a mug. He added just the right amount of milk and dropped in one lump of sugar. I cupped my hands around it and sipped. It was just as I liked it. We said nothing.

Gareth finished his tea and poured some more. His hand moved unconsciously to the satchel that lay beside him. When his mug was empty, he took time putting it back in the basket, as if it were made of crystal rather than tin. His hands were shaking, ever so slightly.

When his mug was safely in the basket, he took a deep breath and turned to face me. A smile moved gently across his face. Without looking away, he took my mug and put it less carefully on the grass. Then he held both my hands in his.

He pressed my fingers to his lips, and the warmth of his breath sent a shiver through me. My whole body wanted to be pressed against him, but my mind was content to look over the features of his face; to memorise every line on his forehead, his dark brows and long lashes, blue eyes like a summer sky at dusk. There was grey at his temples, and I longed to see it spread, over years, through the dark mop of his hair.

I don't know how long we sat like that, but I felt his eyes roam my face as mine roamed his. Nothing obscured us, no polite gestures clung. We were naked.

When our eyes finally met, it was as if we had journeyed together and come home more familiar. He released me and reached for the satchel. A subtle tremor made his fingers clumsy with the buckles. If I hadn't been sure before, I knew then what the satchel held.

But it was not what I expected.

He pulled out a parcel. It was wrapped in brown paper and tied with string: the signature wrapping of the Press. It was the dimensions of a ream of paper, though thinner.

'For you,' he said, offering the parcel.

'Not proofs, surely.'

'Proof, of sorts,' he said.

I released the bow and the thick paper fell away.

It was a beautiful object, leather-bound and gold-lettered. It must have cost Gareth a month's wages. *Women's Words and Their Meanings* was embossed on the green leather in the same typeface used for the Dictionary volumes. I opened to the first page where the title was repeated. Below that, *Edited by Esme Nicoll.*

It was a thin volume, and the type was larger than that of Dr Murray's dictionary – two columns on each page instead of three. I turned to the letter *C* and let my finger trace the familiar shapes of the words, each one a woman's voice. Some smooth and genteel, others, like Mabel's, gravelly and coated in phlegm. Then I came to it, one of the first words I ever wrote on a slip. To see it in print was exhilarating. The limerick fluttered across my lips.

Was it more obscene to say it, to write it, or to set it in type? On the breath it could be taken by a breeze or crowded out by chatter; it could be misheard or ignored. On the page it was a real thing. It had been caught and pinned to a board, its letters spread in a particular way so that anyone who saw it would know what it was.

'What must you have thought of me!' I said.

'I was glad to finally know what it meant,' he said, his earnest face collapsing into a grin.

I kept turning the pages.

'It took a year, Es. And every day that I held a slip with your handwriting, I came to know you better. I fell in love with you word by word. I've always loved the shape and feel of them, the infinite pairings. But you showed me their limitations, and their potential.'

'But how?'

'A few slips at a time, and I was always careful to put them back just where I'd found them. Half the Press were in on it by the end. I wanted a hand in every part of it, not just the typesetting. I chose the paper and worked the press. I cut the pages, and the women in the bindery fell over themselves to show me how to put it all together.'

'I bet they did.' I smiled.

'Fred Sweatman was my lookout at the Scrippy, but none of it would have been possible without Lizzie. She knows your every move and all your hiding places. Don't be cross with her for giving them away.'

I thought about the shoebox in my desk and the trunk under Lizzie's bed. My Dictionary of Lost Words. She was its custodian, I realised. And she'd wanted the words to be found.

'I could never be cross with Lizzie,' I said.

Gareth took my hands again. The tremor in his was gone. 'I had to choose,' he said. 'Between a ring and the words.'

I looked at my dictionary, traced the title with my fingers and heard the words on my breath. I imagined a ring on my hand and was glad for its absence. I wondered how it was possible to feel so much.

No more words passed between us. He didn't ask, and I didn't answer, but I felt those moments like the rhythm of a poem. They were the preface to everything that would come after, and already I was plotting it out. I held his face, felt it differently against the skin of each hand, then brought it near. His lips were warm against mine, the taste of tea still pleasant on his tongue. His hand on the small of my back asked nothing, but I leaned in, wanting him to feel the shape of me. The flan cooled and remained uneaten.

⁓

'Where is it, then?' asked Lizzie when I came into the kitchen.

We both looked at my hand, as unadorned as it always had been.

'Is there anything you don't know, Lizzie Lester?'

'A whole lot, but I know he loves you and you love him, and I thought I'd find a ring on that finger when you came back from your picnic.'

I took the thin volume from my own satchel and put it on the kitchen table in front of her. 'He gave me something far more precious than a ring.'

Smiling, she wiped her hands on her apron, then checked them before touching the leather. 'I knew the words would win you, all bound and beautiful. I told him as much when he showed me. Then he showed me where my own name was printed and made me a cup of tea while I blubbered.' Tears sprang again and she wiped them quickly away. 'But he never said he had no ring.'

She pushed the volume back towards me. I wrapped it in the brown paper and tied the string. 'Can I pop upstairs, Lizzie?'

'Don't tell me you're going to hide it away!'

'Not forever. But I'm not ready to share it.'

'You are a funny one, Essymay.'

If Gareth had fitted, I'd have locked him in my trunk and hidden the key. But it was too late for that. Mr Hart and Dr Murray had been writing letters for months to get him into officers' training.

May 1915

Officers' training finished on the 4th of May. We were to be married on the 5th, a Wednesday. Dr Murray gave everyone in the Scriptorium two paid hours to wish us well.

I slept in Lizzie's room the night before, and in the morning she dressed me in a simple cream frock with a double skirt and high lace collar. She'd embroidered leaves around the cuffs and hems, and added tiny glass beads here and there, 'so when the sun shines on you it will look like morning dew'.

Dr Murray was unwell, but he offered to accompany me to St Barnabas in a cab. At the last minute, I declined. The sun *was* shining, and I knew Gareth would be walking from the Press with Mr Hart and Mr Sweatman. I hadn't seen Gareth for the three months of his officers' training, and I liked the thought of bumping into him as our routes converged on Canal Street.

Mrs Murray took three hasty photographs of me under the ash tree, one with Dr Murray, one with Ditte, and one with Elsie and Rosfrith. As she was packing the camera away, I asked if she would take one more.

Lizzie hovered by the kitchen door, awkward in her new dress. I waved her over. She shook her head.

'Lizzie,' I called. 'You must. It's my wedding day.'

She came, her head slightly bowed against all the eyes turned towards her. When she stood beside me, I saw her mother's pin, brilliant against the dull green of her felt hat.

'Turn this way a little, Lizzie,' I said. I wanted the camera to catch the pin. I would give her the photograph as a gift.

Gareth wore his officer's uniform for the wedding. He stood taller than I remembered, and I wondered if it were an illusion or the benefit of being released from the work of typesetting. He was handsome, and I was as beautiful as I had ever been. These were our first impressions as we approached St Barnabas from different ends of the street.

Inside, I stood with Gareth in front of the vicar. Mr Hart stood to Gareth's left; Ditte stood to my right. Four rows of pews were occupied by Dictionary and Press staff, with Dr and Mrs Murray, Mr Sweatman, Beth and Lizzie in the front. There might have been more, but Gareth's closest friends from the Press were in France, and Tilda had joined the Voluntary Aid Detachment. Her matron at St Bartholomew's in London would not give her leave to come.

I have no memory of what was said. I can't recall the face of the vicar. I must have spent a long while looking into the bouquet that Lizzie had gathered for me, because its delicate white flowers and strong scent stayed with me. Lily of the valley. When Ditte reached to take them so that Gareth could put his ring on my finger, I refused to let them go.

We came out of the church and were caught in a downpour of rice thrown by a small group of women from the Press bindery. Then I saw the choir of printers and compositors, apron-clad. Gareth and I stood, delighted, holding each other's arms as they sang 'By the Light of the Silvery Moon'.

Rosfrith took a photograph. For a terrible moment, I imagined us frozen on a mantelpiece, Gareth remaining ageless; me old and wrapped in shawls, sitting alone by a fire.

We walked in procession through the streets of Jericho. When we got to Walton Street, the bindery women and the printers' choir returned to the Press, and some of Mr Bradley's and Mr Craigie's staff walked back towards the Old Ashmolean. The rest of us continued to Sunnyside, where we had sandwiches and cake beneath the ash. It reminded me of all the afternoon teas we'd had over the years to celebrate the completion of a letter or the publication of a volume. When Mrs Murray helped Dr Murray into the house, we took it as a sign that everyone's two hours were up. Mr Bradley and Eleanor returned to the Old Ashmolean; Mr Hart led the way back to the Press. Ditte and Beth walked Mrs Ballard into the kitchen, and Rosfrith and Elsie insisted on helping Lizzie with the cleaning-up. Of the Scriptorium men, Mr Sweatman was the last to return to work. He shook Gareth's hand and took mine to kiss it.

'How proud and happy your father would have been,' he said, and I held his gaze, knowing the memory of Da was stronger when it was shared.

We stood at the front door of Da's house. My house. As if waiting to be let in. There was some confusion about who should open it.

'It's our house now, Gareth,' I said.

He smiled. 'That may be so, but I don't have a key.'

'Oh, of course.' I leaned down and took the key from under a pot. I held it out. 'There you are.'

He looked at it. 'Well, I don't think you should give it up that easily. It's not a dowry.'

Before I could reply, he bent down and picked me up.

'Right,' he said, 'you open the door, and we'll cross the threshold together. Make it quick though, Es. If you don't mind.'

The house was filled with lily of the valley, and every room was spotless. The range was warming the kitchen against a cool evening, and our dinner was slowly cooking.

'You're lucky to have Lizzie, you know,' Gareth said, putting me down.

'I do know. I also know I'm lucky to have you.' Without discussion, I took Gareth's hand and led him up the stairs.

I opened the door to Da's old room. The bed had a new coverlet, quilted and detailed with Lizzie's delicate stitches. I'd never slept there, and now I was glad of it. It was our bridal bed.

We weren't shy about our bodies, but we guarded what we knew, and what we didn't. When a memory of Bill came unbidden, I was horrified. I remembered his finger tracing the parting of my hair and continuing down my face and the length of my body, making excursions along the way. 'Nose,' he had whispered close to my ear. 'Lips, neck, breast, belly button ...'

I shivered, and Gareth pulled back a little. I took his hand and kissed his palm. Then I guided his fingers down the length of my body, making excursions along the way.

'Mount of Venus,' I said, when we reached the soft tangle of hair.

❧

Gareth had a commission with the 2nd Ox and Bucks but was given a month before he had to report to Cowley Barracks. Though Dr Murray could hardly spare me, he agreed to shorter days. In the afternoons, I walked from the Scriptorium to the Press, where I found Gareth showing men who were too young, too old or too short-sighted how to hold a rifle. The Press was training a home guard.

I watched him, as I'd watched him before. He was showing a boy no older than fifteen how to hold a rifle. He placed the boy's left hand under the barrel; the other hand he positioned around the stock, moving the boy's index finger back so only the tip was resting on the trigger. He was as focused as if he were selecting type and placing it in his stick to make a word. I saw him stand back to assess the boy's stance. He gave an instruction, and the boy shifted the rifle from his shoulder closer to his chest.

When the boy pretended to shoot, as if playing at being a cowboy, Gareth lowered the barrel to point at the ground and spoke to him. I couldn't hear what he said, but I saw something in the boy's face that made me recall something Lizzie had told me when she found out Gareth was to be an officer. 'The army could do with a grown man leading them lads. Posh accents don't seem to be up to the job, according to what I hear.' She was right. Gareth had the authority to lead. I'd seen it with the younger compositors, and in the printing room too. I tried to imagine it in France, but couldn't.

We walked along Castle Mill Stream. Gareth was wearing his uniform, and although he complained that it looked too new, everyone we passed greeted him with a nod or a smile or a vigorous shake of the hand. Only one person looked away as we approached: a young man, his civilian clothes conspicuous.

I'd stopped wishing that Gareth hadn't signed up, but I couldn't stop thinking that he was walking towards death. The notion kept me awake at night and I'd watch him sleep. It had me touching him unnecessarily, and at odd times. I wanted to know what he thought about everything, and I tired him out with questions about good and evil, and whether we English were one and Germans the other. I was trying to uncover more layers so that if he died I would be left with more.

Gareth was recalled from leave after the Battle of Festubert. The 'In Memoriam' list in the *Times of London* included four hundred men from the Ox and Bucks. We'd been married less than a month.

'I'm not being sent to France, Es.'

'But you will be.'

'It's likely. But there are a hundred new recruits who need training before they're sent anywhere, so I'll be at Cowley for a while. I'm close enough to catch one of the new autobuses into Oxford. I could meet you for lunch. And on my days off, I can come home.'

'But I've grown used to your lumpy mashed potatoes – and I think I may have forgotten how to wash dishes,' I said, trying to be lighthearted. But I'd spent too many evenings in solitude over the past few years not to know how lonely I was going to be. 'What will I do with myself?'

'The hospitals are calling for volunteers,' he said, glad to think he'd found a solution. 'Not all the boys are from around here, and some never get a visitor.'

I nodded, but it was no solution.

When Gareth went to Cowley Barracks, he left bits of himself behind. His civilian clothes hung ready to wear in our wardrobe. A comb with strands of hair still in its teeth – black and wiry grey – sat on the bathroom sink. By the bed, a collection of poems by Rupert Brooke was open face-down, the spine bent in half. I picked it up to see what poem Gareth had been reading. 'The Dead'. I put it down again.

I took refuge in the Scriptorium. How long, I wondered, before the slips began to mention this war?

Ditte had sent me *Back of the Front* by Phyllis Campbell. I kept it in my desk and would read it when everyone else had left for the day. Her war was so different from the war in the papers.

It is context, Da had always said, that gives meaning.

German soldiers had skewered the babies of Belgian women, she wrote, then raped the women and cut off their breasts.

I thought about all the German scholars whom Dr Murray consulted about the Germanic etymology of so many English words. They had been silent since the start of the war. Or silenced. Could those gentle men of language do these things? And if a German could commit such acts, why not a Frenchman or an Englishman?

Phyllis Campbell, and women like her, nursed these Belgian women – those who were still alive. They arrived on the backs of trucks, scraps of cloth wrapped around their chests to soak up blood instead of milk, their babies dead at their feet.

My hands shook as I transcribed quotations on slip after slip, heading each with the word *war*. They added something horrid to the slips already sorted and waiting to be turned into copy. When I was done, I was exhausted. I stood up and searched the shelves for the right pigeon-hole. I took out the slips that were already there and shuffled through them. The slips I had just written would bring something new, something awful, to the meaning of *war*. But I couldn't add them. I returned the original slips to the pigeon-hole I'd taken them from, then walked towards the grate. I threw in the quotations from Phyllis Campbell and watched as they became shadows of themselves.

I remembered *lily*. Back then, I had thought that if I saved the word something of my mother would be remembered. It was not my place to erase what *war* meant to Phyllis Campbell; what it was to those Belgian women. Among the propaganda of glory, and the men's experiences of the trenches and death, something needed to be known of what happened to women. I returned to my desk, opened *Back of the Front* and began again. Once more, I forced each terrible sentence from my trembling pen.

If war could change the nature of men, it would surely change the nature of words, I thought. But so much of the English language had already been set in type and printed. We were nearing the end.

'It will find its way into the final volumes, I expect,' said Mr Sweatman when we discussed it. 'The poets will see to that. They have a way of adding nuance to the meaning of things.'

⚜

5th June 1915

My dear Mrs Owen,

I can't imagine I will address you as anything other than Esme, but just once I wanted my pen to acknowledge the woman you have become. I do not place much stock in marriage, but yours to Gareth is right in every way, and if all unions could be as good I would perhaps change my mind about the institution.

You may think my pen has been idle this past month. I assure you, it has not. Each day since you wed, I have had a mind to write to your father and tell him how beautiful you looked, and how perfectly comfortable you were, standing beside Gareth with St Barnabas behind you, lily of the valley in your hand.

I have been writing to your father for four decades, and it has been a difficult habit to break. I tried, but found I was unable to think properly without the prospect of his thoughtful reflections. I am not ashamed to admit (and I hope it does not offend you in any way) that I have decided to resume my correspondence with Harry. Your wedding has been the catalyst for this — to whom else was I going to report the day in all its glorious minutiae? So, when I say I had a mind to write to your father, what I actually mean is that I did write to your father. He is not silent in my mind, Esme.

He would be particularly charmed by your decision to throw your bouquet, even though most of your female guests were married or confirmed spinsters. What a surprise when you turned your back on the little crowd. I saw you take a sprig for yourself and knew what was coming. I hoped the girls from the bindery would step forward, but when the bouquet left your hand it was clear where it was headed. Lizzie and I must have looked stricken — neither of us daring to be the one to catch it, but neither wanting the blooms to fall to the ground. I could see Lizzie hesitate, and it fell to me to put her out of her misery. I must admit to a moment of giddiness (though no regrets); the flowers were my sweet companions all the way back to Bath.

And now I return them to you, pressed and ready to be preserved in whatever way you see fit. I imagine you will use them as bookmarks, and I can think of *nothing better than opening a book you've allowed to languish for months, or even years, and the memory of that day falling from it. Of course, you may choose to have them mounted behind glass to hang beside your wedding photo, but I credit you with more taste.*

Letters to your father have not been my only pastime since your wedding. James Murray's health is not good, as you well know, and I have been sent more proofs than I know what to do with. I appreciate James's confidence in me, but am of a mind to write to the purse-holders and request some small stipend for my contribution. It has increased year on year, and my name in the acknowledgements does not compensate me as it once did. Beth is quite animated on this subject, and has helped to draft a letter of request. But I will not send it yet. It seems mercenary in the circumstances. I shall carry on, as we all must.

I do not want to end this letter without acknowledging Gareth's upcoming deployment. This will test you, my dear, as the war is testing so many. Please keep me close. Write to me, visit me, lean on me as heavily as you must. Stay busy — I cannot overstate the benefits of a busy day for an anxious mind or a lonely heart.

Yours,

Ditte

❧

Lizzie popped her head in through the Scriptorium door. 'Why are you still here?' she said. 'It's gone seven.'

'I'm just checking the entry for *twilight*. Dr Murray wants to see the end of T by the end of the month. It's impossible, but we're trying.'

'I don't think that's why you're here,' Lizzie said.

'Do you know what I do when I get home, Lizzie? I knit. Socks for the soldiers. The first pair took me three weeks, and when Gareth tried them on he said they were so tight that he'd be sent home with gangrene within a week. He accused me of doing it on purpose.'

'Did you?'

'Funny. No, I just hate knitting and knitting hates me. I've made five pairs now and they seem to be getting worse. But I need to do something or I begin to fret about Gareth being sent abroad,' I said. 'How I wish I could fall into bed exhausted each night and sleep without a single thought.'

'That's not a wish you want to come true, Essymay. Have you thought any more about volunteering?'

'Yes, but I couldn't bring myself to sit among the wounded. When I imagine it, they all have Gareth's face.'

'They always need women to roll bandages and such,' Lizzie said. 'And I've heard the men like to chat when the company has a pretty face. If you keep your ears open, you might pick up a word or two.'

'I'll think about it,' I said.

'Have you been talking to Lizzie?' I asked Gareth.

He had the afternoon off from Cowley, and we were eating sandwiches by Walton Bridge. He avoided my question.

'Sam's from the Press,' he said. 'But he's from up north originally. He could use a visitor.'

'Does he have no friends from the Press?'

'He has me, but I barely even have time to visit you. And the others … well, they're still in France.'

Still in France, I thought. Alive or dead?

'He remembers you,' continued Gareth. 'Says I'm a lucky man. I said I'd ask.'

The Radcliffe Infirmary had changed very little since Da was there, except that the wards were filled with young men instead of old. They were enlisted men. Some had all their limbs and all their humour; some were missing both. Those who were able smiled and teased

345

as I walked by. None of them had Gareth's face. I was relieved, and ashamed I'd stayed away.

A nurse pointed to Sam's bed at the far end of the ward. As I walked towards it, I scanned the charts of twenty-five young men. Their names and ranks were written large and clear, their injuries obscured by medical terms and crisp white sheets. It was one ward in one hospital. There were now ten hospitals in Oxfordshire.

Sam was sitting up, eating his dinner. He looked familiar, but only in the way of someone I might have passed a few times in the street. I introduced myself, and he beamed up at me. His right leg was elevated under the covers.

'Foot's gone,' he said, with no more emotion than if he was telling me the time. 'Ain't nothing compared to what I seen.'

Neither of us wanted to talk about what he'd seen. Without a pause he began talking about the Press and asking after anyone we might know in common. I'd paid very little attention to all the apron-clad lads trundling between paper store, printing room, bindery and dispatch, and I couldn't say who remained and who had gone. 'I could tell you who's gone,' he said, with the same dispassionate tone he'd used to inform me about his foot. Then he told me the name and role of each boy he knew had died. It was monotonous in its detail, and he barely took a breath. But he needed to recall them, and as he did I imagined the paths they'd once traversed over a single day as threads stitching the different parts of the Press together. How could it function without them?

'That's all of them,' he said, as if the inventory had been of stores or equipment, and not of men. He looked at me then and grinned. 'Gareth, I mean Lieutenant Owen, says you like to collect words.' He registered the surprise on my face. 'I reckon I might have one that the Dictionary don't know.'

I took out a slip and a pencil.

'*Bumf*,' said Sam.

'Can you put it in a sentence?' I asked.

Someone chimed in from across the ward: 'You do know what a sentence is, don't you, Tinka?'

'Why do they call you Tinka?'

'Shot himself in the foot tinkerin' with his rifle,' said the man in the bed next to Sam's. 'Some do it on purpose.'

Sam made no response, but turned and said quietly to me, 'Hand me them leaflets; I need some bumf for the latrine.'

It took me a while to realise he was providing the sentence I'd asked for. I wrote it on the slip and added his name. 'Why *bumf*? Where does it come from?' I asked.

'I probably shouldn't say, Mrs Owen.'

'Call me Esme. And don't be afraid of offending me, Sam. I know more crass words than you could imagine.'

He smiled and said, 'Bum fodder. There's plenty of it comes from headquarters. Not worth reading but worth its weight in gold when you got the runs. Sorry, missus.'

'I got a word, miss,' another man shouted.

'And me.'

'If you want something crass,' said a man missing an arm, 'come sit by my bed for a while.' With the only hand left to him, he patted the edge of his bed, then puckered his thin lips into a kiss.

Sister Morley, who was in charge of the ward, strode over to me. The banter stopped.

'Could I have a word please, *Mrs* Owen?'

'She's got plenty, sister,' said my one-armed suitor. 'Just check her pockets.'

I rested my hand on Sam's shoulder. 'Can I visit tomorrow?'

'I'd like that, missus.'

'It's Esme, remember?'

'A new patient came in yesterday,' said Sister Morley as we left the ward. 'I was wondering if you would sit with him. I'll give you a basket of bandages to roll; that should keep your hands busy.'

'Of course,' I said, grateful she hadn't asked me to turn out my pockets.

We walked the long corridors to another ward. They all looked remarkably alike: two rows of beds, and the men tucked into them like children. Some were sitting up, almost ready to go back out and play; others were supine and barely moving.

Private Albert Northrop sat up in his bed, but there was something about his vacant stare that made me think he wasn't going anywhere else for a while.

'Do they call you Bert? Or Bertie?' I asked him.

'We call him Bertie,' said Sister Morley. 'We don't know if that's his preference, because he doesn't speak. He can hear well enough, apparently, yet he's somehow unable to comprehend the meaning of words – with one exception.'

'Which is?' I asked.

Sister Morley put her hand on Bertie's shoulder and nodded her goodbye. He just stared ahead. Then she walked me back along the ward. Only when we were out of earshot did she answer my question.

'The word is *bomb*, Mrs Owen. If he hears it, he responds with absolute terror. A learned response, according to the psychiatrist: it's an unusual form of war neurosis. He was at the Battle of Festubert, but he seems unable to recall any of it. When he's shown photographs of the men he served with, he shows no sign of recognition. Not even his own possessions seem familiar to him. His physical wounds were relatively minor; I fear the injury to his mind will take longer to heal.' She looked back towards Bertie. 'If there is reason to take out one of your little slips of paper while you sit by his bed, Mrs Owen, that will be some small cause for celebration.'

Sister Morley bade me goodnight and said she hoped to see me at 6 p.m. the following day.

'And by the way,' she said, 'every patient on this ward has been instructed not to say the word, though none are too keen on it themselves. We would all be most grateful if you could avoid it also.'

I didn't stay long by Bertie's bed that day. I rolled bandages and rattled on about my day. At first, I would glance at his face to see if he registered anything I said. When it was clear he didn't, I took a liberty and examined his features. He was a child, it seemed to me. There were more spots on his face than whiskers.

I continued to visit Sam and two other boys from the Press who soon came through the Radcliffe, but Bertie became my distraction. Talking to Bertie, I was able to enter a bubble where the war did not exist. I spoke mostly about the Dictionary, about the lexicographers and their particular habits. I described my childhood under the sorting table and the joy of sitting on Da's knee and learning to read from the slips. He seemed to register none of it.

'You're not falling in love with him, are you?' Gareth teased when he was home on a day's leave.

'What's to fall in love with? I don't know what he thinks of anything. Besides, he's only eighteen.'

As the days went on, I brought books from the Scriptorium and read passages I thought he might enjoy. I chose them for rhythm more than words, though I was always careful to check that every word was benign. Poetry seemed to steady his gaze, and sometimes he looked at me with such intent that I imagined something of the meaning might have got through. For the rest of June and well into July, I slept soundly.

July 1915

By July, Dr Murray was spending almost no time in the Scriptorium. Rosfrith said he was having trouble shifting a cold, but I couldn't recall him ever letting a cold take priority over the Dictionary – he'd always banished it with the same gruff impatience he used to banish unwanted criticism. But the work continued, with Dictionary staff visiting him in the house, and copy going back and forth. When 'Trink to Turndown' was completed, we celebrated around the sorting table with our customary afternoon tea. Dr Murray joined us, paler and thinner than I'd ever seen him.

It was a quiet celebration. We spoke of words, not war, and Dr Murray proposed a revised timeline for the completion of T. It still seemed optimistic, but no one contradicted him.

As we ate our cake, Rosfrith leaned towards me. 'The *Periodical* is doing a picture spread about the Dictionary for their next publication. They're organising some photographs of the three editors and their staff.'

'How exciting,' I said.

She looked towards her father, his cake untouched. 'It is, but the photographer is not due until the end of July, and I'm worried …' But she couldn't finish the sentence. 'Would you mind taking a photograph with Mother's Brownie? Just in case?'

The Dictionary without Dr Murray. I pushed the thought away. 'My pleasure,' I said.

She rested her hand on my knee, a sad smile on her face. 'I'm afraid it will mean you can't be in it.'

'I'll make sure I'm here when the real photographer comes,' I said.

'Yes, of course. I'd hate you to be left out of the official spread. You've been part of the project for as long as I can remember.'

Rosfrith went to the house to fetch the Brownie. I'd used it once or twice to take photographs of the Murray family in the garden, but she explained the mechanism again. When Lizzie had cleared the sorting table of tea things, Elsie arranged everyone where she thought they should be.

There were only seven of us left. Dr Murray was assisted to a chair in front of one of the bookshelves, and Elsie and Rosfrith sat either side of him. Mr Maling, Mr Sweatman and Mr Yockney stood behind.

I looked through the lens and focused on Dr Murray. It was the same face that used to spy me beneath the sorting table and wink conspiratorially. The same face that looked grave when he read letters from the Press Delegates, or agitated when he read copy from one of the other editors. It was the face that used to delight in slipping into Scottish brogue when he spoke to Da, and that gave way to a restrained smile when Gareth delivered proofs. He sat in the middle of the frame, all the elements of the Dictionary around him: books and fascicles, pigeon-holes bursting with slips, his daughters and assistants. How could it ever be otherwise?

'Something is missing,' I said.

I went to the shelf behind Dr Murray's high desk. There were eight volumes of words, with room for four or five more. In the empty space was the mortar board Dr Murray used to wear when I was a child. I picked it up and beat the dust off it. I let the tassel slip slowly through my fingers and gave myself the briefest moment with memory. I'd worn it once, when it was just Da and me in the Scriptorium. He'd put it on my head and sat me on Dr Murray's stool. With a serious face, he'd asked if I approved of the corrections he'd made to the word *cat*. 'They are adequate,' I'd said, and his face had broken into a grin.

'I think you should wear this, Dr Murray.'

He thanked me, but I could barely hear it.

Rosfrith helped him position the mortar board properly, and I took up the camera again.

'Ready,' I said.

They all looked towards me, their expressions serious. Until the end of time, I thought. I blinked back tears and took the photograph.

I dressed for the funeral while Gareth packed the last of his things into his kit bag. He took his greatcoat from the wardrobe, though the day was warm and winter could barely be imagined.

He came to me and kissed my forehead, brushed his thumbs beneath my eyes and kissed each salty lid. He took up one hand and then the other, buttoning the cuffs of my blouse.

I attached my hat, tucked my curls in tighter and stood in front of the mirror. Gareth passed behind me, out into the hall. When he came back, he had his brush and his comb. I watched his reflection place them in the bag, and I wondered if I could take them out without him seeing and put them back on the bathroom sink.

We were ready.

We stood at the foot of the bed we had shared for barely a month of nights. Our lips came together, and I remembered the first time – the taste of tea sweetened by sugar. This kiss had the taste of oceans. It was gentle and quiet and long. We each imbued it with what we needed it to be. The memory would have to sustain us.

I caught our reflection. We could have been any couple before the whistle blew to board the train. But I wouldn't be going to the station. I couldn't bear it.

Gareth would be leaving after the funeral. He tied up his bag and hoisted it onto his shoulder. I took my handbag and put in a clean handkerchief. I followed Gareth out of the room but turned at the last moment to make sure nothing had been forgotten. Rupert Brooke's poems were still by the bed. I raced back and put them in my handbag, then hurried down the stairs.

At the funeral, I stood with Gareth at the back of the crowd of mourners – two hundred at least, despite the short notice. I wept more than decorum allowed: more than Mrs Murray; more than Elsie and Rosfrith and all the Murray children and grandchildren put together. When the last word was spoken and the family stepped forward, I turned to walk away.

Gareth's hand found mine and I pleaded, as quietly as I could, for him to let me go.

'Walk back with Lizzie when it's all finished,' I said. 'I'll see you at Sunnyside.'

As I came through the gates, there was a strange stillness. The house was nothing more than the stone that formed it, its pulse and breath all gathered in the churchyard. For the first time in my life, the Scriptorium struck me as an impermanent thing – an old iron shed not worthy of its purpose.

I opened the kitchen door. The smell of the morning's bread had grown rich with the day's heat. It tethered me back in place.

I took the stairs two at a time and pulled the trunk from under Lizzie's bed. I felt the weight of it, and calculated the years. Gareth's gift was loosely wrapped, a handful of new slips scattered on top of it; they are bumf, I thought, to anyone but me.

I pulled on the string and the paper fell away, as it had the first time. *Women's Words and Their Meanings.* The same quick beat of a thrill. But there was a sediment of sorrow this time. And fear. I looked more closely at my gift, searched each page. I wanted to find something that would replace his comb, his greatcoat, his book of poems. It was unreasonable to expect there would be anything, and irrational to think it would make a difference. After the last words, there was nothing but blank end pages.

Then, on the inside back cover.

This Dictionary is printed in Baskerville typeface. Designed for books of consequence and intrinsic merit, it has been chosen for its clarity and beauty.

Gareth Owen

Typesetter, Printer, Binder

I raced down the stairs and out into the garden. The door opened, and the Scriptorium took me in. The words I needed were already printed, but I wanted to choose the meaning myself.

I searched the pigeon-holes, found one word and then the other. I took a clean slip and transcribed.

LOVE

A passionate affection.

I turned the slip over.

ETERNAL

Everlasting, endless, beyond death.

Back in Lizzie's room, I put the slip between the pages of Rupert Brooke's poems.

'She'll be upstairs,' I heard Lizzie say in the kitchen. 'Her trunk will be open, I could make a bet on that, and the bed and floor will be a mess of words.'

Then Gareth's heavy boots on the stairs.

'Ah, Rupert Brooke,' he said, seeing the book of poetry in my hand.

'You left it by the bed.' I stood and passed it to him, and he put it in his breast pocket without a glance.

'Find what you were looking for?' he asked, nodding towards the trunk on the floor, *Women's Words and Their Meanings* still open to the back page on the bed.

I picked up his gift and held it tight to my chest. 'Did you know I'd accept?'

'I felt you loved me, as I loved you. But I was never sure you'd say yes.' He enveloped me, the volume of words between us. Then he sat me on Lizzie's bed and kneeled in front of me. The dictionary was on my lap. 'I am on every page, Es, same as you.' He wove his fingers through mine. 'This is us. And it will still be here long after we're gone.'

When he left, I listened to his heavy boots descend the stairs. I counted every step. He said goodbye to Lizzie and must have held her sobbing against him, because all was muffled for a few minutes. Then the kitchen door opened, and I heard Lizzie call out.

'You make sure you come home now, Gareth. I can't have her living in my room forever.'

'You have my word, Lizzie,' he called back.

I sat on Lizzie's bed until I knew the train had pulled out and Gareth was gone. My funny fingers were stiff from holding his gift. I unfurled them, rubbed them, looked at the trunk still open on Lizzie's floor and bent to return my volume of words to its nest of slips and letters.

Then I stopped. A year, it had taken him. Years more, it had taken me. All those women; their words. The joy of having their names written down. The hope that something of them would remain long after they were forgotten.

Lizzie was already laying out sandwiches as I came down to the kitchen. 'They'll have left the cemetery by now,' she said. 'No one will blame you for not staying.' She wiped her hands on her apron and hugged me. I could have stayed there an eternity, but I needed to get to the Press.

❧

Mr Hart was in the printing room. I'd guessed he would avoid the sandwiches and chat after the funeral; the clatter of the presses and the smell of oil were balm to his melancholy. As the war went on he'd been spending more and more time in there, Gareth had said. As I stood inside the door, I understood why. He saw me, and for an instant it seemed he didn't know who I was. When he realised, he took a deep breath and came towards me.

'Mrs Owen.'

'Esme, please.'

'Esme.'

We stood there, silent. I thought about what it might mean to him to lose Dr Murray and Gareth in the same week. Perhaps he thought the same about me.

I held up *Women's Words and Their Meanings*. 'Please, don't think badly of him, Mr Hart, but Gareth did this for me. They're words. Words I collected. He set them in type instead of buying a ring.' I faltered. Mr Hart just stared at the volume in my hands. 'I'm hoping he cast plates. I want to print more copies.'

He took the volume from me and walked over to a small desk at the edge of the room. He sat down. The presses continued their chorus.

I followed and stood behind him as he turned the pages and traced the words with the tips of his fingers, as if they were Braille.

He closed it with extraordinary care and rested his hand on the cover.

'There are no plates, Mrs Owen. It is too much of an expense to produce plates for small print runs, let alone single copies.'

Until this moment I had felt a kind of strength, a clarity of purpose that I knew would hold me up. I reached for the other chair and barely got to it in time.

'If the compositor expects changes – edits, corrections – he'll keep the formes that hold the type. The type is loose, you see. Easy to adjust.'

'Gareth wouldn't have expected corrections,' I said.

'He was my best ... *is* my best compositor. It is a rule that we keep the formes for a period.'

The idea animated us both. We rose together and walked in silence to the composing room. It was half empty, but Gareth's old bench was occupied by an apprentice. Mr Hart opened one of the wide drawers that held formes still in use. He opened another, then another. I stopped shadowing him and began to imagine our empty house.

'Here they are.'

Mr Hart crouched down to the lowest drawer and I crouched with him. Together our fingers traced the type. I closed my eyes and felt the difference under the tips of my funny fingers.

Words, for me, were always tangible, but never like this. This was how Gareth knew them, and I suddenly wanted to learn how to read them blind.

'Perhaps he anticipated additional copies,' the old Controller said.

Perhaps he did.

❧

I was the first to return to the Scriptorium a few days after the funeral. Dr Murray's mortar board was just where I'd left it after taking his photograph less than two weeks earlier. Dust had settled on it again. I couldn't bring myself to brush it off. The photograph,

Rosfrith told me after the funeral, would be in the September issue of the *Periodical*. Even in her grief, she thought to apologise for my exclusion.

But that wasn't the worst news she had to give. 'We will be moving,' she said, her eyes filling with tears again. 'In September. To the Old Ashmolean. All of us. Everything.'

I was stunned. I stood there as if I hadn't understood a word she'd said. September was only a month away. 'What will happen to the Scriptorium?' I finally asked.

She shrugged sadly. 'It will become a garden shed.'

As I walked towards my desk, trailing my fingers along the shelves of slips, I remembered Da reading me the story of Ala-ed-Din. The Scriptorium had been my cave then. But unlike Ala-ed-Din, I'd had no desire to be released. I belonged to the Scriptorium; I was its willing prisoner. My only wish had been to serve the Dictionary, and that had come true. But my service was contained within these walls. I was bonded to this place as surely as Lizzie was bonded to the kitchen and her room at the top of the stairs.

I sat at my desk and rested my head for a moment on my arms.

The weight of a hand on my shoulder. I thought it was Gareth and woke with a start. It was Mr Sweatman. I'd fallen into an exhausted doze.

'Why don't you go home, Esme?' he said.

'I can't.'

He must have understood, because he nodded and put a pile of slips on my desk.

'New words from A to S,' he said. 'They need to be sorted for the supplementary publication, whenever that will be.'

It was the simplest of tasks, but it would take up time. 'Thank you, Mr Sweatman.'

'Don't you think it's about time you called me Fred?'

'Thank you, Fred.'

'How odd that sounds coming from you. I'm sure we'll get used to it,' he said. 'As we must get used to any change.'

❧

10th August 1915

My darling Es,

Ten days since I left and I feel I have been gone an age. Oxford might have been somewhere I visited once, and you a dream. But then I opened my Rupert Brooke, and your slip fell out. The words, your handwriting, the familiar texture of the paper — they will be my daily reminder that you are real.

I have decided to keep Brooke in my pocket at all times. If I am wounded and must wait for a stretcher, I want to have something to read and your words to calm me. But there is no chance of that for a while. We are stationed at Hébuterne, a small farming village not far from Arras. We've been told there is time to settle in, and our days are filled with drills, and loafing. Some of the lads have mistaken the whole adventure for a holiday, having never actually had one, and quite a bit of my time is spent apologising to the mothers of pretty girls. My French is improving.

An Indian bicycle troop is stationed nearby. Have you ever met an Indian? I hadn't. They ride around the village in pairs and are quite a magnificent sight with their turbans and their elaborate moustaches. At least, the older men have moustaches: as with the English, there are plenty of Indian boys who join before they are old enough to have facial hair. I've been told they take them as young as ten, but I've not seen any quite so young. They would be kept well back, one would hope.

Last night, in a gesture of camaraderie, we invited the Indian officers to share our evening meal. They barely touched the food, and drank very little, but it was a late night with a lot of laughter. I was one of the greenest officers there, and it turns out I had a lot to learn. There is a whole vocabulary here that I've been unaware of, Es. Most of it applies to the trenches in one way or another, and there are plenty of words that would sit well against some of Mabel's best. But the word I am sending as a gift has been my favourite so far.

I fashioned the slip from instructions for cooking rice. One of the Indian officers had it scrunched up in his pocket and offered it when I was searching around for a scrap of paper. I was thrilled, knowing how much you would appreciate the Hindi script on the back. The officer's name is Ajit, and he gave me the origin of the word. He also wanted me to tell you that his name means 'invincible' — he insisted I write it on the slip. When I told him I had no idea what my name meant, he gave a wobble of his head and said, 'That is not good. A man's name is his destiny.' By that logic, he is well-suited to war.

At the moment, life is pretty cushy (see how quickly I've absorbed the new vernacular), but I long to hear from you, Es. I've been told that we will start receiving post tomorrow, the War Office having finally registered our whereabouts. I look forward to an account of your days, and any news from the Press or Scriptorium, and Bertie, of course. Don't be afraid to include the boring detail: I will delight in it. Please give my regards to Lizzie and visit Mr Hart for me. I will write to him separately, but I fear his depression will not end until this war does. Your company will cheer him.

Eternal Love,
Gareth

CUSHY
From the Hindi word 'khush', meaning 'pleasure' (Ajit 'invincible' Khatri).
'Don't get used to your cushy quarters, Lieutenant; you'll soon be in the trenches and up to your arse in mud.'

Lt Gerald Ainsworth, 1915

⁕

In the weeks after Gareth left, I had imagined him dying a hundred different ways. My sleep had been restless, and I woke with dread. So his first letter was a tonic.

'Lizzie. A letter!'

'Who from? The King?' She smiled and made herself comfortable at the table, ready to hear it.

'It does sound a bit like a holiday, doesn't it?' I said, when I'd read it through.

'It does. And he's made an interesting friend, by the sound.'

'Yes. Mr Invincible. Which reminds me.' I took the slip from the envelope and read what Gareth had written on it.

'Isn't it a wonderful word?' I said. 'I've decided to use it as often as I can.'

'You'll have more cause than me.'

More letters arrived, one every few days, and August passed into September. There was little sign that work had slowed since Dr Murray died, and as no one packed a box or cleared a shelf I thought, maybe, the Scriptorium would stay as it was. When Mr Sweatman ('Fred' never came easily) started to give me words to research, I felt some equilibrium return to my days. I resumed my errands to the Old Ashmolean and to the Press. Mr Hart was indeed in a depressed mood, but contrary to Gareth's hope, I was unable to bring him any cheer.

Every weekday at five o'clock, I went straight from the Scriptorium to the Radcliffe Infirmary. On Saturdays I was there most of the afternoon. There was almost always a boy from the Press in one of the beds. If they'd just come in, the sisters would make sure I was told and the boy would become part of my rounds, but most were not short of visitors. The Radcliffe was a stone's throw from the Press, and the women of Jericho had claimed it. The wards were full of mothers and sisters and sweethearts fussing over wounded strangers in the way they would fuss over their own, if they could. When a local boy came in they'd swarm around, trading biscuits and toffee for scraps of news that might convince them their own boys were still alive.

I'd always have my evening meal with Bertie.

'He still doesn't comprehend anything,' Sister Morley said. 'But he seems to eat more when you're beside him.'

The Radcliffe provided my dinner on the same tray as Bertie's. It was always bland and repetitive. Sister Morley apologised and blamed rationing, but I didn't mind: it meant I didn't have to go home and cook for one.

'Bertie,' I said. He gave no response. 'I came across a word today that I think you might like.'

'He don't like *any* words, Mrs Owen,' his neighbour said.

'I know that, Angus, but the doctors only use familiar words. This will be *un*familiar.'

'Well, how will he know what it means?'

'He won't. But I'll explain it.'

'But you got to use familiar words to explain it.'

'Not necessarily.'

Angus laughed. 'You got your work cut out, missus.'

'Well, if you keep eavesdropping, you at least will leave here with a larger vocabulary.'

'Reckon I know all the words I need,' he said.

Bertie ate his meal like any other man, and for its duration I could imagine him burping at the end and saying, 'Excuse me, missus,' like so many of them did. But when he'd had enough, he resumed his forward gaze and was as silent as ever.

'*Finita*,' I said.

Bertie's eyes registered nothing.

'What does that mean?' asked Angus.

'It means *finished*.'

'What language is it?'

'Esperanto.'

'Never heard of it.'

'It's made up, in a way,' I said. 'It's meant to be easy enough for anyone to learn – it was created to foster peace between nations.'

'And how's that going, missus?'

I smiled wearily as my gaze settled on the end of Angus's bed: no feet beneath the sheet.

'Still,' he went on, 'if it helps old Bertie here, it might not have been a waste of time making it up.' He nodded towards Bertie's tray. 'Can I have the leftovers if he's finished?'

I picked up the plate of food and took it over to Angus.

'How do you say thanks in Esperanto?' he asked.

I had a list of words in my pocket, but this one I knew by heart: '*Dankon.*'

'Well, *dankon*, Mrs Owen.'

'*Ne dankinde*, Angus.'

❧

Mrs Murray knocked, then opened the door to the Scriptorium. We all looked up from our desks.

'It begins,' she announced, and with a cheerless expression she ushered in a boy wearing the familiar apron of the Press. He pushed in a trolley stacked with flattened cardboard boxes.

'The Press has offered to help with the move and will be sending a boy each afternoon with a trolley. They will take whatever boxes you have packed to the Old Ashmolean.' She looked as though she was about to say more, but no words came. We watched her look around the room, taking in the shelves of pigeon-holes, the books, the stacks of paper. It should have been a private moment. Her eyes settled at last on Dr Murray's desk, on the mortar board resting on the shelf beside *Q to Sh*. She turned and left.

Rosfrith and Elsie got up to follow their mother. 'You can leave the boxes on the floor,' Rosfrith said as she passed the trolley boy. 'I'm sure we'll be able to figure out how to assemble them.'

Work could not stop, but assembling boxes became our morning-tea activity. At lunchtime, we'd pack them with old dictionaries and all the books and journals we could do without. A boy would turn up each afternoon at three o'clock to take them away.

Every day, the Scriptorium cast off a little more of itself. In the last week of September, the final boxes were filled with the paraphernalia that each assistant needed to do their job. The mood was sombre, and on their last day the assistants left without ceremony; there was very little of the Scriptorium to farewell.

I wasn't ready to leave. I volunteered to stay back and box up all the slips for storage or rehousing at the Old Ashmolean. Besides me, Mr Sweatman was the last to finish packing. He closed up his box and left it on the sorting table to be picked up by the Press boy. Then he came to say goodbye.

'Are you thinking of staying?' he said, looking at my desk and its contents, exactly where they had always been.

'Maybe,' I said. 'You were such a rowdy bunch; I'll get more work done now you're gone.'

He sighed, all the chaff gone out of him. I stood up and embraced him.

Alone, I finally dared to look around. The sorting table stood solid and familiar; the pigeon-holes were still full of slips, but the shelves were empty and the desks were clean. The shuffling of papers and scratching of pens had ceased. The Scriptorium had lost almost all its flesh, and the bones resembled nothing more than a shed.

I spent the next few weeks shifting back and forth between the Scriptorium and the Radcliffe Infirmary.

❧

I touched Bertie's hand. '*Mano*,' I said. Then I pointed to mine. '*Mano*.'

❧

'You'll not want to do this alone, Essymay,' said Lizzie. She must have seen me arrive and was coming across the garden towards the Scriptorium.

'You have enough to do,' I said.

'Mrs Murray managed to get an extra girl in for a few weeks. My mornings are yours.'

I kissed Lizzie on the cheek, then I opened the Scriptorium door.

Empty shoeboxes covered the sorting table.

❧

'*Akvo*,' I said, and Bertie took the cup of water. He had long fingers, and the callouses of soldiering had almost disappeared. Beneath them the skin was soft. Not a labourer, I thought. Perhaps a clerk.

❧

It felt like the work of the bereaved. The slips were familiar but half forgotten. I kept stopping to remember.

❧

I lifted my meal from Bertie's tray. '*Vespermango*,' I said. I drank my tea. '*Teon*.'

❧

I stacked the slips in small bundles beside the shoeboxes. If they were loose, Lizzie tied them with string and placed one bundle beside another until the shoebox was full. Then I wrote the contents on the front, adding *Store* or *Old Ash*. It seemed extraordinary to me that the slips were such a good fit, as if Dr Murray had designed the shoeboxes too.

'Why does he always get his *vespermango* first?' Angus asked.

'He doesn't make a fuss, like some,' I said.

Lizzie closed the lid on another box and put it to one end of the sorting table.

'Halfway there,' she said.

'*Amico.*' I pointed to myself. '*Amico.*' I pointed to Angus.

'What makes you think I'm his friend?' said Angus.

'I've seen you talking to him, using the Esperanto words. That's friendship, I think.'

I bundled the last slips and gave them to Lizzie to tie. The pigeon-holes were completely empty. It felt as though my life to that moment was gone.

'This must be what it feels like to be excised from a proof,' I said.

'And that means?' said Lizzie.

'Removed, cut out, erased.'

'This is an important one, Angus,' I said, holding my list of Esperanto words, 'but I have no idea how to define it for him.'

'What is it?'

'*Sekura.*'

'What does it mean?'

'Safe.'

We sat in silence for a while, Angus holding his chin in mock thought, me staring at the word and coming up blank, Bertie between us both, unresponsive.

'Hug him, missus,' said Angus.

'Hug him?'

'Yeah. I reckon the only time any of us feel really safe is when our mum's hugging us.'

❧

The sorting table was covered in shoeboxes, each labelled and full of slips.

'Mrs Murray is organising for the pigeon-holes to be taken to the Old Ashmolean soon,' I said to Lizzie.

'We'll give them a good clean then and our job will be done.'

❧

'*Sekura*,' I said as I hugged Bertie.

I'd been hugging him when I arrived and when I left, and once or twice in between. But he remained rigid. This time, I felt his body yield.

'Bertie?' I said, when I finally pulled back and could look into his eyes. But there was nothing. I hugged him again. '*Sekura*.'

Again, he yielded, his head coming down towards my chest.

September 1915

My darling Es,

My word of the week is doolally. It was used to refer to a lad who was sent a roll of lavatory paper from home and used the whole lot to bandage his eyes. When his mates finally tore it off, the poor bugger was blind. He was ridiculed for faking, but he genuinely couldn't see a thing. War neuroses, according to the doctor. Doolally, according to his mates. I suppose it's an easier word to relate to — leaves room for a laugh.

I'm beginning to feel the English language is burdened by this war, Es. Everyone I meet has a new word for toilet paper, and I've not heard one that doesn't accurately convey its origin or the experience of using it. Yet only a handful of words exist to convey a thousand horrors.

Horror. It's war-weary. It is the word we use when we have no words. Perhaps some things are not meant to be described — at least, not by the likes of me. A poet, perhaps, could arrange words in a way that creates the itch of fear or the heaviness of dread. They could make an enemy of mud and damp boots and raise your pulse just at the mention of them. A poet might be able to push this word or that to mean something more than what has been ordained by our Dictionary men.

I am not a poet, my love. The words I have are pale and slight against the hulking force of this experience. I can tell you it is wretched, that the mud is muddier, the damp damper, the sound of a flute played by a German soldier more beautiful and more melancholy than any sound I have ever heard. But you will not understand. There is not a word in Dr Murray's dictionary that can rise to the challenge of the stench in this place. I could compare it to the fish market on a hot afternoon, to a tannery, a morgue, a sewer. It is all of those things, but it is the way it enters you, becomes a taste and a cramping in your throat and belly. You will imagine something awful, but it is worse. And then there is the slaughter. It comes to you in the Times. *The 'Roll of Honour'. Column after column of names in Monotype Modern. I have no way of describing the wrenching of my soul when the ember of a fag still glows in the mud, though the lips that held it have been blown away. I lit that fag, Es. I knew it would be his last. This is how we do it. We light fags, we nod, we hold their gaze. Then we send them over the top. There are no words.*

And now there is time to rest, but we can't. Our minds will never be quiet. It will start up again, and so everyone is writing home. To the wives of three men and the mothers of four, I will be the letter-writer. We have been told not to describe it, as if that is even possible, but some have tried. It is my job, tonight, to censor them, and I have blacked out the words of boys who are barely literate as well as boys who might become poets, so their mothers continue to think the war a glory and a good fight. I do it gladly, for their mothers, but from the start I have thought of you, Es, and how you would try to rescue what these boys have said so you can understand them better. Their words are ordinary, but they are assembled into sentences that are grotesque. I've transcribed every one, and I include the pages with this letter. I have not corrected or truncated, and each sentence has its owner's name beside it. I could think of no one better to honour them than you.

Eternal Love,

Gareth

P.S. Ajit was not invincible.

Our house was dark except for the hall light, but it was all I needed. I sat on the bottom stair, my coat still on, and read Gareth's letter again.

Then I read all the words he had blacked out for others and transcribed for me. Hours passed, and a chill stole into me. I looked at the date of Gareth's letter; it was already five days old.

I walked to Sunnyside, crept into the kitchen and up the stairs. Lizzie was snoring. I opened the door as quietly as I could, took the spread from the foot of her bed and made a nest of it on the floor.

In the morning, I was roused by Lizzie's quiet movement around the room. When she noticed me watching her, she scolded me for not waking her in the night. I told her about Gareth's letter, and she helped me into her bed. Her body's warmth still clung to the sheets.

'I'll start cleaning the Scrippy. You sleep,' she said, tucking me in like she used to.

But I couldn't sleep. When she was gone, I leaned under the bed and dragged out the trunk. *Women's Words and Their Meanings*: he said he was on every page. I brought it into bed with me, smelled the leather and turned to the first page. I read every word. A year, it had taken him.

❧

When our work in the Scriptorium was done, I was glad to still have the Radcliffe to go to. Perhaps Gareth would end up there, I thought as I walked towards it. What might he be missing? An arm, a leg? His mind, like Bertie?

'Evenin', missus,' said Angus. '*Vespermango's* been and gone. Me and Bertie had a lovely chat about the potatoes. I reckon they was mashed with *akvo*. He silently agreed.'

'I'm quite well, Angus. Thank you.'

'Well, that don't make a lotta sense. I didn't ask how you was, but I suppose I might as well. You all right?'

'Oh, just tired.'

'Well, there's a new one on the ward. A loudmouth. No respect. Giving the nurses a terrible time. One-armed sniper I heard them call him, on account of his sharp shooting in France and his sharp talking in here. Been at the Radcliffe a while, they say. The other ward must have had enough of him.' I followed Angus's gaze.

The new patient was familiar from my first day at the infirmary. When he saw me looking over, he puckered his thin lips into a kiss. I ignored him and turned to Bertie.

'You still collecting words?' It was the one-armed sniper. 'That coward won't give you none. Clammed up at the first sign of trouble, he did.'

'Just ignore him, missus.'

'Good advice, Angus.'

But ignoring didn't work.

'I've got a word that'll blow you away.'

Some men are very kind, and some men are not. It makes no difference whose uniform they wear. There was no mistaking what word was shouted – it was precise and well aimed, and it was repeated over and over, even after it had hit its mark.

'BOMB. BOMB. BOMB. BOMB. BOMB.'

Bertie flattened himself against his mattress then scrambled from the bed, knocking me flat. His screaming bounced off the walls so I heard it from all directions.

I got to my hands and knees and looked along the ward. For a disorientating moment, I thought it might have been a Zeppelin attack instead of simple malice.

The ward was almost as it had been when I came in, but everyone was turned our way. My chair was toppled, and Bertie's bed was askew. He was cowering beneath it, knees up to his chest and hands over his ears. He shivered as if he was naked in a snowdrift. He'd wet himself.

Angus dropped down to the floor behind him, and I thought he'd been tipped out of bed. There were bandages where his feet should have been. Trench foot, he'd said. He dragged himself alongside Bertie.

'*Amico*,' he said in a sing-song way, like a child playing hide-and-seek. '*Amico, amico*.'

The screaming turned to a terrible groaning, and Bertie began to rock back and forth. I crawled towards them and kneeled beside Bertie, wrapping his rocking body in my arms. He was small and frail – barely grown. '*Sekura*,' I said in his ear.

I thought of all the times Lizzie had sat me in her lap and rocked my worries away, her voice a metronome of calm. '*Sekura*,' I said, rocking with Bertie. '*Sekura*.'

Then Angus had his arms around both of us, and I felt him slow us down. Bertie's groaning became a hum, and I whispered my chant. The rocking stopped altogether, and Bertie collapsed onto my breast and wept.

❧

Sister Morley sat me down at the nurses' desk and brought me a cup of tea. 'There are a lot of boys like Bertie,' she said. 'Not his particular war neurosis – I think that's unique – but a lot that don't speak when the doctors say they are perfectly able.'

'What happens to them?' I asked.

'A lot end up at the Netley Hospital in Southampton,' she said. 'They're open to trying all sorts of treatments. Doctor Ostler thinks there might be some merit to your Esperanto therapy and he's written about it to a colleague there. He's aware of your work with the Dictionary and thinks your particular expertise might contribute to their linguistic therapy programme. He's hoping you might make a visit and talk to the staff about what you've been doing with Bertie.'

'But Bertie hasn't said a word,' I said. 'And there's no indication that anything I've done has got through.'

'This is the first time he's been calmed by words instead of chloroform, Mrs Owen. It's a start.'

❧

I dreamed I was in France. Gareth wore a turban, and Bertie could speak. Angus was rocking me, saying, '*Sekura, sekura.*' I looked down and my feet were bloody stumps.

❧

When I arrived the next morning Lizzie was already in the Scriptorium, wiping the pigeon-holes with a damp cloth. I could smell the vinegar.

'Sleep in?' she said.

'A bad night.'

She nodded. 'They'll be taking the pigeon-holes this morning. If you box up whatever's in your desk, they can take that too.'

My desk. Not a thing had been packed away. There were even some slips and a page of copy on top. It was like a room in one of those museum houses. I assembled my box and began filling it.

My copy of Samuel Johnson's dictionary went in first, then Da's books – what he called his 'Scrippy library'. I picked up a worn volume of *The Thousand and One Nights* and turned to the story of Ala-ed-Din. The past came towards me, and I closed the book. I put it in the box with the others.

I cleared the top of my desk and opened the lid. There was a novel I never finished reading. A slip fell from its pages – a dull word, a duplicate, probably. I put it back in the book and put the book in the box. Pencils and a pen. Notepaper. *Hart's Rules* with Mr Dankworth's notes still attached. They all went in.

Then the shoebox full of slips. My slips. The slips Gareth had procured from Lizzie or sneaked into the Scriptorium to borrow. I put them in the box too. Then I folded the flaps down, securing one beneath the other.

'I think we might be done, Lizzie,' I said.

'Almost.' She dipped her cloth in the bucket and squeezed out the excess water. Then she got on her knees to wipe the last row of pigeon-holes. 'Now we're done,' she said, sitting back on her haunches. I helped her to stand.

An older man and a boy arrived while Lizzie emptied her bucket of water under the ash.

'They're all ready to go,' I said.

The older man pointed to the pigeon-holes closest to the door, and the boy bent to lift one end. They had the same stocky build, the same blond hair. I hoped the war would end before the boy came of age. They took the shelves to a small lorry parked in the driveway.

Lizzie came back with a dustpan and brush.

'Just when you think there's nothing more to do.' She brushed up decades of accumulated dust and dirt that had built up behind the pigeon-holes.

Shelf by shelf, the man and his boy removed all evidence the slips had ever been there.

'Last one,' the man said. 'You want me to come back for that box? It's for the Old Ash, I take it?'

Is that where I'll go after this? I thought. It hadn't been a question, and now it was.

'Leave it for the moment,' I said.

The boy walked forwards, the man backwards, turning his head to the side now and then to check he wasn't going to bump into anything. I followed them out of the Scriptorium and watched as they loaded the last of the pigeon-holes into the lorry. They closed the doors, got into the cab and drove out of the gates onto the Banbury Road.

'That's it, then,' I said to Lizzie as I came back in.

'Not quite.' Still kneeling, Lizzie held the dustpan in one hand and a small pile of slips in the other. 'They're filthy, mind,' she said, handing them to me.

The slips were held together with a rusty pin and cobwebs. I took them outside and blew them clean, then returned to the sorting table. I spread the slips out. There were seven, each written in a different hand, with a quotation from a different book, a different time in history.

'Read them out,' Lizzie called from where she kneeled. 'Let's see if I've heard of them.'

'You've heard of them,' I said.

'Go on.'

'*Bonde mayde.*' Lizzie's sweeping stopped. '*Bound maiden, bondmaiden, bond servant, bond service, bond-maide, bondmaid.*'

Their quotations were almost benign, but on three slips Da had written a possible definition: *Slave girl, bonded servant, bound to serve till death.*

Slave girl had been circled.

I remembered the top-slip finding me beneath the sorting table.

Lizzie sat beside me. 'What's upset you?'

'It's these words.'

Lizzie moved the slips around, as if completing a jigsaw puzzle. 'Will you be keeping them or giving them to Mr Bradley?'

Bondmaid had come to me – twice now– and I was reluctant to restore it to the Dictionary. It's a vulgar word, I thought. More offensive to me than *cunt*. Would that give me the right to leave it out if I was editor?

'It means *slave girl*, Lizzie. Has that never bothered you?'

She thought for a while. 'I'm no slave, Essymay, but in my head, I can't help thinking of myself as a bondmaid.'

Her hand went to her crucifix, and I knew she was thinking about the right way to say something.

When she finally let the crucifix rest, she was smiling. 'You've always said that a word can change its meaning depending on who uses it. So maybe *bondmaid* can mean something more than what those slips say. I've been a bondmaid to you since you were small, Essymay, and I've been glad for every day of it.'

❧

I closed the door of the Scriptorium, and Lizzie walked with me through the twilight, back to Observatory Street. We ate bread and butter at my kitchen table, and when my eyes began to droop, I asked if she would stay.

'You'd probably be more comfortable in my old room,' I said, 'but do you mind sharing?'

Upstairs, Lizzie climbed beneath the blankets and folded herself around me. I told her about Bertie. About his fear, and mine.

'I think now I can imagine a little of what it's like for them,' I whispered into the dark. I didn't say Gareth's name. We didn't talk about his letter. The Battle of Loos was hearsay and rumour all over Oxford.

❧

I woke alone but to the clatter of Lizzie in our kitchen. She had porridge on the range, and when she saw me she spooned some into a bowl then added cream, honey and a pinch of cinnamon. I realised she must have been to the market already.

We ate in easy silence. When our bowls were empty, Lizzie made toast and brewed tea. She was comfortable moving around the kitchen in a way that I was not. I was reminded of our time in Shropshire.

'Good to see you smile,' she said.

'It's good to have you here.'

The garden gate sang on its hinges.

'Morning post,' I said. 'He's early.' I waited for the sound of letters being pushed through the slot in the front door. When it didn't come, Lizzie went down the hall to check if there was someone outside. I followed.

'What's he doing?' I asked.

'He's holding …' Lizzie clamped her hand over her mouth and her head shook back and forth, ever so slightly. There was a knock, almost too quiet to be heard. She took a step towards it.

'Stop.' It came out as a whisper. 'It will be for me.' But I was unable to move.

He knocked again. Tears rolled silently over Lizzie's rough cheeks as she looked back at me. She offered me her arm and I took it.

The man was old, too old for the war, and so he was charged with delivering its sorrow. I held the telegram and watched him walk back along the length of Observatory Street. His shoulders hunched under the weight of his satchel.

∾

Lizzie stayed with me. She fed me and bathed me, and held my arm to walk to the end of the street, then around the block, then to St Barnabas. She prayed; I couldn't.

After two weeks, I insisted on returning to the Radcliffe Infirmary. Angus had been sent to a rehabilitation hospital near his home town. Bertie had been moved to the Netley Hospital in Southampton. There were still three other boys there who had been silenced by their experience. I sat with them until the sister sent me home.

A month after the telegram, a parcel arrived. Lizzie brought it into the sitting room.

'There's a note,' she said, taking it from under the string that held the brown-paper parcel together.

Dear Mrs Owen,

Please accept these two copies of Women's Words and Their Meanings, *with my compliments. I apologise I could not print more, and that the binding is not to the standard of the original. Paper is in short supply, as you know. I have taken the liberty of retaining a third copy for the Oxford University Press library. If you ever need to access it, you will find it shelved alongside the Dictionary fascicles.*

Yours, in sympathy,

Horace Hart

Lizzie stoked the coals then sat beside me. I released the bow and the paper fell away.

'It's a good thing,' said Lizzie.

'What is?'

'Having copies.' She took one and turned the pages, counting them under her breath. She stopped on page 15 and found her own name.

'Lizzie Lester,' she said.

'Do you remember the word?'

'*Knackered.*' She ran her finger under the word, then, looking at me recited by heart: '*I get up before dawn to make sure everyone in the big house will be warm and fed when they wake, and I don't go to sleep till they is snoring. I feel knackered half the time, like a worn-out horse. No good for nothing.*'

'Word-perfect, Lizzie. How do you remember it so well?'

'I had Gareth read it to me three times till I got it. But it's not word-perfect. I should have said "till they *are* snoring". Why didn't you correct it?'

'It wasn't my place to judge what you said or how you said it. I just wanted to record, and maybe understand.'

She nodded. 'Gareth showed me every word with my name against it. I memorised where they were and what they said.'

'Why is it a good thing to have copies?' I asked.

''Cos now they'll get an airing,' she said. 'You can give one to Mr Bradley and one to the Bodleian. Anything important that's been written down, they keep. You said that. Every book, every manuscript, every letter written from Lord Whatsit to Professor Who-knows-what.'

'And you think this is important?' I was smiling for the first time in weeks.

'I do.'

Lizzie rose and returned her copy of *Women's Words* to the opened parcel in my lap. She patted it, put her hand to my cheek, then went to the kitchen.

❧

Lizzie came with me to the Bodleian.

Since allowing me to become a reader, Mr Nicholson had softened to the presence of women in his library, but I was not so sure about his successor. Mr Madan looked at the title page. 'I don't think so, Mrs Owen.' He took off his spectacles and wiped them with a handkerchief, as if to remove the image of my name.

'But why?'

He returned his spectacles to the bridge of his nose and turned a few pages. 'It's an interesting project, but it's of no scholarly importance.'

'And what would make it of scholarly importance?'

'If it had been compiled by a scholar, for a start. Beyond that, it would have to be a topic of significance.'

It was ten in the morning. Scholars billowed by in their gowns, long and short – though there were fewer men and more women than the first time I stood at that desk. I turned to where Lizzie sat. It was the same bench I'd occupied years before while Dr Murray argued my case to become a reader. She looked as out of place as I had felt. I rose to my full height and turned back to Mr Madan.

'It *is* a topic of significance, sir. It fills a gap in knowledge, and surely that is the purpose of scholarship.'

He had to tilt his head up a little to look me in the eye. I felt Lizzie shift behind me, saw his gaze flick towards her, then back to me.

I would stay there until *Women's Words* was accepted, I thought. If I had a chain, I would have gladly locked myself to the grille in front of the desk.

Mr Madan stopped turning pages. His cheeks flushed and he covered his discomfort with a cough. He had scanned page 6. C words.

'An old word, Mr Madan. With a long history in English. Chaucer was quite fond of using it, and yet it does not appear in our Dictionary. A gap, surely.'

He wiped his forehead with his handkerchief and looked around, searching for an ally. I looked around also.

Our conversation was being observed by three old men, and Eleanor Bradley – there to check quotations no doubt. She smiled when I caught her eye, nodding her encouragement. I faced Mr Madan again.

'You are not the arbiter of knowledge, sir. You are its librarian.' I pushed *Women's Words* across his desk. 'It is not for you to judge the importance of these words, simply to allow others to do so.'

Lizzie and I walked arm in arm along the Banbury Road to Sunnyside. We came through the gates as Elsie and Rosfrith were coming out. They embraced me in turn.

'Will we be seeing you at the Old Ashmolean today, Esme?' Elsie asked, her hand gentle on my sleeve. 'The pigeon-holes are all in place, and the only thing missing now is you. It's a bit tight at the moment, but Mr Sweatman has made some room for you at his desk.'

I looked from one Murray sister to the other, and then to Lizzie. We were children together, once. Would we grow old together?

'Could you wait a moment, Elsie, Rosfrith? I'll be right back.'

I walked through the garden. The ash was losing its leaves, and autumn winds had already blown them towards the Scriptorium. I had to clear them from the doorway before going in.

It was cold, almost empty, except for the sorting table. The *bondmaid* slips were exactly where Lizzie and I had left them. I sat where Lizzie had sat moving the words around. She couldn't read them, but she had understood them better than I had. I felt my pockets for the stub of a pencil and a blank slip.

BONDMAID

Bonded for life by love, devotion or obligation.

'I've been a bondmaid to you since you were small, Essymay, and I've been glad for every day of it.'

Lizzie Lester, 1915

I pulled the door of the Scriptorium shut and heard the sound of it echo into the almost-empty space inside. Just a shed, I thought, and walked back to where the three women were waiting.

'These are for Mr Bradley,' I said, handing Elsie the bundle of slips. 'Lizzie found them as we were cleaning up. They're the missing *bondmaid* slips.'

For a moment, Elsie wasn't sure what I was talking about, then the crease between her brows gave way to wide eyes. 'Goodness,' she said, peering closely at the slips, not quite believing.

Rosfrith leaned in to look. 'What a mystery that was,' she said.

'The top-slip doesn't seem to be with them, unfortunately.' I gave Lizzie the quickest glance. 'But there are some suggestions about how it might be defined. We thought Mr Bradley would be glad to have them, after all this time.'

'I have no doubt that he will,' said Elsie. 'But surely you can give them to him yourself?'

'I won't be coming to the Old Ashmolean, Elsie. I've been offered a position at the Netley Hospital in Southampton. I think I'm going to take it.'

❧

The trunk sat on the kitchen table. Lizzie and I sat either side of it, each holding a cup of tea.

'I think it should stay here,' I said. 'My accommodation is temporary, and I don't know when I'll get something permanent.'

'Surely you'll collect more words.'

I took a sip of tea and smiled. 'Maybe not. I'll be working with men who don't speak.'

'But it's your Dictionary of Lost Words!'

I thought about what was in the trunk. 'It defines me, Lizzie. I wouldn't know who I was without it. But as Da would have said, I have followed all avenues of enquiry and am satisfied I have enough for an accurate entry.'

'You're not a word, Essymay.'

'Not to you. But to Her, that is all I am. And I may not even be that. When the time is right, I want Her to have it.' I reached over and took Lizzie's hand from where it rested against her chest. 'I want Her to know who I am. What She meant. It's all there.'

We looked at the trunk, worn from handling, like a well-read book.

'You've always been its custodian, Lizzie, from the very first word. Please look after it until I'm settled.'

❧

My own bags were packed when Gareth's kit arrived.

I emptied it carefully onto the kitchen table. There was mud still on the socks I'd knitted; dirt and blood on his spare tunic and trousers.

His or another man's, I didn't know. My letters were all there, and Rupert Brooke's poems. I fanned through the pages and found my slip – *love, eternal*.

I unzipped his shaving kit, emptied his stationery box; I turned every pocket inside out and rubbed lint and dried mud between my fingers. I wanted everything he'd left to touch my skin. I opened my letters to him. The oldest were so worn along the folds, my words were hard to read. When I opened the last, his pages were tucked between mine. The writing was shaky, rushed, but it was Gareth's hand.

1st October 1915, Loos
My darling Es,

It has been three days. Is that possible? It feels like more. They were endless. We were to be kept back for a day to rest and then we weren't. We were already exhausted, but we had to keep on fighting. Is that what we were doing?

Mostly we were dying.

I've not slept. I can't think straight, but I know I must write to you, Es. Es. Es. Es. Es. Es. Essy. Esme. I've always loved how Lizzie calls you Essymay. I've wanted to call you that myself; it's been there, on the tip of my tongue. But it's hers. It's everything you were before I met you. Is that why I love it?

Forgive me. I'm desperate to lie down, rest my head against your belly. I want to hear your heart beating. I rested my head against the chest of my orderly and heard nothing. Why would I? His legs had been blown off. His legs that had done everything I asked of them were no longer attached to his body.

I lost seven of my men, Es. For some, the weeks before this battle were the best they had ever had. Three might be fathers by the time the flesh has fallen from their bones.

I write this, my darling Es, because you say your imagination conjures images that words can't come close to, and you would rather know the truth. I find it is a great relief to write without filter, and it is the closest I can get to resting against your breast and weeping. I am so grateful. But you have not imagined the distress you will feel. My account will seep into your dreams, and it will be me lying in the mud, my eyes like glass, bits of me blown away. Every morning you will wake in fear of what might be, and it will shadow you through the day.

I am spent, my darling Es. There is a buzzing in my ears and images in my mind that get clearer and more grotesque whenever I close my eyes. It is the gauntlet I must run if I am ever to sleep. I would be a coward to share this with you.

When the battle is over, I will tear this up and start again with a more tolerable arrangement of words. But right now, having arranged them exactly as I need to, I feel unburdened. When my lids close, I will be spared the worst, and it will be an image of you that ushers me to sleep.

Eternal Love,
Gareth

I folded the letter and put my slip within it. I turned the pages of Brooke's book until I found 'The Dead'. I read the first few lines in silence.

'All this is ended,' I said to the empty house. I could read no further.

I closed the poem around our final words. Stood. Walked up the stairs to the bathroom. I put Gareth's comb back on the sink. I was leaving; it made no sense at all. But nothing did.

I released the latch and the lid sprang back, *The Dictionary of Lost Words* etched on its inside. The trunk was bulging, but there was room enough.

On top was our dictionary. I opened to the title page.

Women's Words and Their Meanings
Edited by Esme Nicoll

I placed Gareth's Rupert Brooke beside it.

I held the soldiers' grotesque sentences, written in Gareth's hand. I didn't put them in the trunk. He did not mean for me to lock them away.

I could hear no sound from the kitchen and knew Lizzie must be waiting, not wanting to rush me. But she would be worried about the time. The train for Southampton was due at noon.

I took the telegram from my pocket and placed it on top of *Women's Words*. The paper was butcher's brown and sickly against the beautiful green of the leather. Half the message was typed: *Regret to inform you that …* An efficiency when the message was so often the same. The rest was handwritten. The telegraph clerk who transcribed the message had added *Deeply*, before *Regret*.

I closed the trunk.

PART SIX

1928

Wise–Wyzen

November 1928

15th August 1928

Dear Miss Megan Brooks,

My name is Edith Thompson. Your parents may have spoken of me. Sarah, your late mother, was one of my dearest friends and one of the few people willing to accompany me on what she amusingly referred to as my 'history rambles' (it was never clear whether the 'rambling' referred to the walking or my commentary — it amused her to keep me guessing). When you all sailed for Australia, I found her hard to replace, but I delighted in her letters, which reliably shared news of you, her garden and your local politics, all three of which she was justly proud. How I miss her wit and practical advice.

I am sending this letter and its accompanying trunk care of your father, for reasons that will soon make themselves plain. I wanted to be sure you could somehow be made ready to receive the contents of both. How one can be made ready, I am not entirely sure, but a father might know, and of all fathers yours is surely one of the wisest.

The trunk belonged to another dear friend of mine. Her name was Esme Owen née Nicoll. I am aware that you have always known you were adopted, but perhaps you have not known all of the details. I think the story I have to tell will bring on some strong emotions. I am sorry. But I would feel a greater sorrow never to share it.

My dear Megan. Twenty-one years ago, Esme gave you life, but she was in no position to sustain it. These are always delicate circumstances, but your mother and father spent a lot of time with Esme in the months before you were born. It was obvious to me that they grew to love and admire her, as I have loved and admired her. When the time came, your mother was there for Esme in a way that I could not be. It was the most natural thing for her to be in the birthing room, and for a month she sat by Esme's bed, and you, beautiful child, became the bond between them.

It pains me to write these next words. The truth of them will be a sadness I do not think I will recover from. Esme passed away on the morning of the 2nd of July of this year, 1928. She was just 46 years old.

The details seem ordinary — she was struck by a lorry on Westminster Bridge. But nothing about Esme was ordinary. She had gone up to London for the passing of the Equal Franchise Act, not to join the chanters and banner holders but to record what it meant to the people on the edge of the crowd. This is what she did, you see: she noticed who was missing from the official records and gave them an opportunity to speak. She wrote a weekly column in her local newspaper — 'Lost Words', it was called — and each week, she would talk to the ordinary, the illiterate, the forgotten, in order to understand what big events meant to them. On the 2nd of July, Esme was talking to a woman selling flowers on Westminster Bridge when the crowd forced her onto the road.

I feel I should tell you something more of her, besides her death. Our last meeting, I think, is as good an anecdote as any.

I had been invited to sit in the balcony of Goldsmiths' Hall, where a dinner was to be held to mark the final publication of the Oxford English Dictionary. I was accompanied by Rosfrith Murray and Eleanor Bradley, editors' daughters who'd dedicated their lives to their fathers' work. There was some to-do about our presence, owing to our sex, but it was thought only right that, even though we could not dine with the men, we should at least be allowed to witness the speeches. The Prime Minster, Stanley Baldwin, spoke wonderfully, thanking the editors and the staff, but he did not look up to the balcony. The Dictionary was an enterprise I had been involved with from the publication of the first words in 1884 to the publication of the last. I am told that few in that room could claim such a long allegiance. Rosfrith and Eleanor too had given the Dictionary decades of their lives. As had Esme.

She told me, not long ago, that she had always been a bondmaid to the Dictionary. It owned her, she said. Even after she left, it defined her. Still, despite these shackles, she was not afforded even a balcony view.

The men ate saumon bouilli with sauce hollandaise, and for dessert they had mousse glacée favorite. They drank 1907 Château Margaux. We were given the proceedings, and the menu was included — an unintended cruelty, I'm sure.

We were famished when it was all over, but Esme had travelled up from Southampton to meet us, and when we left Goldsmiths' Hall there she was with a hamper of food. It was warm, so we caught a cab down to the Thames and sat under a lamp with our picnic, enjoying a celebration of our own. 'To the women of the Dictionary,' Esme said, and we raised our glasses.

I was not aware of the trunk until after the funeral, when her friend, Lizzie Lester, suggested it should be sent to you. She pulled the battered old thing from under her bed and explained what I would find if I opened it. That poor girl was bereft. But when I assured her that I would send the trunk to you as soon as possible, she was calmed.

The trunk sat at the end of my bed for a week, unopened. When my tears for Esme had dried, I had no need to explore its contents. For me, Esme is like a favourite word that I understand in a particular way and have no desire to understand differently.

The trunk is yours, Megan. To open, or to leave closed. Whichever you choose, please know that it will be my pleasure to answer questions about Esme, if you have any. She called me Ditte, by the way. I will miss answering to it and would be glad to be called by that name again, should you care to write.

With love and great sympathy,
Ditte Thompson

Meg sat with the trunk so long that all the light went out of the room. Ditte's letter lay beside it. Read and re-read. One page was creased from when Meg had screwed it up in a rage. Moments later, she'd smoothed it flat again.

Her father knocked at the door, a light, tentative knock. He offered her tea, and she refused. He knocked again and enquired about her state of mind. Quite all right, she said, though she was quite sure she wasn't. When the hall clock chimed eight, some kind of spell was broken. Meg got up from the chair she'd been sitting in for the past four hours and turned on a lamp. She opened the door to the sitting room and called to her father.

'I'd like that tea now, Dad,' she said. 'With a couple of biscuits, if you don't mind.'

After placing the tray beside her, he poured the tea into her mum's favourite china cup. He added a slice of lemon, kissed her on the forehead and left the room. There was no mention that dinner had gone cold.

It was three years since the cup had been warmed with tea. Meg held it like her mum had done: cupped in both hands with the handle pointing forward, all in an effort to avoid the small chip on the rim where one would normally sip. The gesture blurred the edges of Meg's being, and she imagined her elegant fingers as her mother's fleshy ones, callouses softening under the heat, a hint of earth under the fingernails. Her mother's short, heavy legs had been a better fit for the armchair than Meg's long limbs, but Meg had taken to sitting there. Although the day had been hot, she shivered, as her mother often would, when she came in from her garden to share tea.

What would she have made of the trunk? Meg thought. Would she have told her to open it or to keep it shut? It sat on the chaise longue, where it had been all afternoon. Meg looked at it again and thought it had become strangely familiar. 'In your own time,' her mum would have said.

Meg finished her tea and eased herself out of the old armchair. She sat on the chaise longue next to the trunk. The latch clicked open with no effort at all, and the lid sprang back.

The Dictionary of Lost Words had been clumsily carved into the inside of the lid. It was a child's hand, and Meg suddenly realised that the contents were not just that of a woman who had given up her baby, but of a girl who never dreamed that one day she would have to.

A telegram, a slender leather-bound volume with *Women's Words and Their Meanings* embossed on the cover, letters, and loose bits and pieces – a few suffrage pamphlets, theatre programmes and newspaper clippings. There were three sketches of a woman, naked. She was looking out of a window in the first, the swell of her belly just visible. In the third her hands and gaze embraced the baby that must have been stirring.

But mostly there were small bits of paper, no bigger than postcards. Some were pinned together, others loose. There was a shoebox full of them, sorted into alphabetical order with small cards between each letter, like a library catalogue drawer. Each slip of paper had a word written at the top, and a sentence below. Sometimes there was the name of a book, but most just had a woman's name, sometimes a man's.

❧

Morning light streamed through the bay window, warming Meg's cheek. She woke with a start. Her back ached from the hours she had slept on the chaise longue. Another scorcher, she thought, the trunk and its contents submerged like a dream. But *Women's Words* was open on her lap, and her skin felt tight where tears had dried. Under the glare of the Adelaide sun, Esme's words, in all their forms, lay scattered across the floor, exposed and real.

Meg began to sort them. She gathered Ditte's letters and placed them in one pile, Tilda's postcards in another. Suffrage pamphlets and news clippings had a pile of their own. There was a programme for

Much Ado About Nothing and a handful of ticket stubs that she put with other bits and pieces to form a pile of miscellany.

The slips in the shoebox were almost all written in a single hand. When she checked, they each had an entry in *Women's Words*. She left them as they were and turned to the rest. There were so many, a hundred or more, each unique in script and content. There were ordinary words and words she'd never heard of. Some of the quotations were so old she could make no sense of them at all. But she read each one.

They were a uniform size, more or less, and most seemed made for no other purpose. But some had been fashioned from whatever was to hand: there were slips cut from ledgers or exercise books; from the pages of novels or pamphlets, a word circled and the sentence underlined. One word had been written on the back of a shopping list, the sender presumably having already bought her three pints of milk, box of soda, lard, two pounds of flour, cochineal and McVitie's digestives. Did she bake a cake before sitting down to scribe the sentence that perfectly represented one sense of the word *beat*? The quotation was from the women's pages of a parish church newsletter, dated 1874. The shopping list, no longer necessary, was the perfect size and shape. Meg imagined a woman, not wealthy, not poor, sitting at her kitchen table, the newsletter in front of her, a pot of tea at her elbow, the wait for the cake to rise a welcome pause in her day. And then a child, rushing in, nostrils full of the treat ahead, hovering until it was time to blow out the candles.

A cheer went up from the park across the road, and Meg was brought back to herself and to Esme. The familiar sound of bat on ball, frequent polite clapping and the occasional excitement of a wicket reminded her it was Saturday morning, that she was in the heat of an Adelaide summer and nowhere near the damp and chilly climate of these words and their champions. She felt stiff, dishevelled. She got up and looked out towards the players. It was like any other Saturday, and yet it wasn't.

Another cheer went up, but Meg turned away from the window and walked over to the bookshelf. It contained all twelve volumes of the *Oxford English Dictionary*. They were on a low shelf, so they would be easy to reach, though when she was small Meg could barely lift them. Her parents had been collecting them for as long as she could remember, the last only arriving a week earlier.

Meg pulled *V to Z* from its position at the end of the shelf and opened to the first page. She could smell its newness, feel the spine resist as she opened it. Published 1928.

Only months before, it did not exist. Only months before, Esme did.

Meg went to the other end of the shelf and traced her finger over the gold lettering of Volume I, *A and B*. The spine was creased from opening, the edge at the top damaged from her childish hands levering it out of its place. This time, Meg was careful as she took it from the shelf. The weight of it was always a surprise. She took it to her mother's armchair and rested it in her lap. Then she opened to the title page.

A new English Dictionary
on Historical Principles
Edited by James A. H. Murray
Volume 1. A and B
Oxford:
At the Clarendon Press
1888

Forty years earlier. Esme would have been six years old.

Meg picked up the slip for *beat* and read the quotation.

'Beat until the sugar is well combined and the mixture pales.'

She turned the pages of the Dictionary until she found the word. *Beat* had fifty-nine different senses across ten columns. Violence characterised so many of them. She ran her finger down the columns until she came to a definition that suited the slip. Four quotations, about beating eggs. The quotation on her slip wasn't there.

Meg placed *A and B* on the floor beside the trunk. She opened the shoebox and riffled through it.

LIE-CHILD

'To keep a lie-child condemns her and it. I'll fetch a wet-nurse.'

Mrs Mead, midwife, 1907

Esme's handwriting was already familiar. Meg retrieved Volume VI of the Dictionary and found the corresponding page. *Lie-child* was missing completely, but Meg understood what it meant. She returned to Volume I and turned to *bastard*.

Begotten and born out of wedlock.
Illegitimate, unrecognised, unauthorised.
Not genuine; counterfeit, spurious; debased, adulterated, corrupt.

Meg slammed the volume shut. She rose from the floor, but her legs were shaking. She felt fragile, suddenly unfamiliar to herself. She collapsed into the armchair and began to sob. *Bastard* had two columns, yet what it meant for her had not been captured by a single quotation.

Meg missed her mum, missed all her words and gestures, which she knew would have made sense of the mess that covered the floor of the sitting room. She buried her face in the fabric of the chair and smelled her mum's hair, the familiar scent of Pears' soap, which she'd always used to wash it. And which Meg still used. Deeper sobs. Was that what it meant to be a daughter? To have hair that smelled of your mother's? To use the same soap? Or was it a shared passion, a shared frustration? Meg had never wanted to kneel in the dirt and plant bulbs like her mum; she longed to be considered – not with kindness, but with curiosity, with regard for her thoughts, with respect for her words.

Was that what the mess on the floor was? Evidence of a curious mind? Fragments of frustration? An effort to understand and explain? Were Meg's longings akin to Esme's, and was that what it meant to be a daughter?

By the time her dad knocked at the door, Meg had stopped sobbing. Something was trying to emerge from her grief – to complicate it or simplify it, she did not know.

'Meg, love?' His manner was as gentle as it had been the night before, and he came into the room like a birdwatcher afraid of startling a wren.

Meg said nothing; her mind tripped repeatedly over something uncomfortable.

'Would you like some breakfast?' he asked.

'I'd like some paper, Dad. If you don't mind.'

'Writing paper?'

'Yes, Mum's bond paper, the pale-blue paper in her writing desk.' She searched her dad's face for any sign of resistance, but there was none.

❧

Adelaide, 12th November 1928

As I write all this down, I hesitate. To call Esme my mother feels like a betrayal of Mum, but to deny her that title? Still, I hesitate. All night I have been contemplating the meaning of words, most of which I've never used or even heard of. I've accepted their importance in the contexts in which they were uttered, and for the first time I've questioned the authority of the many volumes that fill one shelf of the bookcase opposite where I now sit.

Mother would be in there. Of course it would, though I have never had any cause to look it up. Until this moment, I would have thought that any English speaker, no matter their education, would know the meaning of that word, know how to use it.

Know who to apply it to. But now, I hesitate. Meaning has become relative.

I want to get up and pull the volume from the shelf, but I'm worried that the definition I read will not apply to Mum. So I sit a little longer and my memories of Mum erase all concern. But now, I fear that mother will not apply to Esme.

Meg folded the page and added it to the trunk.

Later, Philip Brooks placed a breakfast tray on the small table beside his daughter. A pot of tea, two slices of lemon in a little dish, four slices of toast and a newly opened jar of orange-and-lime marmalade. There was enough for two.

'Join me, Dad,' she said.

'Are you sure?'

'Yes.'

Meg picked up her mum's china cup from where she had left it the night before and held it out for him to fill. He poured her tea, then his. He added a slice of lemon to both cups.

'Does it change anything?' he asked.

'It changes everything,' Meg said.

He bent his head to sip his tea; his hands shook very slightly. When Meg looked at his face she saw that every muscle was working to hold back an emotion he wanted to spare her from.

'Almost everything,' she said.

He looked up.

'It doesn't change what I feel for you, Dad. And it doesn't change what I feel for Mum, or how I will remember her. I think perhaps I might even love her a little more. Right now, I miss her terribly.'

They sat in silence among Esme's things, and from across the park the soothing repetition of bat on ball marked the passing of time.

EPILOGUE

Adelaide, 1989

The man standing behind the lectern clears his throat, but to no avail; the auditorium buzzes like a hive. He rearranges his papers, looks at his watch, peers at the gathered academics over his reading glasses. Then he clears his throat again, a little louder this time, and into the microphone.

The clamour dies down; a few stragglers find their seats. The man behind the lectern begins to speak.

'Welcome to the tenth Annual Convention of the Australian Lexicography Society,' he says, with a small quaver in his quiet voice. Then, after a pause that is slightly too long, he continues.

'*Naa Manni*,' he says with a little more strength, his gaze sweeping around the room. 'That is the Kaurna way of saying hello to more than one person, and I'm glad to see there is more than one person here today.' There is the murmur of mild amusement. 'For those of you who are visiting our city, and perhaps some of you who have lived here all your life, the Kaurna are the Aboriginal people who called this land home before this great hall was built, and before English was ever spoken in this country. We are on their land, yet we do not speak their language.

'I use Kaurna words this morning to make a point. Back in the 1830s and 40s, they were used by Mullawirraburka, Kadlitpinna and Ityamaiitpinna, Kaurna Elders known more commonly by white settlers as King John, Captain Jack and King Rodney. These Aboriginal men sat with two German men who were interested in learning the indigenous language. The Germans wrote down what they heard and fashioned meanings that might be understood by others. They were doing the work of linguists and lexicographers, though these are not terms they would have used. They were missionaries, but any one of us would recognise their passion for language, their desire to record and understand the spoken word, not only so it might inform proper contemporary usage, but also so it might be preserved, and its historical context understood. If not for their efforts, the linguistic world of the Kaurna people would be lost to us, and so too our understanding of what was meaningful to them, what *is* meaningful to them. Few Kaurna people speak their language today, but because it has been written down, and the meanings of words recorded, it is possible that Kaurna people – and, dare I suggest, whitefellas such as myself – will speak it again.' His voice has risen to an excited pitch and his forehead shines under the harsh lights of the stage. He pauses to catch his breath.

'Nineteen eighty-nine is a significant year for the English language, though it is probably true to say that few outside this hall would know it.' There is a smattering of laughter, and he looks up, clearly pleased.

'This year, the second edition of the *Oxford English Dictionary* has been published, sixty-one years after the completion of the first. It combines the first edition and all the supplements, as well as an additional five thousand words and meanings. This work – this documenting of language – has been done by lexicographers, some of whom I know are in the auditorium today. For this great effort, we congratulate you.' He claps, and the audience joins in, some with whistles and whoops. 'Settle down, everyone, we have a staid and serious reputation to uphold.' More laughter. He waits it out, relaxed now.

'The great James Murray once said, "I am not a literary man. I am a man of science, and I am interested in that branch of anthropology which deals with the history of human speech."

'Words define us, they explain us, and, on occasion, they serve to control or isolate us. But what happens when words that are spoken are not recorded? What effect does that have on the speaker of those words? One lexicographer, whom we can all be grateful has read between the lines of the great dictionaries of the English language, including Dr Murray's *OED*, is Professor Megan Brooks: professor emeritus of the University of Adelaide, chair of the Australasian Philological Society and recipient of an OAM for services to language.

'Without further ado, I invite Professor Megan Brooks to the podium, where she will deliver the opening address. Her lecture is titled "The Dictionary of Lost Words".'

Applause accompanies a tall, upright woman onto the stage. As she approaches the lectern, she tucks a stray lock of faded red hair behind her ear. The man offers his hand, and she shakes it, a smile on her lined face. He bows slightly and backs away.

From her jacket pocket, Megan Brooks takes a white envelope, and from it she carefully slides out a frail slip of paper, yellowed with age. This, and only this, she places on the lectern, gently smoothing it with her gloved hands.

She looks out to the auditorium. She has done this a thousand times, but this time will be her last. What she is about to say has taken her a lifetime to understand, and she knows it is important.

Her eyes focus on the middle row, and she scans individual faces quickly, not settling. They are mostly men, but there are quite a few women. They are all well into their careers. She can feel a restlessness beginning in the vast space, but she ignores it and scans the row below, then the row below that. She notes faces beginning to turn towards their neighbours, whispering. Still, she continues her search.

At the second row from the front, she pauses. There is a young woman, surely no more than an undergraduate student. She is at the beginning of her journey with words, and there is a curiosity in her face that satisfies the old woman. She smiles. It is a reason to start. Megan Brooks picks up the slip.

'*Bondmaid*,' she says. 'For a while, this beautiful, troubling word belonged to my mother.'

Author's Note

This book began as two simple questions: Do words mean different things to men and women? And if they do, is it possible that we have lost something in the process of defining them?

I have had a love–hate relationship with words and dictionaries my whole life. I have trouble spelling words and I frequently use them incorrectly (affluent, after all, sounds so much like effluent, it really is an easy mistake to make). As a child, when I used to ask the adults in my life for help, they would say, 'Look it up in the dictionary,' but when you can't spell, the dictionary can be an impenetrable thing. Despite my clumsy handling of the English language, I have always loved how writing words down in a particular way can create a rhythm, or conjure an image, or express an emotion. It has been the greatest irony of my life that I should choose words to explore my inner and outer worlds.

A few years ago, a good friend suggested I read Simon Winchester's *The Surgeon of Crowthorne*. It is a non-fiction account of the relationship between the Editor of the *Oxford English Dictionary*, James Murray, and one of the more prolific (and notorious) volunteers, Dr William Chester Minor. I thoroughly enjoyed it, but I was left with the impression that the Dictionary was a particularly male endeavour. From what I could glean, all the editors were men, most of the assistants were men, most of the volunteers were men and most of the literature, manuals and newspaper articles used as evidence for how words were used, were written by men. Finally, the Delegates of the Oxford University Press – those who held the purse strings – were men.

Where, I wondered, are the women in this story, and does it matter that they are absent?

It took me a while to find the women, and when I did, they were cast in minor and supporting roles. There was Ada Murray, who raised eleven children and ran a household at the same time as supporting her husband in his role as Editor. There was Edith Thompson and her sister Elizabeth Thompson, who between them provided 15,000 quotations for *A and B* alone, and continued to provide quotations and editorial assistance until the last word was published. There were Hilda, Elsie and Rosfrith Murray, who all worked in the Scriptorium to support their father. And there was Eleanor Bradley, who worked at the Old Ashmolean as part of her father's team of assistants. There were also countless women who sent in quotations for words. Finally, there were women who wrote novels and biographies and poetry that were considered as evidence for the use of one word or another. But in all cases, they were outnumbered by their male counterparts, and history struggles to recall them at all.

I decided that the absence of women did matter. A lack of representation might mean that the first edition of the *Oxford English Dictionary* was biased in favour of the experiences and sensibilities of men. Older, white, Victorian-era men at that.

This novel is my attempt to understand how the way we define language, might define us. Throughout, I have tried to conjure images and express emotions that bring our understanding of words into question. By putting Esme among the words, I was able to imagine the effect they might have had on her, and the effect she might have had on them.

From the beginning, it was important that I weave Esme's fictional story through the history of the *Oxford English Dictionary* as we know it. I soon realised that this history also included the women's suffrage movement in England as well as World War I. In all three cases the timelines of events and the broad details have been preserved. Any errors are unintentional.

Perhaps the biggest challenge in writing this book was being true to the real-life people who inhabited its historical context. I am not alone in my fascination with the *Oxford English Dictionary*, and I devoured the work of dictionary scholars and biographers. Lynda Mugglestone's book *Lost for Words* gave me the confidence to accept that women's words were indeed treated differently to those of men, at least sometimes. Peter Gilliver's book *The Making of the Oxford English Dictionary* furnished my story with facts and anecdotes that I hope anchor it in truth. Twice, I had the privilege of visiting the Oxford University Press, where the *Oxford English Dictionary* archives are held. I searched through Dictionary proofs for evidence that this word or that had been deleted at the last minute, and I was given access to the original slips, many still tied in bundles by the original string that held them together in the early twentieth century. I found the slips for *bondmaid*: that beautiful, troubling word that was as much a character in this story as Esme. But there was no sign of the top-slip that might have shown the definition – it really had been lost. When the boxes and boxes of papers proved overwhelming, I turned to the people who tended them. Beverley McCulloch, Peter Gilliver and Martin Maw shared stories and insights that could only come from a deep fascination and respect for the Dictionary and the Press that produced it. Our conversations animated the history.

Most of the men of the *OED* can be easily found in the historical record. With the exception of Mr Crane, Mr Dankworth and one or two fleeting characters, the male editors and assistants are based on real people. I have, of course, fictionalised their interactions with other characters in the story, but I have endeavoured to capture something of their interests and personalities. The speech made by Dr Murray during the garden party for *A and B* is taken verbatim from the foreword to that volume.

Mr Nicholson and Mr Madan were the Bodleian Librarians at the time portrayed in this book. Although they have few lines, I hope I have captured something of their attitude.

I have tried to render the characters of Rosfrith Murray, Elsie Murray and Eleanor Bradley as best I can, but there is a paucity of biographical information available, and I cannot guarantee that their nearest family would agree to the personality traits I have assumed.

Perhaps the most important real-life character in this novel is Edith Thompson. She and her sister, Elizabeth, were dedicated and highly valued volunteers. Edith was involved in the Dictionary from the publication of the first words until the publication of the last. She died in 1929, just a year after the Dictionary was completed. I got to know her a little from the materials that have been preserved in the *OED* archives. It is an extraordinary feeling to come across a note penned by Edith and pinned to the edge of a proof. Her original letters to James Murray reveal intelligence, humour and a wry wit. When she wanted to better explain a word, she was in the habit of drawing annotated pictures.

I have taken the liberty of turning Edith Thompson into a key character in this story. As with other women, it is difficult to find a comprehensive account of her life, but what I do know, I have woven through this book. She did, for instance, write a history of England that was a popular school text. She also lived in Bath with her sister.

Her note to James Murray regarding the word *lip-pencil* is real, but the rest is fiction. It was important to me that the real woman behind this character be named and recognised for her contribution. But to acknowledge my fictionalisation of her life, Esme gives her the pet name *Ditte*. As for Elizabeth Thompson (known as E. P. Thompson), she really did write *A Dragoon's Wife* (and I have an original 1907 edition sitting on my desk), but I could find nothing else to guide me as to her character. I have turned her into a woman I would like to know, and given her the nickname *Beth* to acknowledge this fictionalisation.

Finally, to the words. All books referred to in this story are real, as is the timeline of *OED* fascicle publications, *OED* entries, excised or rejected words and quotations. The words collected by Esme are real, though the quotations are as fictional as the characters who speak them.

At the end of the book, I refer to Aboriginal Kaurna Elders who shared their language with German missionaries. It should be noted that the spelling of Kaurna names and words is not a simple matter. The Kaurna language was, for a long while after European settlement, waiting to be spoken and understood. That is now happening, and as more people learn to speak it, questions about spelling, pronunciation and meaning arise and are subject to consideration. I have been guided by the advice of Kaurna Warra Karrpanthi ('Creating Kaurna Language'), a committee set up to assist with Kaurna place naming and translations. Their work continues to enliven the Kaurna language and contributes to Reconciliation.

By the time I had finished the first draft of this novel, I had become acutely aware that the first edition of the *Oxford English Dictionary* was a flawed and gendered text. But it was also extraordinary, and far less flawed and gendered than it might have been in the hands of someone other than James Murray. I have come to realise that the Dictionary was an initiative of Victorian times, but every publication, since 'A to Ant' in 1884, has reflected some small move towards greater representation of all those who speak the English language.

During my visits to Oxford, I spoke with lexicographers, archivists and dictionary scholars, women and men. I was struck by their passionate fascination with words and how those words have been used throughout their history. Today, the *Oxford English Dictionary* is in the process of a major revision. This revision will not only add the newest words and meanings, it will update how words were used in the past, based on a better understanding of history and historical texts.

The Dictionary, like the English language, is a work in progress.

Acknowledgements

ACKNOWLEDGEMENT

The act of acknowledging, confessing, admitting or owning; confession, avowal.

This is just one story. The telling of which has helped me understand things I consider important. I have made it up, but it is full of truth. I would like to acknowledge the women and men of the *Oxford English Dictionary* – past and present; known and unknown.

EDIT

To publish, give to the world (a literary work by an earlier author, previously existing in MS).

This book would be nothing more than an idea if not for the following people. Thank you to everyone at Affirm Press for working so hard to make this a beautiful book that says nothing more and nothing less than it needs to. In particular, I thank Martin Hughes for his extraordinary confidence in this story, and Ruby Ashby-Orr for her consummate skills as an editor. Put simply, this book is better because of her. I also thank Kieran Rogers, Grace Breen, Stephanie Bishop-Hall, Cosima McGrath and the rest of the team.

For their wonderful support of this book and invaluable editorial feedback, I thank Clara Farmer and Charlotte Humphery from Chatto & Windus publishers in the UK and Susanna Porter from Ballantine Books in the US. For the beautiful cover I thank Kris Potter. And I am forever grateful to Claire Kelly for her eagle eye and love of history.

MENTOR

An experienced and trusted counsellor.

I have always loved journeying with people who are wiser than me. Thank you, Toni Jordan, for walking beside me on this adventure and making it a richer and better articulated experience.

ENCOURAGE

To inspire with courage sufficient for any undertaking; to embolden, make confident.

Throughout the writing of this book I have been fortunate to have the encouragement of other writers. For their insights and enthusiasm, I thank Suzanne Verrall, Rebekah Clarkson, Neel Mukherjee, Amanda Smyth and Carol Major. I also thank all the writers with whom I shared residencies at The Hurst, Arvon in the UK, and Varuna, the National Writers' House, in Katoomba, NSW. I also greatly appreciate the community of writers who are part of Writers SA, and I am grateful for the continuing encouragement of Sarah Tooth. A special thank you to Peter Grose for his generosity and timely advice, and to Thomas Keneally, Simon Winchester, Geraldine Brooks and Melissa Ashley for responding so generously when asked to read the manuscript.

SUPPORT

To strengthen the position of (a person or community) by one's assistance, countenance or adherence; to stand by, back up.

This story is woven through the early history of the *Oxford English Dictionary* and I have tried to be true to the people and events of that time. I am indebted to the generosity of three people in particular: without them, this book could not have happened. Beverly McCulloch, archivist for the *Oxford English Dictionary*, brought me the slips, proofs, letters and photographs that furnish this book. She also read the manuscript and told me where I had erred. I am so grateful, and any remaining errors of history are mine. Peter Gilliver, lexicographer at the Oxford University Press (OUP), provided me with a text that became my bible. He also gave generously of his time, and supplied me with wonderful anecdotes that put flesh on the bones of lexicographers past. Dr Martin Maw, archivist of the Oxford University Press, also provided text and rare footage of the processes of compositing and printing the *Oxford English Dictionary*. I am very grateful for the time he spent talking to me about the press during WWI, and walking with me around the OUP Museum.

For their scholarship, assistance or time, I am also grateful to Lynda Mugglestone; K.M. Elisabeth Murray, author of *Caught in the Web of Words*; Amanda Capern for her paper on Edith Thompson; Katherine Bradley for her booklet 'Women on the March'; the Oxford History Centre; and the good people at the State Library of South Australia, especially Neil Charter, Suzy Russell and whoever lugged all twelve volumes of the first edition of the *OED* down the spiral staircase from the Symon Library to the reading room.

I would like to thank Kaurna Warra Karrpanthi for providing advice about Kaurna names and spelling, and Aunty Lynette for sharing her language and stories.

Finally, thank you to my local cafe, Sazón, for all your sustenance and good cheer. I have pushed the limits of time bought by two or three cups of coffee, and I am grateful you allow me to languish in the corner table for as long as a scene requires.

FELLOWSHIP
To unite in fellowship; to connect or associate with or to another; to enter into companionship.

So many friends have listened to me talk about this story and given me the confidence to tell it. Thank you for believing I can do it. Gwenda Jarred, Nicola Williams, Matt Turner, Ali Turner, Arlo Turner, Lisa Harrison, Ali Elder, Suzanne Verrall, Andrea Brydges, Krista Brydges, Anne Beath, Ross Balharrie, Lou-Belle Barrett, Vanessa Iles, Jane Lawson, Rebekah Clarkson, David Washington, Jolie Thomas, Mark Thomas, Margie Sarre, Greg Sarre, Suzie Riley, Christine McCabe, Evan Jones, Anji Hill.

ACCOMMODATE
To adapt, fit, suit or adjust.

Writing can be a crime of passion if the bills don't get paid and the children starve. Many thanks are due to Angela Hazebroek and Marcus Rolfe for understanding that this book was my number one priority and offering me a job anyway. And to my wonderful colleagues at URPS for ensuring my day job is not only possible, but rewarding and meaningful.

AID
Anything by which assistance is given in performing an operation; anything helpful, a means or material source of help.

I am most grateful to Arts South Australia for a Makers and Presenters grant in 2019. I am also indebted to Varuna, the National Writers' House, for a Varuna Fellowship and two Alumni residencies in 2019. The opportunity to write in peace, be fed, and have the stimulation of other writers is an enormous privilege.

LOVE
That disposition or state of feeling with regard to a person which (arising from recognition of attractive qualities, from instincts of natural relationship, or from

sympathy) manifests itself in solicitude for the welfare of the object, and usually also in delight in his presence and desire for his approval; warm affection, attachment.

To Ma and Pa, who gave me a dictionary when I was young and insisted I use it. Thank you for fostering my curiosity and giving me the means to satisfy it. To Mary McCune, my marvellous mother-outlaw, for always listening to my stories as they develop. And to my sister Nicola, for being everything a sister should be.

Thank you to Aidan and Riley for listening when I explain the world, then challenging me to rethink everything. If I could write you into the dictionary, you would be a simple, uncomplicated variant of *love*.

And to Shannon, whose attention to detail and fondness for limericks made all the difference. There is no single word that explains what you mean to me, no dictionary meaning that defines how I feel. Thank you for welcoming my writing life into your everyday, and making generous adjustments whenever it needs a little more space. This book, as with everything, is ours.

RESPECT

To treat or regard with deference, esteem, or honour; to feel or show respect for.

Finally, I acknowledge that this book has been written on Kaurna and Peramangk Countries. For millennia, the languages of these first peoples was shared through oral storytelling, and the words they used gave meaning to their landscape, their cultures and their beliefs. While many of these words have been lost to time, others have been found. They are being shared anew.

I pay my respects to the elders of the Kaurna and Peramangk Peoples, past, present and emerging. I acknowledge their stories and their languages, and I have the deepest respect for the meaning of what has been lost.

TIMELINE OF THE
OXFORD ENGLISH DICTIONARY

1857   The Unregistered Words Committee of the Philological Society
        of London calls for a new English Dictionary to succeed Samuel
        Johnson's *Dictionary of the English Language* (1755).

1879   James Murray appointed as Editor.

1881   Edith Thompson publishes *History of England (Pictorial course for schools)*
        – multiple editions follow as well as adaptations for American and
        Canadian markets.

1884   'A to Ant' published. It is the first of approx. 125 fascicles.

1885   James and Ada Murray move from London to Oxford, erecting a
        large corrugated iron shed in the garden of their house. The house
        is known as Sunnyside. The shed is known as the Scriptorium.

1885   Pillar box placed outside Sunnyside in recognition of the high
        volume of mail generated by the Scriptorium.

1887   Henry Bradley appointed as second Editor.

1888   *A and B* published. It is the first of twelve volumes originally titled *A
        New English Dictionary on Historical Principles*.

1901   William Craigie appointed as third Editor.

1901   Bradley and Craigie move into the 'Dictionary Room' at the Old
        Ashmolean.

1901   *Bondmaid* discovered missing following a letter from a member of
        the public.

1914   Charles Onions appointed as fourth Editor.

1915   Sir James Murray dies.

1915   Staff and contents of the Scriptorium are moved to the Old
        Ashmolean.

1928   *V to Z* published as *Volume 12*.

1928   150 men gather in London's Goldsmiths' Hall to celebrate the
        publication of the *Oxford English Dictionary*, seventy-one years after it
        was proposed. Prime Minister Stanley Baldwin presides. Women are

not invited, though three are allowed to sit in the balcony and watch the men eat. Edith Thompson is one of them.

1929   Edith Thompson dies aged 81.

1989   Publication of the second edition of the *Oxford English Dictionary*.

Staff of the Scriptorium, Oxford. Photographed for The Periodical *on 10th July 1915.*
(Back row) Arthur Maling, Frederick Sweatman, F.A. Yockney.
(Seated) Elsie Murray, Sir James Murray, Rosfrith Murray.
Image reprinted with permission of Oxford University Press.

TIMELINE OF MAJOR HISTORICAL EVENTS
FEATURED IN THE NOVEL

1894   South Australian Parliament passes the Constitutional Amendment (Adult Suffrage) Act. This Act grants all adult women (including Aboriginal women) the right to vote and the right to stand for Parliament. It is the first parliament in the world to do so. (While women in New Zealand won the right to vote in 1893, they were not eligible for election to the House of Representatives until 1919.)

1897   National Union of Women's Suffrage Societies (NUWSS) formed, led by Millicent Fawcett.

1901   Queen Victoria dies. Edward VII becomes King.

1902   The newly established Australian Parliament passes the Commonwealth Franchise Act 1902, enabling all adult women to vote at Federal elections or stand for Federal Parliament (except those who are 'aboriginal natives' of Australia, Africa, Asia and the Pacific Islands).

1903   Women's Social and Political Union (WSPU) formed, led by Emmeline Pankhurst.

1905   WSPU begin militant campaign, including civil disobedience, destruction of property, arson and bombings.

1906   The term suffragette is applied to militant suffragists.

1907   Elizabeth Perronet Thompson publishes *A Dragoon's Wife*.

1908   Adelaide woman Muriel Matters chains herself to the grille of the Ladies Gallery in the House of Commons as part of a protest organised by the Women's Freedom League (WFL), a non-militant suffrage organisation.

1909   Marion Wallace Dunlop is the first gaoled suffragist to go on hunger strike – many will follow.

1909   Charlotte Marsh, Laura Ainsworth and Mary Leigh (née Brown) are force-fed in Winson Green Prison, Birmingham.

1913   8 January, 'Battle of the suffragists'. A peaceful procession of suffragist societies in Oxford is disrupted by an anti-suffrage crowd.

1913	3 June, Rough's Boathouse in Oxford is burned down. Four women are seen fleeing, three in a punt, one along the road. Non-militant suffragists condemn the action and collect money for laid-off workers.
1914	War with Germany is declared.
1914	Sixty-three men from the Oxford University Press march out of the grounds to report for duty.
1914	The First Battle of Ypres.
1915	The Battle of Festubert.
1915	The Battle of Loos.
1918	End of World War I.
1918	The UK coalition government pass the Representation of the People Act, enfranchising all men over the age of twenty-one, and women over the age of thirty who meet minimum property qualifications.
1928	The UK Conservative government passes the Representation of the People (Equal Franchise) Act, giving the vote to all women over the age of twenty-one on equal terms with men.

Reading Group Questions

1. What does *The Dictionary of Lost Words* tell us about power?
2. How do you think not having a mother influenced the trajectory of Esme's life and her character?
3. While this book is based on the true events surrounding the publication of the first Oxford Dictionary, Esme herself is a fictional character. Why do you think Williams chose to have Esme grow up on the precise timeline she did?
4. Is the ending of the book just? Do the characters get what they deserve?
5. Do you think this is a hopeful story? Consider arguments for and against.
6. Consider Esme and Lizzie's relationship. In what ways are the women similar? How are they different? Consider the extent to which nature/nurture shapes their expectations and behaviours.
7. Pip Williams is a celebrated author because of her ability to establish a compelling sense of time and place. How do the changing settings influence the tone of the narrative?
8. Why do you think Esperanto comes to play such an important role in Esme's life, given she grew up with a love of the English language?

9. *The Dictionary of Lost Words* explores linguistic inequality – the idea that not all words are equal. To what extent do you think this phenomenon exists in modern English? Consider the word 'like' and its place in modern speech. Who uses it? How is it used? How has its use changed?

10. Can the evolution of language ever be a bad thing?

11. Williams depicts the lexicographers at the Scriptorium as the gatekeepers to the English language. Should the English language have gatekeepers? Should the dictionaries we use today help us to define our language, or should they reflect it back at us?